PAIN

OTHER PRESS ■ NEW YORK

PAIN

ZERUYA SHALEV

Translated from the Hebrew by Sondra Silverston

Production editor: Yvonne E. Cárdenas
Text designer: Jennifer Daddio | Bookmark Design & Media Inc.
This book was set in Goudy Old Style and Helvetica Neue
by Alpha Design & Composition of Pittsfield, NH

1 3 5 7 9 10 8 6 4 2

LIBRARY OF CONGRESS CATALOGING-IN-PUBLICATION DATA

Names: Shaleòv, Tseruyah, author. | Silverston, Sondra, translator.
Title: Pain / Zeruya Shalev ; translated from the Hebrew by Sondra Silverston.
Other titles: Ke'ev. English
Description: New York : Other Press, [2019] | "Originally published in Hebrew as
Ke'ev in 2015 by Keter Books."
Identifiers: LCCN 2019006874 (print) | LCCN 2019011397 (ebook) | ISBN
9781590510780 (ebook) | ISBN 9781590510926 (paperback)
Subjects: LCSH: Man-woman relationships—Fiction. | Families—Fiction. |
Jerusalem—Fiction.
Classification: LCC PJ5055.41.A43 (ebook) | LCC PJ5055.41.A43 K4413 2019 (print) |
DDC 892.4/36—dc23
LC record available at https://lccn.loc.gov/2019006874

Publisher's Note
This is a work of fiction. Names, characters, places, and incidents either
are the product of the author's imagination or are used fictitiously, and
any resemblance to actual persons, living or dead, events,
or locales is entirely coincidental.

PAIN

ONE

Here it is, back again, and although she's been expecting it
for years, she is surprised. Back again as if it never let go, as
if she didn't live a day without it, a month without it, a year;
after all, exactly ten years have passed since then. Mickey
had asked, "Remember today's date?" as if it were a birthday
or an anniversary, and she wracked her memory—they were
married in winter, met the winter before that, the children
were born in winter, nothing noteworthy occurred in their
lives in the summer despite its length, which seems to call for
countless events—and Mickey looked down, his gaze on her
hips, which have thickened since then, and all at once the
pain was back and she remembered.

Or did she remember first, and then the pain came back?
Because she has never forgotten, so it wasn't actually remembering, but rather existing totally in that burning moment,
in the dawning recognition of the cataclysm, in the ghostly
storm of panic, the solemn inertness of the silence: no bird

sang, no hawk soared, no bull roared, no ministering angels spoke holy words, the sea did not roil, people did not speak—the world was utterly still.

In time, she realized that silence was the one thing that hadn't been there, but nonetheless, only the silence was burned into her memory: mute angels came and bandaged her wounds silently, amputated limbs burned noiselessly and their owners observed them with sealed mouths, white ambulances sailed soundlessly along the streets, a narrow, winged gurney floated toward her and she was lifted up and placed on it, and the moment she was detached from the blazing asphalt was the moment the pain was born.

She had given birth to two children, and yet didn't recognize it when she experienced it for the first time in all its power, drilling into the core of her body, sawing her bones, pulverizing them into thin powder, trampling muscles, ripping out tendons, crushing tissue, tearing nerves, brutalizing the internal pulp she had never paid attention to, the stuff a person is made of. Only the organs above the neck had interested her, the skull and the brain inside it, consciousness and intelligence, knowledge and judgment, choice, identity, memory, and now she had nothing but that pulp, nothing but the pain.

"What happened?" he asks, and is immediately mortified. "What an idiot I am, I shouldn't have reminded you." And she leans on the wall near the door—they are on their way out of the house, each to his place of work—trying to point to the kitchen chairs with her eyes, and he hurries to the kitchen and returns with a glass of water, which she can't hold because her hand is sliding down the wall.

"Chair," she gasps, and he drags one toward her. But to her surprise, he sits down on it heavily, as if he is the one now suddenly seized by the pain, as if he is the one who had been there that morning exactly ten years ago when the powerful shockwaves of the explosion on the nearby bus hurled her out of her car onto the asphalt. And in fact, if it weren't for a last-minute change, he would have been there instead of her, floating in the fiery air like a huge asteroid, landing with a bang among the burning bodies.

And really, why wasn't he the one to take the children to school as he did every morning? She remembers an urgent call from the office, a glitch in a program, a system that crashed. He intended to drive them anyway, but Omer still wasn't dressed, jumping in his pajamas on their double bed, and she wanted to avoid tears and reprimands. "Never mind, I'll take them," she said, which of course did not prevent the regular morning argument with Omer, who locked himself in the bathroom and refused to come out, or Alma's crying about being late because of him. When, completely exhausted, she left them at the school gate and sped up the busy street, passing a bus that was standing at the stop, the most horrendous sound she ever heard smashed into her ears, followed by absolute silence.

Yet it wasn't the intensity of the explosion—that almost volcanic eruption of explosives, nails, screws, and nuts mixed with rat poison to increase the bleeding—that deafened her, but rather another sound, deeper and more horrendous, the sound of the dozens of bus passengers suddenly taking leave of their lives, the keening of mothers leaving behind their children, the cries of young girls who would never grow up, the lamentation of crushed organs, the scorched skin, the legs that would never walk again, the arms that would never embrace, the beauty that would wither into ashes. That is the

3

lamentation she hears again now, and she puts her hands over her ears as she drops heavily onto his lap.

"Oh Iris," he says, wrapping his arms around her, "I thought that nightmare was already behind us."

And she tries to wriggle out of his embrace, saying, "It'll pass in a minute. Maybe I moved in a way I shouldn't have, I'll take a pill and go to work."

But here it is again, every movement breaking down into a dozen tiny movements, each more painful than its predecessor, until even she, so meticulously restrained, known to be the strongest, most authoritative school principal, groans deeply.

But from behind her back, from behind the groan that surprises even her, comes a loud burst of laughter, and they both turn their heads to the end of the hallway where their son stands at the door of his room, tall and slender, tossing his mane of hair, which is bordered by shaved temples. Snorting like a horse, he says, "Hey, what's with you, Momdad? Why are you sitting one on top of the other? Thinking of making me a baby brother?"

"It really isn't funny, Omer," she grumbles, even though she also thinks they must look ridiculous. "The old injury started to hurt me and I had to sit down." Clad only in polka-dot boxers, he approaches them with slow, almost dancelike steps, carrying his beautiful body gracefully—how did their mating produce such a perfect body?

"Great, so feel free to sit," he laughs. "But why on Dad? And why does Dad have to sit? Does it hurt him too?"

"When you love someone, you feel their pain," Mickey replies in the didactic tone that Omer hates more than anything—so, in fact, did she—the tone that already contained the affront he will feel when his son ridicules him.

"Bring me a pill, Omer," she says. "No, make it two. They're in the kitchen drawer." As she gulps down the pain-killers, it seems to her that the force of her will alone would defeat the pain forever, it will disappear and never return. Pain doesn't return for no reason and with such intensity, it makes no sense. Everything was treated, joined together, sewn, screwed, and implanted in three different surgeries during a year of hospitalizations. Ten years have passed, she has grown used to living with pain at the change of seasons or after strenuous activity, and though she never returned to her pre-injury physical comfort, she didn't expect such a new wave, as if this morning, everything is happening again from the beginning.

"Help me up, Omer," she says, and still amused, he goes over to her, extends a strong, thin arm, and she's on her feet. She has to lean on the wall, but she won't give up. She'll go out of the house, walk to her car, and drive to school. She'll run the meetings efficiently, keep her appointments, inter-view new teachers, meet with the supervisor, stay to check on what was happening in the after-school classes, reply to the emails and messages that had accumulated. Only on the way home, in the afternoon, driving with her lips clenched in pain, will she turn her mind to the fact that Mickey re-mained sitting on the kitchen chair near the door, his head in his hands, even after she had already gone—escaped, to be more precise—as if he felt the pain with her, as if he was the one whose pelvis had been crushed that morning ex-actly ten years ago and it was his life that had been brought to a halt.

Trapped among dozens of cars in the crawling traffic on the way home, he had arrived, out of breath, at her bedside in the trauma room, his expression inscrutable. He wasn't the first to arrive—partial strangers had preceded him as the rumor spread quickly. The visitors and consolers came in reverse order, from distant acquaintances to the people closest to her, seven-year-old Omer and eleven-year-old Alma. Her friend Dafna had brought them there a moment before she was taken into the operating room, and when she saw them walking toward her, she remembered in horror that they were the only ones she'd forgotten to call. She had managed to leave a message on Mickey's cell phone and on her mother's home phone, punching in the numbers with bleeding fingers, wiping the blood on her shirt. The only place she'd forgotten to call was the kids' school, and the honest truth was that in all the hours that had passed before she saw them approaching her bed apprehensively, holding hands, she had completely forgotten their existence, forgotten that the woman who had floated momentarily over the flaming street until she crashed onto it was the mother of children.

She even found it difficult to recognize them at first, an odd pair walking toward her, a large boy and a tiny girl, he fair, she dark, he upset, she silent, two opposites walking together slowly and somberly, as if they intended to place an invisible wreath on her grave. She wanted to run away from them, but she was confined to the bed, so she closed her eyes until she heard them bleat in harmony, "Mommy!" and was forced to pull herself together. "I was lucky," she prattled at them, "it could have been much worse."

"You're allowed to show them that it's hard for you," one of the doctors told her later, "there's no need to pretend. Let them help you. That way you're teaching them to deal with their own difficulties as well." But she couldn't expose her weakness to them, and that's why she couldn't bear their presence during the long months of her recovery.

"It's all Omer's fault," she recalls Alma saying coldly, almost indifferently, as if pointing out an obvious fact. "If he didn't hide in the bathroom, we would have left earlier and you never would have been there when the bus exploded." And Omer began to kick his sister, screaming, "No it's not! It's all your fault! Because you wanted Mommy to make you a half-ponytail!" When Mickey tried to restrain him, the boy pointed at him and said, with the same defensiveness that always existed between them, "It's all your fault!"

They might have continued to blame each other, as if they were talking about an event that had occurred in their closed family circle and not a suicide bombing carried out by terrorists who didn't even know their small family, but she was whisked off to the terrible distraction of the long hours of the surgery and the surgery that followed it, of the months of rehabilitation and recovery and the new school appointment that awaited her at the end of the road as if it were a prize. She knew that some people said that were it not for her injury, she would not have been appointed principal at such a young age, and even she herself wondered about it now and then. But the enormous workload left her no time for futile thoughts. She hasn't had any futile thoughts for ten whole years, and as she parks her car and walks unsteadily to her home, it seems to her that she has only just awakened from an operation that lasted ten years, and only now can she think about the issue her children raised then. That's why she has accumulated so much experience, so she can decide once and for all who was actually at fault.

TWO

The elevator opens into the living room, creating the cold, impersonal feeling of a stairwell and lending an air of drama to every entrance, and that evening, when the stainless steel doors open and she enters her home, she once again feels momentarily like a guest, an uninvited guest who has mistaken the day or the time because no one is waiting for her, and she looks around the spacious living room uncomfortably. They moved from the center of town to gain a few more square meters, a separate room for each of their children and a large bedroom with a work area in a nondescript building in a charmless new neighborhood, and they have privacy now, but are unable to fill the shared space. As she looks around the living room, at the large couch, the small couch, the two armchairs, the coffee table in its center, the windows that usher in an urban landscape tinged with desert dust, the clean bright kitchen, the two pots on the polished gas range, she wonders for a moment whether real people live in this house, because it suddenly seems to her that it is empty, that it lacks substance.

Neither she nor Mickey has ever been interested in matters of design, caring only that the place be pleasant, comfortable, and visually neutral. They come home late anyway, and after dinner with the kids, she spends hours in front of the computer writing emails to teachers and parents, resolving conflicts, setting dates for appointments and meetings, planning her weekly principal's letter to parents, so what difference does one sort of flooring or another, one sort of upholstery or another really make. The important thing is to have a place to rest a tired body.

The door to Omer's room opens and she is about to make herself smile at him when she sees that it isn't Omer who comes out, but a slender, orange-haired girl in a tight tank top and tiny underpants hurrying in embarrassment to the bathroom, and Iris sighs in relief as she stares at her supple hips. The many fears she had while raising Omer were proven false, and this girl is further corroboration. When she emerges from the bathroom, Iris tries to see the face behind the curtain of long hair—has she already seen her before? Over the last several months, when she wakes him in the morning a girl sometimes emerges from his bed, even though she saw him get into it alone, as if she had hatched during the night.

Pleased, she watches the girl disappear back into Omer's room and turns to go into the kitchen. She has to eat something, if only so she can take another pill. Steamy white rice and beans as orange as the girl's hair await her in the pots. Lately, she's been asking the cleaner to cook for them occasionally. Omer is always hungry, and who has enough strength left to cook after work? What a pleasure it is to find two full pots on the gas range, to be rid of the endless burden of preparing food, however easy it has become to attain. But the taste of it seems to have changed, and a vague feeling of strangeness has intensified, as if this were a modest neighborhood restaurant, a mundane hotel—anything but a home.

Nonsense, she laughs at herself, nonsense has been fermenting in her mind since this morning like garbage in a khamsin. A home, not a home—what difference does it make? The main thing is that they don't go hungry, that there's a roof over their heads, that they're working, that the kids are more or less okay. If only this torture would stop, because she is swallowing a couple of pills again to push away the waves of pain. Like labor pains, they come every minute or two and wrap themselves around her body, sawing through her pelvic cage bone after bone, and she lies down on the couch, groaning deeply. An early summer wind, hot and ominous, blows into the house, but she is so cold that she feels as if her bones are being ground under her skin. It seems to her that, in a moment, the wind will carry off the bone splinters and perhaps then the pain will stop. She'll give them up, and not only them, she'll give up all her painful organs, let her body empty out, if only it would stop. She can't allow herself to rest, she has messages to write, crises to resolve, she'll get up in a minute and drag herself to her work area, sit down in front of the computer, gird her loins—she wonders about that expression, which apparently was coined for her because that's precisely where the pain begins, in her loins, which were once as slender as the waist of the girl who has just gone into the kitchen, clad for some reason in Omer's polka-dot boxers. Will he appear wearing her tiny underpants?

Through closed eyelids she peers at him with that old fear—he was always unpredictable. "Madam Principal!" he calls to her, saluting for some reason, and she sees with relief that he's wearing exercise shorts. He is in excellent spirits—if somebody's heart is going to be broken here, it won't be his, and she watches them as they eat across from one another in the dining room, filling and refilling their plates. "Delicious!" they purr with full mouths as if they are complimenting each other, chewing and laughing, and she's surprised at how little they speak. Does her presence silence them, or do they have no need of words to make them feel close?

How different they are from the way we were, she thinks. I was exactly Omer's age and Eitan was slightly older, and we talked endlessly and laughed very little. There wasn't much to laugh about then, when his mother was dying and Eitan, her only son, nursed her devotedly, sitting at her bedside in the hospital for hours and hours. From there, he would come to her house, tall and gaunt, his pale eyes burning with sad bewilderment, and she would feed him, console him, soothe him with her love.

What do they understand, she thinks angrily, observing with sudden hostility as her son and his girlfriend chew across the table from each other, forage around in the fridge, then return to the table with something else that is delicious, "really delicious," they say, trying to be exact, their fingers brushing. Why does the happy sight make her feel so nauseous? Or perhaps there is no connection, after all, she has been feeling nauseous since morning. She isn't jealous of her son, heaven forbid, on the contrary, she's grateful that he has been spared Eitan's torment or her suffering when he abandoned her, because immediately after the seven days of mourning for his mother, after the last mourner left the house and before they went to visit her grave, he told her clearly and coldly, as if he had prepared it all in advance, that he planned to start a new life, a life without pain, and she had no part in it.

"It's not personal, Rissi," he had added generously, "I'm just tired of being weighed down," as if she were the one weighing him down when all she wanted was to ease his burden. "Try to understand me. I'm not even eighteen yet. I want to live," he said, "I want to forget this terrible year, and you're part of it." She listened to him horrified, and even years later, when she remembered his words, her teeth chattered, and she could still see the way his jaws moved incessantly beneath his smooth cheeks.

"I don't believe it. You're punishing me for being with you, for supporting you this whole year," she had said in a stunned voice.

"It's not punishment, Rissi, it's inevitable," he said, "if I met you now, everything would be different. I would definitely fall in love with you and we'd be together, but we met too soon. Maybe we'll have another chance someday, but now I have to save myself."

"Save yourself from me?" she asked, astonished, "what have I done to you?" He took her hand and for a moment seemed to share her feelings, to be sad along with her about this inevitable turn of events. But he quickly withdrew both his commiseration and his hand, for which she has never forgiven him, Eitan Rosenfeld, her first love and maybe her last, because never again did she feel that absolute, indisputable emotion. To this day, she hasn't forgiven him for feeling no remorse for her, for their love, or for the cruel breakup he forced upon her, because even if he had believed it necessary, he should have mourned along with her and not left her that way, alone with the fate he sentenced her to, alone with the loss of purpose and hope, of trust and youth, the loss that, for her, was on a par with the loss of his mother, the loss she barely recovered from.

"What's with you, Mom?" Omer says, walking over to her. She must have groaned unintentionally. "Why are you lying there like a sack of potatoes? Is there a strike I haven't heard about?" His chest is long and narrow, compact and smooth, and his cheeks are still almost hairless, like Eitan's.

"My own personal strike," she says, "I'm in terrible pain. Get me a pill from the drawer and a glass of water, Omy." If the pain stops, she thinks, so will the memory. She hasn't allowed herself to think about Eitan for so many years, nor has she lain idly on the couch for many years, and in the meantime, her son has almost reached his age without her noticing and his girlfriend is giving her the same curious glance that she herself gave Eitan's mother when she saw her for the first time, lying on the couch in the living room of their small apartment.

Eitan was the only son of a single mother who had only one breast. She had fallen ill and undergone surgery when he was a child, and Iris remembers the surprise in his eyes at the sight of the perfect symmetry of her upper torso when he undressed her for the first time. She also remembers looking surreptitiously at the neckline of his mother's worn pajama top when she sat beside him at her bedside in the hospital, and the scarred crater that showed when she leaned toward them did not look like anything she had ever seen before, nor did the large moonlike skull that hung swaying above the thin neck. She loved going to see him there, stroking his free hand as the other held his mother's, she loved the silence in

13

the ward, the sacred silence of a battle of titans, of the expectation of miracles, of life that was being peeled away, layer by layer, until only the exposed, trembling inner core was left, the essence of existence that refused to depart. She pictured herself at his side, walking through a forest of withering, breaking trees of life. How could she possibly have imagined that her devotion to him in his distress would arouse such antipathy in him? For her, those had been hours that bound them together in a holy mission—he and she, a young boy and girl in the world, trying to lessen suffering, he trying to alleviate his mother's, and she trying to alleviate his. For long months, she felt that her home was there, at the bedside of the noble, sick woman, that they were her true family and not the harsh, demanding mother, a war widow who gave little and expected much, not the twins who were born four and a half years after her and filled the house with noise. No, she belonged to them—the refined woman suffering in silence, and her only son, who was so devoted to her. But if she had become less involved in their pain, if she had kept herself separate, she would not have been abandoned, for she quickly realized that his extreme abandonment of her was the other side of his extreme devotion.

Until one day in early summer she went there again after school, a sour apple and a carton of chocolate milk in her bag for him, and before entering the room, she saw through the curtain the smooth skull swaying back and forth in an aggressive, rebellious way she had never seen before. Eitan, looking pale, came out to her and said, "Come back later, Rissi, this isn't a good time," but she stood frozen in place at the door to the ward, knowing she'd never be coming there again, unable to leave.

She saw two nurses hurry to the room and heard a terrible, animallike voice coming from inside. She couldn't believe it came from the throat of that most delicate of women. In awe, she watched from behind the screen as if she were standing before a divine revelation, before a miraculous, supernatural sight of the sort you learn about in Bible lessons, a burning bush, the giving of the Torah at Mount Sinai, until one of the nurses closed the door in her face and she walked away on trembling legs. She sat down on a bench in the lobby of the building, the neutral territory between the land of the sick and the land of the healthy, and took tiny bites of the apple she had brought for him. When evening fell, Eitan emerged, his shoulders stooped, his gaze lowered to the coarse floor tiles of the lobby, not surprised to find her there. They walked slowly, the way they would walk the next day behind her body, wrapped in a white sheet, as if both of them had been orphaned.

She continued to walk beside him that way during the seven days of mourning—she was his seventeen-year-old wife receiving the mourners, including her mother and brothers. At night, she stroked his back until he fell asleep, and in the morning, she got up before him and readied the house for a new day of mourning. That, in fact, was how she saw their future—an endless shiva, a comforting, painful, and sometimes happy din of seven days of mourning that fused them together so they would grow as one, like two plants in a single pot, nourished by the same soil.

It was her second time being born, her second time losing a parent, choosing to be born and to mourn at his side. And so she became his mother, his sister, his wife, and the mother of his children, because her young body burned with the desire to give birth to a baby girl and name her after his mother. At night, when he wept in his sleep, she felt the little crown emerge from between her legs. Only she could give birth to her again and honor her memory, only she could console him, but when the shiva ended, she found that she was not only an orphan and a widow, but also bereft of all her dreams.

She packed her belongings in two large garbage bags and walked resolutely, her head held high, from his house to the bus stop without looking back. She boarded the right bus, got off at the right station, reached her house, and climbed into bed with her clothes on, the bags of her belongings at her side, and lay there with dry, open eyes until her mother arrived. She didn't answer her questions because she didn't hear them, and she didn't respond to her pleas to get up and eat or shower. Beneath her dry eyes, her body had frozen and remained in the same position for days. "Once I was so sad that I was paralyzed," she told Mickey a short time before they got married, "I was paralyzed for a few weeks, but I'm fine and it won't ever happen again."

Mickey, of course, wanted to hear more, and she disappointed him in that as well, but her mother occasionally mentioned it, giving away one detail or another, and the menacing looks she shot her way were of no avail. "Yes, I was depressed. Who doesn't get depressed about love when they're seventeen?" she summed up in an effort to convey how unimportant the memory was to her, focused more on her mother's betrayal than on the matter at hand. And what was the matter at hand, she sometimes wondered. That she had almost died of the disease called love? And what was more surprising, her disease or her recovery? The fact that, in the end, she chose life, chose to be born again, all alone, into the emptiness that slowly filled up?

As her daughter has grown into a young woman, she has followed her love life with apprehension, frightened that she would have a similar breakdown, but for the time being, Alma has only brief, superficial relationships. She can, of course, find something in that to worry about, but not to the same degree, and in any case, Alma doesn't tend to keep her in the picture. Her son seems calm and relaxed with the girl wearing his underpants, and apparently her fears on that front will not be coming true in the near future, she can stop watching the young couple taking shape before her eyes. Meanwhile, the pain has lessened, leaving her body stunned. She senses it observing her from a distance, permitting her to get up from the couch slowly and sit down at the computer as she does every evening to write her weekly principal's letter to parents along with messages and instructions, questions and answers. What will she write about tonight? Perhaps she'll try to breathe life into the last few weeks of the school year between Memorial Day and the Festival of Weeks, the tired time after most of the year has passed but before it has ended, the time that is much more crucial than it seems, because if something can still change, that's when it will, in the tension between memory and renewal.

THREE

She hasn't seen that time on the clock for years: 3:40 in the morning. An unbearable hour. For years she has been as protective of her sleep as if her life depended on it. At ten o'clock, she already begins her going-to-bed rituals. "Wait a while, what's the rush?" Mickey occasionally complains from in front of the TV, "The movie Dafna and Gidi recommended is just starting," or "This series is really terrific, you'll love it." And sometimes he says nothing, merely observes her departure with bitterness in his eyes.

"I need to sleep, I have a very busy day tomorrow, a meeting first thing in the morning," she says, but even when there is no teachers' meeting, she is always the first one at school. Standing at the entrance gate every morning, winter and summer, she says good morning to the pupils as they arrive, remembers them by name, exchanges a few words with their parents. But he isn't impressed. "You're not the only one who works hard, you know. You're not the only one who gets up early."

"Sorry, Mooky, I'm dead tired. My eyes are closing," she mutters, evading his arm, which is trying to hold her back. It isn't only the early hour that angers him, she knows, but mainly her decision to turn Alma's room into her bedroom when she left the house a few months earlier. "It doesn't mean anything, Mooky," she said, trying to mollify him. "It's just more comfortable sleeping alone, that's all. Sleeping together is a primitive custom—we only disturb one another. There's even been some research on it. Don't you hate it when I wake you up because you're snoring?" Yes, he expected her to accept his snoring with love, and he certainly didn't expect her to desert to Alma's three-quarter bed and close the door in his face.

"It's not against you, it's for me. It's only sleep, it doesn't have to affect intimacy," she kept telling him, honestly and truly believing that it wouldn't have an effect, why should it? After all, couples don't make love while sleeping, don't have heart-to-heart talks while sleeping, and anyway, when Alma comes home, she'll give her back her room and return to their double bed. But who would have thought that Alma would come home so infrequently, barely once a month, and that the things she now kept on the night table beside Alma's bed would settle there. The eye cream, the glass of water, the socks—her feet were always cold—the hand cream, a book or two, slowly their number increased until, on her last visit, Alma said, "Great job Mom, you've taken over my room! You want me to sleep with Daddy in your place?"

Of course, she collected her things quickly and put them back in their former place, already deciding that she had no choice, she'd go back to sleeping with Mickey. But to her great dismay she discovered that all the things that had disturbed her before disturbed her a hundred times more now that she had grown used to the freedom of having her bed to herself. After a totally sleepless night at his side, she found herself waiting impatiently for her daughter to leave her bed and go back to her roommate in the apartment they had rented for her in Tel Aviv, which she did in the evening. She was so tired that she couldn't even have a serious conversation with her daughter that weekend to hear a bit more about what she was doing and what her plans were, though Alma would probably have avoided such a conversation even in the face of a much more alert mother, because she wasn't doing anything and had no plans except to waitress at night in a restaurant in south Tel Aviv and sleep during the day.

How could they have produced such a daughter, so lacking in ambition and direction? Even as a child, she never stuck with any after-school activities, never took an interest in anything, sat for hours in front of the TV or the mirror, who knows which is worse. For all these years, she saw her parents working hard, but it seemed to have had no impact on her. Even if Iris managed to have a conversation with her on the weekend, her daughter would surely have mocked her, "It's all good, Mom, lighten up. I'm not a pupil in your school, or maybe I should say not a soldier. After all, they're like little soldiers there."

"So why do they come en masse to register if it's so terrible?" she'd defend herself quickly, re-creating in all its details a conversation that never took place, though similar ones have buzzed between them these last few years, fragmented, oblique conversations that were meant to bring them closer but always drove them further apart, meant to clarify but always obscured. Naively, she expected her daughter to be proud of her, to value her life's work—transforming a failing school in a poor neighborhood into the most sought-after school in the city—and she certainly didn't expect such ridicule. "I guess it suits them, but not me," Alma would say, looking up at her defiantly. How could they have produced such a short daughter? All her friends' daughters were taller than their mothers, and only Alma remained short, even though both she and Mickey were tall.

As a young child, she hardly ate, and all their pleas and threats were futile. Only when she was distracted in front of the TV did they sometimes manage to get some food inside her, shoving a wedge of omelet, a slice of cheese, a vegetable patty into her mouth, and she would move her jaws absently, chew and swallow, until she suddenly shook herself as if waking from sleep and protested loudly.

How her heart had pounded during those stealthy feedings, as if her daughter were standing on the edge of a high roof and she had to sneak up behind her and grab her before she became aware of her presence. Every omelet bite took her one step further away from the edge. She was a young mother and thought that her daughter's thinness reflected very badly on her, so she tried to fight it with every means possible, until Omer was born and his demanding presence drained her strength so much that she couldn't continue all the maneuvering, wheedling, pleading, and threatening, which naturally benefited everyone. The fact was that the girl survived. She must have eaten enough to exist, and during adolescence, she even developed a healthy appetite while all her girlfriends tortured themselves with fasting. But by then it was already too late to affect her height, and she remained so short and thin that she looked like a twelve-year-old, but breathtakingly beautiful with those huge black grape-colored eyes, that long straight hair, the combination of her childlike body and mature, seductive expression.

Who can say exactly whom she is seducing? Definitely not her parents, whose questions she pushes firmly away. Since she moved to Tel Aviv, they have completely lost any chance of supervising and gathering information and are now dependent on whatever she deigns to tell them. She occasionally provides some bits of information, but all attempts to get her to expand on a party she went to or a waitress she's become friendly with fail miserably, and if they try to use what she tells them to draw closer to her, the next time they speak to her, she denies everything she said as if it were a figment of their imagination.

"She's punishing us," she sometimes says to Mickey, who shrugs dismissively. "What are you talking about, why would she punish us?" If it weren't so pointless, she could list the reasons easily: letting Omer steal all our attention, and later, you know what, that terrible year, the hospitalizations, the operations, the rehabilitation, an entire year when her mother barely functioned. When she was home, she was totally dependent on them, but most of the time she was in hospitals because she had pelvic fractures, openings in her legs and shrapnel in her chest, her pelvis had to be stabilized with fixators, her broken legs had to be set and skin transplanted over the lesions. There were parts of her body she did not feel at all, and others she felt much too intensely. She had to relearn how to walk and how to sit, she had to wean herself from painkillers, from her fear of leaving the house, from the terror she felt at the screech of a bus engine every time it pulled out of a stop.

When she returned to life, she found a different child there, closed and almost hostile, attached to her father, looking at her accusingly. That was when Alma started doing the minimum required of her at school, just as she did at the dining table, tasting only a bit of what was offered, not with curiosity, but just enough to survive. And Iris? She had just won her bid to become principal of the school and had returned to life hungrily, busier than ever before, so perhaps she hadn't paid enough attention to her daughter. Omer always knew how to demand, but Alma was apparently the kind of person who waited and was disappointed, like her father, and the two of them saw her through her rehabilitation and recovery with a mechanical devotion that was both desperate and cool, sometimes making her feel as if the few seconds she had floated in the air had propelled her into a different country, from which she could never return.

Every now and then Mickey came into the bedroom, where she was confined to her bed for long months, carrying a plateful of a strange-looking concoction he cooked and a cup of tea that had already cooled, and asked how she was and what she needed. But even the rare times she asked him to stay, "Come and sit with me for a while, tell me what's happening," it seemed to be more than he could manage. He was undoubtedly drained and exhausted from taking care of her and the children, in addition to going to work, but beyond that, it seemed to her that he was as cold as the tea he brought her and as strange as the food he cooked, because he avoided her gaze for months, as if he were to blame for what had happened to her.

She even joked about it sometimes. Less than a year ago they moved to that apartment with the elevator that Mickey was so excited about. "Why do we need an elevator at the age of thirty-five?" she wondered, preferring a different apartment altogether with a view of the Dead Sea and a large balcony, which seemed to her immeasurably more exciting. He, who bragged that he always saw one step ahead, said, "You can never know what's going to happen. An elevator is always necessary," which turned out to be so true a short time later when she was injured, and caused her to joke about his access to intelligence, saying that he would be more useful in the secret service than in high tech.

But he never found that funny, and now, at 3:40 or a bit later—she doesn't dare look at the clock again—when the pain won't let her fall back to sleep, she finds herself re-creating moment after moment of that morning, wondering once again about the most random combinations of time and space that lead to the greatest disasters, as well as the most awe-inspiring miracles.

She remembers that Mickey had stayed at work until late the night before. She was already asleep when he came home, and when she woke up in the morning, he was already dressed and said he was in a hurry, they'd called from the office. During those years, he was at home much less than now. When the children needed him more, that's when he was rarely around, and today, when it doesn't matter one way or the other, he comes home early, plays chess at the computer for hours, and then stretches out with a sigh on the couch in front of the TV. But he was always with her in the mornings, helping with the kids—with Omer, that is, who was in the first grade and suffered so much there, he claimed, that they could barely get him out of the house. He would lock himself in the bathroom, and no threats or promises, no rewards or punishments helped.

But on that morning, Omer was relatively cheerful. She remembers that he was jumping wildly on the double bed, Mickey was already dressed and she was just waking up. It was a clear, almost cool, early summer morning, and Mickey was wearing the old, thin, mustard-colored jacket she didn't like but that he refused to get rid of. Omer was singing so loudly that they couldn't hear one another, making up the words; "Little kids paint with pee and poop," he screamed, managing, as always, to make everyone tense and irritable.

"You're leaving already?" she asked. "No one's ready yet, it's not even seven," and Omer screamed, "I'm seven already! Did you forget that I'm seven?" Mickey said, "They called from work, the system crashed, I have to fix it." And she asked again, "At this hour?" as if it were the middle of the night. "Omer," he said, "be quiet already," even though at that particular moment, the boy was jumping in silence, which immediately became loud wailing and then turned into a very annoying song: "Daddy's pee, Daddy's poop, talks to me like an asshole." That forced her to intervene: "Enough, Omer, I don't allow you to talk to Daddy like that!" And Mickey, whose will always ebbed and flowed, had already started to unzip his jacket and said, "Never mind, I'll stay with you and drive them like always."

Their school was on his way and not hers, and she was on sabbatical then anyway, had completed her master's degree, and loved to shower leisurely and drink her coffee after everyone was gone. But she saw in his face that it was important for him to go, that the glitch in the system was bothering him.

So she decided to forgo one leisurely morning for his sake, to make up for something else much bigger that always made her feel a bit of compassion for him, a bit of guilt, which made her angry, sometimes at him and sometimes herself.

She sat up in bed across from the mirrored doors of the closet. Her face looked white and tired, her hair black and unkempt, and she smoothed it down and looked at his worried profile. Omer had already left the room and was apparently beginning to cause a commotion in Alma's room, because they immediately heard her familiar shouting: "Get out of here! Dad! Mom!"

She leaped out of bed, and as she passed him, she said, "Go fix your system. I'll take care of them." He pulled the zipper of his jacket up and down indecisively, and the slight movement of his fingers on the zipper put an end to their indecision and sealed their fate. And the fates of dozens of other people were sealed as well as they began their daily routines, washing bodies that would soon be buried in the ground, bending to put on shoes that would be ripped off in exactly one hour, spreading moisturizer on skin that would burn, saying a quick goodbye to the child they would never see again, changing the diaper of a baby who had only another hour to live. She also began her morning routine, put on a loose striped shirt and jeans and pulled her hair back carelessly because she'd be home soon, promised Omer pizza for lunch if he came out of his hiding place quickly, made sandwiches and put them in their backpacks, and even managed to comb Alma's hair into an especially nice half-ponytail before they left. In the car, she heard the end of the eight o'clock news and Alma screamed that she was late again because of him, but in less than ten minutes they were at the school gates and she was speeding up the hill with a pleasant sense of liberation, passing a bus that was standing at a stop.

Why the sense of liberation, she wonders now, what was it that had made her suddenly feel relief several seconds before her life imploded? Can she attribute such great significance to that moment when she told him he was free to go? Because only now does she understand that it was a special morning, a morning that heralded change. Perhaps that was why she had insisted on passing the bus that had already signaled it was pulling out, had tailgated it and even honked her horn, driving with an impatience that was completely uncharacteristic of her. But that honking was swallowed up in the shock waves of the explosion.

He was in a hurry and all she did was tell him he could go, how much significance could that possibly have had? In retrospect, every detail seems momentous, but she needs to examine them at face value, in their real time, stripped of the clothes the future clad them in. She strains to turn over in bed, supporting her thighs with her hands, remembering once again how painful even the slightest movement can be. To her surprise, she hears sounds in the kitchen, then water flushing in the bathroom. It isn't Omer's rapid movements, so it must be Mickey—funny that he can't sleep either. It's already five in the morning, how will she survive tomorrow, hour after hour?

"Mickey? Is that you there?" she groans. He opens the door and peers inside, his shaved skull looking momentarily as if it were hanging in the air, reminding her suddenly of the bald head of the sick mother, and she is horrified. What happened to her today, what is happening to her tonight—it can't go on. It's all his fault. Why did he have to remind her, as if it were a wedding anniversary or a birthday. Omer was right when he said it was all Daddy's fault.

"What's up?" he asks in a soft voice, "Why aren't you sleeping?"

"I'm in terrible pain," she says. "Bring me another pill."

He comes back from the kitchen with a packet of pills and says, "You've emptied the drawer, aren't you overdoing it with these drugs?"

"Do I have a choice?"

"Apparently you do," he says as he sits down on her bed. "I heard that there all sorts of new improvements in pain treatment now. You should check them out. There's laser therapy, cortisone injections, all kinds of methods. Maybe you should make an appointment at a pain clinic?"

"Pain clinic? Already?" she says, surprised. He always thinks ahead, as with the elevator. She's thinking only about tomorrow morning, it never enters her mind that the pain might continue for days and weeks. "So you figure it'll continue for a long time. How depressing. I've learned to take you seriously after you foresaw the terrorist attack."

"Right, I really foresaw it," he laughs bitterly, "it's a good thing you're not saying I carried it out." She swallows the pill and tries to sit up, leaning on the large pillow Alma received from her friends as a gift when she went into the army.

"Then why were you in such a hurry that morning? Usually, when you work late, you don't go into the office so early."

He answers quickly, as if that same thought woke him up in the middle of the night. "Don't you remember? There was some kind of glitch, the system crashed."

"It's strange," she says, "that such a thing never happened before or after, not at that hour anyway."

"Come on, enough already, Iris, let's not open that wound again. You know how it torments me. If I had taken the kids, I would have been injured instead of you, and there's a good chance I wouldn't have been injured at all because we would have left a few minutes earlier. Everything would have been different if I hadn't been in a hurry that morning. We might have had another child, or maybe we would have separated."

"Separated?" she says, astonished.

"Yes, maybe you would have left me. You always felt you deserved someone better. But after I took such good care of you, you couldn't allow yourself."

She stares in surprise at the shaved skull—how mysterious another person's brain is, even more mysterious than the future. "What are you talking about? You didn't take good care of me at all! The food was horrible, you avoided me all the time, you acted weirdly. If I'd wanted to leave you, that would definitely not have been a problem. Maybe you're the one who wanted to leave me, but couldn't anymore?

"Tell me," she says as his large head moves closer, "what exactly was wrong with that system?"

"And what exactly is wrong with your system?" he teases and tries to kiss her. "Since you left me alone in bed, I've already forgotten how you look at night."

She tries to push him away, saying, "Don't change the subject, Mickey. What was so urgent? You came home in the middle of the night, almost morning. Why didn't they call someone else to fix the glitch?"

"What's going on with you?" he protests. "Why are you bringing this up now, all of a sudden? That was ten years ago, Iris, it's been behind us for a long time!"

"It hurts me as if it happened yesterday," she says with a groan, and he whispers, "Show me where," pulls her nightgown up to her waist and begins caressing her. His breath burns on her scarred skin, and under it, platinum plates, bone transplants, wires and screws, the shrapnel left in her body—all of it clatters in protest against his touch, and she cries out more loudly than she intended, "Don't touch me, Mickey, it hurts!"

"Great, you've found the perfect excuse! Maybe you should just admit that you were never attracted to me," he mutters, taking his hands off her, placing them on his knees and staring at them for some reason.

"I don't believe what I'm hearing," she gasps furiously. "You picked one hell of a time to settle old scores!"

"You're the one who's settling old scores with me," he says. "All of a sudden you just have to know what made the system crash? You're interrogating me as if I went rushing out to see a lover."

"That never entered my mind," she says in a hollow voice. "What are you talking about? What do you want from me now?"

"Not a lot, really," he says. "A little love, a little warmth so that I feel I have a wife at home."

"I'm so tired of your self-pity. We're not talking about you now, we're talking about me. I'm in pain and all you can offer is sex? Why can't I ever get a little empathy without sex?"

"I'll never understand you," he protests, putting his head in his hands. "There's always something wrong! Either you complain that I avoid you or else that I get too close to you!"

Once again feeling that old compassion for him, she says, "It's just a matter of timing, Mooky. There are no rules of behavior here. Sometimes we want closeness and sometimes we need distance. We've been together for one hundred years already, don't tell me you don't understand that."

"Of course I understand, Madam Principal. It's just that I'm sorry to say that you want less and less closeness."

"There are all kinds of closeness," she says, "too bad that you only know one of them."

He straightens up with a sigh and fragments of morning light are reflected in delicate stripes on his bare back, like zebra skin. "There are all kinds of distance," he says, "too bad that you know only one of them. Have a great day."

FOUR

She never imagined she would find herself in this place again so soon, as if she is sentenced to relive the entire history of her injury, because the pain that suddenly returned dictates its own schedule, disrupts her routines like a new baby. Those mornings of rising early and hurrying to school to wait at the gates and welcome every student seem far off, rooted in another time. She hasn't left the house in ten days, hasn't visited her kingdom bustling with obedient young subjects in ten days, and it seems to her that her home can no longer contain the pain, so it pushes her out into the sickeningly familiar corridors of the hospital she hoped not to see again for many years, preferably never.

She rests her head on Mickey's shoulder, glad he's at her side in this place that swiftly erases the vestiges of her identity that the pain still hasn't managed to wipe out. A woman in pain, that's what she is now, which is why she's here, waiting her turn to see the senior physician. But the man at her side is proof, at least on the surface, that there are other things in her life aside from the pain, so when it's their turn to go into the office, she leans on his arm conspicuously and allows him to respond in her place to the first, simpler questions posed by the doctor, who doesn't look at all senior.

Not the least bit senior, he truly looks like a child, Mickey must have grabbed the first appointment offered him, or tried, as usual, to save money. She is already giving him an angry look, which he doesn't notice, but the skeleton hanging behind him gives her an empty-eye-socket look in return. To her horror, she sees that it's missing a leg, and she looks at it in alarm, it seems real to her, the legless corpse that burned beside her on the street.

Why did you hang a skeleton without a leg here, she wants to ask. Is it so hard for you to attach a leg? You manage to do much more complicated things! But the doctor is already speaking to her, asking her in a slightly chirpy voice to walk across the room and sit down on the bed, then to bend and stretch her legs, and he taps her knees with a hammer. "Please lie on your back," he says, "roll up your pants and tell me where it hurts when I press down and how much it hurts on a scale of one to ten." His touch burns as if his fingers are on fire, and she cries out involuntarily.

Does the scream frighten him, or does he need an adult's help, because after the initial examination, while she is still lying on the narrow bed, her pelvis exposed, he mumbles, "I want the unit chief to see you," and immediately presses one of the numbers on the old-fashioned phone on his desk. "Dr. Rosen, are you free by any chance?" he asks hesitantly, and a moment later the door opens and a tall, slightly stooped man in a white coat, his hair graying and his beard whitening, enters. At first, she focuses on the fact that the man has covered himself with so much hair, totally unlike the completely shaven Mickey, who lately looks like a cat without fur, that they appear to be two different species of the human race. The unit chief barely looks at her, but carefully examines the x-rays displayed on the small screen and listens to the young doctor describe her history in detail as if they were old friends—the complicated injuries, the surgeries she underwent, the shrapnel still left in her body, the pelvic pains radiating to her legs that began all at once—and perhaps that's why he doesn't recognize her.

And how could he recognize her? She was seventeen when he saw her last and today she is forty-five, almost thirty years have passed. Before the injury, she maintained her youthful appearance—long hair and slender body despite the births—but after the explosion, when her hair had almost gone up in flames, she cut it quite short and in no particular style. Her no longer active body widened, to her dismay, but she is too busy to spend time on her appearance, and he sees before him now a woman who is no longer young, her hair graying and neglected, her heavy, scarred pelvis exposed to above her groin. Will he recognize the two beauty marks on the left side of her navel which, together, create an astronomical trio? The sun, the moon, and the earth, he used to call them, and she thinks that they are the only detail of her physical appearance that hasn't changed over the years. His appearance has also changed radically, she honestly didn't recognize him at all under that cloak of hair, not even the blue eyes, which are slightly darker against the background of the grayness of his cheeks. But her body suddenly begins to tremble uncontrollably and Mickey asks, "Are you cold?" He immediately covers her with a sheet patterned with a Star of David, as if he is deliberately hiding the sun, the moon, and the earth, and she looks at him hostilely, forgetting how happy she was to lean on his arm only a few minutes earlier.

Why didn't she come without him? How will she reintroduce herself to her first love with him there? Or is it better this way, to cover the identifying marks, to avoid eye contact? He certainly doesn't recognize her, she changed her surname, she looks different, and anyway, it's the x-rays he is studying so carefully, not the actual person, in the way of all senior physicians. If she doesn't identify herself, he won't recognize her, and she won't identify herself because Mickey is beside her and because she isn't prepared for this meeting. She steals glances at him, pulling the sheet up almost to her eyes, maybe it isn't him at all, maybe he merely looks like Eitan, or more precisely, the way Eitan might look today.

He appears older than his age, maybe this isn't him at all. It isn't probable that Eitan would become a doctor because like her, he was much more interested in literature than science, and unlike her, he wasn't at all a good student. Nonetheless her body insists it's him, and she watches him breathlessly, hears him explain to the young doctor as if he is the patient and not she, that he believes this to be a case of damaged nerves that didn't heal properly and are transmitting pain to the brain even when there is no problem in the tissues.

"Send her for a pelvic ultrasound," he says, "though I don't think they'll find anything. Give her the minimum dose of painkillers for the time being and set up an appointment with her in a month. There is sometimes a delay in nerve pain, so let's hope it passes just as abruptly as it appeared." Leaving his diagnosis behind, he walks out of the room quickly without even glancing at her.

"What does that mean?" Mickey asks just as she asks, "Who is that?" and the young doctor looks at them dubiously, like a boy embarrassed by his dimwitted parents.

"That's the unit chief, Dr. Rosen," he says.

"Did his name used to be Rosenfeld?" she asks at the same time that Mickey asks, "So the pain isn't real?" His question drowns out hers, the doctor can't hear it and she can't hear his answers in the extreme agitation in the room, which they all feel in some way and are unable to shake off.

"So it turns out that the pain is a defense mechanism." Mickey repeats the doctor's explanation as they drive up the hilly road. "The nervous system produces the pain to warn you that something is wrong with the tissues, but when it's damaged, it's like a smoke alarm that keeps on beeping even after the fire is out. Do you get the picture? It's absolutely fascinating! He says that sometimes, it's actually the healing process that causes the problem. The damaged nerve that heals and comes back to life begins to transmit distress. It's called post-traumatic pain."

"I'm glad you find it so exciting," she says, "because I find it depressing." She fixes her glance on the window, and the sickeningly familiar scenery looks suddenly new because Eitan sees that tree every morning, because he takes this bend in the road. She wants so much to be back there that she can barely keep herself from saying to Mickey, Take me back to the hospital, drop me off and drive away, or alternatively, from opening the car door while it's still moving and getting out without saying anything. In that brief, wordless meeting, her life had appeared to her as a worn-out body, scarred and useless. She hasn't recovered and never will, she has only been pretending for thirty years. Maybe the time has come to give up, today, after seeing him again, and that meeting filled her with dread, as if she were seeing the terrorist who had exploded the bomb on the bus. When that happens, you can either cling to life with all your strength or give up on it, there is no middle way, so she will open the door and let her pain-wracked body fall onto the side of the road. Cars will pass her, and maybe on his way home to the family he must certainly have, he will pass her too and not stop. After all, she reminds him of that terrible year, of his sick mother, which is why he ran away from her then. But now he has returned and dedicated his life to illness by becoming a doctor, he has returned to the same place he fled as a young man, though not to her.

Did he search for her, did he ever try to find her? It's so much easier to locate people today than it was twenty or thirty years ago, but if he really wanted to, he would have succeeded. Probably he eventually married a woman he loved who didn't remind him of the wretched young man he had been, and with her, he ultimately returned to the world of the sick not as a powerless orphan, but rather as someone who could help, and by doing so heal himself. And what about her? Has she been given the chance to find the light in a sea of darkness, to turn weakness into strength, anguish into achievement? Has she given herself that chance? On the surface, it seems as if she has, her mother often praised her for that over the first few years. In fact, until recently and on less appropriate occasions, of course, she had said, "I thought that dreadful boy had ruined your life. I didn't think you'd ever have a family or a career. Do you have any idea what became of him?" She spoke with complete disregard for her daughter's clear aversion to the subject, and Iris would reply coldly, "I have no interest in knowing. I'm not in contact with anyone from those years." But her mother would reproach her, "How could you not? You had such good friends. What about Dina, or Ella?" and then she would say again, "I have no idea, Mother. Why do you care so much?"

Of course, she knows that her mother was making a valiant effort to keep her daughter's youth fresh because that was when she'd still had a share in her life, and she seemed to remember it better than Iris herself did—her girlfriends who slept over, her girlfriends' parents, her teachers at school. She loved to remind her of significant events, mostly embarrassing trivialities, loved to describe enthusiastically her random encounters with one girlfriend or another, taking a crumpled bit of paper from her bag with a phone number on it that she'd gotten for her. "Na'ama would be really happy if you called. I gave her your number too," she'd say with pleasure, even though Iris had asked her over and over again not to force her to hear voices from the past.

Thinking about it now, as they are nearing home, she can't help gloating over the fact that her mother's brain is withering away quickly and she can no longer set such traps for her. Nonetheless, she feels an urgent need to tell her, even if she won't understand: I saw him, Mother, I saw what became of him. So when Mickey turns off the engine in the building parking area, she says, "You know what, since I'm already in the car, I should drive over to see my mother. I haven't been there for two weeks."

"You're sure you can drive?" he asks, as surprised as if she has been resurrected, and quickly offers, "I'll go with you," and restarts the car. But he would be superfluous there—to speak privately with her mother, to return to being a teenager with a secret she will tell only to her mother, that is what she wants, even if she can no longer understand what is being said to her.

"No, it's all right," she says, getting out of the car and walking around it, slowly and resolutely, leaning on the hot metal for support, until she's standing at his door. He gets out, the familiar complaining expression on his face: I'll never understand you, and alongside it, a look of relief: You're yourself again, it's a good thing we didn't make an appointment with that specialist and pay that outrageous fee. But that's what she does a second or two later as he is disappearing in the elevator—she calls the hospital and tries to arrange an appointment for the beginning of next month, a private appointment, at an obscenely high price, with the unit chief, Dr. Eitan Rosen.

"Dr. Rosen no longer accepts new patients," the receptionist informs her in a metallic voice, and she hears herself say, "I'm not a new patient. I was his first patient, actually his second, after his mother." The receptionist ignores that bit of intimate information and asks, "What's your ID number? You're not in our files." And she persists, "He examined me an hour ago, your computer hasn't been updated." But after the receptionist is convinced, she herself begins to feel uncertain, she won't go back there at the beginning of the month, she won't ever go back there. She is no longer a teenager in love, she is a busy woman with a full life, almost too full, her cell phone is overflowing with messages, her mailbox is flooded with emails she doesn't even have time to read, hundreds of people await her recovery, her decisions, her solutions to various problems that have arisen. Tonight she will take the strong pills prescribed for her and return to running her life without looking back. The fire has long since gone out, even if the smoke alarm continues to buzz.

Once again, she is surprised when a man opens her mother's door, the door to the house a man hasn't set foot in since her father died in the Yom Kippur War. This is the house of a woman who has avoided every attempt to find a replacement for her deceased husband, and not because of her great love for him or the depth of her loyalty to his memory, but rather out of an existential anger and profound contempt for what life offers. And now, at the end of her days, she is forced to share her life with a man she would never have deigned to look at—short and smiling, a sagging potbelly, fleshy lips under his black mustache, and when they open to speak, appallingly ungrammatical sentences emerge in both Hebrew and English. She wonders once again how her mother, who always used precise, elevated language and never ceased correcting them even after they were grown up, has become accustomed to the way he speaks.

We finally found you a match, Mother, she thinks as she stands in front of him. You were so picky, no one was right for you after Dad, who wasn't really right for you either—your list of complaints against him expanded after his death. Perhaps this is our bittersweet revenge on you for being so stubborn and proud. But on the other hand, she reminds herself, they brought one female caregiver after another and her mother threw them out of the house one after the other until one of her brothers suggested that they try a male caregiver. To their surprise, that seemingly hopeless idea turned out to be the perfect solution, because their mother became attached to the kindhearted, devoted Parshant in a way she had never become attached to anyone else.

"Oh, your mama said you not come!" he says as she enters. "Now mama happy, Iris come!" He is using the masculine form of the verbs and she can't help making the necessary corrections, saying, "Mother is a woman, not a man." But she thinks there may be some truth in what he says because, as they near her mother, who is sitting in the living room in front of the TV, which is showing a muted Indian film, she thinks that she might easily be mistaken for a man, with her short white hair, her gaunt body, her flat chest. She has always been slightly masculine, and now, in her old age, when the differences are blurred in any case, the masculinity has triumphed over the femininity. And what about me, she thinks, catching a glimpse of herself in the hallway mirror? He also uses the masculine form when addressing me. Her pale reflection looks at her with dissatisfaction—years of neglect have left their mark, but it isn't too late, she can still grow her hair, color it, lose weight, wear makeup, emphasize the light-colored, wide eyes she inherited from her father, which are so different from the small brown ones fixed on her now.

"Welcome to my home!" her mother says loudly.

"I'm delighted to be here," she replies, once again embarrassed to hear her mother speak to her in the formal language she always reserved for strangers.

"Do come in, sit down! How many years has it been since we've seen each other? How are things with all of you? Are you still in America? Have you come back home for a visit?" She showers her daughter with eager questions, and Iris looks at her hopelessly, trying to identify the character she is playing in her mother's imagination this time. Sometimes she is willing to accept the role her mother assigns her, avoiding corrections that would be received with ridicule in any case, in the hope that she can clarify the mysteries of the old woman's inner world.

But now, this afternoon, she longs to be her daughter Iris, sharing with her the memory of a dark time, and so she protests firmly, "Enough Mother, we don't live in America, we live in Jerusalem, not far from you, and we saw each other two weeks ago. Listen, Mother, I have to tell you something! You won't believe who I saw today."

Her mother suddenly bursts into laughter and says, "You won't believe who I saw!" Then she gestures for Iris to come closer as if she wants to share a secret with her. "I saw Parshant, and he proposed to me again! What do you say about that?" She chuckles smugly and quotes Sarah from the Bible, "Now that I am old, I shall have pleasure."

"Congratulations, well done!" Iris sighs, staring distractedly at the Indian movie, which also appears to be showing a festive marriage proposal. What distortions lie in wait for us at the end of our lives!

Not long ago, during a rare moment of lucidity, her mother had said to her, "You all left me, and the empty space was filled by strange creatures. They felt the vacuum around me and pushed their way in," and she said, "We didn't leave you, Mom, we only left the house. That's the way of the world. Listen, Alma isn't living at home anymore either." Remembering Alma now, she again feels the familiar waves of concern. Yes, Alma left the house and is making her own way in the world. What sights does she see there? She tells them so little, and it's convenient for them to believe that if she doesn't get in touch, it means that everything is fine, the important thing is that she's happy, she tries to believe, more important than her relationship with us. But is she happy? Is that what her silence means?

She herself never dared to cut herself off from her mother so openly, even if she had profound misgivings. A parental child, that's what it's called nowadays. A poor child, that's what it was called then, a child whose father was killed when she was four and she had to help her mother raise the twins born after his death. Today, many women raise their children without a father and do it so naturally that men seem to have become a burden, that's how greatly their status has declined. But back then, the father was the knight who protected the family, he was the rock, the foundation, and a family without a father was like a house without a door.

She remembers how much pleasure she took in the word "Daddy" after she gave birth to Alma. "Daddy's coming soon," she would promise the baby girl who still understood nothing. Maybe that was why she was in such a hurry to get married and become pregnant, to savor raising a little girl who had a father, who wouldn't be jealous of others the way she had been, who wouldn't ask the electrician who came to repair a short circuit to teach her how to play chess. During those years, she thought that a father was all a little girl needed to be happy, but apparently she was wrong, because her little girl was tense and worried most of the time, even though she had a father, and only now that she is far away from both of them does she seem to be a bit more relaxed.

"Mother, listen to me for a minute," she again asks the old woman, who is totally focused on some sensational events taking place on the TV screen—has a marriage promise been broken, why is the future bride crying so bitterly? But Iris won't give up on her this time, there has to be a way to bring her back, if only for a moment, and if not to the present, then at least to the past. She moves closer to her, and a pungent odor rises from her skin, as if she had washed with bleach. "Mother, you won't believe who I saw today!" she shouts into her ear, "Eitan Rosenfeld! You remember Eitan?"

"Of course I remember that dreadful boy," her mother says with a snort of victory, abandoning the screen with surprising ease, "him and his dreadful mother! I saw her at the clinic recently. She bragged that he became a famous doctor and his wife was a doctor too and they had three children. But I didn't let her act superior to me. I told her that my daughter was a school principal—do you know that my Iris is a principal already, or didn't that news reach you in America?"

"What are you talking about? His mother died almost thirty years ago," Iris protests in a weak voice. "You couldn't have seen her!" Nonetheless, she seems to have met someone who knew Eitan, because at least one correct detail is buried in that mishmash, which means that other details might be accurate as well. Why shouldn't he be married to a doctor, why shouldn't he have three children, why shouldn't he have forgotten her, erased her? What is the point of appearing before him with her scarred pelvis, with the pain caused by nerves that hadn't healed properly? She'll cancel the appointment or she just won't show up and he'll wait in vain, so at least his wallet will suffer. Maybe she'll make an appointment every week and not show up, maybe she'll even ask to be listed by her maiden name—that will arouse his curiosity— but will never show up. Or maybe, instead, she'll go there every day, sit in the corridor among the waiting patients and tell them the real truth, tarnish his good name. "That doctor increases the amount of pain in the world," she'll whisper to them, "how does he dare to call himself a pain specialist?!" The rumor will spread quickly and the number of appointments will decrease until she is the only one waiting in the corridor when he opens the door, surprised that no one needs him. Then he'll see her, his only patient, the last one left to him, and he'll take her in his arms and heal her.

Her mother laughs defiantly once again, and as she moves her mouth closer, Iris can smell the pungent odor of disinfectant—does she brush her teeth with bleach? "Don't tell my Iris," she whispers, "no one knows about it, but that dreadful boy is still trying to find her! Can you believe it?" Now she begins to shout. "But I gave him a piece of my mind, I told him that if he tried to get in touch with her, he'd have me to deal with!"

Stunned, Iris listens to her, shakes her head, and mumbles, "You didn't, Mother, you're just saying that. You wouldn't do such a thing to me." But she quickly gets a grip on herself, and having no other choice, takes on the role of the guest from America. "Well done," she praises her, "that's the way a dreadful person like him should be treated! When was that?"

Her mother peers at her suspiciously. "Many years ago. Before Iris was married, he tried two or three times and then stopped. I think he went off to study where you live, in America. Did you happen to see him there?"

Iris shakes her head. No, I didn't see him, I didn't know, and I don't know if I believe you now either, I don't even know if I want to believe you. She puts her head in her hands as the dragon of pain begins to raise hell in her body once again.

"You cup tea?" Parshant says, bending over in front of her.

"I am not a cup of tea," she replies angrily, but immediately apologizes. "Thank you Parshant, but it's too hot for tea."

He sits down beside her mother on the couch, puts his arm around her shoulders, and says, "Mama is good boy." He pats her on the shoulder and adds, "Mama behave good." Her mother giggles at him like an old baby. In her light-colored cotton pants and checked blouse, she lacks not only gender, but also age, and her fading awareness has transformed her into a much more frivolous and relaxed person than she had ever been.

"Parshant proposed to me and I accepted," she announces, resting her head on the shoulder of her caregiver, who has not only a bulging potbelly but also the hint of a pair of breasts above it. "We're going to Sri Lanka to get married, we're sailing there on a ship!"

Iris averts her gaze hopelessly. Mom's in love! Even that old dream has turned into a nightmare! Her mother has lost her sanity and won love, but first she drove away her daughter's chance for love without even asking her, and now Iris insists on setting things straight. "Mother, Parshant has a wife and children in Sri Lanka," she informs her with vengeful sweetness. "He's not your fiancé, he takes care of you."

Her mother shakes her head in shock, pales, and says, "That can't be! He never told me he had a wife and children! Is it true? What my guest is saying, is it true? Get out of here right now, you charlatan! Deceiving a war widow!"

"Maybe mama salad?" Parshant scrambles to his feet and asks automatically, clearly unable to follow the conversation. "Maybe mama lentil soup?"

Iris closes her eyes. Her mother struggled to raise three children, none of whom take care of her, and now this stranger calls her "mama" as if he is her fourth child, gives her food and drink, while she is convinced that he is her fiancé. What distortions await us at the end of our lives! But now she is more concerned about the distortions of the beginning of life, and she almost pleads, "Mother, try to remember, are you sure he was looking for me? When exactly was it? How come you didn't tell me?"

For a moment, the familiar, hard look jumps out at her. "You were pregnant with Alma. Alma's your daughter's name, right? You became pregnant right after the wedding, right? I couldn't tell you, so you wouldn't regret it, right?"

"Right," Iris mutters distractedly, and immediately becomes skeptical once again. "But a minute ago you said it was before I got married."

To her surprise, her mother's withered lips smile broadly. "Right," she says, her trembling hands reaching out for the bowl of soup Parshant hands her.

Iris shakes her head, it can't be, either she's fantasizing or she's lying. She enjoys tormenting her, was always jealous of her father's great love for her, and now old age lets it all show without defenses or restraint. The slow, heavy overhead fan squeaks, pushing blazing air from place to place through the tiny living room, hurling the conflicting words at her, words that sting like wasps. Her mother was also jealous of Eitan's love for her, and especially envious of her devotion to his sick mother. "Why are you pushing yourself into their lives? Let him say goodbye alone. She's his mother, not yours, thank God!" She commented on it at every opportunity, refusing to understand that it was through Eitan's prolonged parting from his mother that Iris was trying to part from her own father, drafted at noon on Yom Kippur while she was taking the afternoon nap her mother was never willing to forgo. But later she realized that her mother had been absolutely right, even though she didn't understand her reasons, for if she had listened to her, Eitan would not have seen her as part of the contaminated circle and might not have abandoned her. Did he really look for her?

"This is unbelievable! Why didn't you tell me sooner?" she says. "You've been hiding this from me for more than twenty years?"

But her mother looks at her calmly over the bowl of soup and says with extravagant politeness, "Eat with me, I'm sure that they don't have soup like this even in America."

Though she isn't hungry, she has some of the murky lentil soup and grimaces. She has no doubt that Parshant keeps most of the generous allowance he receives for her mother's food. She doesn't check the receipts, but of course she would do the same if she had hungry children in a far-off country. Nevertheless, she asks him, "When did you make this soup, Parshant? Do you cook for my mother every day?" and he replies, "Today morning, I swear, Iris, you come tomorrow morning you see."

"And how are your children?" she asks.

He rolls his eyes heavenward and says, "Thank God."

"And how are your children? Remind me how many you have," her mother asks, and immediately clucks her tongue when she hears her answer. "Only two children, are you sure? Didn't you have three?"

"You have three, Mother," Iris taunts her, even though she thinks of her twin brothers as almost a single body, and to her great surprise, her mother suddenly begins to cry.

"I had three, but only two are left! Didn't you hear that my Iris was killed in a terrorist attack a few years ago?"

"Stop it, Mother," she bursts out and shakes her mother's emaciated arm. "It's me, I wasn't killed, only injured, and now I'm fine. This is me, Iris, your daughter. Recognize me already."

But her mother, always repelled by any extreme emotion, looks at her reproachfully and says, "Enough! Why are you so upset? It only proves that you're not my Iris. That's not how I brought her up."

"Oh really, you're just impossible," she mutters. "Why do I bother to come here at all if you're convinced I died?" But she knows that today, at least, she didn't come for her mother's sake, but for her own, to share the secret with her. And in return, she has been told another secret, a more shocking and depressing one. Did Eitan really look for her?

FIVE

They are always tired, her teachers. Especially in the morning, at the first meeting. They yawn, nod off, those poor, exhausted creatures. Some of them drink more and more coffee in order to wake up, others overeat. By noon, their facial features will stabilize, but in the morning, this one is droopy-eyed and that one slack-jawed. The younger they are, the more tired they are. She was like them once, but now she can hardly remember why. What a waste, and to what end? Those babies that keep you up at night become angry adolescents in no time at all, and the homes you work so hard to cultivate will be a prison for them. The family you make so much effort to build and watch over will become a burden to them, and even worse, to you. That husband of yours you sacrifice your time for so he can finish his degree or move up at work will leave you in another twenty years for a younger woman, and even if he doesn't leave, he will most likely become aging, grumpy, and ungrateful, and you'll find yourselves wishing for a different life. Some of you may try to realize your dream, but only a few will be lucky enough to get another chance, which won't necessarily be better than the previous one.

Yes, ladies, she wants to say as they sit around the large, elongated table in her office, I too have been young and tired, and now, in retrospect, it seems totally unjustifiable. Again and again, we make life difficult for ourselves just to see how much we can cope with, how much we can take upon ourselves, another child, another job, another mortgage, ridiculous Sisyphuses that we are. Perhaps that's what we need to talk about, dear ladies, and not about the discipline problems in one of the fifth-grade classes or the new program for multiculturalism. Let's talk about the pointlessness of female effort, which overlaps with the pointlessness of human effort. But this morning, it seems even more blatant when you're collapsing, bleary-eyed, on your chairs around me.

"What's going on, Sharoni? Everyone's waiting for you," she says to one of the teachers, who is whispering feverish instructions into her cell phone, and she ends the call quickly. "She's sick all the time," she complains about her one-year-old. "From the minute I put her into day care, she has been home all the time with my mother, who is collapsing."

Iris tries to give her an encouraging smile. "It's always like that at first, but in a few months she'll be immunized." She finds it strange to be older and more experienced than any of them. She was always the youngest, the youngest mother in the kindergarten, the youngest principal. In the early years, she was also the youngest teacher, but recently all of that has changed, and only the secretary and counselor are older than her. She has lost her youth, so much so that he didn't recognize her.

When they exit her office, leaving behind the familiar atmosphere you can almost feel with your hands, a blend of complaint and hope, she leans back with a sigh of relief. She managed to run the meeting as if nothing has happened, as if she hadn't seen him with his white coat and gray beard, like an angel of destruction. She won't let him destroy everything she has built since then—did he really look for her? Exhausted from the effort, she stands up and stumbles to the secretary's office adjoining hers.

"Do you have anything for pain, Ofra? I've finished off my daily dose."

The longtime secretary, looking concerned, hands her a packet of pills. "You can't go on like this. It can't be that there's no solution!"

"Why not, Ofra?" she chuckles. "Since when is there a solution to every problem? If only the world worked that way. Usually you just have to adjust." She pours herself a glass of water and limps back to her desk, which is almost entirely covered with yellow Post-its, each noting something else she has to do. Set a date for a Home Front Command training session, secure city funding for the third-grade field trip, set up an appointment with parents threatening to take their children out of school, find a new assistant teacher to replace the one who left this week even though she had promised to stay until the end of the year, send an email about a community welcoming-the-Sabbath ceremony, sit with the Arabic teacher on the "Language as a Cultural Bridge" program, write her weekly principal's letter, complete the discussion on basic guidelines for filling out report cards—and all that in addition to the daily chores written on the huge calendar on her right, which covers almost the entire wall.

Every Sunday there is a meeting with the homeroom and subject-area teachers of a particular class, during which they discuss the emotional, social, and scholastic performance of each child. At noon on every Tuesday, there is a meeting of all the homeroom teachers to discuss educational programs, and in the evenings, the meeting with the Central Parents Committee, the meeting of the Educational Forum, and of course there are days of principal training courses and seminars. There's no room on that calendar for days of pain, there never has been, but her hand tightens on the eraser as she struggles with the urge to erase everything and leave a clean slate, to begin afresh. If he did look for her, if he did want her, then she can't continue her previous life. It changes the entire picture, the entire calendar.

Did he really look for her? She sits down in her chair with a sigh, peels off and sticks more and more yellow Post-its on her desk. Did she really miss her chance with him? Bile rises in her throat—for almost three weeks, she has been living mainly on painkillers. Did he really regret leaving her? Did he want to take her back, to give her back his love? Even if she was about to marry, even if she was about to give birth, she would have gone back to him. What vile news her mother gave her, sawing off the branch on which she built her flimsy nest. She puts her head down on her desk, eyes closed, lids as sticky as the yellow Post-its, but then there's a knock on her door and the custodian comes in to complain about vandalized school property, followed immediately by two pupils in the heat of an argument—when the homeroom teachers are out, the pupils always come to her with their disputes. Then a pupil who doesn't feel well comes in with his father, who came to pick him up, and since he's there anyway, offers to help with the new computers. Whenever the door is open, they enter en masse. Today, she actually welcomes it, but Ofra protests out of habit.

"Hey, leave my principal alone," she says as she strides into the room and tries to empty it. "You won't believe it, I saved us five hundred shekels," she announces happily, as if it were her own money. "I received a refund on the water bill we paid."

"You're the best, Ofra, what would I do without you?" Iris says, observing her lively gestures with affection. She has surrounded herself with good people, people who care, and she sometimes thinks that, despite the heavy workload, managing a school with three hundred pupils and forty teachers is easier than managing a family of four.

It's when the room empties that she becomes restless, so she goes out to the corridor, walks slowly past the closed classroom doors. Everything is quiet at the moment, the days of her absence haven't cracked the strong structure she built with so much effort. A pupil returning from the bathroom enters his classroom immediately without lingering at the game corner, and when the door opens, she can hear verses from a Bible lesson taking place inside. Sharon is reading the end of Genesis to her pupils:

Then Joseph could not refrain himself before all them that stood by him; and he cried: "Cause every man to go out from me." And there stood no man with him, while Joseph made himself known unto his brethren. And he wept aloud; and the Egyptians heard, and the house of Pharaoh heard. And Joseph said unto his brethren: "I am Joseph; doth my father yet live?" And his brethren could

not answer him; for they were affrighted at his presence.
And Joseph said unto his brethren: "Come near to me, I
pray you." And they came near. And he said: "I am Joseph
your brother, whom ye sold into Egypt. And now be not
grieved, nor angry with yourselves, that ye sold me hither;
for God did send me before you to preserve life."

Iris stands beside the slightly open door, her body trembling involuntarily at the sound of the verses. Yes, for years she too hoped to learn that she was cast into that pit to preserve life, and yes, there have been many such moments in her life, proof that, in the end, everything has worked out. But this moment is not one of them. Her gaze wanders down the corridor, stopping at the large stone plaque carved with the names of school graduates who fell in Israel's wars. Not far from where she stands, on another stone plaque, her father's name, Gabriel Segal, is carved. He was the first casualty of the school he had attended, her first casualty. Will he be the last? As Omer grows older, she is haunted by the letters of his name inscribed on a memorial plaque. OMER EILAM, the letters assemble for her, beautiful, symmetrical, bowing their heads in subdued pain. She shifts her damp eyes to the new poster about Eliezer ben Yehuda, reviver of the Hebrew language. They hang across from each other like cause and effect, and she stands between them. Is it for the sake of the Hebrew language that we die? Do we bury our young fathers and young men just emerging from childhood only so that their names can be written in Hebrew on cold stone plaques throughout this turbulent country?

You must not think such thoughts, she chides herself, what choice do we have? It's not the language, it's our very existence, for we have learned time and time again that we cannot exist anywhere else, even if such an illusion sometimes crops up. But lately she has become more convinced that it is actually Jewish existence here in the land of the Hebrew language that is an illusion soon to be shattered, perhaps not in her generation, perhaps not even in Alma and Omer's generation. Once again she sees the name engraved on the memorial plaque, OMER EILAM, and once again she averts her gaze. Stop it, she thinks, he hasn't even received his first draft notice. Maybe they'll take pity on her, after all, she's a war orphan, she was injured in a terrorist attack, maybe they'll take him off their list. Until the first draft notice arrives, she can still hope, and until then, he's hers, or rather he's his own person.

Farther down the corridor is a poster she is especially proud of, THE OTHER IS ME, a project they have invested heavily in that teaches tolerance. But at the moment, it is the archaeological display that attracts her more, and she walks toward it slowly, passing the closed classroom doors. "The Past Creates the Future" is the name she thought up at the beginning of the year, but it seems so farfetched to her now. The past creates the future? The past destroys the future, the past turns the future into ashes. Furious, she rips the sign off the wall, looking around to be sure no one saw her. She can already hear the whiney voice of the custodian reporting on more vandalizing of school property.

"Dear Parents," she writes when she returns to her office,

This week, the fourth-graders are studying the gripping story of the biblical Joseph making himself known to his brothers. His brothers hurt him in the most dreadful way imaginable. They separated him from his beloved father, his home, his future, dooming him to a life of slavery and wandering. Daily injuries and affronts are an inseparable part of our lives and the lives of our children and pupils. Every day, children who hurt each other come into my office, and I try to make each of them see the pain they have inflicted on their fellow pupils.

But how can Joseph truly reconcile with those who have inflicted such a mortal blow on him?

When we are hurt, we expect those who hurt us to acknowledge the pain they have caused us and accept their responsibility and guilt. When the injury has humiliated us, we expect the person who has inflicted it to humiliate himself by asking for our forgiveness, asking us to believe that he has changed so much that we need not fear he will hurt us again.

Joseph tests his brothers in various ways to make sure that they have really changed, and he seems to be punishing them for the suffering they have caused him. Even when he makes peace with them in the end, the most important element seems to be missing—their apology to him. Hard feelings linger between Joseph and his brothers, which is why they begin to be suspicious of each other right after their father Jacob's death, leaving the following generations with much to set right.

The following generations are us and our children, and the children you place in our care in our school, which holds that justice is nothing more than forgiveness. The process of forgiveness, in which both sides take part, begins with the acknowledgment of the pain inflicted on us and on the other. It is the ability to see the other's viewpoint

along with our own. It is the humility that enables us to see
the other as a separate, independent being and not simply
someone who exists merely to satisfy our own needs. It is
the mutual commitment to help each other prevent further
injuries, in the knowledge that genuine change can only
come about through cooperation.

Dear parents, we encourage your children to ask their
friends to forgive them if they have hurt them. Please serve
as models for them by apologizing to them for any injury
you may inflict. Help them to see how the ability to forgive
enables healing to take place and alleviates the pain.

Yours,
Iris Eilam

That is the verse that stays in her mind as she enters the
blazing heat of her car a few hours later, after she has written
her weekly principal's letter, after she has persuaded the assistant to stay until the end of the year, has observed a substitute
teacher's lesson, has stepped in herself to teach a civics lesson:
"Then Joseph could not refrain himself before all of them
that stood by him; and he cried: 'Cause every man to go out
from me.' And there stood no man with him, while Joseph
made himself known unto his brethren." Therefore, instead
of driving home, she drives west to the place where she saw
him. She has no idea whether he'll be there or how she can
get in to see him without having an appointment. And even
if she does get in and lifts her shirt to show him the three
birthmarks—the sun, the moon, and the earth, as incontrovertible proof—she has no idea what will happen then.

Will he throw his arms around her and cry as Joseph did
with Benjamin, his brother? Will he hold her hand as they

both weep for the lost love of their youth? Or will he be cold and distant, continue that conversation as if most of their lives hasn't passed since then, explaining that he had to get away from her because he wanted to live, because he had to forget? Whatever happens, there is only one thing she actually wants to know: did he look for her, and why, did he want only to ask her forgiveness or did he regret leaving her and did he want to live his life with her? That life seems so exhilarating to her now that the sun is shining on it, dazzling her, its glitter extinguishing the life she's had since then as though it were time wasted. A sunlight storm, Omer called such moments in summer, and she was impressed by the originality of the phrase, but now, even the children she bore seem as bitter as the spilling of seed.

Mickey occasionally amuses himself by judging how well suited couples are based on the children they have. "Those two really shouldn't have hooked up. Look at the kids they had," he'd say decisively, and of course, at those moments, he considers their own children the epitome of perfection, even Omer, whom he used to complain about frequently. But at the moment, she is the one being skeptical about their children, even Omer, whom she has always defended. Now his number appears on her cell phone just as she finds a parking spot, almost miraculously, near the hospital, and is squeezing between two cars that have not left room for her. Her car seems to respond to the intensity of her desire and shrinks so it can fit.

"What's up, Omer?" she asks, and he replies with a question, "Where are you, Mom?" Reluctant to offer information, she says, "Why? What do you need?" How strange that now, as a teenager, he has returned them to the beginning of his life, to the time he was a baby totally immersed in his most rudimentary needs, which she had to fulfill. Now too, they deal with his most basic needs: food, transportation, financial support, help with his schoolwork. He doesn't say to her, as he did when he was a child, "Let's go out and have fun, Mommy," and she actually has no problem with that, unlike some of her friends, especially Dafna, who lament the fact that their children have grown up. That's the way of the world, and in any case, those outings were difficult for her, he was so frenetic, hot-tempered, and controlling. She definitely prefers the way he is now, more distant, calmer, expecting her to perform only a few clearly defined services for him.

"I don't need anything, Mom," he says, to her surprise. "When are you coming home?" She hears the rush of bad news hurtling toward her, recognizes it immediately. It was imprinted on her soul the night they received the news of her father's death and her mother struck her stomach over and over again, where, unbeknownst to anyone but her, she already carried Iris's twin brothers, Yariv and Yoav. For many years, she was convinced that those strong blows caused her mother's stomach to fill with babies, that her mother conceived that night. She even argued heatedly with her girlfriends, who had already heard rumors of the mysterious joining of sperm and egg, and said with conviction that it was a lie, that all you needed to do was pound your stomach all night. Later on she told Eitan about it, and he laughed and covered her stomach with kisses. She told Eitan everything without a second thought, as if she were speaking to herself, that's how close they were.

"What happened, Omer?" she asks tensely, "tell me already, has something happened to Alma? To Dad?"

"Cool it," he says, "nothing happened, it's just that yesterday, a few of my friends were at the bar where Alma waitresses."

"So, what happened? She miscalculated their bill?"

"Forget it, we'll talk when you get home, it's not for the phone." But he can't restrain himself and blurts out almost involuntarily, "They said she was weird."

"Weird?" she asks. "What does 'weird' mean? What exactly did they tell you?"

"Enough, Mom, don't interrogate me like that, we'll talk when you come home."

Unhappily, she parts from the rare parking spot she worked so hard to find and says, "I'll be home in fifteen minutes. Wait for me, okay? Don't go anywhere!"

But her trip home takes longer than an hour because the car, it seems, has returned to its regular proportions and even swelled. She barely manages to move it out of its tiny parking spot, only to discover, to her dismay, that there is a huge traffic jam up the hill, with no end of it in sight. An obese driver gets out of his car and goes to see what's happening. "If there's going to be an accident, this is the best place for it, a minute away from the hospital," he chuckles. But when he returns, the smile is gone from his face and he says, "Someone was killed. I can't believe it, actually killed."

She nods somberly and rolls her window up in his face, momentarily frightened that it's Eitan, that she has missed her last chance to see him again. After surviving countless road accidents over the past thirty years, he will elude her now, a moment before she could make herself known to him.

How strange it is to suddenly add Eitan to her list of people she worries about, after so many years of wishing him only torment and a variety of painful deaths. But when traf-fic finally begins moving again, she is relieved to see that the crushed car on the hillside is facing the hospital, surrounded by police cars and ambulances. This isn't the time people go to work, but rather when they leave it to hurry home to the wife and children, and the thought of them fills her with anger, as if she herself is alone, as if she has been waiting for him all those years. Does he have a son, a tall, handsome, slightly stooped young man? Perhaps he'll meet Alma one day and together they will consummate the love that was stolen from their parents. She tries to picture her thin, dark daugh-ter, who bears no resemblance to her, at the side of that young man she loved so much—how surprised he will be to learn that she's her daughter—but then Omer's disturbing words strike at her again: she was weird.

What does "weird" mean? Alma was always quite aver-age, never showed striking tendencies in any area, no special enthusiasm or talent. That itself seemed weird to her, not to mention disappointing, as disappointing as her inordinate preoccupation with her appearance, mainly her hair. She would stand in front of the mirror for hours, painstakingly arranging it, not leaving the house until she was satisfied, and sometimes she would come home if she had been upset by her reflection in some random mirror. How much they fought about that, with Iris reprimanding her impatiently, "Why are you looking in the mirror? What difference does it really make? You're late!" and Alma would slam the door in her face. Is that what Omer was talking about? Was she looking in the mirror instead of serving customers?

Don't be tempted to speculate, you'll know the facts soon enough, she tells herself out loud, you'll be home in a minute and everything will become clear. But awaiting her at home is a note from Omer in his strange handwriting—"I have a driving lesson"—and she crumples the disappointing piece of paper in her fist. What a shame she hurried home, she could be sitting across from Eitan now, could be asking him, do you remember how I believed that children would come out of your stomach if you hit it hard enough?

But perhaps it's better this way, perhaps it's better for her to wait for the appointment at the beginning of next month. And there's no reason to make herself known to him as soon as she walks into his office, but rather she should wait to see if he recognizes her. That way she'll have the advantage over him, as Joseph did with his brothers, the same advantage he had over her back then. After all, he knew he was planning to break off their relationship while it had never occurred to her. She was as clueless as a sacrificial chicken he was spinning in the air in the Yom Kippur *kapparah* ceremony.

Nevertheless she calls the clinic and hears herself ask if her appointment with Dr. Rosen can be moved up. But while she is still waiting for the reply, the silver wings of the elevator door part and Mickey lumbers out of it, wearing a huge blue polo shirt—the elevator opening always seems too small for him—so she ends the call and puts the phone down before receiving an answer.

"When did you speak to Alma?" she asks quickly as he pours himself a glass of water and looks disappointedly at the pots—Alma calls him more than she calls her.

"Yesterday. Why rice and beans again?"

"So cook yourself if you don't like it."

"You know I have no problem cooking. The problem is that you and Omer don't like my food. Only Alma does."

"Really?" she hisses. "She likes your food so much that she's anorexic." But she regrets her words immediately. What made her say anorexic? She's just thin, lots of girls would gladly change places with her. Why hurt him only because he came in at the wrong moment, only because Alma prefers him to her, only because when she married him, it never entered her mind that Eitan was looking for her. Did he really look for her?

"How did she sound?" she asks.

"Fine. She's slightly overdrawn at the bank and asked me to cover it. She was sweet."

"Sweet? Not weird?" she asks.

"Weird? What does that mean? Why would she be weird?"

Sitting down at the dining room table across from him, she says, "I have no idea, Mickey. Omer said something that worried me. He'll be back soon and we'll know more. How much is she overdrawn? Maybe she's spending money on drugs?"

"If she is, then it's soft drugs," he says chuckling. "Four hundred shekels all in all. I wish that was all we spent."

"You're sure she didn't sound high?"

Surprised again, he says, "High? Are you kidding? Don't you know Alma? She was never attracted to things like that, she always puts down her friends who drink and smoke. Don't you remember how we used to laugh when she sounded like some old Victorian spinster?"

But she persists, "Things change, Mickey, now she's alone in Tel Aviv and we have no idea where she goes and who she hangs around with. We gave her too much freedom."

"I trust her! And what choice did we have? I trust her," he repeats as if trying to convince himself. They listen tensely to the sound of the elevator straining to rise, as if it is carrying a particularly heavy load, bringing their son to them with the information they are so concerned about.

"Hey, Momdad, what's happening? You're not getting a divorce or something, are you?" he asks immediately.

She is surprised. "A divorce? What are you talking about?"

He laughs, "You're waiting for me at the table like you have some dramatic message for me."

"Have you forgotten, Omer? We just happen to be waiting to hear what you have to say. What exactly did your friends tell you about Alma?"

He pretends he forgot, but she recognizes the tension in his laugh. "Come on, you don't have to make such a big deal of it," he says, "the girl went to the big city and seems to be horny as hell."

"Horny as hell?!" Mickey spits out the words in disgust. "What kind of way is that to talk?"

Omer approaches them and stands there at his full height, forcing them to look up at him like a couple of young children. "Call it what you like, Dad, but if she sits on Yotam and tries to make out with him, then on Ido, and then asks Yonatan if wants to go to the restroom with her, and they're kids she knows from the first grade, then she must be horny as hell."

"Or high on drugs," Iris hears herself say in a cold metallic voice, the sound of a knife twisting in her guts. "Can I talk to one of your friends, hear more details?"

"Forget it, Mom, that's all they told me, and it really embarrassed them. Don't worry, they won't take advantage of her condition, but I figure that there are guys who will. So that's the latest news from Tel Aviv. I have to study now, I have an exam day after tomorrow." He disappears into his room.

She turns to look at Mickey and is surprised to see him stand up quickly, as if he too has an exam the day after to-morrow, and go over to his desk at the end of the hallway. She hears his computer awaken, and in another moment or two, when she manages to pick herself up and go over to him, he is already engrossed in one of his speed chess games, five minutes each at the most, a new form of his old addiction.

"Mickey, let's drive over to her place," she says. "I have to see her."

"Not now, I'm in the middle, give me another minute." From behind his back, she watches the chessboard screen, which seems ancient, for some reason.

Her father also loved chess, was an excellent player, and he even managed to teach her a few moves. She has only a single black-and-white photo showing her sitting across from him, a chessboard between them, a worried expression on her face for some reason, and he is pictured from the back, his face not vis-ible. That was what attracted her to Mickey in the university cafeteria twenty-three years ago. She was sipping her hot coffee when, from the corner of her eye, she saw a large man bent over a small board. He was immersed in thought, occasionally moving the pieces, both black and white, because there was no one sitting across from him, and she immediately thought of her father, who was huge in her memory, though he had actually been physically unassuming—Alma undoubtedly in-herited her thin, delicate build from him. As if in a trance, she approached the broad back and sat down on the empty chair opposite him, and the moment she realized she was there, she felt oddly certain that the empty chair was meant only for her, even though she didn't know how to play—after her father's death, there had been no one left to teach her.

That's what she told the surprised young man who looked at her questioningly. "I don't know how to play." He smiled and said, "That's okay, what I really love the most is playing against myself," and in retrospect, that sentence takes on an additional meaning that neither of them was aware of then, because life with a woman who almost died of love is a game against yourself, and in any case, not for yourself. She found herself telling him about her father, who had been addicted to the game, which was why her mother had to go looking for him at the chess club and force him to come home. If he lost, he was despondent and angry all evening, but if he won, he'd take her in his arms and whirl her around, so happy that it was impossible to be angry at him.

The large young man listened to her patiently, and his black eyes, which at first seemed slightly veiled, showed greater depth when he heard how young that chess lover had been when he died and how young his daughter had been. "Do you want me to teach you how to play?" he asked cautiously, as if he were afraid of making a wrong move.

"No," she said, "I'll just watch," and so she observed in silence as he played against himself, his large, dark, slightly doughy face changing expression rapidly from trepidation to satisfaction, from arrogance to frustration. It occurred to her that had her father played against himself, her mother would have been spared those humiliating forays to the chess club and she herself would have had more hours with him—their time together had been so short. As she watched the young man, who seemed gentle despite how large everything about him was, she tried to calculate how many father hours she'd had in the few years that their lives had overlapped. So focused was she on her calculations, counting on her fingers and mumbling, that she didn't see that now he was the one watching her, and when she did notice, she laughed in embarrassment, he must think she's weird.

She placed her pale hands on the sides of the board and looked at his dark hands, thinking that if they laced their fingers they would look like pawns lining up to face each other in battle. She wanted so much to lace her fingers through his that she heard herself say suddenly, "I've saved my father's chess set all these years. If you want, I'll give it to you."

Surprised at the gesture, he said, "Wow, thanks a lot, but I can't take it from you, it should stay with you."

She replied quickly, "You're right, it should stay with me, but I really want it to be yours too. After all, I don't know how to play."

"I have the perfect solution," he said, "we can live together," and they both laughed as if it were a joke, which turned into reality faster than expected. She was enchanted by his enthusiasm and total lack of doubts about her. But how could she have known that while they were planning the merger that would enable her to give him her father's chess set without parting from it, Eitan Rosenfeld was climbing the steps to her mother's house to ask about her, and her mother was throwing him out as if he were a beggar or a criminal.

How could she have known that as time passed, she would begin to hate the very thing that had attracted her to him, just as her mother had hated it in her father, even though the chess clubs had become the computer screen and the long games had become lightning-fast ones. The addiction and the complete disconnect from his surroundings only became worse, until she could barely speak to him in the afternoon and evening because he was utterly focused on the games. Even when she called him during work hours, she sometimes thought she could hear the impatience so typical of addicts.

"Not now, I'm in the middle," he'd say curtly when one of the children asked him for a ride somewhere or help with homework. And she would take consolation in the thought that if this was the father she had lost, perhaps the loss wasn't so great. Now she says to his back, the same back she walked over to, trancelike, twenty-three years earlier, "They say that the tendency to addiction is genetic. She saw her father addicted to chess, and now she's addicted to drugs."

"Not now, I'm in the middle," he mutters.

"Maybe if you weren't so involved in your games, Alma would be in better shape today," she says, even though she knows that Alma is the only one who sometimes manages to get his attention even in the middle of a game, the only one willing to be shown a brilliant move he made and be happy for him when he won, but mainly to console him when he lost. The loss was utterly meaningless in the real world, after all, he didn't know who his opponent was in most games, and no one had the slightest interest in the points he won or lost. But it stung him deeply, as does the loss he is suffering now on the screen in front of him. Making no effort to hide the pleasure she takes in his defeat, she says, "Don't start a new game now so you can make up for the one you just lost. We're going out."

"Where to?" He stands up and trudges into the kitchen as if he has only just awakened from a deep sleep.

"To see our daughter," she says.

He yawns. "Aren't you getting a little carried away, Iris? She just wanted to have some fun."

"Have some fun," she repeats the hackneyed phrase derisively. "What planet do you live on? Seducing her brother's best friends indiscriminately—you think that's normal?"

"Who am I to say what's normal? At least I know now that she's not asexual like her mother."

She flinches as if he'd slapped her and walks in stunned silence to her bedroom. Asexual? Where did that suddenly come from? It isn't like him to talk to her that way! She knows he was hurt because she left their bed that way and because, like many friends her age, she hasn't been particularly excited by sex these last few years, but to say such a thing to her? He must be more stressed than he's been willing to admit. She sits down on the bed—she'll take another painkiller in a minute and drive to see Alma without letting her know she's coming, go directly to the bar and surprise her there. She'll certainly resent the invasion, but she won't be able to do anything about it, or maybe she'll be able to watch her from outside without attracting her attention, if there is a window, and the thought of what she might see through it horrifies her.

She'll see her daughter's sexuality. Parents aren't supposed to see such things. Maybe Mickey is right, the normal state of affairs is that children should see their parents as asexual and parents should see their children the same way, anything else would be extremely uncomfortable. But that's irrelevant at the moment because if Alma is behaving strangely, she has to help her, even if Alma doesn't want her help. She undresses and lingers in front of the closet. She doesn't usually take much care about her clothes, but tonight she wants to look good so that her daughter won't be ashamed of her. She chooses a tight black skirt—since the pain came back, she has hardly been eating and the skirt is no longer as tight as it used to be—and the white blouse with the black polka dots that always looks nice on her. But as she hurriedly puts on lipstick, he comes into the room, the phone in his hand, a supercilious smile on his face.

"Mom's already getting dressed in your honor, sweetie," he chats comfortably into the phone. "She wants to drive over to see you, she's worried about you."

Then she hears their daughter say quickly, "There's nothing to worry about, Dad, I'm really fine. I'm doing a double shift today, there's no reason for you to come. I'm always on my feet and I won't have a minute for you, and I'm closing the bar, get it?"

"More or less," he chuckles. "I get that you don't need to see us urgently." And the conversation continues before Iris's blazing eyes. "I heard that Omer's friends were there yesterday. How was it?"

"Don't ask," she complains. "They're nerds like you wouldn't believe, they totally don't know how to drink, one shot of vodka and they're groping everything that moves. I had to throw them out. They really messed up, and I had to lie for them and tell Boaz they were eighteen! Tell Omer not to send me his friends anymore."

Mickey listens to her gleefully, his smile broadening. "Who's Boaz, the owner?"

She sings into the phone, "Yes, my boss. He's really thrilled with me. Next week I'm going to be shift manager."

"So when are you coming home? How about this weekend? We haven't seen you for almost a month."

"But Dad," she protests, "we get the best tips on the weekends. It's a real bummer to miss shifts like that. You know what? Maybe I'll come on Sunday, okay? It's the slowest day."

"Sure, sweetie, whenever it's good for you." He purses his thick lips to the phone. "Kisses, sweetie, take care of yourself."

"Bye, Daddy."

In the silence that ensues, Iris's anger at him for giving away her secret plan is mixed with a host of other things: enormous relief at hearing Alma's steady, cheerful voice; the reassuring uncertainty about the information Omer conveyed; the realization that despite his chess games, he has greater success than she in his relationship with their daughter; an acutely painful sense of failure that momentarily masks the pain in her pelvis, which radiates to her leg; the foolishness of the fancy outfit she put on as if she were going to her daughter's wedding; the discovery that she is still applying the red lipstick, coating her lips with a thick layer of the sticky substance; and his smile, which appears in the mirror behind her, pleased and expectant, as if he has given her an offering and is waiting for her cries of surprise and joy.

"What are we going to do, Mickey?" she mumbles, her lips stiff with color.

And he, pragmatic as always, says, "Let's go out for something to eat. We haven't eaten out in a long time, and you're already dressed."

She gives up on all the excuses because despite her pain, despite the fact that she isn't hungry and has to get up early the next day, despite the fact that he hurt her, she knows that this is a moment she cannot not let pass.

"Anything but rice and beans," he jokes as he reads the menu. "What do you have that's as far away as possible from rice and beans?" The waitress doesn't really understand what he says.

Iris looks at him warmly. This is her Mickey, who loves her in his way, who loves their children, who saw them being born, who disappoints but also pleasantly surprises her. Who took such good care of her when she was injured, who supported her when she decided to apply for the principal's job and was so proud when she got it. She feels a profound sense of security beside his large body, as if she were a turtle and he her shell. The closeness she feels toward him is growing stronger from minute to minute, until she almost tells him that the doctor with the white beard is apparently the boy she loved when she was young, Eitan Rosenfeld, and that from the moment she saw him again, she has been totally preoccupied with him. The words are already on her heavily coated lips, but she swallows them with the spicy cold pepper soup. What is the point of telling him something that will never happen, because she has already decided not to return to the hospital and try to see Eitan again, she won't open the door to her life for him to enter. The pain he caused her belongs to her former life, and even if he throws himself into her arms or prostrates himself at her feet to beg forgiveness, he cannot undo what he did. Her mother was right to send him away just as he had sent her away, and she will do the right thing by not allowing that old-new pain to lead her to him, because he can't heal her, and she will not allow him to make her sick again.

SIX

Absolutely not, she decides once again the next day, and the day after that, I will absolutely not try to see him again, I will absolutely not make myself known to him. Sitting in her office and staring at the pupils' drawings that hang on the wall, she thinks about the childhood she never had because of her father's death, which placed an enormous responsibility on her shoulders, instantly catapulting her from childhood to maturity. Perhaps that is why she sometimes feels so old, because at the age of four, she was already a grown-up, which might explain why she feels a bit fed up and vaguely angry with elderly people. But none of that is important now, she breaks off her reverie, she will stop thinking about her own youth and focus on her daughter's. Today she'll leave work early because Alma promised to finally come home, and even though she has her doubts, she'll act as if the visit is a sure thing and make the biscuit cake, sweet layers of biscuits and vanilla and chocolate cream that her daughter loves so much. They used to make it together every Friday, and Alma's face would be covered to her forehead with creamy smears, but after Omer was born, that became a rare event reserved mainly for birthdays.

How difficult it was to raise Omer, she thinks resentfully, staring at his smile in the family photograph that hangs on the wall across from her. It seems to her that from the moment he came into the world, he decided that nothing would remain as it had been, neither the nights nor the days, and even a minor domestic ritual like baking a cake came up against countless obstacles. Either he would scream in fury about not being included or he would hide the ingredients throughout the house. But if they finally agreed to include him, he would argue endlessly, insist on playing a bigger role, and wreak havoc with the quantities if they didn't agree to his demands, turning the task into a nightmare until Alma walked off in tears. She recalls how she once decided to trick him and asked a babysitter to take him to the playground so she and Alma could make the cake together for her eighth birthday. But he came back home with the expression of a suspicious, jealous lover on his face, immediately discovered the cake in the fridge, and took advantage of a moment when they were distracted to throw it on the floor in a rage. The sound of the dish shattering under the rich creamy mixture appalled her, and she looked at her little boy with horror and almost appreciation—see, you really are capable of doing anything, just as I feared you could, just as I felt you could.

From the time he was born, her friends tried to reassure her, "That's what boys are like. You're used to a girl, and such a quiet one at that. Boys are wild, he's like the rest of them, he doesn't have a problem." She, of course, was quick to accept all the reassurances, but the reality confronted her each time anew. He was different, he wasn't like all the others, he was wilder, more violent, and at that moment, in front of a loudly sobbing Alma, she realized that the time for denial had passed. She had to prepare for difficult years, and her daughter, whose birthday cake had been deliberately destroyed, would most likely pay the price.

After coming to terms with the situation, she rose to the challenge. She had chosen education for a reason, and if she succeeded with her little boy, she would also succeed with others like him from all over the city who had left many kindergarten and elementary school teachers feeling frustrated and helpless. And she succeeded quite well—within a few years, Omer became easier to handle and more disciplined. Years of consistent effort transformed him from an impossible child to an almost average one, a boy like all boys, though slightly more volatile. But during all that time, Alma was neglected, and it's clear that today, no cake will make up for that birthday cake, even the new one she made for her in the middle of that night didn't make up for the one Omer had destroyed. Nonetheless, she hurries to the grocery store now to buy the ingredients, having convinced herself that this time, the visit will go well.

But the biscuits she just bought so cheerfully would remain forgotten and crumbling in the bowl because the sound of the elevator surprises her too early, while she is still dipping them in milk and arranging them in the pan, and she turns around with a smile of happiness and anticipation on her face. But the girl who steps out is so different from her daughter that she almost doesn't recognize her. For a moment, she seems to have changed into a boy, so short has she cut her hair, but chopping off her gorgeous chestnut tresses wasn't enough for her. She has dyed the thatch that remains a deep shade of raven black, which brings out the features she inherited from Mickey's mother and gives her face an entirely new expression. The shocking change fills Iris with such anxiety that she completely gives up on the idiotic attempt to make the cake and lets the biscuits drown in the pool of milk mixed with a teaspoon of instant coffee that gives it a soft mocha color.

"Alma? What happened to you?" she asks, wiping her sticky hands on a kitchen towel and hurrying over to her, as if she is about to faint and needs her support.

That, of course, is not the right question, because her daughter, as expected, says defensively in a cold voice, "What happened to *you*, Mom? You're looking at me as if you've seen a ghost! It's only a haircut!"

Iris, immediately sensing her daughter's regret for having bothered to come, tries to rectify the situation. "No, it's not just the haircut, it's the color, it changes you completely. All of a sudden, you look like Grandma Hana." She hugs Alma's tense, thin body, which seems to have a new stiffness. What is that body hiding from her, what is happening to it, that body that took root in her womb and emerged from her own body and now moves out of her embrace quickly, as if fearing that its secret will be revealed.

"Hey, what's up, Sis?" Omer says, suddenly appearing from his room. "Congrats on the haircut. Why do you remind me of Grandma Hana now?"

She laughs with him, even though he deliberately destroyed her birthday cake thirteen years earlier, and in a chatty, brittle voice, she explains, "Every girl in Tel Aviv tries to be the most beautiful, so I decided to go against the flow and not try to be beautiful. I'm even trying to be the opposite, you know, unbeautiful," adding a slim question mark.

He laughs, "That's cool, Sis, as long as you like it."

"You bet I like it," she says, peering into the wall mirror and ruffling her hair, her smile both provocative and apologetic, Grandma Hana's annoying smile. But her mother, anxiously observing her movements, knows what Omer and his sister don't, that their Grandma Hana, who died of cancer when they were children, had been a battered woman for many years.

Let's see what Mickey says, she thinks as her children speak together easily and laugh, let's see if he's so calm now and makes fun of her for worrying for no reason. His mother's pain tormented him throughout his childhood and adolescence, though she did everything to protect him from his father, who was many years older than she and insanely jealous and violent. It wasn't until Mickey was a married man that together they managed to help her leave his father. But she fell ill a short time later, and instead of enjoying her new life as a free woman, she became totally enslaved to her illness, her treatments, and her suffering, until she died exhausted, almost with a sigh of relief. Meanwhile, his father was growing older with a new wife, and since Mickey had cut off all contact with him, they never knew whether she had enjoyed a better fate than her predecessor.

"He reminds me of my father," Mickey would occasionally admit, mortified, when Omer was having one of his tantrums. "It must have skipped a generation and gone straight to him." But it would be worse for him to feel what she feels now, that their daughter, who has come home from the big city for a short visit, has brought with her an alarming whiff of enslavement.

"Hi sweetie," he says joyfully when the elevator ejects him straight into her arms, and Iris sees that she also moves quickly out of his embrace and avoids his glance with the same forced cheerfulness. Then Alma hurries to the kitchen counter, grabs the packet of biscuits that weren't dipped in milk, and eats them nervously one after the other.

"Don't fill up on biscuits," Iris says quickly, "there's a ton of food," because she thinks that's what a normal mother is supposed to say at such a moment. Then she adds with a bright smile, "I was just making you the cake you love." A normal mother in a normal family consisting of two parents and two children, because look, Omer snatches a few biscuits from her hand and goes to stretch out on the large blue couch, Alma sits down beside him, Mickey pours himself a glass of water and joins them. They seem to be waiting for Iris to sit down on the flowered couch across from them and enjoy a tiny bit of well-being, a tiny bit of pride in the normal family they have built despite the fact that they don't come from normal families, but she is unable to feel part of the pleasant gathering. The sight of her daughter pains her so much that she can't sit down across from her and pretend to be content. So she mumbles, "I'll just make a salad," and turns her back to them.

"Is everything okay, Iris?" Mickey asks, and he explains to Alma that Mom's pelvic pain, which radiates down her leg, is back and she's been suffering a lot lately.

"Everything's perfectly fine," Iris says, because she doesn't feel comfortable taking refuge in the shadow of the event that caused her daughter more than enough suffering in the past.

She takes the vegetables out of the fridge and cuts them into thick pieces, trying to calm down. What happened to her daughter? But perhaps Alma was right when she asked, what happened to you, Mom, because no one has noticed anything and everyone looks pleased, she is the only one whose heart is pounding with apprehension, and it isn't clear why.

So she cut her hair, threw the long hair she took such care of for so many years into the trash can of some hair salon, or maybe she did it at home, considering how sloppily it was cut. Then she turned the beautiful chestnut brown into jet black, which isn't a disaster either, but the change upsets a certain balance in her face, and together with the clothes she chose to wear, a tattered black T-shirt and gray jeans, she looks very unattractive. No one will turn to look at her the way they used to when she wore her very short dresses and had long flowing hair. But why the panic? For years she had chided her daughter for spending so much time on her appearance, so she should be happy about the sudden turnabout. But it isn't the temporary loss of her beauty that bothers her so much, it is the loss of something—freedom, perhaps?—in her expression.

It's hard to define an expression, and perhaps it's the sudden resemblance to Grandma Hana that is causing her to make a mountain out of a molehill. What connection can there be between that hardworking woman who married a violent, controlling man against her will and the young girl living alone in the big city who has her entire future before her? She takes a few deep breaths, sprinkles coarse salt on the salad, and squeezes lemon juice over it. The quiche she put in the oven is bubbling. "Come eat," she calls, "Omer, where are the lentils? Don't tell me you finished them off."

"We have fantastic lentils at the bar," Alma says as she sits down in her usual place. "We serve them with melted goat butter."

Iris tries to smile at her daughter and says, "Sounds like you're really happy at work."

Alma nods, "I really am! It's like home, all the waitresses are my friends, and Boaz is thrilled to pieces with me, starting next week, I'll be a shift manager." She attacks her food and eats with a healthy appetite, so there seems to be nothing to worry about, but the way she says Boaz echoes in her ears even after she moves on to another subject. She said his name with special emphasis and pride, and there was an aura of secrecy about it.

"How old is Boaz?" she asks as if trying to remember.

Her daughter evades the question. "I don't know exactly, about your age."

"And he's nice?" Iris asks with great affability to avoid arousing her daughter's suspicion. "He treats you all well?"

Her daughter falls right into the trap, saying, "He's a very nice person. He runs the bar to make a living, but what he really cares about is guiding us back to our true inner selves. There are a few girls there that he really saved."

"Saved from what?" she asks, the fork in her hand beginning to shake, which her daughter notices and tries to ignore.

"Nothing," she replies, "just, you know, they were kind of lost, looking for themselves, he helps them do the spiritual work to find their true inner selves."

Trying to steady her voice and her hand, she asks, "Did he help you too, Alma?"

Immediately arming herself with her disdainful tone, her daughter says, "What kind of help do I need, in your opinion?

I'm a kid from a good home, I have parents who worry about me, I don't need any help."

Alma adamantly refuses to sleep at home, even though Iris has taken everything out of her room, changed the sheets, and urged her to stay. "You can sleep late, and when you get up, I'll leave work and we'll have coffee together," she says, trying to tempt her. But it must sound like a threat, because her daughter promptly refuses, saying that she likes to sleep at home, and it turns out that the place she calls home is no longer their home. She feels more comfortable going back at night than in the afternoon when it's hot and traffic is heavy. So after a quick hug, she disappears into the elevator with her father, who volunteers to drive her.

Iris remains frozen in front of the stainless steel doors, waiting for Mickey to return so she can repeat to him those prickly words, spoken so ironically, "What help do I need, in your opinion? I'm a kid from a good home, I have parents who worry about me, I don't need any help!"

"Don't tell me that you took it at face value!" she reproaches Mickey when he comes back from the central bus station.

"I understood it exactly as she meant it," he replies in surprise. He pours himself a glass of water from the fridge and sits down across from her at the dining room table. "She saw that you were worried and wanted to reassure you. What irony are you talking about? She doesn't have parents who worry about her? Just look at how worried you are about her now! Listen Iris, I'm afraid that something's gone wrong with you. Maybe it's because of all those painkillers. Everyone knows they cause hallucinations. We need to go back to the pain clinic and start serious treatment. Maybe we'll go straight to the unit chief, even though he seems to be a bit of a psycho."

"Psycho?" she says in surprise. "Why?" She feels oddly cheerful, perhaps he's right, perhaps she is hallucinating, perhaps she needs to see the unit chief. Of course she needs to see him again, just look at how eager she is now, despite all the decisions and vows, to gossip about him with Mickey, and she asks again, "Why do you think he's a psycho?"

"You didn't notice that he's strange?" Mickey says with a laugh. "He literally ran out of the office without even looking at us, afraid of his own shadow."

"Or of ours," she says, because for the first time, the possibility occurs to her that he recognized her and ran for his life.

Now it's Mickey's turn to wonder, "Why should he be afraid of us?" Immediately he tries to answer his own question: "He's probably just a misanthrope. But I heard he's a good doctor. There's a girl at work who said he really helped her."

"Really? Who is she?" she asks, surprised at the flow of information suddenly gushing from an unexpected source.

He stands up and says, "Someone new, you don't know her. She's the one who told me to take you to him when the pains started, but I didn't want to wait that long for an appointment, and he costs an awful lot."

"Oh, Mickey," she sighs, "you have no idea." She follows him to the bedroom, where her things are now, back home, the earplugs, eye cream, nightgown, open book. The small bathroom mirror shows her the top of her head beside his ear, her high forehead and straight, faded hair. Standing side by side, they brush their teeth thoroughly, but just as she plans to spit the contents of her mouth into the sink, a strange new feeling of embarrassment stops her. She feels uncomfortable spitting out the repulsive stream, which is pink from bleeding gums, and she expects him to precede her. But he seems to be uncomfortable as well and continues to move the brush in his mouth until she turns aside and spits into the toilet, wondering what it says about them, about their intimacy. He takes advantage of her turned head to get rid of the mixture of toothpaste and water in his mouth, spitting it out hard into the sink. Almost against her will, she remembers that there was never any barrier between her and the boy she loved so much, neither when they woke up in the morning nor when they went to bed at night, she fell asleep in his arms, inhaling the air he exhaled.

We were children, she sighs, there's no comparison, and she looks at her graying hair with dissatisfaction, maybe she'll go to the hair salon near the school tomorrow and have it dyed the same jet-black color as her daughter's. Maybe the artificial resemblance it creates will bring them closer even now at this late stage, when she surprises her at the entrance to the restaurant, because she is not reassured, she is not convinced.

"To what do I owe this honor?" Mickey says when she lies down beside him in bed. "I've already gotten used to sleeping alone. You're sure you haven't started snoring in the meantime?" She moves closer to him, puts her head on his smooth chest—she has always loved the feel of it, soft and hard at the same time.

"Tell me," she says, stretching out the words as she formulates the rest of the sentence, "what else did she tell you, that girl from work? What kind of pain did she have? How exactly did he help her?"

To her surprise, he replies eagerly, "She had unbearable lower back pain, she suffered terribly, couldn't function at all. And she has a little girl she's raising alone. Nothing helped her until she went to see him. He gave her a cortisone injection that absolutely saved her."

"Wow, you really are up to date! I didn't know you took such an interest in the people around you."

Immediately defensive, he says, "I don't take any special interest, but when a girl sitting next to you cries all day, you can't remain indifferent."

"Now I understand why you even thought of that clinic. I really did wonder," she says, trying to shift the subject to the doctor, not the patient—what does she care about her.

But Mickey does seem to care about her, so much so that he attacks. "What's been going on with you lately? I can't talk to you! Everything makes you suspicious, first the morning of the explosion and now the poor girl I tried to help."

"Exactly how did you try to help her?" she asks.

"Nothing special. I once drove her to see that doctor when she couldn't drive herself because she was in so much pain."

"Good for you, Mickey," she laughs. "I didn't know I was married to such a good Samaritan. So how come you always get annoyed when Omer asks you to drive him somewhere?" But what's the point in letting the conversation go there, that isn't the main thing, and she tries again: "What else did she tell you about him?"

"Nothing special. He's treating her and her condition has really improved."

Iris sighs. "Great, I'm happy for her."

She hasn't received the information she hoped for. Instead, she's received different information that is almost upsetting—to him, apparently—because he gets out of bed angrily and says, "I'm going to the computer. I'm not tired anymore."

"What's going on with you, Mickey? You've become as sensitive as a teenage girl," she calls after him. "It looks like you really do have something to hide." But he is already moving his pawns and doesn't hear her words. Maybe that's better, she thinks, because something about our use of words has gone awry lately, we use them to hide instead of to reveal. We have betrayed our words, and perhaps that's even worse than betraying each other. We have betrayed our words and now they are punishing us.

SEVEN

"*Jet black,*" she tells the hairdresser, "the blackest black there is." As the color is being absorbed by her hair, which has grown longer lately, she looks in the mirror expectantly. She has never done anything extreme with her hair, she has never done anything extreme at all, but this morning, her youth seems to be sneaking up on her through a mysterious window she unconsciously left open, stirring the spirit of rebellion in her. She won't go back to work today, she'll do something different. For too many years, she did what she had to do, now it's time to do what she wants. After the dye is washed out of her hair, she looks at herself curiously. Not bad at all, she thinks, her hair reaches almost to her shoulders, and its darkness brings out her pale complexion and green eyes. Since she's lost weight recently, her cheekbones are prominent, and the blue linen dress she bought a few days before the terrorist attack and has never worn fits her well now. And here she is—different.

"See, you look ten years younger!" the hairdresser says enthusiastically, and Iris smiles, she really didn't expect such a big change. Uncharacteristically, she takes a picture of herself and sends it to Alma, who, also uncharacteristically, replies immediately, "Cool!"

"Are you free in the next few hours?" she asks after Alma swallows the bait. "I have a meeting in Tel Aviv. Can I come to see you afterward?"

But to her disappointment, her daughter rebuffs her quickly. "No way," she writes, "I have a really crazy day! A double shift and I have to close up too."

What did you think, that if you dyed your hair black like hers, the new color would erase everything? Do you think you can buy her off so cheaply, although it isn't really cheap, she thinks as she pays the hairdresser, not for me and definitely not for her. How many shifts does she work to make herself so ugly? The new black hair suits her, but not her daughter, that's how different they are in looks and coloring.

"Hi, Dafi," she says when, in the stifling heat of the car, she hears her friend's voice sounding exhausted and impatient.

But Dafna revives immediately. "Iris, I didn't notice it was you! Finally! To what do I owe this honor?"

"What's this honor thing you all have? How are you? How was Barcelona?"

Dafna sighs, "I have so much work that I've already forgotten. How's the pain?"

"With the pills, it's bearable. Listen, I think I understand why I was injured."

"You were injured because of a conflict that's been going on for at least one hundred years. But let's not get into politics."

"It's not politics, Dafna," she says. "I was injured because Mickey was having an affair, that's why he didn't take the kids to school that morning."

"That's crap! Mickey? It can't be! Where'd you get that idea all of a sudden?"

"I think he's having an affair now and that's a sign he was having one then. How can we learn about the past if not from the present?"

They meet in the café next to Dafna's office.

"All he did was help a poor girl, what do you want from him?" Dafna's expressive face is agitated. "What's happening to you? We haven't spoken for two weeks and the sky has fallen! I don't believe that I left work for crap like this on the busiest day of the year!"

"Alma has a busy day too," Iris says.

They're used to talking about their daughters, Dafna's Shira and her Alma, who have been close friends since kindergarten, and their mothers have followed suit. She still hasn't told her the main thing, and she can't decide whether she will—that she saw Eitan. Remember my telling you about Eitan? My first boyfriend? Sometimes Dafna can't control herself and tells her husband, and he, with his big mouth, might say something when the four of them get together. No, she won't tell her because she needs to tell Eitan first, it's their secret, after all, because now, after almost thirty years of total separation, they have a common secret. Even if he's still unaware of it, it exists and connects them to each other, or perhaps he does know, and that's why he left the room in such a hurry. Perhaps since then he has been waiting for her to come to see him alone, looking for her name on his list of appointments, peering occasionally into the corridor. She remembers how sometimes he used to wait for her after school, and when she came out of class and saw him, she would feel a sense of pleasure unlike any she had ever known. She would walk over to him as excited as a bride walking to her groom as he waited for her under the wedding canopy. She feels suddenly breathless now, she feels that she can no longer restrain herself, just as the biblical Joseph felt when he sent everyone away before making himself known to his brothers.

"I have to get going," she says to her friend, whose jaw drops in puzzlement.

"I don't believe it," Dafna says. "What's going on with you? You got me out of my office and now you have to go?"

"I'm sorry, Dafi, I forgot that I have a really important meeting. I'm so sorry. I'll make it up to you."

Dafna looks hopelessly at the huge plate of salad that has just arrived and says, "Okay, I'll ask them to bag it for me," then adds reproachfully, "I really don't understand you. You tell me that Mickey is cheating on you but you haven't looked this good in years. Maybe you're the one having an affair? Who is this important meeting with?"

Iris bends down, kisses her cheek, and whispers in her ear, "With the past. I have a rendezvous with the past."

"What are you talking about?" Dafna tries to hold her by the arm.

"I'll tell you later. I have to go before I lose my nerve."

But she's feeling braver, as if she had been put under a spell at night as she slept alone in the double bed, with Mickey on the other side of the wall, in Alma's bed. For the first time in a long while, they switched beds, for the first time in a long while she focused her mind entirely on him, the way she sometimes focused on her pupils, the difficult, baffling ones. She would focus on a particular one and try to understand what made him tick, how she could reach him. That was how she concentrated on Mickey for that entire, long night until the picture became perfectly clear. But the moment it did, it became just another fact in the world, not even one that concerned her in particular or one she had to do or feel something about.

No, she feels nothing but the urgent need to return to the place where she saw Eitan, an urgent need she remembers so well from her youth. That made it seem as if she hasn't actually met Mickey yet, as if the day Eitan suddenly reappeared in her life belongs to an earlier time, before she met him, and so his life doesn't touch her at all.

But what does touch her? The sounds spilling out of the loudspeakers spin around her like spools of spine-tingling electricity, cello and piano accompanying each other, echoing, beckoning. As she drives down the hill, she sees in her mind's eye a winged young boy and girl ascending and descending on a ladder that reaches to the sky, meeting for a brief moment and separating again, forced to move in opposite directions, he is life and she is death, he is death and she is life. Who doomed them to eternal separation? Life and death are, after all, intertwined, she recalls, thinking about the weeks she lay in her bed, dry-eyed, neither hungry nor thirsty, unmoving in her small, dark room as the angles and intensity of light shifted along the floor tiles. But that meant nothing to her because if she never saw Eitan again, she didn't want to see anything, if she couldn't speak with Eitan again, she didn't want to say anything, if she never heard his voice again, she didn't want to hear anything. Sometimes, it seemed to her that he was calling her name, that he had come back to her, but that was no longer him because the Eitan who was capable of leaving her that way was no longer the same person, he was lost forever. So she lay on her back, diminishing, absorbed into the mattress that was absorbed into the bed that was absorbed into the floor that was absorbed into the ground. She didn't have to do anything, for she would get there sooner or later, all she needed was patience and she would disappear forever.

Occasionally, strange bodies would enter her room and try to disturb her, disrupt her plan: the family doctor, the school guidance counselor, her homeroom teacher. They would sit at her bedside and plead with her, but she didn't hear a thing because it wasn't Eitan's voice, and later, there was whispering in the next room, talk about hospitalizing her, but her mother objected strenuously. She vaguely remembers how frightened her twin brothers were, and Yoav, the more sensitive one, would sometimes crawl over to her bed and beg her to get better, but she didn't care about his pleas, didn't care about getting better.

Give up on me, she wanted to tell them, give up on me the way I gave up on you, it might seem difficult, but it's so easy. That is the great deception that allows humanity to exist, the deception that is meant to hide the fact that giving up is actually easier than persisting. But the moment we understand it, like a stolen bite of the fruit of knowledge, we discover the terrible taste of pointlessness and then there's no going back, because there is no point in eating and drinking, no point in washing and dressing, no point in going out and coming back, no point in working and studying, no point in marrying and giving birth.

In fact, to this very day, she doesn't know how she got well. Probably the IV the family doctor inserted into her veins when she was too weak to object also released drops of the spice of life into her bloodstream, for they finally managed to pull her up from the depths of her misery and give her, even if only artificially, the minimum necessary to recover. As a baby learns to walk, she relearned the necessary life skills that had been almost completely lost to her, and she slowly and carefully returned to the world. But Eitan Rosenfeld was no longer in that world, so she did not experience it as a return but rather as a first encounter with a new world, one that was quite bland and left her almost indifferent. It was only a basic impulse to do what she had to do that allowed her to move from one day to the next, and later, to do it well, until finally, the impulse expanded and the new world grew fuller. But now that she is once again squeezing into that small parking space, which has apparently been waiting for her since the last time, she thinks that it was nothing but an illusion.

And so she crosses the corridors now with her jaw clenched as if they were raging rivers. Heart pounding, she climbs the hilly steps quickly despite the pain, which wastes no time in coming. She glances at her watch every now and then, as if she has an appointment, it is almost noon. Is he also glancing at his watch now, wondering when she will arrive? How has she gotten stuck in this strange, overheated corridor facing the wooded hills, a corridor that leads nowhere just when she is in such a hurry, and, perspiring, she has to backtrack and ask the passersby. Last time, with Mickey leading her, the walk was much shorter, and naively, she didn't wonder why he knew his way around so well. Now the arrow points straight ahead, so she goes straight ahead, then it says to turn, so she turns, and there it is, she has reached him. Agitated, sweaty, panting—that is apparently how you arrive at a rendezvous with the past.

But his door is closed and a long line of people is standing beside it, all of them waiting for him to help them. How will she break through the blockade of pain, how will she get inside? None of them will give up their eagerly awaited visit with the doctor for her sake, and her own appointment is a long way off, almost two weeks away. Under the watchful eye of a stern-looking receptionist, she hesitates at the closed door, the situation is more complicated than she expected. Maybe she'll push inside when the door opens just to tell him she's there, that it's her, but they will all attack her immediately, people in pain are not particularly patient. Tensely, she looks at the first people in line. The one closest to the door is a pretty, plump girl with flowing brown curls, her eyes glued to a small tablet as her fingers fly across it. Iris speaks to her in a whisper, as if they are conspiring against the other people in the line, "Are you next? Could you let me go in with you for just a minute? I just need a quick word with him and then I'll leave. It's really urgent, okay?"

The girl frowns at her, surprised at her chutzpah, but gives her a quick, angry nod as if she is annoyed at herself for being unable to refuse and at her for knowing how to exploit that. "Okay, if it's only for a minute," she says, quickly returning her gaze to the tablet, and Iris thanks her warmly, leans against the wall, and looks at the door and the name written on the wall beside it. What an amazing coincidence, who would have thought it possible that she would one day find herself standing in front of a door that has Eitan's name hanging on the wall beside it.

Suddenly, her certainty is shaken, sometimes doctors switch shifts and don't take the trouble to inform the people waiting in the corridor, that has happened to her more than once, so she asks the girl, "It's Dr. Rosen in there, isn't it?" The girl, torn away from what she's doing, looks at the sign on the wall, and then focuses on her tablet again as if that is where the answer can be found.

"I think so," she replies coolly. She doesn't appear to care one way or the other, and as Iris thanks her again, she glances at the screen, freezing in shock as she recognizes the familiar, old-looking chessboard in a creamy brown color reminiscent of the one her father played on. Why didn't she think of it sooner! This is probably the girl Mickey told her about the day before, the girl from his office, perhaps his lover, even though, looking at her, it seems unlikely, she's too young and good-looking in her short striped dress, why would she want Mickey? Nonetheless, not many women play speed chess while waiting to see a doctor, and it isn't unreasonable to assume that Mickey infected her with his rare hobby. Perhaps that's why she agreed to Iris's request, apparently her reward for lending her husband to this girl, and she asks chattily, "You're playing speed chess? My husband is addicted to it!"

The girl gives her a blank look similar to the look Mickey gives her when she interrupts him in the middle of a game. "Not now," she mutters, and goes straight back to moving the pieces with her fingers, her curls covering the screen. Iris looks at her uneasily, is this Mickey's taste? Actually, she doesn't know much about his taste in women. Is he attracted to women who are thin or plump, short or tall, fair or dark? When they met, she was thin and long-haired, and a few years later, when her appearance changed, he didn't seem less attracted to her. The girlfriend he had before her was totally different, red-headed, lively, curvaceous. Appearance, it seems, doesn't really matter, and why shouldn't he be attracted to this girl, who has eyes as brown as her hair, smooth skin, feet encased in gold sandals, nails covered in glittery red polish.

But a moment later, all of that is forgotten. The door opens and a short, white-haired old lady comes out carrying a pile of forms, one of them falls onto the threshold. Iris bends down to retrieve it for her and when she straightens up, she sees him standing in front of her, his eyes fixed inquisitively on her, the wrinkle between them deepening.

She walks toward him slowly, a step, perhaps two, longer than infinity, because she doesn't know how to walk. She left her bed for the first time only today so she has to learn everything all over again. She reaches out and puts her arms around his neck in a trembling embrace, even though the door is open, even though the girl is standing in the doorway to his office making sure she doesn't lose her turn. To her surprise, he responds immediately, his arms encircle her back, and since she can't see his face, she says, "It is you, isn't it?" But he neither confirms nor denies, only whispers, "Wait for me," and walks her to the door. As if in a dream, she sits down on the chair the girl has vacated, her body is still trembling, she feels the touch of his cold fingers on her arms, crosses them and covers his touch.

In the hours that follow, it happens again and again. She once again walks slowly toward him, arms extended, once again places them on the back of his neck, once again asks him, "It's you, isn't it?" Only the end changes occasionally:

did he say, "Wait for me," or did he say, "Don't wait for me"? Did he walk her out or send her away, as he had then, saying, "I'm tired of this burden, I want to live." She sits unmoving, the girl who went inside with her has already come out, stealing a curious glance at her. A frighteningly gaunt man enters after her wearing phosphorescent running shoes, even though he can barely walk, much less run. Now he too comes out holding forms, and a woman about her age hurries inside, her hairless skull exposed, she will definitely remind him of his mother, will he throw her out of his office, will he tell her that he wants to live?

She is surprised when that patient remains inside longer than the previous ones, and when she does leave, there is a paleness still hanging on her face. Then an old man is led into the office by his impatient son, and she doesn't move the entire time, doesn't open her handbag even though her cell phone occasionally rings. She is waiting for him, as he asked, and even if he didn't ask, she is waiting for him. Or perhaps it isn't him she is waiting for, but rather for the past, which partly belongs to him, because it seems to her now that nothing she has done since then, no experience she has had since then, no feeling she has felt since then can rise above that past.

There is life, it appears, that progresses step by step, brick by brick, reaches its peak and stabilizes there, and when decline begins, it is expected and natural. But there is life that declines almost from its beginning because its peak comes early, as it did with hers, that is clear to her now and she did in fact know it even then. It seems to her that there is only a loose connection between the girl she was and the woman she is now, a loose connection that does not allow for a full life because the main link is missing. How was she naive enough to believe that she could construct the framework of a life without it, without the main link that is sitting behind that closed door now. She fixes her eyes on that door, not daring to look away, afraid she will miss an opportunity to see him, if only for an instant, to hear his voice.

How strange it is that he doesn't come out. Is he afraid of her? She hopes to catch an occasional glimpse of him, to glance surreptitiously at him as he walks through the corridor, called out for urgent consultation as he was with her. When she lay there totally exposed to him, did he rush out because he recognized her? Did he return home that night and tell his wife that he saw his first love? You won't believe who I saw in the clinic today, my first girlfriend, the one I left, I hardly recognized her, she's changed so much.

But the thought of his wife disturbs her, and she stares impatiently at the line of people, which isn't getting shorter because new patients are replacing those who leave. The world is full of pain and it all flows here. This must be what the cycle of life looks like to God on high, people leave and new ones come, and it's difficult to tell them apart. They all look alike because they are in pain, and it is he of all people who presumes to ease pain, the man who hurt her so much at the beginning of her life. What a paradox! Is this how he atones for his sin? You're missing the point, she will tell him, you can only make amends to the ones you have injured, there are no substitutes, there is no way around it, not even God can grant atonement for such sins, let alone mere mortals.

On the other hand, how can she blame him or expect him to atone? He was a child, only slightly older than her Omer, a neglected child, lost, frightened. It wasn't his fault that she reacted so badly, nor was he to blame for running from her as if she were the angel of death. That was his way of coping with the death of his mother when he was mad with sorrow, fleeing from the grief and leaving it behind with her, otherwise he would not have disappeared so cruelly, for such a long time. Did he really look for her?

A woman sits down beside her with a sigh, her face yellow from her illness, her head wrapped in a kerchief. But printed on her blouse are smiling hearts—how striking is the gap between the people here and the clothes they wear. Like them, on the morning of the attack, she wore a light striped shirt as if she were going out to jog. Indeed, she flew through the air as if she were weightless, but when she landed among the burning bodies, broken glass, shrapnel, the objects that flew out of people's bags, her cheerful shirt became covered with blood and her mother threw it out even though she explicitly asked her to wash and keep it. She always had reservations about her daughter's striped shirts, which she thought were too young-looking, and she took advantage of the opportunity to get rid of at least one of them. Even she herself liked those shirts less after her injury and finally gave them, along with most of the clothes that didn't fit her anymore, to a shelter for battered women. Now she recalls the striped dress that the girl who played chess was wearing, and once again the seemingly random facts join together in a taunting, ominous image of parallel lives suddenly clashing though they were never supposed to meet at all. Only now that image threatens her less because the meeting she awaits so eagerly was not supposed to take place either, or was it the parting that never should have taken place.

How long will she wait? It seems to her that at least ten people have come out of his office since she arrived, and she can already see the cycle. Each one remains inside for about fifteen minutes, sometimes longer, so on a full day, he sees dozens of patients. How many does he succeed in helping? And for how long? She sees that no one leaves his office empty-handed, they all carry white forms and they all look slightly more relaxed, apparently smiling their thank-yous as they leave, because there is the tail end of a smile on their faces when they come back into the corridor, back to their lives. Will she also come out of there smiling? Will he give her white papers too?

She smiles as she recalls how they used to sit on his bed, surrounded by papers, when she tutored him for his exams. Even though she was a year younger and a grade below him, she was able to teach him material she hadn't learned yet, with patience she didn't know she had, that's how much she loved him. He found it difficult to listen, he was distracted, who knows how he managed to study medicine, because without her, he wouldn't even have passed his matriculation exams. She always breezed through school, while he found it difficult to concentrate, he never had enough time in exams, and the system was far less forgiving than it is today. A boy taking care of his sick mother alone was given no special consideration, nor did he give himself any. How frustrated he was when again and again, he couldn't finish exams in the allotted time, or forgot to answer certain questions and lost points out of carelessness, and even worse, forgot the answers she had taught him the night before. She would sit beside him on the bed covered with papers and try to console him—don't blame yourself, Tani, your head is somewhere else, of course it's hard for you to remember, there are extenuating circumstances.

He would lie on his back, straighten the pillow behind him, his long, beautiful body tense, and she would give lectures one after the other, teach him about equations, world wars, the beginnings of Zionism, the legislature and the executive authority, the rules of syntax and vocalization, a later novel by Agnon and an early poem by Bialik—neither of them studied the sciences. She remembers the relief on his face when he managed to understand something difficult, how sweet he was, kissing her excitedly, singing the answer in her ear. She loved teaching him, and perhaps when she finally recovered and had to choose life, that was what she held on to, the gratifying memory of teaching, of instilling knowledge, love, and joy. And so she was a teacher in the army and studied education afterward, to the great disappointment of her mother, who wanted her to go to law school, while her first pupil, so slow to learn, miraculously succeeded in medical school without her help and without even her knowledge.

When the door opens, the boy with the crutches limps out and the next patient in line, a potbellied man, leaps impatiently out of his chair intending to go inside. But there seems to be a sudden disruption of the familiar rhythm of those exiting and those entering, because another man comes out of the room and closes the door behind him and no one goes inside. Without his white coat, he looks like one of his patients, thin, slightly stooped, his bearded face tired, his shirt wrinkled, a patient coming out of the doctor's office, empty-handed and heavy-hearted, who says to her unsmilingly, "Come with me."

He always walked more quickly than she did, his steps longer, and now too, she practically runs after him through the corridors. She was elated when he chose her from among the lineup gathered at his door, but now she's embarrassed by the way he is running down the steps as if fleeing from her, floor after floor, until she recognizes the cool operating rooms, where he turns around for the first time to make sure she is actually there and points to one of the waiting rooms.

It's a windowless room and no one is there, no one can see him throw his arms around her. "Rissi," he whispers, "Rissi," and he strokes her hair, runs his fingers across her face as if he is blind, his touch strange and familiar. She closes her eyes and presses against his thin body, it's him, her hands remember, it's her and her body knows, it's them and their severed love. It has always been there, beyond time and place, almost forever.

Then he moves her away slightly, sits her down on a hard armchair, places another one in front of her, so close that their knees touch, and stares into her eyes. He says in a soft voice, "You found me, Rissi. I feel like a criminal who's been caught."

"Don't worry, I already release you," she says quickly, offended, embarrassed, because his words are inappropriate to the emotion in his movements.

"Don't release me," he says. "I'm happy to be caught. I've wanted to ask your forgiveness for years."

Once again she is offended if that is the only reason he's happy to see her, just so he can return to his life with a clear conscience. She says coldly, "I forgave you a long time ago. You were a child, an orphan." Her eyes examine every wrinkle and blemish on his face, even his beard is deceptive, because most of it is gray, but it still looks white. His lids droop slightly over his young-looking, pale eyes, and though the wrinkle between them is deep, his forehead is smooth. One moment she sees him as he is now, and the next as he was then. Does he see her that way too as his eyes examine her face? For some reason, she isn't embarrassed, as if her skin is as smooth and radiant as it was then.

"We were both orphans," he says, "but I have a daughter your age, and if anyone did to her what I did to you, I'd kill him."

"My age?" she laughs. "I'll be forty-five soon."

"The age you were then, of course."

"But unfortunately, I didn't have a father who would kill you. That's why you're still alive. What's your daughter's name?"

"Miriam," he says with longing, and she nods, of course, there was no other possibility but to name her after his mother. The noble Miriam Rosenfeld had become Miriam Rosen, probably a tall, slim girl with light-colored eyes.

"Does she look like her?" she asks, whispering for some reason.

"Less than I hoped. I didn't make her alone, of course. She's much fairer than my mother, but there is a resemblance."

She suddenly chokes up as she thinks about the girl she should have given birth to, their Miriam, with dark hair and blue-green eyes, their Snow White. Is that why Alma is so angry at her, because she sensed from the day she was born that she wasn't the daughter her mother hoped for?

"Don't be sorry," he says. "You have children too, right? I saw it in your file, married plus two." But tears glisten in his agitated eyes as well.

"Did you recognize me right away?"

"Of course! How could I not? Flesh such as yours will not soon be forgotten," quoting from one of the books she taught him then.

She smiles gratefully. "I thought I had changed completely."

He shakes his head over and over again, a youthful smile on his lips. "For me, you are the same, Rissi," and his fingers confirm his words, caressing her face as if they had never stopped.

"How can that be," she protests happily, but for her as well, his present face becomes blurred, and she sees the face of the boy he once was, the boy who was hers. She feels her body fill with love as if it is an empty well finally filling with blessed rainwater, a cracked well that has been repaired and is whole now, able to contain the copious waters that cannot extinguish love. The streams that cannot wash it away are flowing inside her now, obliterating time, repairing the rift. The wounds of love can be healed only by those who cause them, she recalls a saying she once heard, her fingers covering his as they stroke her face, and her mind fills with all sorts of maxims: all's well that ends well, better late than never. Day after day, night after night, we were together, all the rest has long since been forgotten.

"I have to get back to the clinic," he says, taking his vibrating phone out of his pocket and looking at it. "They're waiting for me." He pulls her to him, raises her chin and presses her mouth to his, her lips trembling breathlessly, as if they have never been kissed. It isn't the touch of his beard that she feels, but the cheeks of the boy he was then, when his lips were fuller, and then too gave off a hospital smell of antiseptics and drugs.

"Thank you for forgiving me, Rissi," he says hoarsely, breathing the words into her ear as if that is the purpose of their meeting. "I have to go." He releases her suddenly and opens the door.

"Eitan, wait a minute," she says, and he turns to her, but a young doctor in blue scrubs stops him in the corridor and she stands off to the side and watches him, his expression once again stern and remote. When the young doctor continues on his way, she says, "Eitan." She is ready to speak his name all day, day after day, until they see each other again. "Eitan," she hears herself ask, "when will we see each other again?"

"Whenever you want," he says, as if nothing could be simpler, and she is shocked by the incomprehensible change. How is it possible that this memory, this dark, sick part of her life she could barely allow herself to think about, has suddenly opened, awash in airy, pleasant sunlight, like a torture chamber that has become a health resort.

He takes a small business card out of his pocket and hands it to her. "Call me," he says, and disappears from sight on the staircase.

She walks back along the bustling corridor. Here is the door he opened for her, the cool, windowless room, the two armchairs looking at each other with longing. Here she is, trembling with excitement, her hands on her lips that were kissed here, on her face that was caressed here. She sits down on the armchair, puts her feet up on the one in front of her, and closes her eyes.

The face of the boy he was moves closer to her, mouth slightly open, thick lashes shading his eyes, cheeks as pink as a baby's from the sun, and if she opens her eyes, she'll see the top of the mulberry tree that shaded them. They walked down the hill from Eitan's house to the spring under the tree on the most golden day, through the narrow space between the cold that had been and the heat that was coming. The late winter flowering was at its height, and the air was saturated with honey. It might have been the only day they had allowed themselves to act like a pair of lovers and nothing else, and it was also, she has to admit, the happiest day of her life, happier than her wedding day, happier than the days her children were born. The touch of the hot stone on her back, her handsome boy caressing her breasts, the pink berries at their tips, and she wound herself around him on the ancient terraces in the absolute certainty that nothing would ever separate them. She remembers picking leaves from the tree for the silkworm larvae her brothers were growing in an old shoebox, remembers dipping her feet in the spring water while he immersed himself in it. "Come into the water," he said, but she said skeptically, "Isn't it too cold?"

Yes, the air-conditioning is getting stronger and she shivers—after all, not only thirty years have passed, but the few moments of their meeting, only just ended, also belong to the past she so yearned to revive. What precisely was said and what can be learned from it? What does she know about him? Almost nothing. He has a seventeen-year-old daughter, that he needs her forgiveness, that in his eyes, she hasn't changed, which is almost too good to be true, or bad, actually. Because her life is now pouring into this new opening like sewage, because she doesn't want to go home now, because the only thing she wants is to see him again, as if thirty years haven't passed. So she will stay here in this room and wait for him, leave him a message that she's still here, in this tiny waiting room known apparently to only a select few. Appearing on the blue screen that she now notices for the first time are the initials of the patients undergoing surgery, perhaps her initials, I.E., will be added, for she still hasn't recovered from an operation that lasted almost thirty years. Now it turns out that it was all in vain, the teams of surgeons worked in vain to remove him from her body because, in an instant, he has come back and filled the space that nothing else has managed to fill, not Mickey, not her children, not her work, leaving it still hollow, ill, and painful.

Her eyes fix on the screen, she stretches her legs a bit. The armchair is hard, but she arranges her body on it as if she is planning a long wait, watching the scanty, fateful information flash on the screen: initials, date of birth, sex, length of surgery. M.D., born 1938, has already been taken to recuperation. He is exactly the age her father would be now if he were alive. Would he have killed Eitan if he had been alive then? Would she have been less devastated if she'd had a father?

R.L., a woman her age, has been in surgery for such a long time, she notices, since five in the morning. Where is her family waiting? She thinks about her own family waiting for her in one of these rooms ten years ago, Mickey, the children, and her mother, who seemed okay until the symptoms of her illness began to appear exactly when she needed to help Mickey with the children. Her help turned out to be a burden, even dangerous, when the three of them were almost run over because she insisted on crossing at a red light, when she was confused about the direction of the traffic on a one-way street, when she kept making chicken soup for them, forgetting that they were vegetarians. They were a family unraveling then, at the time her bones slowly knit together for hours and days, for weeks and months, with the help of screws and pins, as if she were Pinocchio, a wooden marionette. They never again became the family they once were because the absolute certainty of their fragility and vulnerability was burned into their minds and has never faded.

On the surface, they were united in their concern for her, in their nursing of her, but deep down, they had broken apart, like her pelvis, because in a single day, they had changed from an innocent young family into a bitter old one that had no illusions, that had nothing to look forward to. She knows all that now, as she sleeps, sees it with her eyes closed. She has to get out of here, but is still sleeping, how can she dash like a doe into the depths of the forest? Her cold eyelids cover her eyes, her arms hug her icy ribs, the air-conditioning is becoming more aggressive every minute, as if her body had been placed in the morgue while she was still alive.

She was brought to this room in order to freeze time, in order to take them both back to those years, because what is the point of loving anew when the world has changed in the meantime? New stories are being told in it, new matches are being made, new people, like her Omer and Alma, like his daughter Miriam, are being added, people who stand between them. Even as he hugged her, she sensed the presence of outsiders, her Mickey and his wife, their apartments, their mortgages and their friends, everything they have accumulated since then. She tries to picture his house, but can't. Obviously it's a large and elegant house not far from here, but she can see him only in his mother's small, ground-floor apartment in a suburb of the city, standing there at the end of the seven days of mourning and informing her of his decision. Are the tears that have been hidden behind her dry eyes for years suddenly pouring out? Alarmed, she pulls herself together, shaking with cold, her fingertips frozen and her throat burning. A tidal wave of weeping is moving toward her, flinging open the door of her secret waiting room, gushing from wide-open mouths. Horrified, she knows immediately that her unwanted guests are no longer waiting, they are in mourning, and it's because they have no one to wait for that they have come here and are standing in front of the screen, crying "Mama, come back, Mama!"

She looks at the screen and sees that R.L. has disappeared from it as if she had never been there, leaving behind numerous confused mourners now gathering around her. Pretending to be one of those waiting for a loved one to come out of surgery, she looks worriedly at the screen as the others, stunned, lament their loss.

"The doctors here are butchers," a man of about her age, a black kipa on his head, shouts at her. "They killed my wife, they murdered her in cold blood. There was nothing wrong with her, just a simple operation. They destroy families! Is your husband having an operation? Get him out of there while he's still alive. This place is hell!" The minute they see her, they crowd around her as if she has it in her power to save them, telling her detail after detail as if she can still fix the one detail that proved fatal. They remind her of her pupils, clamoring for her to resolve an argument and find the guilty party. "I told her, to me you're beautiful just the way you are, why do you need that ring in your stomach?" he says, swaying back and forth as if praying. "She wanted to lose weight. She got fat after the babies and wanted to be thin, and now the children have no mother. God have mercy on us!" He sobs, and at his side, a heavyset woman wearing a headscarf, probably the dead woman's mother, screams, "Eight children! Last time she had twins! In two months, they'll be three!"

Iris listens to them, shocked. Did they expect her to take in the motherless children? With a slight stammer, the father continues describing the final hours before the operation, and it is no longer clear to her whether they are telling the story to her or to each other. How they realized that there were complications, that nothing would be the same, how they read from Psalms, "The Lord answer thee in the day of trouble, may he send forth help from the sanctuary, and give thee support from Zion." Their presence has raised the temperature in the room, she feels her body defrost slightly, and she wants to get out of there, but how can she abandon them in their time of trouble? Every now and then a different family member speaks to her, adding another detail, as if she is supposed to document the event, but she gives most of her attention to the husband, whose name turns out to be Zion. He shouts over and over again, "A ring! A ring in her stomach! What are all these inventions? I sanctified her with a ring! To die for a ring! To be thin, that's what she wanted. Now you'll be thin. After the worms eat you, you won't weigh anything at all!" He sobs and all his siblings and the deceased's siblings and her older children cry their hearts out until they once again begin to vent their anger at the doctors. "They're murderers, they killed her, they destroy families. Get your husband out of the hospital before he dies," they warn her. She listens to their advice, and as if hurrying to do what they ask, mumbling words of condolence, she walks quickly out of the room. It is only when she reaches the ground floor that she realizes it is already evening, the crowds have thinned, even the corridor outside his office is empty, the receptionist is gone and his door is locked.

She is the only one in the clinic now, as if pain has passed from the world while she slept, and the frightening tumult coming from the adjacent emergency rooms is the only sound she hears. Maybe she'll go there and not to the parking lot, because she feels as if she's burning up with fever. Her throat hurts, her teeth are chattering, her body is transforming the cold it absorbs into intense heat that freezes her and then into intense cold that burns her. She staggers to her car, turns on the heater, stares at the fogged-up windows. Black heat enfolds her, the heat of a summer night, a night that doesn't end in the morning. She takes her phone out of her bag, she muted it hours ago, and there are dozens of unanswered calls, written and spoken messages, dozens of emails: her assistant called her almost every hour; Rachel from City Hall called over and over again; Arieh from the Ministry of Education; teachers, parents, the supervisor, Dafna; Parshant called on behalf of her mother; and Mickey left a curt message, "Where are you?" Omer asked for a ride to Yotam's house and then back. Mickey asked again, "Is everything okay?" then made do with only a question mark, but she doesn't respond. If she starts answering, there will be no end to it. She doesn't want to answer, she wants answers, so she takes out the business card he gave her hours earlier and copies the numbers into her cell phone, but instead of entering his name under the letter *E*, the first letter of his first name, or under *R*, the first letter of his surname, she enters it under the letter *P*: Pain.

EIGHT

What were you thinking, that he'd answer you in the middle of dinner? That he'd say to his wife, "Excuse me, it's my former lover," get up from the table and speak quietly to you on the balcony so no one could hear? That he'd say to his daughter Miriam, "It's someone who was once your age, and I loved her until I left her. If anyone leaves you like that, I'll kill him"? Or maybe he also has small children and he's reading them a bedtime story and doesn't notice that her call is waiting to be answered, so she leaves a bland message and tosses the phone onto the seat beside her.

Why did you wait for it to be so late? You fell asleep on the refrigerated morgue slab as if you hadn't slept in years. Even if he was excited to see you, he has probably calmed down since then, understands what is at stake and has decided to break off the new-old relationship before it begins. If he left you when you were seventeen, at full bloom, when your love was at its most intense, then he'll have no problem leaving you again now that you're forty-five and already withered, despite the dyed jet-black hair. You should have struck while the iron was hot, should have called immediately and arranged to see him, or ambushed him in the corridor when his last patient left, but the iron apparently froze in the morgue. No wonder you are still shivering with cold and there are pins stuck in your throat, you have to get home quickly, have to get into bed. Mickey is worried about you and even Omer said that he felt your absence, you promised to help him study for a Hebrew test tonight.

But it isn't to them that she drives, her teeth chattering, but to the house she saw in her sleep, his mother's house. She feels her temperature rising and her head is already lolling the way his sick mother's did. She knows she won't find either one of them there, the small apartment has certainly been sold or rented. Their meeting won't continue there, only their parting remains in that house like a burnt-out corpse with smoke still rising from it.

She didn't dare to go anywhere near it for decades, and now she is driving with her eyes almost closed, much too fast, as if someone is waiting for her in that neglected ground-floor apartment in a neighborhood that looked old right after it was built. The car seems to remember the way it never knew, and she parks at the bus stop where they used to sit on their way to school or the hospital, their arms around each other, after nights of making love as they slept and sleeping as they made love. Sometimes she had to go home to help her mother with the twins, and he usually waited with her, always holding her hand or putting his arm around her shoulder, their young bodies intertwining effortlessly, wordlessly.

These days, the buses come more frequently—two had already passed the empty stop—but back then they came rarely. If she missed one, she had a long wait, and sometimes, if she had to sit there without him in the morning, she would return to him for another sweet farewell and climb into his bed if he was still sleeping. By the time she left, she would have missed another bus, but never regretted it because she had gained more time with him. It was from there that she left that morning at the end of the shiva when he sent her away, and that morning, she suddenly remembers, when she had nowhere to go, the bus came right away.

A high, thick hedge surrounds the ground floor of the building, which the years have been kind to, lending it an aura of dignity. She walks toward the main entrance, trying to find a way into the garden, where she can look into the windows of the apartment. Apart from several carob trees and one plum tree, nothing grows in that garden, which was always empty and neglected. It was only during the shiva that it filled with life, when group after group of visitors sat there in the pleasant breeze of an early summer evening. Some lit candles, some played guitar, and she would walk among them, gathering consoling words for him, appropriating a few for herself. Eitan almost never got up from his seat, she remembers now, but she walked among the round tables the neighbors lent them, speaking with friends and relatives, secretly enjoying her role. Occasionally, she would join his table, sit on his lap if there wasn't an empty chair, put her arm around his shoulder. "You two look so much alike," someone said, "just like brother and sister," because they were both tall and thin, had dark hair and light eyes. She thought he was much more beautiful than she, even though when she glanced at her reflection in the mirror hanging in the hallway, she was very nearly satisfied with the reedy girl who had flowing hair and eyes that glowed like a bride's on her wedding day. Yes, that was the heart of it, she thought in horror now, that must have been the original sin she was punished for—feeling like a bride in that small garden during those seven days of mourning that had been like the seven days of her wedding celebration, saturated with solemn joy, with bitter pleasure, spurting now like water from a sprinkler through the hedge, directed entirely at her. She can almost hear them there, singing and playing guitars, laughing and crying, drinking and smoking. Day after day, night after night, we were together, all the rest has long since been forgotten.

What is the point in returning to that garden now, in peering into the windows of the apartment he has obviously not visited for years. There is no point, and yet she doesn't leave. It's the only thread she has that leads back to the past, and she will pull it, or let it pull her, because an unfamiliar force is pushing her through the hedge, pulling her to find an opening. A thorny branch scratches her cheek, but she is already there, inside the hedge as if it were a living creature that has swallowed her up. Suddenly she is alarmed by the sound of steps approaching the building, apparently those of a father and his son, who speaks in a shrill voice that sounds familiar, perhaps one of her pupils, she thinks in horror—she has several from this place. If only they don't see her, the rumor of their principal losing her mind will spread like wildfire.

"Daddy, thieves wear white clothes, right?" the boy asks. "Daddy, thieves only come to the ground floor, right?" The father nods distractedly, lingering at the entrance, foraging around in the mailbox—she'll never be able to explain her presence here in the bushes. But now they're walking up to the safer first floor and the boy continues to voice his fears, saying, "Daddy, thieves make a lot of noise, right?"

Only then does the father listen for the first time, and instead of reassuring him, he decides to go for accuracy: "No, of course not, thieves try to be very quiet so they won't get caught."

"No they don't," the frightened boy protests. "You don't know anything about thieves!" But luckily for him, the door closes behind their conversation at the exact moment a branch snaps under her weight and, surprised, she falls deep into the bush. She tries to forge a way out, or rather a way in to the garden. It seems as if she will be trapped there forever, but the branches enclosing her don't let go and she stretches her legs inside the tangle of shrubbery, flails her arms and bangs her head against the thick greenery as if she is a baby trying to pass through the birth canal. She feels a branch scrape her other cheek, her hair catches on the thorns, but she can't stop. She grabs hold of the branches and pushes them back until her body falls forward and drops onto the other side of the hedge.

She never imagined it was so difficult to break through a hedge, and now she doesn't know how she will get out of there, unless she is discovered in the garden and the residents of the ground-floor apartment call the police, who will make sure she is thrown out. Or perhaps it will be the first-floor residents, because she can already hear the screams of the frightened boy, "Daddy, did you hear that noise? There are thieves here!" But fortunately for her, his father pays no attention and admonishes him to finish his cornflakes instead of talking nonsense. So she stands up cautiously and, holding on to the building walls, tries to walk silently around it to the large living room window.

To her sorrow, it is completely dark, as is the garden on this moonless night, and she continues on to the bedroom window, where the shutters are half closed. The light is dim, and the sound of running water is the only indication that the apartment isn't empty. She waits, her eyes fixed on the window as they were earlier on the small screen. She has been waiting all day, all her life. What is she doing here, shivering with cold, though her breath is burning, her face scratched and her dress torn, clutching the bars of the window as if she has taken leave of her senses? Does he still have the power to unhinge her so much that she will return home soon to lie motionless on her bed as she did then? A broken heart at the age of forty-five—who would have believed it?

What is she looking for here? The apartment is probably rented to a pair of students or a young family, although there are no toys in the garden to indicate the presence of children. In fact, there is no evidence at all of anyone's presence or of the time that has passed. In the weak light, it seems to her that nothing has been added or removed from among the scrawny carob trees and the plum tree she remembers so well. During the shiva, they decided to start cultivating the garden, they'd plant flowers and maybe even vegetables, but then he deserted her and certainly this place as well, which reminded him of the illness. He probably planted flowers and vegetables in a different garden, the one where he lived with his family, his daughter Miriam and her mother, and perhaps another child or two. Though he caressed her face and kissed her lips, he will give her up because it was first love, which has nothing to do with adult life, because they are no longer what they were then, because a lifetime has passed and all the momentous choices are already behind them, because encounters with the past are barren, like this garden, because their good years are already behind them and there is no going back. She will return to her car now, in the hope that the branches take pity on her, and drive home. The present tenants of that apartment do not know the noble woman who once lived here with her only son and can shed no light on either her past or future life, so she walks slowly back, holding on to the carob trees.

For a moment, she is terrified by the sudden appearance of light, but it is only the light being turned on in the bedroom she is standing in front of. Through the slats, she is shocked to see a bearded, older man who turns his skinny back to her, clad only in underpants. She shakes her head in disbelief, or is it the chill she feels that is causing her head to move back and forth? It can't be, it's inconceivable, but it seems to be him, he lives here, this is the place he returned to in the end. Where is Miriam, his daughter, where is his wife? There don't seem to be any other people in the house, will they be returning soon? Is it possible that he lives alone, waiting only for her? She watches him go into the living room, where the light comes on, then he opens the fridge and takes out a bottle of beer. If he sees her here, he won't believe his eyes, won't believe that she has willingly returned to the place he banished her from.

The apartment has barely changed since then, and is as gray and shabby as she remembers it, showing no signs of a woman's presence. Is he alone, available to her, available to continue that mourning? She watches him put on a gray button-down shirt and light-colored shorts and she knows that he will leave the shirt open, that the water dripping from his hair will leave spots on the fabric. She sees him go into the living room, then sit down in front of a computer that is on the kitchen table and begin to type quickly, his expression grim and his back slightly stooped. Will he be happy to see her, or will he be alarmed—after all, he didn't bother to answer her message. Perhaps he thought it was from an annoying patient and didn't even listen to it. She'll try again now that she can watch him, she'll try again and discover the truth in real time. She sees him stand up slowly, probably looking for his cell phone, and then he disappears into the bedroom and she hears his voice twice, through the phone and through the window, drifting out to her on the evening breeze.

"Hello?" he says, and when she doesn't speak, he continues. "Is that you, Rissi? I didn't know if it was appropriate for me to call you back at this hour. You might be with the family," he explains—using the word "family" as only a general term.

She murmurs in reply, "I'm not with the family, Eitan. I'm with you, I'm here in the garden."

"You're in the garden?" he asks in surprise, his voice smiling at her. "You're not!" And she drops to the dry ground, her teeth chattering, knowing that he will open the living room door and walk down the four or five rickety stairs, the cell phone in his hand, its bluish light illuminating her. "Here you are," he says, and instead of taking her hand and leading her into the house, he lies down beside her. "What are you doing here, Rissi? I don't believe you're here," he whispers, examining her face in the light of the phone. "You look ill." He puts his hand on her forehead. "You have fever. Your face is scratched and your dress is torn. Why didn't you come in through the door? How did you even know I was here?"

"I didn't," she mumbles. "I didn't know who lived here."

"You always had a strong sense of intuition, always knew what had to be done and what was going to happen."

"Absolutely not," she protests, "the fact is that I had no idea you were going to leave me."

Surprising her, he says, "Neither did I." He glances at his watch. "How will you get home? What will you tell your husband?"

"I'll tell him that I ran into some thieves," she whispers.

"Really? And what did they steal from you?"

"Everything, my entire life. I gave them everything so they would leave me alone."

"You did the right thing. You think he'll believe you?"

"Of course he will. I never lie."

He laughs, "My good little girl. You always were a good girl." He tries to cool her forehead with his beer bottle. "When I saw you earlier, you didn't have fever. Are you ill because of me?"

"Obviously. Now you have to heal me."

"I'll do my best," he says and offers her some beer. She drinks it thirstily, and his hair, damp from his shower, drips onto her face as he leans on his arm and looks at her, lying limply on the ground at the foot of the plum tree.

She's more comfortable on the dry ground than in her bedroom, more comfortable on the ground with his familiar body at her side because this ground is hers. It seems to her that her footsteps from then have remained imprinted there, like the footprints of the first man to walk on the moon, because in the absence of wind and rain, in the absence of weather, nothing changes. She has returned to her moon now, the ground beneath her embraces her body, the sky rises above her and she lies between them. This is where she belongs, to this plum tree whose fruit was always a bit unripe or slightly rotten, it was good only one day a year. Nonetheless she used to devour the plums, hot from the sun, and when she strains her eyes, she can see tiny fruits among the branches now. "Have the plums improved since then?" she asks.

He looks indifferently at the tree and says, "Not really. They taste like olives. The tree must be an olive-plum hybrid. I haven't improved either, by the way," he adds with a smile.

Mesmerized, she looks into his deep-set eyes, which are shaded by thick, dark eyebrows, and whispers, "You weren't supposed to improve. I thought you were wonderful just the way you were."

"Funny, no woman after you ever thought that."

"You see," she says with a smile, "you should have stayed with me."

He sighs loudly and says, "Oh, Rissi, you think I don't know that?"

"Daddy, there are thieves in the garden! I hear them! I hear voices!" The boy's sharp cry from above interrupts them, and his father admonishes him, "Enough of that! A new story every night, anything not to go to sleep!"

"I want to sleep with Mommy," the boy wails, "there are no thieves there!"

Sighing, Eitan says, "Poor kid, he's so anxious. He reminds me of my little boy."

Surprised, she asks, "You have a little boy? How old is he?"

"Nine."

Then she asks, her tone suddenly formal, as befits the nature of the question, "So how many children do you actually have?"

"I have two children and two wives. From two different wives, I mean. Neither one of them lives with me."

She gives a sigh of relief at this new information, as if she really believed that he was not only unavailable, but also married to two women. How wonderful the new information is, even if the smallest doubt stirs in her as he describes what seems to be an especially disastrous love life. She cannot dwell on it. This isn't the time for interrogations and demands, it's the time to delight in the incredible encounter she supposedly hasn't anticipated, hoped for, fantasized about, or expected. But now she realizes that it is only for this encounter that she has lived since then, that everything she has done since then—her studies, her marriage, her children, her career—has been merely passing time in a waiting room, doing what was expected of her.

"Come," he says, standing up and giving her his hand, "let's go inside. Take pity on my upstairs neighbor."

She stands up heavily, the night darkness penetrating her eyes so she is almost unable to see, and without his support, she would fall. He leads her inside, almost carries her, the way a groom takes his bride into the home he has prepared for her, returning her to the place he banished her from almost thirty years earlier. Just as she sees the face he had then when she looks at his face now, so she sees the apartment both as it is now and as it was then, a double, deeper image that seems now to be the only image of any value. From the threshold, she sees the small living room. The couch has been changed, but it stands on exactly the same spot the old one did then, when she came there for the first time and saw a narrow back covered by a blanket, the long, well-groomed hair flowing onto it, and heard Eitan say softly, "Mama, Iris is here."

The blanket moved slowly, with effort, and the face that was turned to the wall turned to her, examining her with huge, blue, surprisingly young eyes. "Welcome, Iris," his mother said in a warm, gentle voice, shifting onto her side and leaning on her elbow, supporting her head with her hand and extending her other hand. "Nice to meet you. I'm Miriam. Forgive me for not getting up. My legs hurt."

Iris shook her hand emotionally—she loved her deeply from that first moment—and said, "You don't have to get up for me. I'll be happy to help Eitan take care of you."

"It's enough that you take care of him," his mother said, smiling. "It's a great relief for me to know that he's not alone." When she tried to straighten up a bit more, the flowing hair suddenly detached from her head, leaving her bare skull exposed, humiliated, and she flushed in embarrassment. "I can't seem to manage with this wig," she mumbled, shaking it out and placing it on the pillow. She never put it on again, and now, as Iris sees her image in the mirror that has remained in the hallway since then, she runs her fingers through her own hair, which has remained smooth and shiny even after she rolled around on the ground.

"Do you remember her wig?" she asks, and he knows immediately what she means.

"I was just going to say that you really look like her, not only the hair. It's incredible how much you've grown to look like her."

"She died at the age I am now," she says. "What does all this mean?"

He runs his fingers through her hair. "Let's wait and see. Who knows." For a moment, she trembles as if she has heard something ominous in his words. "You're shaking, you have a high fever. Let's finally take care of you. I don't know how to begin. Do you want to lie down"—he points to the couch— "or maybe take a shower?"

"Both," she replies.

"We'll start with the shower." He leads her gently to the bathroom from which he emerged a short time ago. "Hold on to the railing so you don't fall," he cautions her, pointing to the aluminum bars his mother used to hold on to, "and call me if you need me." When he comes back and hands her a towel, she is almost naked, and he hurries out while she, surprisingly, feels no embarrassment. It's not her that he's looking at, not at the stretch marks on her stomach, the surgical scars, or the general flaccidity of her body. It's the young girl she once was that he sees, and the image of his mother superimposed on her. For better or for worse, let's wait and see.

And so, when she emerges from her brief shower—the thought of missing precious time with him suddenly made her unbearably sad—she isn't surprised when he hands her a faded flowered robe she vaguely remembers. "Maybe you can wear this for the time being," he says, and she wraps herself in the robe, which smells surprisingly good, as if it has just been laundered for her. She lies down on the couch, drinks the tea he brews for her and swallows the pill he gives her, putting herself totally in his care. He cuts a slice of watermelon into small cubes and hands them to her, places a cool towel on her forehead, pours her a glass of water, and it seems to her that everything she did for him in the past is being returned to her in concentrated form. In a moment, he'll sit down beside her and begin tutoring her for exams.

"What's funny, Rissi?" he asks gently.

"I remembered how I used to teach you before your exams. It was really hard. How did you actually manage to get through medical school?"

"There were always girls who thought the effort was worth it," he laughs.

"I never thought otherwise," she says, clearly displeased.

He lies down beside her. "The truth is that in a few years, my brain cleared. After the army, I discovered that I actually liked to study. Don't judge me harshly. I know I was a complete idiot, but there were extenuating circumstances. You said so yourself."

"Of course," she smiles, "I don't judge you at all," even though she doesn't know whether he is talking about his learning difficulties or his abandonment of her. But it doesn't matter to her now as she closes her eyes and holds his hand. She feels as if her flesh is melting from the fever, melting and blending with his into a single, indivisible mass. "What did you give me, morphine?" she asks with a smile. "Medical cannabis? I feel like I'm hallucinating."

"Just Optalgin."

She protests, "Optalgin I have at home. I don't need a pain specialist for Optalgin. Why did you choose that specialty?"

"Someone who doesn't believe in cures goes into pain," he says. "It's a totally different worldview. For most doctors, disease is the main thing, but for us, it's only of secondary interest. We don't try to cure, just to reduce the suffering. You're the last person who needs to ask that. You were there with me."

"Her suffering was terrible," she says, the horrific cries that came from the other side of the curtain on the day of his mother's death echoing in her ears. For a moment, they seem to be coming from her own throat. Has he given her his mother's disease so he can tend to her as devotedly as he tended to his mother, reduce the pain he caused? She will accept it only if he remains with her here until the day she dies, only if she never goes back to her home. She needs time with him, she has so many questions to ask— she doesn't know anything yet, doesn't know, for example, what he did after he banished her, on that day and on the day after it. In fact, she wants to go through the calendar with him, through all the weeks and months that have passed since that day, even if it takes almost thirty years to re-create the large and small details in the order in which they occurred. What did he do in the army where did he go to school whom did he marry where did he live why did he leave whom did he marry next where do his children live when does he see them does he still love sour apples? But the feeling of infinite time blows around her with the night breeze, she has no idea of what time her watch shows, her time is different, she is in another country, inside the planet, where the years gather.

"Are you sleeping?" he whispers.

She shakes her head, adding, to her surprise, "I'm happy."

He strokes her bare arms, his fingers graze her breasts through the robe. "Rissi, what about your family? Aren't they waiting for you? Won't they be worried?"

"So let them worry," she whispers.

But he pleads with her, "At least send a message. Where's your cell phone? I don't want to get you in trouble."

He puts the phone in her hand, it's only 10:30, she discovers, she can still stay with him, she can't leave him again, so she sends a terse message to Mickey, "I'm in Tel Aviv. Be back late. Don't worry," and he responds immediately, "What are you doing in Tel Aviv?"

She quickly sends a message to Dafna: "I'm with you in Tel Aviv, okay? I'll explain tomorrow," and only after Dafna confirms does she text him, "With Dafna. Don't wait up for me."

She arranges it all with astonishing skill, as if her life with him has been filled with lies, but she never cheated on him, never lied to him, always wonders at her friends who have affairs. It seems to her like an unnecessary burden on both body and soul, and until now, she has never met a man she felt was worth carrying that burden for. Every now and then, a pupil's father would linger in her office longer than necessary. In meetings at the Education Ministry, she would sometimes notice suggestive looks, especially before she was injured. She never responded, not only out of loyalty to Mickey and the family, but out of the certainty she felt that they would not satisfy her hunger. Now, however, she is in another country where her great hunger has ended, she is in her own land of Egypt, and so she will lie brazenly to her children as well. To be on the safe side, she also texts Omer: "I'm in Tel Aviv. We'll study tomorrow." He replies immediately with a smiley face and "Have fun, Mom." What does he even care where she is as long as his clothes are washed and his plate is full.

The entire time, Eitan putters around in the kitchen, giving her privacy although she hasn't asked for it, and while she is still spinning her lies, he takes another bottle of beer out of the fridge and sits down in front of the computer again. She watches him as if she is still in the garden on the other side of the window as he types quickly, and for a moment, he seems to forget that she's there at all, his brow furrows above his eyes, his already dry gray hair is brushed back, his clenched lips are dark, his expression grim. She closes her eyes and listens to the sounds of the keyboard. "What are you writing?" she finally asks, and only then does he stand up and go over to her, stretching his youthful arms above him and to the back.

"I'm answering patients' questions," he says with a sigh. "There's no end to it. I sit with these emails for hours every night."

She spreads her arms for him and whispers, "I have questions too, but I want the answers orally," and he lies down beside her again. He has turned off all the lights, the room is illuminated only by the bluish glow of the computer monitor, and from the window, fingers of the cool, summer, plum-scented night breeze of the Jerusalem Hills caress them.

"Can I answer orally, but without words?" he asks hoarsely.

"How?"

"Like this," he whispers, his lips on hers, and she feels as if, with the long, ardent kiss, he is pouring into her the essence of the life he has led until now, without her, even lonelier than she. Yes, she already knows everything, she has no further questions, except perhaps why he isn't worried about catching her throat infection.

Under the flowered robe that once covered his mother's body, her body is covered by kisses, her skin is blooming, she is a flowering plum tree, she is a hedge, she is magically transformed from animal to vegetable, her needs now simple, and she is planted in the ground. She suddenly remembers teaching him for his Bible exam, and he couldn't understand that verse, "A man is like a tree of the field." How exhausting it was trying to give a clear and simple explanation of the conflicting interpretations: is it possible to say that a man is the equivalent of a tree in the field? On the face of it, yes, because he too is created from a tiny seed, he too grows and is cut down like a tree. But the verse, from Deuteronomy, which is about the rules of war, is saying the opposite—is the tree of the field like a man who must endure the siege? A man can flee and a tree cannot, a man can attack and a tree cannot, and so it should not be destroyed.

They sat here at the table and studied, and he kicked his chair in frustration, his eyes filling with tears. He always cried more easily than she, though on the day he banished her, he didn't cry. But now he can't banish her again because she is planted here like the plum tree, she has never so truly belonged, has never had such a profound sense of home in any of the apartments she has lived in. Now he carries her to the bedroom and takes off the robe, and there is nothing separating his cool skin and her burning skin—it is like an encounter between two climates, two continents caught in a single storm cloud, heavy with thick steam, hailstones crashing into each other, laden with electrical currents exploding in flashes of light. It is the encounter that creates the lightning and thunder that rolls through the skies like her voice, which keeps repeating, "My love, my love." There is no end to the words she yearns to say to him, and each word yearns to be said endlessly in a single sentence that is as long as her life. To her surprise he suddenly answers her, begins to speak as his body intertwines with hers, telling her of the first years after their parting, his voice growing hoarse, and she listens intently, devouring every whispered word before he can no longer speak. "I was so lonely, Rissi. Do you understand what it means not to have anyone in the world? I was thrown straight into the army, I wanted combat, I wanted to die. I spent every weekend with a different friend. I chose them on the basis of how far from Jerusalem they lived, the farther the better. I didn't want to see this house or my grandparents, who were devastated themselves. I don't think I came to Jerusalem for about three years."

"And what about me," she asks, "didn't you want to see me?" Suddenly, her mother's story becomes simply one more hallucination of her withering brain, and she doesn't know whether to be happy or sad about it.

He rests his gray head on her breasts and says, "Don't be silly, of course I wanted to. You were the person closest to me, but I was afraid of that closeness. I ran as far away as I could from it, just so I wouldn't feel anything. If you don't feel, you don't suffer. That was my dream for years, to numb my emotions. I had a reason for doing a residency in anesthesiology. I slept with women without feeling anything, I married without feeling anything. I didn't feel again until Miriam was born."

"And what was it like to feel again?" she asks, suddenly realizing that her months of suffering, which he knew nothing about, were inconsequential compared to the long years he was describing. She may not even tell him about them, especially if he doesn't ask. Because what can she say? I lay in bed without moving, frozen in one position for days on end? I didn't eat or drink, I didn't speak or hear? I was like a vegetable, because a man is a tree of the field? How can she even be angry with him? He left her because he loved her too much, hurt too much.

He repeats her question, "What was it like? It was wonderful and terrible, and it destroyed my marriage."

"Really? Why?"

"Because then I realized that I didn't love her mother, and that was not a happy discovery. I left the house fairly quickly. It was Miriam's loss when I began to feel again."

"I'm sure she also gained," she says, finding herself consoling him, just as she did then, when they were young, when she was quick to take his pain upon herself.

"Not enough, I'm sorry to say. With all the pressure at work, all the night shifts I had, and her hostile mother, it was very hard to build a relationship. She was too young when we separated. And later I went abroad to study and hardly saw her."

Iris eagerly absorbs the abundance of surprising new information. For some reason, she always imagined him happily married to a woman more accomplished than she, a woman it was impossible to leave, raising accomplished children with her. It never occurred to her that he might be divorced and was alone the entire time. And for the entire time, he is making love to her, speaking to her with every part of his body. She forgot that he is like this, that they are like this, she has become so used to Mickey's down-to-business approach that separates words from touch. But here, with them, everything merges in the face of his past and her own, which she is re-creating in parallel to his. His daughter Miriam was born several months before her Omer, which means that when he left his wife, Iris was already in her second pregnancy, undecided about why she was actually having another baby. The question grew more pressing after Omer was born and drained all her strength, but she let it go because she didn't have the time to think about it in depth, and also because, despite herself, she was grateful to the active, hot-tempered baby who constantly caused chaos and distracted her. As she re-creates her life in parallel to his, she is surprised to discover that she was happier than he, at least during those years, in spite of the vague sense of defeat she felt. Since recovering from her breakdown, when she felt profoundly close to destruction, a simple, low-intensity life was usually enough for her. But just when she seemed to have forgotten the lesson, a suicide bomber came into her life, a Palestinian policeman from Bethlehem, who reminded her once again how close the abyss was, and that solid ground was better. Now everything that happened takes on a new meaning, has a double significance, like the double face of her young man who has become a middle-aged man, and apparently not an easy one, with thick dark eyebrows, beautiful eyes, and lips only fully revealed when he kisses her. Once again she wonders at the double vision, layer upon layer—that must be how we see ourselves and those close to us. But she didn't see the beard grow on his cheeks, and now it is turning white, she didn't see him reach his full height, and he is already beginning to stoop. They have so much to fill in, almost thirty years were stolen from them.

Now they have to be twenty or thirty years old again, marry and give birth to the children of their deep, old love, to their Miriam, because his seed is flooding the corridors of her body now and she knows that a forgotten egg of her youth must be waiting for it. He moves above her as if he is praying, and with his beard and the devout expression on his thin face, he looks like a cantor chanting the final Yom Kippur prayer a moment before judgment is passed: Open the gates for us when the gates are closing, for the day wanes. The day is waning, the sun is setting, let us come into your gates! Oh, God, please! Please pardon! Please forgive! Please wipe out! Please atone! Please have mercy! Please suppress anger, sin, and transgression! She joins in his prayer, her body pulsing with his in pleasure and joy, your prayer is answered, my prayer is answered, our prayer is answered.

NINE

When she opens her eyes in the morning, she still feels blessed, despite the raw throat and high fever. Slowly and gradually, images clear. The interrupted story of her life comes together in a colorful chain like the ones she used to make for the Sukkoth holiday when she was a child. Longing so much for a sukkah of her own, she used to cut and paste endless strips of paper in the belief that the longer the chain she offered to her neighbors, the happier they would be to welcome her into their sukkah, because there was no one in her own house to build one. So she cut and pasted and put on her holiday clothes, but on the way to the neighbor's sukkah, the too-long chain tore under her feet and she returned home in tears. Now she is pasting again, a strip of red paper to a blue one, a blue one to green one, each strip adhering to its companion, suffusing it with its color and changing it completely, the way she has changed beside Eitan. Even the mere thought of him now changes her very being. Parting from him the night before, she felt that nothing would remain as it was. He was afraid to let her drive alone and followed her in his car, its headlights caressing her with two glowing eyes, imbuing her with a thrilling sense of peace as she led him to her home, to her life.

He parked next to her in the residents' parking area, helped her out of her car and supported her as she walked into the elevator that in no time at all opened into her living room. From there she walked gingerly to Alma's bedroom, a profound sense of alienation separating her from the apartment and its residents. Mickey's door was closed, and gratefully, she didn't have to see him or be seen by him when she belonged to another man and another time, and Omer was asleep as well. With a sigh, she fell onto her daughter's bed, feeling that she had returned from a long journey, though it wasn't to her home that she returned, but rather to a stop along the way, a sort of hotel, because though the journey was long, it had only just begun.

Now too, with closed eyes, she listens to the sounds of the house, hurried steps in the hallway, the fridge opening and closing, the elevator going up, its doors opening and closing. Only when it is quiet does she go cautiously out of her room like a guest who would rather not bump into her hosts. They must have left together, Mickey to work and Omer to school, but she nevertheless looks all around to avoid being caught off guard, following the traces of their morning routine. She herself left no traces last night, keeping close at hand all the things that might incriminate her—her dress, her handbag, and of course her cell phone, adopting overnight all the necessary rules of caution. She hurries to wash her dress, scrubs her body with soap and shampoos her hair, applies makeup to hide the scratches made on her face by the branches, puts on a clean nightgown. Now she is ready for them, primed and ready, because a person with a secret must always be primed and ready, even in his sleep. But no soap can wash away the truth that is beyond one stain or another, the truth that her very being has changed, that her inner core has come suddenly and powerfully to life—no makeup can hide that. She takes a cup of hot tea and a slice of bread and honey into the bedroom and goes back to bed to continue pasting her paper loops together.

How he stood in front of her, his eyes fixed on her questioningly, the wrinkle between them growing deeper as she walked slowly toward him and wrapped her arms around his neck in a trembling embrace, and to her surprise, he responded, his arms encircling her back. "It's you, isn't it?" she said, because she couldn't see his face. How he said, "Wait for me," and led her to the door, and she waited for him, waited for hours until he finally came to her. How she hurried after him to the icy waiting room where they made themselves known to each other, the way Joseph made himself known to his brothers. How she found him in his mother's house and he lay on the ground beside her, under the plum tree, and she was once again united with his familiar, precious body, as if she had never been away from it. How he drove here behind her, his headlights accompanying her like two glowing eyes. It happened in only a single day, if it happened at all, too good, too easy, contradicting everything she has learned about life in the meantime.

But her cell phone is signaling now, and breathlessly, she reads the message that has just that moment been sent, "How are you, my love?" the sender called Pain asks. Her eyes and her fingers caress the letters he sent her, and she writes back, "I'm sick and happy."

"Are you alone?" he asks, "Can I come to see you for a minute?" And so excited by the possibility, she replies immediately with all the words at her disposal, "Of course, definitely, absolutely come." She doesn't want him to feel any hesitation or reluctance on her part, although she actually does feel some. She is alone in the house, waiting for him almost thirty years, Mickey is at work and Omer at school. The chance that they may return suddenly in the late morning is as slim as the chance was that she would ever see him again. She hurriedly smooths her hair with the hot straightening iron she saves for special occasions and quickly applies lipstick, and while she is still searching the closet for a dress that will be more flattering than the old nightgown, the bell rings, causing her to tremble with anticipation. He came, he's here, and she coughs into the intercom, "Eitan? I'm sending down the elevator." But there's no one, and the bell keeps ringing, confusing her, until she realizes that it is the infrequently used front doorbell. She opens the door with shaking hands and falls into his arms, her body aflame with her illness and her heart pounding with emotion.

"You walked up six flights?" she asks, her cheek on his shoulder. "Why didn't you take the elevator?" as if this is the most important thing between them.

"I never use elevators," he replies, "they're swarming with germs." But apparently he isn't afraid of the germs she's growing in her mouth, because he raises her chin and devours her lips with his; in a moment, he will draw her entire body into his hungry mouth. Through the thin nightgown, his hands are on her breasts, the breasts that have nursed two children who are not his, but no man had ever touched them before him. She is in his arms once again, she is his once again, a flame burns between her legs and her body fuses with his in the total giving of herself she remembers from then and has never felt since. Panting and quivering at his touch, she feels as if she isn't standing on her feet, but on his, because his arms raise her up as he bends her backward and kisses her hot breasts through the fabric of the nightgown, the pleasure so intense that she no longer remembers where she is. Even if Mickey comes in right now, she won't stop, even if Omer suddenly emerges from his room and looks at her in astonishment, she will continue, she will not give up this total pleasure, she will not let go of his body as it becomes joined to hers, joined from head to toe. This is nature's gravitational force, this is how we were created, as two particles of a magnetic field, another inevitable phenomenon of the planet, one of many that are much worse, she hears herself rationalizing, gasping.

"What did you say?" he whispers in her ear.

"Nothing. I'm hallucinating because of the fever. Let's sit down for a minute." She leads him to the couch. The moment they sit down, before she has time to take her hand from his, she hears the familiar breath of the elevator stopping, and to her horror, it opens and emits Shula, their housecleaner.

She always dresses nicely for work, a miniskirt and heels, which are immediately replaced by an old apron and flip-flops. Iris always tells her he how nice she looks, and even now, out of habit, her stunned brain tries to produce a comment about her red blouse. "That color really suits you." But the shocked expression of their longtime cleaner brings her to her senses like a pail of cold water, and she stands up quickly. "Don't ask, I feel terrible! I was so lucky that my doctor was in the neighborhood and agreed to examine me. This is Dr. Rosen, chief of the Pain Unit," she stammers.

Shula walks toward them, still stunned. Her awe at his profession tempers the shock slightly and offers a reassuring interpretation of the suspicious scene, especially when the distinguished doctor stands up and shakes her hand gravely. But Iris knows that her lips are swollen, her hair is a mess, and there are incriminating spots on her nightgown.

"So what do you advise me to do? Take antibiotics?" she asks in a formal tone when Shula goes into one of the bedrooms to change clothes.

"The truth is that I have no idea what you have. The only thing I understand is incurable disease," he says, and they both burst out laughing.

She can't stop even when Shula returns to the living room wearing her apron and asks, "Should I start in Alma's room so you can go back to bed?"

Iris nods enthusiastically. "Thank you, Shulinka. You're the best," she calls to her back as she moves away.

"I hope you don't plan to fire her," he says with a chuckle. "You're in her hands now. Tomorrow she'll ask for a raise."

Iris protests, "Don't be silly, she's not like that. She would never hurt me." Yet she feels threatened by the sense that things have changed.

He glances at his watch and says, "I have to get back to the clinic. I'm sorry if I've made trouble for you, Rissi. You should be the one to set the rules. You have more to lose than I do."

She walks him to the door and says, "I have nothing to lose but you."

Nonetheless, she hurries back to Shula to see how suspicious she is and gets into bed while she is still running the vacuum cleaner. "I was really lucky," she says again, "I felt so bad and I didn't have the strength to go to the clinic. Then I remembered that Dr. Rosen went to high school with me, so I called him and he just happened to be in the neighborhood."

"Ah, you went to high school together!" Shula says. "Isn't that something!"

For a moment, she seems to accept the explanation for the unmistakable intimacy, but she still has that look of displeasure she always has when she sees that Omer has again left his wet towel on the rug in his room. She puts on her earphones now—she is always tuned in to the radio and happy to share the reports with anyone who is at home. "Isn't that something!" she suddenly calls out again, "they say that the percentage of infidelity in Israel almost doubled in the last decade. I wonder how they know that. I mean, people keep their infidelities a secret." The noise of the vacuum cleaner drowns out everything that is and isn't said, and Iris closes her eyes. Clearly there is a problem, but she'll deal with it later, when she feels better, because that problem is a small babushka doll in the stomach of a larger problem. In order to solve it, she has to forage around in the stomach of the larger problem, so she'll wait, she won't think about the word that had just been tossed into the dustless air of the bedroom— too bad it can't be sucked into the vacuum cleaner. Infidelity.

Is it infidelity, when she feels with such absolute certainty that it's a miracle? Is it infidelity, when she feels that she has never been more faithful to herself? Have she and Mickey grown so far apart that being faithful to herself means being unfaithful to him? And if that is so, doesn't it prove that their relationship is fundamentally a mistake? Infidelity is such an ugly word, how can it apply to such a beautiful encounter so filled with bliss? Shula has spread the new word through the house, an uninvited guest. It's bliss, not infidelity, she protests in the silence. When Mickey comes home, will he sense that a stranger had been here, an invader from the past? And what will she do then?

"You should be the one to set the rules," Eitan said, standing tall and slightly stooped at the door, his long dark lashes lowered toward her. Although that seems convenient, it is impossible because she now senses that she will never be able to refuse him, will never be able to forgo even one brief, reckless meeting like today's. She is too hungry for him, he is too precious to her. Let's break the rules, throw caution to the wind, she wants to say. Perhaps when she gets well, she'll be able to manage the relationship, just as she has managed her school until now, but for the moment, she feels as soft and borderless as a pool of water that will pass through any opening it finds. How thirsty she is for water, but it's hard for her to get up, so she gulps down the tea that has cooled beside her bed. In a minute she'll call Shula, ask her for a glass of water and casually hint that she shouldn't say anything to Mickey about the doctor's visit. You know how difficult he is about money, she will malign him behind his back, better he doesn't know that I paid for a private visit instead of going to the clinic. But before she can carry out her plan, which seems clever if a bit despicable, she falls asleep.

When she opens her eyes, it is already evening, Shula is long gone, a bluish darkness has spread like a curtain over the open window and she hears the rhythmic beeps that announce the beginning of the evening news. She hopes they won't broadcast the item that Shula reported to her about the percentage of infidelity in Israel that has doubled recently, an item that may cause Mickey to ask where she was the night before. It was only yesterday that she suspected him, and now the suspicion has shifted to her. Perhaps it's actually both of them who have been unfaithful, perhaps they are the ones who have raised the statistics in one fell swoop. She tries to hear the news, but the reporter's words are swallowed up by the loud clattering of a spoon or fork on a plate, creating a link between the two, as if the glamorous anchor is reading the news while dining in their living room.

Staring at the darkening window, she recalls the days she was confined to her bed, listening to the sounds of her family as if they were in an old radio play about family life from the distant days when sounds were more accessible than sights. It was a radio play that had no special connection to her, or so she felt at the time, about a father and his two children trying to maintain their routines as they clung to the fantasy that their sick mother would return, a fantasy that the listeners tended to doubt.

"Your food is disgusting. I want Mommy's food," she used to hear Omer cry. "Then don't eat," Mickey would scold him, then immediately regret it and try to calm him down. "We all want Mommy to get well fast, Sweetie. But we have to be flexible now."

Alma actually showed great flexibility. Far from her anxious mother's eyes, she wolfed down Mickey's strange concoctions—he liked to cook a mishmash of soup leftovers in the same pot with fresh pasta and old rice—at least that was what she understood from the praise she heard coming from the dining room. She listened to that drama every evening, recognizing the psychological mechanisms and analyzing the goings-on, but a new feeling of apathy, a screen of tedium separated her from the characters. Does every relationship we were once part of look so insipid when we observe it from a distance? she wondered. Is it only the profound, indisputable sense of belonging that causes us to be drawn in, to love a tiny baby, to devote ourselves to our mate? Because the moment an arbitrary force suddenly cuts off the continuity, everything becomes pointless.

After the meal and the showers, Omer and Alma would come into her bedroom to say good night to Mommy, and she tried to focus on their stories, making sure to smile at them even if she was in agonizing pain. She never cried in their presence, always tried to show restraint and self-control to make it easier for them, but deep down, she didn't want anyone with her during those difficult months, certainly not a child. She always felt more protected in the hospital, and after the third and last surgery, she actually begged to remain there for a few more days. She remembered that they sent the hospital psychiatrist to check that everything was all right at home, and she, of course, didn't open up to him, saying only, "There's no problem at home, I'm just more comfortable here."

"You're hiding too much from them," the psychiatrist said in his American accent. "Show them that it's hard for you and give them a chance to help."

"That contradicts my worldview," she said condescendingly, unconsciously imitating his heavy accent. No wonder he didn't dare approach her bed again.

Did she also deny Mickey a chance to help? On the surface, he helped her constantly—she couldn't stand, was totally dependent on him the way she had been dependent on her mother during her breakdown. Perhaps that was why she felt strangely adept at being disabled, why she was so bothered by the presence of the children. And Mickey did try, but the coffee he made her was always cold, the food was strange, and so was he, cold and strange, and here he is now, opening the door, a bowl of soup in his hand, letting a painful shaft of light into the room.

"You're here?" he asks with a smile as he eats the soup. He seems to be in a good mood for some reason, maybe he beat an anonymous opponent at chess. "Shula must be in love. She poured like a cup of salt into the soup. Who even needs soup in this heat?" he complains, the slightly foolish smile still on his face. Iris stares at him with half-closed eyes, he still hasn't asked how she is, doesn't notice that she's sick, is concerned only with the taste in his mouth, speaks to her without noticing whether she is asleep or awake. Is that why she chose him? Because from the beginning, she had something to hide, so she preferred a man with such a limited ability to notice other people?

"Mickey, I don't feel well," she says, opening one eye at him. In the light coming from the hallway, he looks almost like an abstract figure, devoid of details.

"That pain again?"

She is frightened for a moment, but his question is an innocent one. "No, it's not the pain. I must have caught a cold in Tel Aviv, from the air-conditioning. I have a high fever."

"What were you doing in Tel Aviv?" he barks.

She still hasn't spoken to Dafna so they can get their stories straight, and she tries to make do with a general answer. "Dafna asked me to go to a meeting with her. Please bring me a bowl of soup."

Her plan is working well for the time being—he's happy to return the conversation to the subject that has preoccupied him from the beginning, grumbling once again, "Who needs soup in this heat?"

"It's probably because I'm sick. Bring me some too? I haven't eaten a thing all day." He goes back to the kitchen and she sighs in relief. On the surface, he's suspicious, but much too focused on himself to act on his suspicions, to draw conclusions. It's too exhausting, he's too lazy, and it's convenient for him to return to what interests him, his chess. He doesn't notice that her cell phone is suddenly beside her bed. He still hasn't even noticed her new hair color or the scratches on her face. He isn't used to looking at her attentively, but to be on the safe side, she should stay in the dark, and when he returns with the bowl of soup, she asks him not to turn on the light. "It hurts my eyes," she whispers, immediately surprising herself with a new evasion. "Just listen to me, my voice is gone now." It seems that all the lies her pupils, and occasionally her teachers, told her over the years have been preserved in her memory and are at her disposal now that she needs them. "You can go back to the computer. It's hard for me to talk anyway," she adds generously, using clean language to describe what she usually calls "your fucking chess games." He stands there between the bed and the door, hesitating, surprised at being released but afraid to disappoint, in case she is deliberately tripping him up so she can add this to his list of offenses and use it against him in the future.

"Don't be silly," he finally protests gallantly. "I won't go to play when you feel so bad. I'll sit here with you." Suddenly all the arguments they've had over the years about his chess seem so inane. What does she want from him? After all, he can't give her what she needs even if he remains at her side every minute of the day, and for a moment, she feels sorry for him, lump of a man that he is. In fact, he is also her son, her ungainly older son, who unlike his siblings won't leave the house when he grows up. How could she have suspected him of infidelity? Dafna is right, it's so unlike him. He is naive, honest, and guilty of nothing. He simply isn't enough for her, he simply isn't Eitan. She has to continue taking care of him the way she takes care of Omer, but she will keep her emotional life for herself, as mothers do. A mother has the right to fall in love as long as she doesn't neglect her children, and she won't neglect them. She'll stay here with them, preserve the family unit, and occasionally slip away to her other life. You can't even call it a double life because there is nothing double about it. She is a woman there and a mother here, two parts that make up a whole, and that's the solution that presents itself almost naturally, considering the circumstances of her life.

After all, if Eitan Rosenfeld hadn't left her, she would be living a full life to this day with him and the children they would have had together. But that didn't happen, and now there are three people in the world she has an obligation to, an obligation she will honor only if they honor her needs, her feelings, her loyalty to the young girl she once was and the woman she has grown into.

"Why are you looking at me like that?" he asks.

She snaps out of her reverie. "Me? Like what?"

"Like you're seeing me for the first time, or the last time."

She is seized by a paroxysm of embarrassed coughing. "I'm going to die of the flu, Mooky, so maybe this really is the last time. Someone is always dying of the flu." She tries to make light of his words, to gloss over the accuracy of his perceptive comment.

"Usually more elderly people," he says, oddly serious.

"I'm pretty elderly," she says quickly. The more he thinks about her in those terms, the less he will suspect her and maybe he'll even want her less. Is that why he's still here, in the doorway, hoping that her passive presence in bed will grant him access? The thought of his touch seems vaguely perverse, like the inappropriate touch of a child who has already grown up, and her patience is already coming to an end. "I want to sleep," she whispers.

"But you still haven't eaten the soup I brought you," he protests.

"I feel nauseous all of a sudden. Maybe later." And in order to leave no doubt, she calls after him as he leaves, "Close the door. Good night." She tries to hide the smile that appears on her face, as involuntary as a baby's twitch.

Because she actually likes this illness. How good it is that the air conditioner in the waiting room devastated her, it allows her rest, privacy, freedom, everything an unfaithful person needs. To her dismay, the word that emerged from Shula's mouth is still drifting through the house, and she's amazed again and again at her resourcefulness and creativity, at how much more accomplished she is becoming from moment to moment, as if she were born to be an unfaithful woman, a woman with a secret. Maybe I'll open a workshop in infidelity, she thinks, I'll instruct men and women on how to be unfaithful without arousing the slightest suspicion. Naturally I'll start with the parents at school, then the rumor will spread and I'll become a much sought-after lecturer.

She observes her progress in amazement, because the next morning, he is there again. It isn't Shula's day to clean, but, learning from experience, she takes him into her room and locks the door, and on her daughter's bed, she experiences the greatest of all encounters. Her body, now thinner, becomes the body of the young girl she once was, and the undivided, passionate soul that lives within her comes alive as well. Whenever she thinks she is sated, she wants him again. "Don't go, stay with me," she says, but he doesn't have time, he has to return to his patients, he'll try to come tomorrow.

But the next day, he can't get away when she's alone at home, and she tosses and turns in bed, disappointed. Her skin needs him urgently, the way it needs a warm coat on a winter's day or a cool breeze in a khamsin. Has he already grown tired of her? She can't endure that again. But the following day, he comes early, a few minutes after Mickey and Omer have gone, smelling fresh, his eyes glowing. "I can't go another day without you. I'm completely addicted," he whispers.

"Me too. I could barely get through yesterday," she admits happily. She locks the door, takes off his clothes, and drapes them across the back of Alma's chair, which stands at the desk where she used to do her homework, beside her now-empty aquarium. She caresses his body with every part of herself. What does that body possess that makes her so hungry for it? It is thin and sensitive, it makes her weep with pleasure, laugh with pain, it speaks to her constantly, demands all of her, the totality of her, every fiber of her being, all the sweet spasms of her passion. The bare walls of the room observe them, only the outlines of the pictures that once hung on them are left, their various sizes marking Alma's growth from child to teenager to young woman: family pictures, drawings she made, posters of the TV stars she liked.

"It reminds me of your room," he says. "You had a bed like this that was too large for one and too small for two. We used to say that your mother should switch with us because she always slept alone. How is she? Still alive?" He doesn't ask about Alma, even though he is a guest in her bed, and she herself manages to shut out all her upsetting thoughts about her daughter.

No worrying about Alma while he's here, she warns herself, and not after he's gone, because then she will think about him, re-creating every moment and doubling the pleasure, the miracle of his reappearance in her life. Not in the afternoon, when Mickey comes home from work and she really tries to be nice to him, and not when Omer comes in from school and sits down across from her with a full plate and chats with her. Unlike Alma, he likes to share with her, and now he's trying to decide whether to tell his girlfriend that he needs a little more space. And not when she reluctantly answers the dozens of emails, trying to pass on as many as she can to her assistant principal, a young woman she trained who is still enthusiastic and grateful for every expression of trust from the principal.

Now Eitan looks around the room. "Are you in quarantine because of your illness?"

"No, because he snores."

He laughs in relief, delighted at the snorer's misfortune. Until now, he has asked very little and she has told him very little, not even about how sick she was after he abandoned her. It would be a shame to waste time on things I know, she thinks, better to hear from him what I don't know, or simply to be with him, to rediscover him. She seems to have fallen in love before learning who he is now, returned all at once to the forgotten experience of an emotion so intense that it fills all the spaces, leaving not a single one free of him.

When they were young, the opposite happened, of course. First she got to know him and then she fell in love with him. Well, maybe she didn't really know him, but became used to seeing him, even though he was a year ahead of her at school and there was hardly any social interaction between the grades until he was in his senior year and his class had to organize the Memorial Day ceremony. These days, it horrifies her to see young men about to be drafted reciting commemorative verses as if they were preparing themselves for their own deaths, but back then it seemed natural, just as her participation in the ceremony seemed natural. There were several bereaved parents in her school, but only she had lost a father in war, so she was called to the stage every year to talk about his heroism in a burning tank on the banks of the Suez Canal, a story that obviously did not change from year to year. She also sang two memorial songs in her beautiful voice, songs that actually did change from year to year. That year, unsurprisingly, Eitan had been chosen to host the ceremony because of his height, his blue eyes, and his serious expression, which seemed perfect for the occasion. So it happened that she spent much time with him during the weeks of rehearsal and preparations, and even though he was surrounded by the girls in his class, he clearly preferred to be with her.

She felt as if the loss of her father interested him, but still didn't know why, and tried to give weighty replies to the questions he asked: Had her memories dimmed with time? Was she angry at her father for leaving her, or at the country that took him away from her, or at the Egyptian soldiers who killed him? She tried to gather all her memories of her father for Eitan, even the uncomplimentary ones, such as his terrible fear of insects, which she inherited from him. To keep her safe from the creepy-crawlies, even just a roach or a tiny mouse, he would pick her up and spirit her away, to the sound of her mother's strong objections. She also mentioned his terrible taste in women, as evidenced by his choice of her mother. She even told him that she thought it was only an unplanned pregnancy, or more accurately, an unplanned daughter, namely her, that might have forced him into marrying her, and that he had chosen to die in order to get away from that woman, who was wrong for him. "It's her fault that I never said goodbye to my father," she told Eitan. "She wouldn't let him wake me up when he was mobilized and had to go off to war because she didn't want our routine to be disrupted." But mainly she told him how everything had changed abruptly after his death. It was as if they had moved to another country, as if their lives had been transformed, and her greatest loss had been the loss of anticipation because all of a sudden, there was nothing to look forward to. Until then, she had spent her days waiting for her father to come home in the evening, waiting for their little talks, sitting in his lap, encircled by his arms, observing the world triumphantly. The loss of anticipation was harder than the loss of her father because he spent only two or three hours with her, while the expectation of seeing him filled her mind for most of the day. Without it, she turned into a hardworking, gloomy little girl who unhappily helped her mother raise two unnecessary babies. Her only wishes were negative ones—for them not to wake up at night, for them not to be sick, for her mother not to be angry.

She loved the way Eitan's neck bent as he listened to her speak, the way he looked at her with an interest she was unused to, and she loved his mature and direct questions, the glowing depths of his eyes and his full lips. But she never dared to hope that he was interested in her and assumed that after the ceremony, they would once again be as distant as they had always been. But to her surprise, to her joy, that did not happen, because right after the ceremony, after the national anthem had been sung, he asked her what she was doing that evening, Independence Day eve, and invited her to go with him and some other friends to a spring not far from his house, a spring that no one knew about, under a beautiful mulberry tree.

"Does our spring still exist?" she texts him right after he leaves, and he replies after a while, "They built a housing project in the wadi and destroyed it. I heard that now they're trying to restore it. I'll check on Saturday when I go out to ride my bike." On Saturdays, she learned, when his children are with their mothers, he rides his ultramodern bicycle, and the thought of him going back to that place where they knew such bliss thrills her. So she texts, "Wait for me, I want to go there with you," and he replies two hours later, "I'll wait."

But in the evening, when he has more time to write than she does, he texts her long messages, mixing memories and desires with plans of action. "My mother loved you so much," he writes suddenly. "Before she died, she told me to marry you. I was so stupid. What do you say we get married at her grave?" She hears Mickey come into the house and sends a quick reply under the blanket: "We were supposed to get married at the spring. Have you forgotten?" "No I haven't," he replies, and adds that it's impossible that night because his son is with him and they're playing Snakes and Ladders. "I have to see him," she writes, and he sends a picture. Again she ducks under the blanket to take a covert look at it. How young the boy is, she thinks sorrowfully, he's nine, but looks six, there's an impish gleam in his eye and he doesn't resemble his father in the slightest. She still hasn't heard anything about his mother, their conversations jump from one subject to another, constantly fragmented by touch, memory, constraints. "How sweet he is," she texts right back, "I'd love to be with both of you now." "Come," he replies, just as, several days earlier, he said, "Call."

Just then, Mickey peers in from the door and says, "What are you doing there under the blanket?"

She pops out immediately, blushing and excited. "Nothing. The light bothers me."

"What light? It's completely dark in here!" he says, then complains, "Why don't you go to the clinic? It's been a week already and you're not better."

"Probably complications from the flu...I don't have the strength to go there, Mickey. I'm really weak."

"So we'll call a private doctor to come here. It'll cost whatever it costs," he offers generously, and she apologizes silently for planning to badmouth him to Shula. Or has he heard about the doctor's visit from Shula and is in fact testing her? She should close her eyes and pretend to be sleeping until the subject runs its course. Her cell phone vibrates in her hand, and she yearns to crawl back under the covers to see what he's written, but Mickey is still there, staring at her in concern. For a week, he hasn't seen her out of bed, which has become her fortress, the bed that does not call to him but rather rejects him. It has become a hiding place for her body, which has a secret, and for her cell phone, which has a secret, and he is not pleased. Through her slit eyes she sees him walk away, slack-jawed. "I'm making an omelet," he calls from the kitchen. "Want some?" Why is he suddenly offering her food when she is supposedly asleep? Her phone vibrates again and, unable to restrain herself, she peers at it and her hand trembles as she reads, "I'm making an omelet. Want some?"

What does it mean? She is alarmed, could Mickey have read the text even before it reached her? He is, after all, a high-tech person, maybe he has some secret way of catching messages in the air like butterflies in a net? What nonsense, she tries to calm herself, it's just a coincidence. People are making omelets for supper now in many homes, but nevertheless, she won't reply so quickly this time. Under the covers, her heart pounds. Maybe she isn't cut out to be an unfaithful wife after all, maybe lying, concealing, looking for meaning in every word and gesture doesn't suit her. It's oppressive, it's humiliating, and when she gets better and goes back to work, it will keep her from doing her job well. Maybe she'll get out of bed now, sit at the table across from him, and tell him everything as she eats his omelet. It isn't his fault, it isn't her fault, it isn't anyone's fault. She has the right to fall in love and he has the right to know. Married people are also free people. He'll be free to choose how he wants to continue his life and she will be free of the need to lie. She begins to straighten up in bed, her feet on the floor, her head spinning.

"Mickey?" she says as she walks toward him. In the distance, she can see his back in front of his computer screen, an empty plate at his side.

"Not now," he says automatically, "I'm in the middle."

Perhaps it's better this way, she can confess anytime. Everything is still so fresh, she doesn't even know Eitan, she doesn't even know herself anymore. Her life has turned upside down in a single week, it's too soon to take steps there is no coming back from. And yet she returns to her bed with the feeling that she has missed an opportunity.

"I almost told Mickey," she texts, and he replies immediately, "Too bad." She wonders what he thinks is too bad. That she hasn't told him or that she was about to confess impulsively and endanger her marriage? How enormously different those two possibilities are. Should she ask him? If he hasn't explained, he probably assumes she understood, and if she doesn't understand, then she probably doesn't know him well enough, and that means it's fortunate that she didn't confess. But she has a vague, disturbing feeling that the moment will not return and she will regret not having given Mickey, herself, their years together, and the two children they brought into the world that basic respect, the right to know.

TEN

Dear Parents,

Love has many faces—soft and hard, imprisoning and freeing, permissive and restrictive, expanding and limiting. As parents and educators, we choose which face to pick from the supply at any given moment, depending on the current circumstances. But as our children grow up and gradually become more independent in greater areas of their lives, we usually set clear boundaries for them between the inner and the outer—teach them how to identify strangers, how to distinguish the foreign from the familiar, friends from foes.

But how and when do those definitions change and turn into traps that ensnare us? The realities of Israeli society pose a constant challenge—how to approach and how to behave toward the other, the stranger who resides with us. In a city inhabited by both Jews and Arabs, Sephardim and Ashkenazim, religious and secular, refugees and foreigners, parents who want to protect and educate their children must reexamine those definitions and boundaries they have set. We have decided to integrate the children of foreign workers into our school and design a curriculum based on multiculturalism as part of the broader program, called "The Other Is Me," being implemented in our school.

Next year, as part of the program, our pupils will meet with peers from the Arab sector and celebrate Jewish and Arab holidays, learn about their common traditions and get to know each other directly. If there is any hope left here, it will grow from this encounter.

Exhausted by the writing, she puts her laptop on the bedside table and closes her eyes. She'll continue tomorrow, she isn't focused, and no one reads her tiring manifestos to the end anyway, brimful of good intentions though they might be. They are ineffective in any case. The power of the street is always stronger, and the street has become more and more extreme. It is easier to hate than love, even though, recently, she herself has been finding it so easy to love. She has been implementing the "The Other Is Me" program fiercely, with every inch of her being. The Other is part of her flesh and blood, she herself is the Other, the betrayer is now the beloved, the stranger who now resides within her, the many faces of her love, all directed at him.

In amazement, she remembers the long years during which school was the center of her world, because now it merely flickers at the edges of her life, and her main concern is to avoid disaster. Meanwhile, she tries to put out the fires from her bed, aiming water hoses at the various conflagrations.

The end of the school year is approaching and the burden is doubled: she has to close the year and open the next one; many teachers are sick and there aren't enough substitutes; they haven't yet finished the protracted discussion on report cards, an issue she thought was crucial until only a few weeks ago—on what basis should a child be evaluated, how much of a part should the personal touch play. For years, she has been trying to turn report cards into a report with greater depth. But now she thinks it is too late, it no longer interests her, they will have to continue the discussion without her. She also has to interview teachers and meet with parents. Her assistant seems to be growing quickly into the job of principal, justifying her belief in her. She will clearly be happy to replace her, and at the moment, Iris likes that idea much better than the idea of getting out of bed.

How can she go out into the world if she hasn't recovered yet? It seems to her that her life has been knit together again in a complex surgery, because the time she has been lying ill in bed at home is directly connected to that time in the past when she lay almost motionless in her mother's house. It seems that her prayers from then are being answered now. Then is joined to now and the years between have vanished, as if her head has been sewn onto her legs, leaving the organs in the middle outside of her new body. In the middle are Mickey, the children, and her job, in the middle is everything she has built in her adult life, which now seems lackluster, a faded substitute for the true joys of life. Now that he has come back to her, she knows that it is to that girl he has returned, the girl who prayed for that miracle night and day as she lay on her bed in her mother's house: come back and say you made a mistake, come back and say that the separation is over, that you can't live without me just as I can't live without you. We are a pair from the beginning of creation, like sand and sea, thunder and lightning, clouds and rain, like bow and arrow, like sound and echo. She used to listen for hours, against her will, to the sounds of the house and the street, the twins fighting and her mother scolding them, news broadcasts beginning or ending, neighbors talking on their balconies, steps hurrying along the street. Come, if only to see whether I'm dead or alive. It can't be that you don't care one way or the other, she prayed, repeating the syllables of his name over and over again. And now he has finally heard her, has come back to her, knocking on the door when the house is empty, her mother at work and the twins at school. All at once, she is borne aloft on a wave of joy and hope, all her pain gone, all her suffering eradicated.

"Today we sit in the living room," she says, pulling him to the large couch. Omer didn't feel well in the morning and might suddenly appear. "Today we have coffee and talk like old friends."

He smiles his boyish smile at her, the smile that lights up his face, and says, "I can't talk to you without touching you. It's too harsh a prohibition for me."

She reprimands him with pretended severity. "You managed for almost thirty years without touching me."

"It really was very hard."

She ruffles his hair. "You poor thing. I feel so sorry for you."

"In my way," he protests quickly, "I was faithful to you. It's a fact that I didn't last with anyone, which can't be said about you." He gestures at the apartment. "You built a home and a family." It seems to her that she hears ridicule in his voice.

"You didn't leave me much choice, my dear," she says. "Don't forget that you left me."

"Believe me, I haven't forgotten it for a minute. I was an idiot." He pulls her to him and says, "But you forgive me, don't you? I'll kiss you until you forgive me."

In an instant she is on his lap, her short housedress exposing her thighs. "I won't forgive you if it means you'll stop kissing me." Did she say those words or did she only think them? The boundaries are blurred, and does it matter? Nothing matters, neither age nor family situation. They are acting like teenagers with no worries or responsibilities, like Omer and his redheaded girlfriend. The thought of Omer makes her move away from him, hurry to the kitchen, and return with two cups of coffee and a bowl of grapes. I still haven't seen you eat, still haven't seen you sleep, show me more of yourself. But the clinic calls him again and he has to leave again, and tomorrow is Friday and the day after, Saturday. So many hours would pass until she sees him again.

"Hurry and get well so we can be at my place. We've played doctor long enough, let's move forward," he says.

"Forward to where?" she asks.

"That's a good question, Rissi."

"Do you have a good answer?"

He stands in front of her, leaning against the door, looking intently at her, the wrinkle between his eyes deepening. "People don't usually get a second chance in this life," he says quietly. "But we've been given one. This time it's your turn, Rissi. I chose wrong last time, now you choose." He kisses the tip of his finger and places it on her lips as if she is a mezuzah. Then he opens the door and goes out, leaving her standing at the door that has just closed, so stunned and agitated by the explicit words that she doesn't see the elevator stop in their living room or hear Omer's chuckle behind her.

"Hey Mom, what do you see there? Ghosts?"

She turns slowly and looks at him, her little boy who has become a young man. Projected before her eyes is the crucible in which they were fused together, and now they are about to split apart. Will he forgive her? Will he identify with his abandoned father and punish her? Will this morning be engraved in his mind as the morning his life changed?

"What's with you? Did you see a thief? A rapist?" he asks with a smile, but he doesn't wait for an answer. Interest in others is limited at that age, the age that many of his sex never grow out of. "I caught your flu," he complains. "I feel awful."

"Get into bed," she says quickly, "take your temperature while I make you some tea." She calms herself with the traditional role. Her lips, only just kissed, now graze the forehead of her son—he is the young man now, not Eitan, she must not mistake the time periods even though everything is so confused. She gives him tea with lemon and cooks the cereal he likes. In the future, when he is so very angry at her, will he remember how devoted she was? After all, it was so difficult to raise him, with his frequent tantrums and extreme reactions, his aggressiveness and constant provocations, and Mickey, who retreated from him again and again, was of very little help.

With perseverance and consistency, aided by professionals and all the knowledge and experience she had accumulated, she did almost the impossible, helping him to develop his ability to control himself, to empathize with and consider other people. She never gave up, neither on him nor on herself, and succeeded beyond expectation. Her success was so great that even now, at the height of adolescence, he is relatively pleasant and easygoing and hasn't worsened or weakened. As if she wants to plead her case to him before he falls asleep, she sits on the edge of his bed and looks at his cheeks, flushed with fever, his fleshy open mouth, his brushed-back mane of hair stiff with gel.

On the wall behind him is a picture of the boy he was, laughing with missing teeth, holding high some basketball championship cup from a camp he attended. How much he has changed since then, and how much more he will still change. She tries to imagine him as an adult, the slight hint of a line between his beautiful eyebrows will become a wrinkle, the thin hair on his cheeks will become thick, and in another few years, when she is no longer here, it will turn gray like Eitan's beard. How will he remember her? Will she become the woman who destroyed his family, shattered his youth? But he is no longer a child, and he will leave home anyway to make his way in the world. But the home he leaves—what will it be like? Whether he leaves behind a solid base or the broken pieces of a family depends entirely on her, on her decision. It seems to her now that the issue is between Omer and Eitan, not between her and Mickey, as if she has to choose between two young men and two futures, between the familiar one awaiting her in this house and an exciting new stomach-churning future. She strokes her son's burning hand, he radiates heat like a huge oven, inflaming her as well. They say that fever is healthy, heat destroys germs, but with her illness, the germs of infidelity are thriving.

She remembers how frightened he was of germs when he was a child, always refusing to drink from a bottle she drank from. If she absentmindedly touched one of his friends, he went crazy, jealous and controlling. "You'll never touch me again," he would scream, his two anxieties blending. How will he react? It's true that he has become more moderate the last few years, but a crisis like that might rouse all the demons, especially now that the army is waiting impatiently, threatening both him and her. And how will her daughter react? Obviously she will side with her father without hesitation, will give her the cold shoulder—her shoulders are cold as it is, she thinks, recalling the stiffness of her touch the last time she was home, she is angry at her anyway. And Mickey himself, what will his life be like? He certainly won't remain alone, but he'll be hurt forever, he'll never forgive her. She shakes her head, trying to rid herself of the weight of the future, the enormity of the price. Why are you in such a hurry? What's the rush? This is not the time to decide! You don't know Eitan, he's a complete stranger as far as you're concerned. He isn't that boy anymore, and you didn't really know that boy either. It's a fact that he surprised you when he so surely and unhesitatingly delivered the ax blow to your love, to your neck. How can you trust him again?

Sweat drips from her body, and she stands up from her son's bed angrily. "Second chance," he said, his eyes clouded. But once again, she is the one who will pay the price, just as she did then. "I felt nothing," he said, and now too, if he grows tired of her he will feel nothing and lose nothing, but she will hurt the people most precious to her. "Now it's your turn," he said, as if they were playing Snakes and Ladders. Now it's your turn. Either you'll land on a ladder that will raise you up high or on a snake that will push you all the way down to the tip of its tail.

"For you it's easy," she mutters angrily, "you have nothing to lose. How dare you talk as if it's such an easy step for me to take." She showers quickly, her strength returning and along with it, anger and anxiety. She strips her bed and washes away all signs of her illness in the washing machine. I'm cured now, she thinks resolutely, I'm cured of you, I have a family, I have a school to run. It was nice of you to come back, but for me, it's too late. Moving brusquely, she returns the bowl of grapes to the fridge, washes and rewashes the coffee cups that are contaminated by the germs of infidelity, puts them in the dishwasher and turns it on, even though it is almost empty.

The humming of electrical appliances usually soothes her, but not now, as she stands at the kitchen window, straining to see signs of the desert between the buildings. To her dismay, the neighbors have the view of the Dead Sea, leaving them only the banal landscape to the west. She remembers that Alma took her side in her dispute with Mickey about the view, and she took pleasure in her rare support, intensifying the argument only to bring her closer. "What's the point of living in Jerusalem if we don't see anything that's special about the city from the window? We might as well live in Tel Aviv," she and Alma said to him when they were still trying to decide which apartment to buy. But there was a big difference in price, and Mickey really craved the elevator, so the connection to Alma faded completely when she was injured a short time after they moved to the new apartment. To this day, she cannot understand why her daughter became estranged from her at that terrible time, as if she chose to be away from home, to be confined to bed. Since then, Alma has only grown further away from her, and in the end, she actually did move to Tel Aviv, and not only because of the absence of the Dead Sea. There she cut off her gorgeous hair and dyed what was left of it black, and her face has taken on an unfamiliar, sickly hue, as if she is rotting from within.

Suddenly, Iris feels sharp stabs of anxiety at the thought, mixed with anger: at her daughter, who did not forgive her for being injured in a terrorist attack; at herself for never clarifying the situation and not fighting for her, but letting her grow distant; at Eitan, who suddenly returned and made her forget her concern for her daughter. Now he wants her to forget all her obligations, wants to turn her into his beloved with nothing in her life but him.

To her surprise, her anger keeps growing, and she goes back to the computer to read the emails she only skimmed this week because she has been so preoccupied with him. What a nerve he has, assuming that if he's available, she is too, that if it's easy for him, it's easy for her too. "You built a home and a family," he said mockingly, gesturing at the bourgeois living room. But the family she built is not to be mocked and will not crumble just because it suits him now to take her back into his life for a brief trial period and toss her back after a while, as he apparently did with his two wives. Naively, she didn't even ask, didn't demand to know. She stupidly believed that he was waiting for her and that was the only reason his marriages failed, when the real reasons are undoubtedly much less complimentary to both him and her.

Deceived, deceived, deceived, she hears herself muttering. She won't be enticed this time, she'll text him now. Let's stop before it's too late. I was happy to see you and I wish you a painless life. Yes, that's what she'll write to him and end this madness. She walks firmly to her cell phone to compose the right words, but awaiting her there is a message from him.

How can he still sense her thoughts the way he did then, when they were so profoundly close? "No pressure, my love," he wrote. "I'm ready to wait for you for another thirty years," and she throws the phone onto the rug exactly the way Omer used to when he was having one of his tantrums. I hope it breaks, I hope it breaks and I never get his phone number again. But she immediately kneels down to pick it up, breathing a sigh of relief when she sees that it isn't broken.

No pressure, my love, she reads over and over again, memorizing the words before she deletes them. I'm ready to wait for you for another thirty years, no pressure, my love. It's difficult for her to delete the message, but she has no choice, she has to be careful so that when the right time comes to make the right decision—is there even a right decision?

ELEVEN

"*Now everything is clear!*" Dafna announces with a sour smile. "I finally understand why you've disappeared on me recently. To meet your first love! I'm almost jealous of you."

"I'm jealous of myself too," Iris chuckles, "it's crazy, it isn't just that I met him, I met with my youth itself, with love itself. Time suddenly froze, it's like nothing else!" She feels as if she can go on describing it until dawn, can tell her friend every single detail, because, until now, she has told only herself, reliving the miracle again and again in her mind. She expects Dafna to be excited as she listens—she always encouraged Iris to deviate from her workaholic routine. "You live like an ant," Dafna sometimes said, but now she looks troubled and doesn't share her enthusiasm.

"What's wrong, Dafi? Another fight with Gidi?" she asks.

Her friend studies the menu. "Absolutely not. Who has the strength for those fights?...What do you feel like eating?...There's nothing like first love. The truth is that not too long ago, I looked for my first boyfriend on Facebook, but he doesn't exist, he completely evaporated." Her eyes are glued to the menu, as if she might find him there.

"Put the menu down. You'll only order a salad anyway," Iris says.

Dafna finally looks at her. "I'm starving, sweetie. Not everyone lives on love, like you. You've become anorexic! I'll eat whatever you eat, maybe your luck will rub off on me. Tell me more. What does he look like? Is he married? Have you slept with him already?" But above her smile, her narrow eyes avoid Iris's gaze, and despite the plethora of questions, Iris feels as if her friend isn't open to hearing anything.

"Not really," she hears herself lying even to her best friend, to be on the safe side. She suddenly doesn't feel sure about her.

"Not really? What are you waiting for? Until you're eighty? Do it, sleep with him already, get over it and move on. Life moves forward, not backward!"

"Enough, Dafna." Iris shakes her head. "Let it go. I don't understand why you were so anxious to see me today if you have absolutely no patience. What happened? Where's your head? Something wrong at work?"

"The truth is that I wanted to see where your head is. You don't return calls, don't answer messages. Who would have believed that you have a lover!"

Iris hurries to correct her. "I don't have a lover, Dafna. Eitan isn't a lover, he's the love of my life, do you understand? He's closer to me than anyone has ever been. I almost died when he left me. And now everything is coming alive again, do you understand?

"I understand mainly that you've lost your mind. Eitan was your first love, but that doesn't make him the love of your life. Look, you've lived most of your life without him! Everything you've done with yourself since you were seventeen has nothing to do with him. You're not the girl you were then. You're on the verge of menopause, sweetie."

"So what are you trying to say," Iris mumbles uncomfortably. "It's hard for me to follow. Let's order already." Through the open windows she can see the wall of the Old City illuminated by golden light. How beautiful this new place is—the always up-to-date Dafna suggested it. Would she ever be able to come here openly with him?

"I'm saying that you should enjoy it, but don't do anything stupid." Dafna moves her head closer, the ends of her blond hair dancing on her high forehead. "Have your affair, but be smart about it, don't hurt anyone, don't make any radical moves."

"I understand you," Iris says in annoyance. Every one of her friend's words angers her tonight. "But why? Of course we have to wait, but if after a few months I feel that this really is the love of my life, then I have to make a radical move. You said it yourself, not to wait until I'm eighty."

But her friend shakes her head firmly. "I don't think, Iris, that this is really the right time—"

Iris interrupts. "You did it when you had a four-year-old girl, which is a lot harder. My kids are grown up and living their own lives. Many couples separate at this stage, after they've finished raising their children."

"You never finish raising them," Dafna says. "Shira still calls me twenty times a day. The family will always be important to them. When Omer is in the army, he'll need a stable home behind him, and Alma still needs it. Maybe more than you know."

"What do you mean?" She tenses just as the waitress approaches to tell them about the specials. It seems to her that Dafna is deliberately keeping the girl there with all sorts of pointless questions, in order to avoid explaining the phrase that is reverberating in her mind—maybe more than you know, maybe more than you know.

"What do you know that I don't?" she almost shouts as soon as the waitress is gone.

Dafna shushes her. "Calm down. Not much, only that she's drifted away from Shira recently, sets a date to see her and then cancels, things like that. Shira's a bit worried."

"She's like that with me too," Iris blurts out. "It's become much worse since she started working in Tel Aviv. And she hardly ever comes home. So you see, she doesn't need me or the family at all. I gave her what I could, she's not interested in getting anything from me. And Omer is completely involved in his own things. He'll hardly notice if I leave the house. The truth is that Mickey will hardly notice either."

"That's what you think," Dafna says with a chuckle. "But family is more than that, more than Mickey, Alma, Omer and their situation at this particular moment. The whole is more than the sum of its parts. When I was young, I didn't understand that, but now it's clear to me. And the alternative is also clearer to me now. How long will this excitement last? A year at the most. And then all that's left for you is to grow old with him, with all the complications of his family and yours, and the guilt and disappointment. It's inappropriate, it's pathetic, it's like older women who wear young girls' clothes."

"How can you be so sure?" Iris says, angry once again. "There are many cases of late love that work out. There are endless numbers of men and women who break up families for less than what I have. Do you even understand what kind of love this is? It's the deepest love there is, it's a relationship that died and has suddenly come back to life. Imagine that you meet someone you were sure had died, someone you had mourned for years. Do you understand what a miracle that is?"

As she speaks, she too begins to understand the enormity of what has happened to her. She becomes agitated and breathless, suddenly afraid that she hasn't completely realized it until now and has already lost part of it, because the relationship was so natural that they adapted to it too quickly. It's natural for her to talk with Eitan, natural for her to make love with Eitan, and that naturalness has turned the miracle into something almost routine. She wonders if the miracle she wished for on all her birthdays had actually happened and her father had suddenly come back to her—would she have grown used to that too quickly as well? But her father's return did not come with a price and Eitan's does, which is what causes her friend's expression to darken and her brow to furrow in displeasure as she listens to Iris's emotional words.

"I don't believe in miracles," Dafna says, "and I don't believe in great loves either anymore. Naturally there has to be a strong affinity, but in the end, it's all about hard work. In that sense, Mickey is right for you. There's something stable about him, reassuring. I wouldn't give up on him so easily."

"He's so reassuring," Iris repeats sarcastically, determined to tarnish his image. "He won't even kill a cockroach for me when I'm about to faint. You should see how gently he tries to toss it out the window. What you see as stability looks to me like apathy."

"There's no point in arguing with a woman in love," Dafna says with a smile, "and what do you even know about that walking miracle of yours? Is he a fierce warrior against cockroaches, for example? Give me facts, not impressions. Is he married? Does he have kids? How serious is this for him?" When Iris tries to be precise about facts, Dafna shakes her head skeptically and says, "On the surface, it's convenient that he's single, but not necessarily a good sign. Something here looks too easy, but maybe I'm wrong. It's just a gut feeling. Speaking of guts, where's the food we ordered?"

"Our waitress just went into the kitchen now. You kept her here with that interrogation of yours. Tell me, don't you find it depressing that every good thing immediately makes us suspicious? As if we've lost all hope that life could be happy?"

But her friend is busy looking for her phone, which is shrieking in her huge handbag, and she is not receptive to her thoughts. "Hi, Shirush," she smiles at the cell she finally pulls out of her bag. "What's happening? Did he answer you? No, you definitely cannot text him again. Of course he got your message, there were no breakdowns in the network. You have to control yourself! Listen for a minute," she says, trying to interrupt the emotional monologue so typical of her daughter. "I'm sitting with Iris now. Do you want to talk to her?"

Iris looks at her in surprise. What's going on here, what are they hiding from her? She reaches out for the phone, but the call has ended, Shira cut it short, which is not like her.

"What's going on here?" a tense shout bursts from her mouth, and she covers it. "What was Shira supposed to talk to me about?"

Dafna hesitates. "That's why it was so important to meet today, Iris. I told you that Shira was worried. Yesterday she went to the bar and Alma practically threw her out, claiming that her boss didn't like it when girlfriends came by. She says that Alma looks weird, but you know Shira, she always exaggerates."

"So what are you telling me, that I shouldn't think about myself for even a minute?" Iris hears herself whispering aggressively. "—that if I forget for one minute that I'm a mother, I'll pay for it? What am I supposed to do now? Hire a private detective to follow her? Give up on the chance of love, the only chance I've ever had, for her sake?"

"Oh, Iris, you sound really deranged. Where is all this pathos coming from? You're not supposed to give up on love or hire a private detective. You're just supposed to keep your eyes open. It's like in your school, you have to worry about everyone all the time. And you're good at that. Didn't you win the education award last year?"

"I'm sick and tired of education. The only thing I care about now is love."

"So go make love," Dafna grumbles. "Why are you wasting a night on me? Go, I'm your alibi until morning."

"I love you too, Dafi, and besides, he's with his kids tonight."

Dafna shakes her head. "See? It's not simple! You want to hurt your children for that? So you can make omelets for kids who aren't yours?"

"What's all this talk about omelets lately? You don't understand. I'm so much in love with him that I'm ready to change their diapers if I have to."

"Great, because soon you'll have to diaper him too. How many good years can you have left together? He's not young anymore, and old men are a bitch."

Iris protests immediately, "Like Mickey isn't aging too? Did you happen to bump into his potbelly recently? And Gidi isn't exactly the picture of eternal youth."

"Right," Dafna laughs, "but we're used to them, don't you see the difference?"

"Mainly I see the miracle that happened to me. I can't let him go."

"It's not that I don't understand you," Dafna placates her, "I was once in love with Gidi like that, and in less than a month after meeting him, I took Shira and left the house. That's exactly why I'm more realistic, because in the end, I'm not sure that all the suffering was worth it. The crazy love ends quickly, that's a law of nature. So if it comes easily—why not? Go for it! But to leave a husband and children? Definitely not."

"With all due respect for your experience with Gidi, there are other possibilities." Iris always thought that her friend made a mistake when she chose that loud, controlling man, and she secretly hoped they would separate, which they decide to do almost monthly after a heated argument. But they always make up a short time later and neither of them can remember what their latest fight was about. The one who paid the heaviest price was Shira, who shuttled back and forth between their house and her father's. He also remarried, and a stepparent who was not especially happy about her presence lived in each house. Perhaps that's why she hasn't been able to separate from her mother to this day, and here she is, calling again.

"He texted me!" Shira's joyous voice booms from the phone even though the speaker is not on. "He asked if I wanted to go out with him tomorrow night. What should I tell him?"

"Text him that tomorrow you can't," Dafna instructs her in a serious voice.

Shira protests, "But I can! I'm free tomorrow night!"

"Of course you can, and you'll definitely have lots of other free nights if you keep on being so eager."

But Shira revolts and replies defiantly, "I'll tell him that I can see him tomorrow. He'll be hurt if I say no and he won't try again."

"Do whatever you want," her mother says, shrugging. "Just don't come crying to me after he runs away too."

Iris reaches out impatiently and takes the phone from her friend, who doesn't object. "Shira'le," she says, "sorry for mixing in. Do what you feel and stop asking your mother for advice."

Shira, immediately ready to look to her for support as well, asks hopefully, "So I should go out with him?"

"Definitely!" Iris replies. "If it's the real thing, you don't have to play games, and if it isn't, no game will help. Now I want to hear the whole truth about yesterday. What happened in Alma's bar?"

"That's just it, nothing happened," Shira says evasively. "But there are bad rumors about that place. That's why I went there, but she practically threw me out."

"What rumors, exactly? You have to tell me everything you know."

"Maybe there's nothing to it, but they say that the boss, that Boaz, controls the girls who work for him, like a kind of guru? Takes them away from friends and family? A little bit like a kind of cult?"

The phone drops out of Iris's hand when she hears the explicit word, and Dafna bends to pick it up and continue the conversation with her daughter, who already regrets giving the upsetting information. "It's good that you told her," she supports her. "Alma has parents and they have to know. That's what a good friend should do, not show blind loyalty but offer good judgment. And I advise you to use good judgment about tomorrow night too."

Iris is only dimly aware of their goodbyes, images float before her eyes, connected one to the other. Two little girls dancing ballet in a crowded hall, Shira a head taller than Alma, a bit clumsy, her skin fair, Alma thin and dark. Neither moves very well, both will soon drop out of the class, but in that eternity that follows the terrifying words, they dance and dance, their hips not yet curved, their chests still flat, smiling at each other as they strain to be precise. For a moment, she thinks she can freeze the scene, she and Dafna sitting beside each other, Omer the baby in her arms and Dafna pregnant, Shira not yet a neurotic young woman and Alma not yet lured into a cult. A cult! What exactly does that mean? Is he the one who told her to cut her hair, dye it black, seduce Omer's friends? What else has he told her to do? Nausea rises in her throat and she clenches her lips. Dafna puts an arm around her shoulders and whispers reassuringly, "It's not the end of the world, Iris. Shira is probably exaggerating a little, and if Alma really is in any trouble, you'll get her out of it."

"How will I get her out of it?" she says with a groan, her breathing labored. "She isn't Shira, who reports everything and does what she's told. Alma's a tough nut! I can't even talk to her, I have no influence over her! Neither does Mickey, even though he's sure they have a great relationship. I don't know what to do with this information, how to verify it, where to start."

"Tonight you should just go to sleep. You're in no condition to do anything. But tomorrow you have to talk to Mickey and make some kind of plan. There are experts in things like this, but I actually trust you. The main thing is not to attack her and not to do anything that will push her even further away. Try to be accepting."

"Yes, we'll go to see her," Iris mumbles. "I've wanted to go there for a while now to see how she lives. We'll go to the bar after work, see that Boaz, and mainly he'll see us, he'll see that she isn't some waif whose mind he can control, that she's a girl who has parents who look out for her, parents who have—how did Eitan put it—built a home and a family."

TWELVE

"*I won't get up and drive to Tel Aviv* because of some hysterical rumors," he says angrily and turns his back to her. "What's going on with you? Those pills have made you completely crazy!" He's trying to belittle her so that the rumors she is handing him this morning will shrink as well, fighting her in an effort to eradicate the upsetting news.

She wakes him up with Shira's story after tossing and turning all night, every movement painful, stabbing, as if pebbles were strewn on the mattress. Here's a good-morning story for you, who's the good guy in it and who's the bad guy, a wake-up story about a young girl in trouble. But it's always so difficult to wake him, she recalls angrily. Your daughter's in trouble and you're asleep, your daughter has fallen into the trap of a slimy guru and you're sleeping. What does that say about you? He's still in bed, always finds it hard to get up in the morning, constantly fights the alarm clock. Who knows, maybe his entire life has been a failure because of that weakness, maybe that's why he hasn't advanced enough at work even though he was an excellent computer student, why he has never moved up to a managerial position. It seems to her now, as she stands angrily facing his unmoving back, that he rose early only once in his life, unwittingly resulting in her being injured.

He was already dressed when she woke up, as if he hadn't even undressed, as if he hadn't slept at home that night, standing in front of her in that mustard-colored jacket. Why, in fact, did he wear that jacket on that morning? After all, this isn't Europe where it can rain in summer, it's a country of endless dry sunshine where only at night do you occasionally need a jacket in their city. Maybe he came home in the early hours and was still in his clothes?

Where's that jacket?" she asks suddenly, "I haven't seen it in years."

To her surprise, he understands and answers immediately. "It got too small for me a long time ago, so I gave it to Shula, for her husband." She turns away from him, goes into the kitchen, and brews fresh coffee. How difficult it is to isolate a single moment in your life, this moment, for example, because it is always joined by another moment. Anger is joined by anger, worry by worry, and in the transparent morning light, events join together in a thorny, merciless chain. He wore the mustard-colored jacket, he hurried to work because of a breakdown in the system, Omer wasn't ready on time, she offered to take the kids in his place and sent him on his way, Omer hid in the bathroom and Alma wanted a half-ponytail, so they left home a bit late, she went to the wrong place at the wrong time and was seriously injured, Alma never recovered from her injury and in her turn went to the wrong place.

But that chain of events can be joined together in a different order that will give them a different meaning.

She married that large, persistent boy out of gratitude and a profound sense that they shared a common fate. She felt too hurt to fall in love, so she never gave him a chance, and even worse, never intended to give him a chance. No wonder he tried to find love in another place, at another time, which unfortunately was the time when people who turned themselves into walking bombs roamed city streets, trying to send as many human beings as possible to their deaths, including her. Alma, who only wanted a half-ponytail that morning, didn't pay the price for the cruel, hundred-year Israeli-Palestinian conflict, but for Eitan's cruel abandonment, because it was Eitan Rosenfeld's daughter that her mother had wanted so passionately to give birth to. That's the reason Alma, like her father, was not given the chance she deserved, that's the reason she distanced herself from her mother, why she hasn't taken better care of herself. But it is possible to build a different chain of events that began with the death of her father, or even earlier, with her parents' mating, which was commemorated by an unplanned pregnancy and an unplanned death, leaving her to grow up alongside a hardworking, hard-hearted mother who was blind to her emotional needs, which prevented her from maturing into a proper mother to her own daughter, which pushed her daughter into the arms of that man who was—how had Shira put it—like a kind of guru, like a kind of cult leader?

Coming from the open window, a rush of dusty wind strikes her like a slap, and she hurries to close it. She needs to act now, not analyze. She hears Mickey's steps behind her as he pours himself coffee and sits down across from her in his checked boxer shorts, his chest broad and heavy, his dark potbelly sagging. He has gotten fatter recently, or perhaps she has already grown more familiar with Eitan's thin body, and Mickey's flesh surprises and repulses her, as if she is seeing it for the first time. "We'll drive down to see her after work," she repeats, "we have to be more present in her life."

"I am not participating in this drama," he insists, running his hand over his shaved head, which is tilted slightly forward as if it is about to butt something. "Shira is a hysterical girl who likes to exaggerate, and you know that. I won't just get up and drive down there because of an unfounded rumor. What's happening to you? It's not like you to react like this. What cult? What guru? I talk to Alma every day and she sounds perfectly fine!"

"What's your problem with driving to Tel Aviv?" she says, hearing her voice shrill with anger. "It's less than an hour's drive! People do it every day!" They both know that under-lying this complaint is another one about a wonderful job offer with a much higher salary that he turned down a few years before only because it meant driving to Tel Aviv, which meant getting up earlier.

Immediately defensive, he says, "I have no problem about driving to Tel Aviv, it's a matter of principle! I trust her and you don't. I believe in her and you don't!"

"Enough of that ridiculous competition!" she counters angrily. "You know what, I don't believe you! It's just more convenient for you to deny it so you don't have to deal with it! You'd rather play chess with people you'll never meet than try to solve your daughter's problem. When you say you trust her, you're actually saying that you don't care, that you want to be left alone. Maybe that's legitimate, but at least don't act superior with me!"

"How dare you talk to me like that," he says heatedly. "I don't care? Which one of us would rather spend her life with kids who aren't theirs, you or me? You have more patience for every kid in school than for your own kids!"

"You blame me for being dedicated to my work?" She shakes with rage. "You fat chauvinist! You would never talk to a man like that. Maybe you're jealous because I'm more successful at my work than you are!"

"No way," he hisses, "I'm not competitive like you! I'm successful enough, I don't have to be the best in order to be happy, I don't constantly look back to see if anyone's passing me."

She takes a sip of her coffee. It's bitter, like those words, like seeing herself through his eyes, seeing the amount of filth that has accumulated during the years of their life together. Only a thin line separates the routine of their daily life from piles of garbage, she thinks. Maybe I should write about that in my next letter to the parents? We think our home is clean when we throw bags of trash into the bin every day, we think that our bodies are clean when we shower every day. But the really dangerous garbage accumulates under our skin, and there is no way of throwing it away because even when we spew it out the way he has just done, it doesn't disappear, it only multiplies. And now it has taken up residence inside her as well. Every person is a small universe that accumulates trash, and even when we shower and perfume ourselves, even when we dress well and go out to a restaurant, to the theater or the opera, even when we converse politely, even when we make love, we are two piles of garbage. It becomes apparent at the first opportunity, like now, when he refuses to stop.

Buttoning his light-colored shirt over his potbelly, he says, "I have no problem with your success, it's just too bad that it comes at the expense of the children."

Slamming her mug down on the table, she shouts, "Just exactly how did it come at the expense of the children?"

"It's a fact that you know every kid in your school better than you know your own daughter!"

It's almost funny that, through the window, she sees the garbage truck stop in front of their building as if it's an ambulance come to take away someone.

Suddenly, she doesn't know how to reply, maybe he's right, I hope he's right, and she asks in a thin voice, "So you won't go with me?"

To her surprise, an answer comes immediately, "I'll go with you," but the words don't come from Mickey's mouth. Omer says them as he stands at the end of the hallway, clearly upset. "I'll go with you, Mom," he repeats, emphasizing the first word, exposing in the merciless morning sun the almost transparent cobwebs along which they move as Mickey predictably grumbles, "Of course, you'll always take Mom's side."

"What does Mom's side have to do with it?" Omer says. "I just happen to think that Alma's in a bad way too."

She feels compelled to say to Mickey, "Is that all you have to say to him instead of praising him for being worried about his sister?"

"I apologize, Omer," Mickey mutters as he hurries into the elevator. "I just think this trip is unnecessary, and I hate unnecessary things."

"You yourself are unnecessary," she blurts out, but the elevator doors drown out her words. "I'm sorry, Omer," she groans, utterly drained. She sits down on the couch, her eyes burning. "I'm so sorry you heard that."

"Never mind," he says, "I can handle it. I'm a big boy." With an innocent voice that doesn't go with his height, he announces, "I'll have a different kind of marriage, Mom."

She smiles at him and says, "I hope so. Even though we're really not the worst. I don't know how we deteriorated so much this morning, usually it doesn't go that far."

"I have a problem with Dad," he says, sitting down on the couch across from her, so good-looking in his denim shorts and green tank top, which brings out the brown-green of his eyes.

"I know Omy," she says with a sigh. I hope your relationship with him improves when you get older."

"What's it got to do with age? It's the kind of person he is, the kind of person I am! He has a problem with me."

"Don't be silly," she denies quickly, "he has no problem with you. He loves you very much. If anything, he has a problem with me."

"So what does that have to do with me?" he asks, so naive.

Her heart goes out to him. "It really shouldn't have anything to do with you, but in families, things get mixed together. We all have good and bad qualities, Omy. I hope that in the future, he'll let you see more of his good qualities."

"Why did you marry him?" he asks. "Were you really in love with him once?"

Trying to curl her lips into a smile, she says, "Love has many faces." The wall clock above his head reminds her how late it is, but she can't get up from the couch, can't cut their conversation short. How many intimate conversations do they have left? Is she doomed to replay them in her mind for the rest of her life? Once again she sees the letters of his name seeping into the plaque, the older he gets, the worse it is. "It's late," she says, "what kind of sandwich should I make you?"

While frying the omelet for him, she thinks about how wrong Dafna was with her hypocritical advice, as if she were a rabbi. What is the point in working so hard to preserve the family? Maybe there are families that are worth the effort, worth making sacrifices for, but unfortunately, the family she built with Mickey is not one of them. They never had special Sabbath or holiday meals, didn't take many family trips. The few traditions they had managed to maintain crumbled after she was injured, and she never bothered to restore them be- cause when she came back to life, she was so busy. Is he right, does she really know her pupils better than her own daughter? And even if he is right, who knows whether work pressure is to blame. Dafna works hard in her architects' office, and it never keeps Shira from being close to her. But all of that is irrelevant now, past its time, like yesterday's sandwich, which she takes out of Omer's backpack before she puts the new one, fresh and fragrant, inside. Everything Mickey said to her is irrelevant, as is everything she said to him this morning and all the other mornings they spent together, even the one when he stood in front of her in his mustard-colored jacket. She doesn't look back, she looks forward, through the kitchen window, and sees the edge of the desert momentarily peek out between the buildings in a rare appearance. In that at- tempt to see into the distance, it seems to her that this family she built over a quarter of a century has run its course and no longer has a reason to exist.

How quickly morning turns into afternoon, and how much work she still has waiting for her. One meeting after another, one appointment after another. The yellow Post-its mushroom on her desk like groundsels after the rain, and the painkillers mushroom in her stomach, blending with strong coffee. She sees that Mickey called her and Omer left a message: Yotam has a birthday that evening so he can't go to Tel Aviv with her. She didn't plan to take him with her anyway, she was just happy that he offered. Before she can reply, a young teacher who has come for a work interview enters her office. She's wearing a long, light-blue dress and has light-blue eyes, and Iris likes her immediately.

"I was accepted by a university in London, and quit my job, but then I met the love of my life and decided to stay in the country," she says candidly. "So now I have love but I don't have a job."

"You're just beginning your life," Iris hears herself say. "How can you know that this is the love of your life?"

The young woman's beautiful eyes flash as she says, "I just know. When it happens, you know. Otherwise I wouldn't have been willing to pay such a price."

Iris listens to her with concern. I hope you won't be disappointed, that you won't be abandoned. I hope that in another year, he won't tell you that you remind him of a tragedy. I hope that in another twenty-five years he won't tell you that you neglected your children, that he won't ever look at you with eyes full of anger and complaint. Right then and there, she decides to hire her as a substitute teacher even before the end of the year, to lessen the price she will have to pay for love. And what about the price she herself will have to pay?

Tired, she stares at the accumulating Post-its on her desk. During these sweltering afternoon hours, the price seems negligible. Even if Alma needs them now, that doesn't mean they have to stay together. Separated couples take care of their children too. Alma and Omer have grown, and along with them, the frustrations, angers, resentments, disappointments. Only the love hasn't grown, and even if it hasn't diminished, its place in the scheme of things has become limited. If at least we knew how to love as well as we know how to argue, knew how to be kind as well as we know how to be mean. If only we knew how to enjoy and give pleasure as well as we know how to torment and be tormented. It seems as if, with the years, their ability to hurt has improved while their ability to enjoy has atrophied. Does it have to do with our age or the age of our relationship? Or perhaps, in the end, it's about the nature of the relationship, its qualities and abilities. She and Mickey have apparently taken the connection between them as far as it can go and haven't left behind any still-unrealized possibilities. Though she sometimes feels that she never gave him a chance, she certainly can't do it now, not after seeing Eitan again, not after she has stepped onto the lost continent of the pleasure that will never end, after she has become immersed in a body of water that will never dry up.

When she thinks about him, she can't concentrate on work, can't respond to the demands of the yellow Post-its, so she tries her best to avoid doing it. She sends a short text saying that she will drop by his place in the afternoon, on her way to Tel Aviv. She hasn't seen him since she recovered from her illness, and this meeting will be brief as well. She glances at the clock—four hours left. How hard it is to wait; the closer the day comes to its end, the slower it moves, as if it has grown tired from the race. This week, she has been trying to weave the elements of her life together, because she cannot devote her entire life to love. She neglected her school and now she has to gather everyone around her all over again, project the confidence she knows how to project, infuse them with the necessary certainty that they are in the right place, are doing the right thing. Alone in her office, her mind wanders, but when someone comes in, she manages to pull herself together, so she's relieved when there is a knock at her door and a woman her own age walks in, her expression grim. "Do you have a minute for me?" she asks.

Surprised, Iris says, "About what? Did you make an appointment?"

"No," the visitor says, "I only came to have a look at the school and decided to see if you're free. I registered my son here, but I'm worried. I'm afraid that your program may be too rigid for him."

"Were you at the parents' meeting last winter?" Iris asks. It feels to her as if many seasons have passed since she gave a talk before dozens of parents, speaking proudly about the school's principles and the path it is taking. Today, it's difficult for her to feel pride. She may know her pupils well, but not her own daughter, she may have succeeded with other children, but not with her own daughter. She listens to the woman describe her son's difficulties: ADHD, behavioral problems, rebelliousness. "On the one hand, I know he needs a framework, but on the other, I'm afraid that an overly rigid framework will make him even more frustrated. I'm totally helpless. I must be a failure as a mother."

"You're not the only one in this room," Iris hears herself say, then laughs as if she were joking. "We have a lot of experience with children like him, and in most cases, we succeed." The woman reminds her of Sasha's worried mother. Sasha was the most difficult pupil she ever had, and Iris gave his mother her constant support. Can she devote so much time to this mother as well? "Send me his diagnoses," she says, "I'll go over them and tell you honestly whether we're the right school for him." She never makes such generous offers, but the uninvited guest's distress touches her. When she leaves full of gratitude, the room fills with the familiar faces of the Integration Committee members, the guidance counselor and the psychologist, the homeroom teacher and the parents. Iris tries to be as she has always been, believing in herself, in the system she built, but her concern about Alma deepens, and she wants to send the confused parents away and discuss her own daughter with the professionals.

Theoretically, she can consult with the psychologist at the end of the meeting, but she shouldn't—she is still the principal and it isn't a good idea for her personal failure to resonate between these walls. There are only two possibilities for her now, to speak only about Alma or not to be Alma's mother at all, to be with him, seventeen years old, before Alma was born. But for the time being, only the middle road is open to her, and she pretends to listen to what is being said around her table. How young these parents are, the mother still looks like a girl. She too was a young mother, only a few years had passed between her breakup with Eitan and Alma's birth, fewer than those that have passed between her injury in the terrorist attack and now. Obviously she had not recovered, obviously she had not matured. She had been so anxious to have a family, to prove to herself that her life was good despite everything, to belong to a family that had a father. But apparently a father isn't enough, there has to be a mother.

"Of course she had a mother," she hears herself argue with her thoughts out loud, to the surprise of everyone in the room. Embarrassed, she pulls herself together immediately and says, "Forgive me, I was someplace else for a moment," hurriedly restoring the vestiges of her authority. "We'll give him four hours of integration and try to hire an assistant," she says firmly. That may be more than the boy needs, but she has to compensate the parents for her lack of attention. When the next pair of parents comes in, the discussion shifts to another pupil, a girl whose difficulties are completely different, though the extent of her distress is similar, and Iris steals a glance at the clock. In another hour, she will be in her car on her way to Eitan. She knows that without the promise of seeing him, she wouldn't be able to endure all this. She no longer understands how she could have lived so many years without the expectation of seeing him, unless it has always been there, invisible but persistent, pushing her onward from day to day, year to year.

Finally, she is on her way to him, stopping at a roadside store, undecided about what to buy. How can someone be so familiar and so unknown at the same time? Does he prefer wine or beer, red or white, sweet or savory, vegetables or fruit, cheese or meat, tea or coffee? She knows so little about him— even about Alma she knows more—so it's probably better to choose what she likes, salty cheese, olive bread, cherry tomatoes, walnuts, red wine. What did they take with them then, when they walked along the blossoming wadi on their way to the spring, on the only day between winter and summer that was no longer cold and not too hot yet, and the air was filled with the aroma of honey? In those days, teenagers didn't drink liquor, even if they were about to be orphaned. She has a dim memory of a package of plain cookies, and she looks for something similar on the crowded shelves, but what's the point, her arms are already full with too many things for the too-short time they will have together. After all, she will have to be on her way to Alma soon.

The last time, ill and afraid, she crept toward the building like a thief, but now, she returns on the wide path to the front door, unconsciously running her hand along the hedge before she rings the bell. The door has certainly been changed, but his childhood surname is still inscribed on it, alongside the surname of his adulthood. He opens it quickly, wearing gray shorts and a faded T-shirt, his appearance combining both periods of his life. Once again, his youthful body, almost completely incongruent with his middle-aged face, surprises her, but when he smiles, the years are erased from his face as well.

"Rissi," he says softly, "it feels like another thirty years have passed since we saw each other. What did you bring? You were right not to trust me. I didn't have time to prepare anything. I thought we'd order something or go out to eat. Ah, I forgot, you can't be seen with me. Tell your husband I was here first." He prattles on entertainingly. "How much time do you have for me? Until midnight, let's say? I've never been with a married woman, I feel like a mistress."

She unpacks the bags in the small kitchen. How will she tell him that plans have changed, that she has to go to see Alma tonight? She doesn't want to tell him about Alma, she doesn't want to burden their young relationship with that weight. In any case, she isn't a mother when she's with him, mothers don't have this feeling, this egocentric and domineering love that excludes all other things.

For the first time, it occurs to her how alien the totality of feeling actually is to her. She has been without him for decades, shifting between her fear of pain and the inconstancy of happiness. For the first time, it occurs to her that her daughter may be feeling the same thing now, that it is what she is missing in her life. Does Alma feel that totality of emotion for Boaz, and has it led to blind obedience? She is horrified by the thought, but she won't tell him, even though he keeps asking what's bothering her. Once again, she thinks about the daughter that wasn't born to them and whether she would have been a better mother to her because of the total love she feels for her father. But sometimes it's like that, and sometimes it's the opposite, when the intensity of the parents' relationship leaves no room for the child.

She has seen so many possibilities during these years of being responsible for hundreds of children and knowing their families. Sometimes children end up receiving vestiges of their parents' unreciprocated love, they win or lose, it is difficult to set rules. But Alma has surely lost, not only because her mother didn't love her father with every fiber of her being, but because, when she gave birth to her, she had not yet recovered from her breakdown and was still grieving for the life she had lost. That means that he is to blame for all this, so she can tell him and even be angry with him. But how can she be angry with him when he is so charming, opening the bottle of wine she brought, pouring her a tall glass and saying, "To you, my beautiful love, I've missed you. Every day that I don't see you, my heart breaks."

"To you," she says, thirstily drinking in those glorious words. What has she wished for her entire life if not precisely those words? She thirstily drinks the dark wine, her face suddenly burning with a hot flash that reminds her of her age, her situation. Have the words come too late, like dreams that come true in inappropriate circumstances and instead of a blessing, become a curse? What will she do with those words, she thinks as her phone rings and Mickey's name flashes on the screen. She won't answer, she has the right to ignore him after he hurt her so much that morning, and she will ignore her age as well. The years vanish when she is with him anyway, and the pain has also vanished suddenly, though she hasn't taken a pill for several hours. Even her concern for her daughter fades when she is with him. Maybe Shira was exaggerating after all. A cult? A guru? Why should she believe unfounded rumors?

"Is that your husband?" he asks, placing a large pot of water on the gas range. "Leave him, Rissi," he says quietly.

She looks at him, her heart pounding. "What did you say?"

He goes over to her as excited as a young boy, with his beautiful long legs and shining eyes. "Listen, I've been thinking about this constantly on the days we weren't together. Something phenomenal has happened to us, Rissi, do you realize that? Do you understand what's happened to us, against all odds, almost at the last minute?"

She smiles at him, of course I understand, she wants to say, that's the only thing I think about all the time instead of thinking about how to help my daughter.

"We've been given a second chance," he says, "a last chance. We can't let it go by." His fingers stroke her face, his upper lip trembles. "Come back to me, Rissi, there's a reason we met again after all those years. We've never stopped loving each other, that breakup was a terrible mistake. I thought I was choosing life, but it was suicide for me."

"It was probably an especially fatal combination of murder and suicide," she says, "because I almost died too." She sits him down on the couch and tells him what she never intended to tell him, what she has never told any living soul, what she has never spoken about even with the few witnesses. It isn't about herself that she speaks, but about a seventeen-year-old girl who didn't get out of bed for long weeks, who didn't speak, didn't eat or drink, didn't respond to her surroundings, whose body was frozen in a single position. "They wanted to hospitalize me, but my mother wouldn't let them," she says. "They went along with her only because she was a nurse and they let her hook me up to an IV at home."

He listens to her, sorrowful, mortified, his eyes downcast, his hand covering his mouth. "I didn't know," he mumbles, "I didn't think."

She almost reprimands him, "So what did you think? Did you even think about me?"

"Not enough, apparently. I felt so guilty. Now I understand why your mother threw me out."

Iris protests, "She didn't, that didn't happen!"

"She did, she screamed at me like a madwoman. She had a cup of tea in her hand and threw it at me and it shattered."

Stunned, she asks, "When was that? Why haven't you told me until now?"

"I was ashamed, Rissi. It was one of the most shameful moments of my life. I don't know what I was thinking. It was a short time before I got married. I was in the neighborhood and decided to try. I thought maybe you still lived there, but she opened the door and the minute she recognized me, she started screaming like a crazy person."

Listening to him, Iris suddenly has a vague recollection of a scorching afternoon when she brought Alma, still a baby, to her mother's house and found her furiously cleaning the

stairwell. "A cup broke. Watch out for the glass," she said angrily, as if they were to blame. Iris picked Alma up quickly
and asked, not really interested, "How did it happen?" Her
mother muttered some complaint about the neighbors as Iris
took Alma into the living room and then hurried off to a
meeting. "Mickey will pick her up at six," she said on her way
out, unwittingly stepping on the shards of her wish, which
had almost come true.

"What are we going to do about all this?" Eitan mumbles,
resting his elbows on his knees, his back bent, like someone
standing before a pile of ruins. Out of an old habit, she runs
her fingers along his back, up and down, along the prominent vertebrae, feeling his heavy breaths, and for a moment,
it seems as if he is about to burst into tears as he did at his
mother's grave after saying Kaddish. His legs had buckled and
he fell onto his knees, remaining there, stooped over before
the mounds of earth. "Come back to me, come back to me,"
he cried, and she knelt beside him and stroked his back just
as she is doing now. Suddenly she is choked by such intense
sorrow that she can hardly breathe, because it seems to her
that, in fact, they are both already buried under the earth,
and even if they manage to dig a dark, narrow tunnel between their graves where they can entwine their dirt-covered
fingers, their meeting is merely an illusion.

Alarmed, she runs her hands over his body and says,
"You're real, you're alive?"

"As far as I know," he says with a sigh. "Only a living
person could feel this kind of pain." She presses closer to him
and rests her head on his shoulder, the heat of his body soothing her a bit, the smell of him, his breathing, the steam rising
from the bubbling pot. They sit side by side on the couch,

their backs bent like survivors of a pogrom who know that their persecutors will soon be back. Finally he stands up, adds water to the pot and wine to the glasses. "Let's make love," he says, "we have thirty years to catch up on. You know how much lovemaking that is?"

She can tell that he is trying to sound cheerful, to erase the oppressive past, but what do we have left without it, she thinks, the past brought us here, for better and for worse. Nonetheless, she still tries to respond so that he will not say again, you remind me of that terrible year, you remind me of the disease. She sips her wine, turns a blind eye to how quickly he can shrug off the past, she is even happy about it. She lies down under him on the couch, the water in the pot boils as he kisses her. A toy car suddenly lurches along the rug, and he pulls the remote out from under her back. Inanimate becomes animate, so animate that she can feel his closeness on the tender, underside of her skin, not on her rough outer skin, making the feel of him on her body so intense and piercing that it is almost painful. This is surely the way a newborn feels when it is touched for the first time. Does he feel as she does? There seem to be tears in his eyes—he always cried easily. She still remembers how embarrassed he was when he told her tearfully of his mother's illness, and her heart went out to him, the empty heart of a longtime orphan opening to embrace the pain of a soon-to-be orphan. She pulls his face close now and kisses his damp eyes. "My love," she whispers, her fingers at the roots of his hair, his fingers at the roots of her body, coaxing from it pure bliss, thick and sticky, for a layer of hot glue joins her to him. When the glue cools and coagulates, she realizes that she cannot pull herself away from him even if she wants to, and she does not want to. There is nothing that makes it worth separating her arms from his, her stomach from his, her thighs from his.

"I have to put more water in the pot," he whispers, "it's going to burn in a minute." But he doesn't break away from her body.

"Let it burn," she whispers, and she repeats a haiku Mickey once recited to her about a poet who came back from a period of seclusion to find that his house had gone up in flames. Instead of mourning, the poet wrote, "The storeroom burned down, nothing hides the moon."

"That's interesting," he says, "to call the house a storeroom is powerful, very appropriate to this particular house." He repeats the words loudly and points to the full moon shining in at them through the window, a giant orange egg, like that of a huge extinct animal.

"The world is full of miracles," she says.

"Yes, miracles and disasters." In the glow of the moonlight, he points to the scar on her lower abdomen, near her thigh, "I'm so sorry I didn't know, I would have come to treat you if I had known, I would have transferred you to my department. When exactly did it happen?"

Although it turns out that he was in the States at the time, he continues to lament the lost opportunity. "I wouldn't have let any other doctor touch you without my supervision, I would have anesthetized you myself before the operation, I would have been there for all the operations and kissed the inside of you. We lost ten years." She thinks about those ten years, about her school, her life's work, could she have done that with him at her side? Would it have been possible not to be swallowed up by his love?

"We would have had time to make a baby together," he goes on, as if he is enjoying the sadness.

"I don't think so. Everything down there was injured."

"I would have fixed it. I've done more complicated things, believe me."

She smiles. "I believe you. I love you." Day after day, hour after hour, lost moment after lost moment—what can we do with all of this? She caresses his face, lingering on the curly gray beard. "Since when have you had this?" she asks.

"Many years, forever, in fact. After all, I'm in mourning, did you forget?"

"But I don't remember you with a beard."

"Because I hardly had any hair on my face then. But when it grew, I left it, at first because of the mourning, and then because I got used it."

Unable to restrain herself, she says, "I thought you wanted to escape from the mourning, that's what you told me. It seems that in the end, I was what you wanted to escape from."

"Enough, please," he begs, "let's not go over that again. I was in mourning for my mother and for you too. I couldn't separate the two of you."

"The mourning for me is over. Can you shave off the beard? I want to see you the way you were."

"Are you sure that the mourning for you is over? Because I'm afraid it's just starting all over again."

"Yes, I'm sure," she whispers, and looks around for a moment as if she wants to be certain there is no witness to her promise.

He follows her gaze and suddenly remembers, "The pot!" and hurries into the kitchen naked and fills it with water. When he returns to the living room, he's wearing black underpants and has a razor and a shaving cream brush in his hand. He looks intently at himself in the hallway mirror and says, "Come here, I'm in your hands.

"Come on, they do heart surgery faster," he laughs as she moves the razor hesitantly and gently along his face, afraid to injure the white skin being exposed. "My patients will be frightened. I'm as white as a ghost." The steam rising from the pot smells of scorched metal, fogging the mirror in the hallway, and their images are as blurry as a hallucination in the turquoise-painted wooden frame.

"You keep moving," she scolds him. "I forgot how fidgety you are."

"Because you're tickling me. Being overcautious is dangerous. Will you let me finish it?"

But she refuses. "Of course not. Just look at me without moving. When did you get so tall? I don't remember you so tall."

"Sorry, I developed late in every sense of the word. But you, unlike me, have become more beautiful."

"Really?" she protests happily. "That can't be!"

"It absolutely can. There's more life in your face. You were so delicate and thin and pale, like an idea. Now you're much more womanly. Come on, let me finish this." He takes the razor from her and in two quick strokes exposes the high cheekbones she remembers. Her breath catches at the sight of the face restored with such spine-tingling accuracy.

"Only now do I really believe it's you," she gushes. "I've been pretending until now. Look, you've hardly changed at all." His face is still soft and smooth, and except for the slightly sunken cheeks and the drooping skin around his chin, he is her young Eitan. At the sight of him, tears rise in her eyes as she shakes her head again and again and bites her lips in wonder. The face emerging from his face fills her with painful longing the way suddenly discovered pictures of deceased loved ones do after many years, shedding bright light on the unknown past.

Here is his face in their school, coming into her classroom at recess, smiling bashfully. Here is his head resting on a pillow on her bed, his thick lashes shading his eyelids as he sleeps. Here is his face glowing at her on that most golden day in the narrow interval of spring after the cold and before the heat. The feel of the hot stones on her back, the lush foliage of the mulberry tree a canopy above them, her handsome boy stroking her breasts, his mouth slightly open, his blue eyes flashing, his cheeks slightly pink from the sun like a baby's cheeks, and she curls herself around him with the utmost certainty that nothing will ever separate them.

"Who is that? I don't know him!" he says, examining himself suspiciously, feeling his cheeks, twisting his lips. "What did you do to me? I feel like I've switched identities. The children will be in shock! I'm completely exposed." He covers his face with his hands and walks into the kitchen, fills the pot with water for the third time. Then he takes some tomatoes out of the fridge and cuts them into small cubes, leaving her alone in front of the mirror.

It appears that recently, a covering has been removed from her face as well. Since she met him again, she looks different, everyone tells her that, bigger eyes in a thinner face. Teachers in the school who have seen her every day for ten years wonder, "How come I never noticed that you have such beautiful eyes?" Perhaps it's her expression that has changed—how had he put it, "There's more life in your face." Unwilling to lose even a single minute, she quickly returns her gaze to him.

How swiftly time passes when she's with him. It's already eight, and she can hear the opening of the evening news broadcast coming from the apartment above them. The worried little boy is apparently with his mother today and the father is free to watch the depressing events of the day, which are far more upsetting than thieves in the garden. She'll go in about an hour. She can't leave him like this, cooking them dinner, she hasn't even told him that she's pressed for time.

"What can I do, Tani?" she asks.

"Leave your husband," he replies quietly, still chopping vegetables.

"I mean, what can I do to help make dinner. It wasn't an existential question." The deprecation in his voice when he said "husband" was a bit hurtful, and she looks over at her cell phone, momentarily afraid that Mickey can hear them in some mysterious way, perhaps even watch them, as round and silent as the moon.

"Set the table in the garden."

She walks down the rickety steps. A round, unsteady wooden table stands there, covered with dry leaves, which she sweeps away with her hand. Then she goes back to the kitchen and easily finds a rag, a tablecloth, plates, and silverware. After all, she knows this house as well as she knows her own, she even recognizes some of the items.

"Since when have you actually been living here?" she asks. "Did you live here with your wives?" Despite her curiosity, she still hasn't dared to question him about his adult life. Focusing on their past, she was afraid to ask about the course his life took after they went their separate ways, in case the thirty years they had lived apart had triumphed over their year together.

"You're my wife," he replies immediately, "there were no other wives."

"Right," she chuckles. "All you did was marry twice and make two children."

He sautées the garlic and tomatoes, drains the spaghetti, and adds it to the frying pan. "The fact is that I didn't stay with either one of them."

"That fact is open to many interpretations, some harsher than others."

"Women always interpret more harshly," he smiles. He hands her the bowl of spaghetti with sauce, then puts the bottle of wine, a plate of black olives, and a bowl of yogurt on a tray. When they finally sit down, they hear the sound of movement approaching and she is momentarily shaken. Maybe it's Mickey, maybe he followed her here and has been hiding in the hedge, but it's only a scrawny cat, the worried expression on its face almost funny.

"Come on, Gulliver, the coast is clear," Eitan tells it. "Itamar's not here, you can relax." He stands up and pours some cat food nuggets into a bowl under the steps. "Itamar tortures him a little. When he stays over here, the cat is always shaken up."

"So who's Itamar's mother?" she asks hesitantly.

"Not you, I'm sorry to say. Do you remember how sure we were that you were pregnant after we took a bath together in your house?"

"Of course. It was so scary, I started taking pills right after that."

"We could have had a twenty-seven-year-old son."

"Daughter, not son," she corrects him.

"How can you be so sure?"

"Because it had to be a daughter, and we would have named her Miriam."

"So I've already done that," he says wryly, wiping his mouth with a napkin. The absence of his beard now completely exposes lips red from the sauce, his white face appearing to be made up.

"But not with me," she says, suddenly tormented by her guilt at betraying her daughter, a betrayal no less cruel than his betrayal of her. "So who is Miriam's mother?" she asks.

To her surprise, he isn't evasive this time. "Her name's Susan. She's a gynecologist." She trembles for a moment at his words. So he did marry a doctor, and he did look for her. Bits of correct information blend with lies—this is what her mother told her, married to a doctor and the father of three bright children.

"You went to medical school together?" she asks. "She tutored you for your exams?"

"Of course," he laughs. "Without her I would have failed."

He seems to be weary of the subject, but she doesn't let up, she wants to know everything, despite her fears. Where they married, where they lived, what they talked about, how they made love, what sort of husband he was, what sort of father. And she wants to see pictures, all the pictures he has. Maybe she's making the same mistake now that she made then, not separating herself from him, because she wants to be under the wedding canopy with him and in bed with him, she wants to see his daughter emerge from another woman's womb. If that's how it was meant to be, at least she would be there, beside him. But on the other hand, she doesn't want to tell him anything about her own marriage and children, particularly not about her Alma, who was born very small and remarkably beautiful. But Iris looked at her with disappointment because she wasn't the daughter she saw in her mind's eye, long-limbed, blue-eyed, and black-haired, because she wasn't their Miriam.

"What do you want to know?" he asks. "I told you, didn't I?"

She glances at her watch. That baby is apparently in trouble and she has to rescue her, atone for that first look of disappointment she gave her. But how will she tell him that she has to go? How will she walk out of here when it is so pleasant sitting across from him in the neglected garden, which belongs to her no less than her own home, because in this garden, redolent of tree resin, a perfect fossil of the young girl she was has been preserved.

He fills her plate and her glass over and over again, how will she even be able to drive? The paling, shrinking moon hangs like a yellow plum above the tree, the world is filled with miracles and disasters, and now she's on the miracle side of it, no wonder she can't get up and move from here to the disaster side. But she has no choice. She stands up and, weaving slightly, goes over to him, holding on to the rickety table.

"Where are you going?" he asks, and sits her down on his lap. "It's incredible how much you look like my mother now."

"It's only my hair that reminds you of her wig."

But he shakes his head. "It's also the eyes and something in the way you walk, it's amazing, I don't understand what's happening to me, what time I'm living in." He grasps her hair tightly as if trying to pull off the wig, crushes her lips with his until she can't breathe, unbuttons her shirt and buries his head between her breasts.

"My love," she mumbles, "I have to go."

And he whispers, "Don't go, stay with me."

When she looks at her watch again, it's past midnight and her body is filled with his love, with the resin of their youth, with crumbling dry leaves, with promises and vows and with longing as old as their unborn children. When she breaks away from him, her heart pounding, she too no longer remembers who she is and what time she is living in, where she came from and where she is going. Will she have to answer for her actions, and to whom?

As her car ascends the hill, worry attacks her like a highway robber of old, and she tries to calm down. She'll go to see Alma tomorrow, another day won't matter, and at home, Mickey is probably asleep, convinced she drove to Tel Aviv. It isn't likely that he's waiting up for her after he refused to go with her, and Omer said he would sleep at Yotam's house. No one will see her when she arrives, her kissed lips and love-sated body redolent of intimacy. She tiptoes inside, she'll shower in the morning, better not to make unnecessary noise. She brushes her teeth quickly at the kitchen sink, then goes into Alma's dark room and closes the door. But when she undresses silently and climbs into bed, she is horrified to feel another body under the blanket and cries out in fright. Is Mickey lying in wait for her there, shrunken with jealousy? But it isn't his large body. She leaps out of bed, gasping, and opens the shutters. In the light of the full moon that followed her here, she recognizes Alma, whose mouth is slightly open in surprise and disgust, as if she has just seen an especially disturbing sight.

Unnerved, Iris stares at her alibi fading before her eyes, a skinny, mysterious, fragile alibi. What will she say to Mickey? Why didn't he tell her that Alma is home and there's no point in driving to see her? He must have deliberately laid a trap for her and now she has to deceive him in return, even though she doesn't have enough information. When did Alma arrive? What time did she leave work? She may be able to say that she went to the bar and Alma wasn't there, but she has to wake her if she doesn't want to be caught in a lie.

"Alma?" she whispers. "I'm so glad you're here! When did you come?" as if she hasn't noticed that her daughter is sleeping.

To her surprise, Alma responds to her forced cheerfulness, mumbling in her sleep, "Mom! I waited for you, where were you?"

"At work. When did you come? Why didn't you let me know you were home?"

But Alma has already turned onto her side, showing her narrow back clad in one of Mickey's huge T-shirts. Iris closes the shutters quietly and tiptoes to Omer's room so she can sleep in his bed, anything to keep Mickey from waking up. She can't face him like this, with her skin coated in a layer of love and her brain empty of lies.

How can it be? He told her he was sleeping over at Yotam's, but he's in his bed, the heat of his body radiating from it. He's snoring lightly, his presence clear and vibrant even in his sleep, and she hurries out, staggering her way to the couch. All their linens are stored in the bedroom and she will absolutely not go in there, so she has no choice but to lie down on the couch in her clothes, without a blanket, even though the night coldness is making her shiver. Maybe she'll get up, take two used towels and cover herself with them even though they are slightly damp and cold, someone showered recently. The house is sending her mysterious clues, its residents are unwittingly punishing her, changing their plans without telling her, giving her false information, banishing her to the couch. She trembles under the damp towels. Why didn't Omer go to the birthday party? Is it because Alma came? Did she come because she wanted to or did Mickey call her again, supposedly to alleviate Iris's fears, but actually to show her that he's right. Maybe he is right, maybe he does know Alma better than she does. There was such a rare sweetness in her voice when she said, "Mom! I waited for you."

Maybe Shira really is exaggerating. She'll talk to her daughter tomorrow and try to understand what this is all about. After all, she's so young, and at her age, things change quickly. Perhaps by tomorrow morning she'll be able to stop worrying and in fact—she giggles under the damp towels like a girl in love—she will be able to keep walking undisturbed along the miraculous path being paved under her feet to the world where the years fall away, where she can step back among the flowering plazas of time, walk over and over again in the perfumed wadi, among the clouds of honey, on the only day of spring when it isn't too hot or too cold.

THIRTEEN

She'll be the first one up, shower in the children's bathroom, and go into the bedroom, alert and resolute, to get dressed and put on her makeup. When she's efficient, she arouses less suspicion, particularly when Mickey isn't completely awake. And when he gets up, he might forget what happened the night before, her prolonged, ludicrous absence on the pretext of having driven to Tel Aviv to investigate Alma while Alma came to Jerusalem—clearly an especially botched investigation. She'll get organized quickly, slip out of the bedroom just as his alarm clock rings, waking him for a new day. For what, actually? She knows so little about his daily routine, his relationships with his bosses and underlings, the work he has to do. How many women in distress does he help, driving them to and from various doctors? How many chess games does he manage to play secretly during work hours? Who are the people he talks to? And if he does suspect her, whom will he share his suspicions with? His need to socialize is limited, always has been, and since his close childhood friend left the country, he hardly ever spends time with other people.

She makes a sandwich for Omer hastily and peeks into Alma's room. It's still dark in there and she seems to be sleeping deeply. She'll text and ask her to call when she wakes up, she'll even cancel a meeting to see her. "Mom! I waited for you," she had said, such rare words. Did she want to share what's happening in her life with her? She, of course, will listen with love, no judgments and no criticism. She'll be supportive, we all make mistakes when we're young, she'll assure her, every mistake is an important lesson.

Now here's Mickey, lumbering his way toward her like a sleepwalker, surprising her with a smile on his way to the kettle, asking her nothing. Or perhaps it isn't exactly a smile, but a sleepy nod of recognition, as if he has bumped into a neighbor on his way to the garbage bin. "I have to run," she says quickly, "wake Omer, okay? His sandwich is in his backpack, we'll talk later." Then she's in the elevator, in the car, trapped in moving objects, up and down, right and left, anything not to be in his line of vision.

It's good that she left early, she'll have time to prepare for the end-of-year meeting with the supervisor. But it isn't really that early, the first pupils are beginning to arrive, some emerging from moving vehicles, some walking, heavy bags on their backs, the younger ones accompanied by their parents. She didn't walk Alma and Omer to their classrooms that morning, there was no need. They got out of the car together, walked through the gate together, and then separated to go to their classes. If she had been with them, the bus would have exploded without her. But what sort of conclusion can she come to, what lesson can she learn from that mistake?

Learn from your mistakes—how hollow that saying is. Eitan made a mistake by leaving her, and both their lives were fatally damaged. Even their children, who owed their lives to that mistake, were damaged. Suddenly anxious, she recalls the Talmudic story of the man who breaks his promise to marry a young girl he comes across on the road, and marries a different woman instead. His children meet with mysterious deaths until he goes back to her. Whenever she taught that story, she thought of Eitan, but in the legend, the young girl continues to wait for him, even pretending to have lost her mind to avoid marrying someone else. But Iris didn't wait, she has a family, which means that her children are in danger, not only his.

She must send an urgent text to her daughter before she gets out of her car and is besieged on all sides—sweetie, she'll write, call me when you wake up and I'll come right away, we have to talk. But her fingers groping in her bag can't find her phone, and she upends the bag on the passenger seat angrily. So many necessary and unnecessary things fall out, pain pills, chewing gum, Brazil nuts, shopping lists, sunglasses she's been looking for these last two weeks, an open lipstick, pens, pencils, yellow Post-its, hand cream, sunblock, wrinkled forms. But her phone, her essential, incriminating phone, has apparently remained behind on the kitchen counter and she can't text Alma, and even worse, with a single tap, Mickey can find out where she was last night. Or a random glance may reveal to him a new text that was sent in the meantime, several stolen words of love for the morning after, a text you can't help noticing even if you aren't prying.

One of her teachers knocks on her closed window, neon orange fingernails dancing on the glass, but she signals her that they'll talk later. She feels a sharp pain between her temples, what a fateful mishap, to escape him so quickly and still reveal her secret to him. She has to go back home and get her phone, but then she'll be late for the meeting. That's all she needs— the supervisor has been much too interested in her recently. Pretending to be concerned about her well-being, she takes note of how poorly she is doing her job. The day is coming when she will recommend firing her, and anyway, there's no point in hurrying home, Mickey is already on his way to work. Maybe she left it on the seat and it fell, she thinks, foraging around under the mats, trying to recall which texts from Pain are still on her phone. She usually deletes them in the elevator before she goes into the apartment, and forgot to delete only the latest one. But that is definitely enough for Mickey, he doesn't need a historical survey of their love.

And if the phone miraculously escapes Mickey's notice, Omer might see it, or Alma, she thinks in horror as someone taps on her window again. She straightens up and again signals that she can't talk now, but to her surprise, a large hand holding the familiar phone waves at her. She opens the window, trying to hide her agitation.

"Is this what you're looking for?" he asks, the same strange and polite smile from the morning frozen along the width of his swarthy face. He must have enjoyed watching her search. "I figured you'd have a hard time without it," he says, and climbs back into the car parked next to hers. How long has he been there? She didn't noticed him arriving, just as she doesn't notice him leaving now before she has time to mumble a word of thanks.

She just grabs the phone hungrily from his hand and immediately checks if there are any new texts from Pain, if there is any sign in the texts that they have been seen. "When are you coming? I'm waiting for you. Come soon, my love, I'm home," she reads the last text that says everything to anyone who wants to know, but it doesn't tell her whether anyone else has read it. Fortunately, there are no new texts from Pain since they said goodbye the night before, unless they were erased in fury, and that, at least, she can check. "Good morning, love," she writes hurriedly, "did you text me anything this morning?" To her great relief, he texts back immediately, but doesn't answer her question. "Why do you ask?"

"Yes or no," she writes, tapping nervously, but this time he doesn't reply. Perhaps a patient has just come into his office, or maybe this is his way of protesting against the circumstances that require him to hide his love for her, turning his texts from a source of supreme happiness into a dangerous threat to her peace of mind. She puts her head on the steering wheel, what a revolting situation, those two men hiding essential information from her, each for his own reasons. Now she has to go into a meeting without knowing what she will have to deal with when she comes out of it. The bell rings and she drags herself out of the car straight into a swarm of pupils flocking to their classrooms. She is losing everything, all these pupils she knows so well, this place she built with her own two hands, she is losing Mickey, Alma. Before she can text her, the supervisor is standing in front of her. She'll text her right after the meeting, Alma loves to sleep, like her father, and she probably won't get up till noon.

"Good morning, sweetie, call me when you wake up and I'll come right away," she taps into her phone when she returns to her office and drops onto her chair, drained. This time a reply comes quickly, but not the one she wished for:

"I'm in the central bus station already," her daughter writes, "bye for now." What rotten luck, her daughter has eluded her again, the information has eluded her again. But she won't give up easily, after all, last night she clearly said, "I waited for you," so Iris calls her immediately. "Alma? Wait for me at the bus station, I'll be right there," she says. "We'll have coffee together and then you can go."

But Alma says, "I'm in a hurry, I'm just getting on a bus."

"What time did you come home? I'm so sorry I missed you. Why didn't you let me know you were coming?"

"I didn't know myself. I had a ride and all of a sudden I found myself in Jerusalem."

"What do you mean, you didn't know where you were going?" she asks sharply, which of course closes the gates with a bang.

"It doesn't matter, it's hard to explain," Alma mutters. "I'll come next week."

But Iris won't let it go. "It matters to me. Who gave you a ride? You got into a car without knowing where it was headed?"

"Can't hear you, Mom, there's a lot of noise on the bus, bye for now."

What did she give in exchange for that lift? Did it have anything to do with the cult? Maybe Shira wasn't exaggerating, but actually minimizing? The most terrible images fill her mind now, fucking in the back seat, strange men, drugs, violence, what can she do about those hideous sights? Should she get into her car and block Alma's bus before it leaves the station, threaten the driver? Let me see my daughter or I'll hurt you all, she'll say. It will be a new kind of terror attack, a maternal terror attack, that's what they'll probably call it in the news reports, because she thinks she is capable of anything now. For years she hasn't been able to look at buses, but today that seems to be the least of her problems. She'll take control of the bus, hold the passengers hostage, and say to her daughter, I won't release any of them until you come home with me. Or maybe she herself will be injured, a totally personal suicide attack. Come home or I'll throw myself under the bus that's taking you to disaster.

"Is everything okay?" her secretary asks her as she enters her office with a pile of forms to sign.

"Nothing is okay today," she replies.

"Just today?" Ofra asks. "It seems like a long time already. Can I help you, Iris? You take care of everyone here and you never let anyone help you."

"No one can help me," she says in a cold voice and repeats the words in surprise, as if only now has she recognized that sad fact. "No one can help me."

Ofra looks at her sadly. "So make just this one last effort to end the year, it'll be vacation soon."

"What vacation?!" she says. "You know how many teachers I still have to interview, how many seminars I have to organize, not to mention the renovations of the first-grade classrooms."

"That's small change for you." Of course, Ofra is right. Iris is ready to renovate the entire building and replace all the teachers just so she doesn't have to think about that daughter who is making her worst nightmares come true with such shocking thoughtlessness.

In the teachers' room, she sees the young woman who has just joined the staff. She isn't much older than Alma, but a huge abyss seems to divide them—one has work and love, and the other is involved in something shady that horrifies her more the more she thinks about it. "I found myself in Jerusalem," Alma said, "I found myself in Jerusalem." Iris sits down across from the young teacher, seized by a powerful urge to know her better, to hear about her family, especially her mother. Maybe it will become clear that the difference lies there. But what will she ask, was your mother abandoned by her first love, which caused her to have a severe breakdown? Did your mother marry your father without passion, without joy? Was she disappointed when she looked at you the first time, realizing that you weren't the baby she had dreamed of because you weren't the daughter of the man she loved?

She can ask all sorts of other questions, but what's the point, after all, whether she is or isn't to blame for everything or anything, she has to do all she can to rescue her daughter. Nonetheless, unable to restrain herself, she asks with a forced smile on her face, "So how's it going? Are you still in love?"

Ya'ara replies with a broad smile that is both embarrassed and certain, "Yes, it's a dream, just a dream."

"I'm so happy for you. Did you have a model for that kind of happiness at home? Are your parents in love that way too?"

To her disappointment, the young teacher replies enthusi-astically, her eyes glowing. "My parents are really something. After thirty years, they still hold hands!"

Iris nods sadly, absorbing the information, until another teacher interrupts the conversation: "That doesn't mean anything. My parents separated when I was little, but I still have a good marriage." Then the science teacher contributes contradictory information about lovebird parents who have a twice-divorced daughter, but Iris clings to the most depressing story, "They still hold hands after thirty years!"

Did Alma ever see them holding hands? Not very often, that's not their style. They quickly became sarcastic and unromantic with each other, but they didn't function badly as parents, as a family. No, it wasn't her relationship with Mickey, it was her relationship with Alma, that's where the failure lay, her failure to make her daughter feel unequivocally that she loved her. Devastated, she returns to her office, leaving behind the ongoing conversation.

She needs to talk to Mickey, whatever he saw. It doesn't matter now, they will always be Alma's parents and everything between them is irrelevant at the moment. Once again, she reads the text that he may have seen: "When are you coming, I'm waiting for you, Come soon, my love, I'm home." Poor Mickey, how terrible to find a text like that on your wife's phone. Such disappointment, such deceit, and yet he didn't seem upset, he seemed almost excited, amused, his broad hand handing her the phone through the window, his large face composed. Is he also having an affair, as she recently suspected, and did this discovery liberate him? She has to call and talk to him about Alma, but her finger hesitates above the touch screen. She taps the name of the bar, which is called, for some reason, Sinai. The Sinai Bar-Restaurant.

Apprehensively, she reads the information that leads her to the name Boaz Gerber. Why hasn't she done this sooner? But on the other hand, it would have been pointless, because even the sophisticated search engine can't tell her a thing about her daughter and doesn't upload even a single photo of that Boaz or link him to any cult or to Alma. But it does have an abundance of frightening information about cults and leaves her to navigate her way through the links by herself. She reads with horror about the enormous number of people damaged by cults in contrast to the scanty public debate on the subject, about the critical importance of locating them in the early stages, and on the other hand, about how difficult it is to locate them. She reads with alarm about the warning signs, changes in the manner of dress and behavior, severed relations with family and friends. Nausea rises in her throat and her stomach roils. "Alma, no," she mumbles, "Alma, no," as if her daughter is on the roof of a tall building, her legs already dangling in the air, and she remembers all the tension related to her eating. Even then, she pictured her that way, in constant danger, in need of rescue.

"I finished early today, want to meet up?" Eitan's text overlays the ominous reports, and she swoops down on it as if it were prey. "Sure. Where?"

It's good that he suggested this place outside the city, in an Arab village on a hilltop where there is no chance they will see anyone they know. She has never been here, and she stares at the serene pastoral sights, the chickens pecking the ground, two skinny cows ambling through a dry field. Of course, it's an illusion, disasters can be hidden under every roof in the city and outside of it, in palaces and in tents. The simple life is no guarantee, and yet the clean, harvest-scented air soothes her a bit. She sits down at the last table in the garden, almost outside the restaurant, where she can look out over the road that leads to the hilltop, can see his silver car speeding toward her. What a miraculous, incredible sight—sunbeams collect on its roof, and for a moment she thinks it is going up in flames, like the chariots and horsemen described in the Bible. She stands up to greet him, overwhelmed, as she is every time she sees him. So many years have passed, and she has already been nearing the end of her life without seeing him. Many people her age fall ill and die, even on that morning ten years ago, death was closer to her than life. And yet, if it hadn't been for that catastrophe, they would not have met again, and that thought is just as unbearable as the thought of the catastrophe itself. When the car door opens and he gets out, tall and disheveled, she can't believe it's him, her Eitan, who has come back to her. It is inconceivable that the pain, which split them apart, has now brought them together again only to have them separate once more.

His pale, beardless face is astonishingly beautiful, surrounded by a full head of gray hair, and the sun in his eyes illuminates the mesmerizing blue rings around his pupils. She gives him a long hug, almost hanging on his thin body. There is no one there but the owner, who is busy in the kitchen and doesn't know her, but he apparently knows Eitan well because he hurries out to them, waving his arms in excitement and almost pushing into their embrace. "Doctor!" he shouts. "Welcome, I was worried about you, you haven't been here in a long time."

Eitan claps him on the back affectionately and says, "You know how it is, no time to breathe. How's everything with you? How's your mother?" Then he explains to her, "Moussa's mother is an old patient of mine."

"He saved her," Moussa adds. "She suffered so much, she used to cry from the pain. Thanks to him, she goes on with her life, even takes care of the grandchildren." He leads them to the table and begins to fuss around them. He turns the fan in their direction, brings them a jug of cold water with mint leaves and lemon, and three glasses of arak, one for himself, because he immediately sits down beside them.

"Orit will be sorry she missed you, she's working late today."

Eitan asks, "How is she? How is life together?"

"What can I tell you, it's not easy, as you know."

Eitan explains, smiling broadly, "Moussa made the mistake of his life by marrying a Jewish woman. Instead of taking a simple girl from the village, he got mixed up with an opinionated city girl who argues with him about everything."

Moussa laughs, picks up his glass and drinks to his wife. "I'm nuts about her, but she drives me crazy. When will you find a cure for that disease?"

She listens to their conversation, fascinated. Since finding each other again, they have always been alone, only the two of them in the oasis of their return to the past. In fact, even when they were young, they didn't socialize very much, they were so preoccupied with his mother's illness. Now she enjoys seeing him in a lighthearted conversation, enjoys being this man's woman, in this place, which is almost utopian anyway, in this beautiful, friendly Arab village in the Jerusalem hills, in the home of this mixed-marriage couple who are living the most exciting fantasy in the region—coexistence.

The drink makes her dizzy, and she looks admiringly at Eitan's sharp face. If they can do it, so can we, she promises herself, we haven't been given a second chance only to fail again. Maybe Mickey will be pleased about it as well and it will be astonishingly easy. They'll separate as dispassionately as they had married, and the first love of her life will become the last love of her life. She must have unintentionally laughed, because they break off speaking and look at her. "What's funny, Rissi?" Eitan asks softly and puts his hand on her thigh. She drapes her arm around his shoulders and rests her spinning head in the hollow of his neck, her lips longing to kiss him in the sight of the slowly departing sun, in the sight of their host. Here is a witness, and she has to prove to him that it's real, that she had belonged to this man from the days of her youth. As her fingers caress his cheek, she realizes that she wants to live in this village with him, in an isolated house on the hilltop, to raise cows and goats and never leave. She laughs again, inhaling deeply the familiar smell of him that she loves so much, the smell of soap and medicine, the smell of his orphanhood. She's a bit disappointed when her witness leaves the table hastily, as if fleeing from their intimacy, but he returns immediately with full plates. He covers the table with a profusion of dishes that Eitan has clearly eaten before and likes. She's so hungry, but except for a plate of yellow rice, everything is meat, and she is slightly put off.

"Dig in," Moussa urges her as Eitan attacks the food.

She explains, somewhat apologetically, "I'm a vegetarian."

Eitan puts down his fork in surprise. "I didn't know!" He adds almost angrily, "You didn't use to be a vegetarian!" Turning to Moussa in disappointment he says, "What are we going to do with her?"

But Moussa reassures them, "No problem, I'll make a vegetable dish for you." She is sorry once again that he leaves their table and watches him move away, clad in a white shirt and bursting with goodwill. Then she returns her gaze to Eitan, who is chewing away at pieces of a pinkish steak, a kind of juicy kebab, and a chicken cutlet, his jaws moving quickly. A cloud of burnt blood rises from their table and nausea rises in her throat.

"How long have you been a vegetarian?"

"More than twenty years. When I married Mickey, we decided that we wouldn't eat dead animals." She feels uncomfortable about admitting the existence of the person she has spent so many years with, who shares her worldviews, her eating habits.

Eitan shakes his head in annoyance. "You take B-12, I hope."

"Of course, when I remember," she replies, happy to reduce the subject, so important to her, Mickey, and the children, to an insignificant detail. Couples overcome such large differences, she thinks, trying to cheer herself up, and yet it is hard to watch him chewing away so comfortably, as if it isn't a living creature that once had a conscious mind lying there on his plate, as if he has never even thought about it.

"I didn't know you were so unevolved," she finally says, unable to stop herself. "They're animals like you and me! How can you eat them?"

He recoils as if he has been struck. "So go back to your husband if it bothers you so much," he hisses, his jaws moving constantly, and when he takes a sip of arak, the inside of his mouth looks black and hollow.

"I haven't left him yet."

He moves his face closer to hers. "Of course you've left him. You wouldn't be here otherwise." His eyes, grown dark in the sunset, fix on her. "You're coming back to me." He shoves a piece of meat into his mouth and chews it defiantly. Then he raises her chin and crushes her lips with his until they part and her mouth fills with the forgotten, repulsive taste of roasted blood. To her horror, she feels a lump of chewed meat being thrust onto her tongue. She tries to break away from his lips, tries to push the lump back into his mouth, but can't. Her stomach churns and her lungs empty of air until her power to resist weakens and she swallows the lump of chewed meat from his mouth with a bitter sense of defeat. Only then does he take his lips from hers.

"You've gone too far," she says, gasping for air, knowing that she sounds like a self-righteous old schoolteacher. "What was that supposed to be?"

To her surprise, he laughs. "Lighten up. Where's your sense of humor? Are all vegetarians so uptight, or is it just you?"

She leaves the table angrily and hurries to the restroom, fills her mouth with water and soap, and spits it out over and over again. No, she doesn't think it's funny, definitely not. But neither does she think it's funny when she recalls feeding Alma the same way when she was a baby, shoving mashed-up globs into her small mouth as she begged, threatened, coaxed, persisting even when she felt the child's revulsion. How could she have done that? How could he have done that? She hears the sound of a moving car, and for a moment, she hopes it's him, that when she returns to the table he will no longer be there—is that what she really hopes for? Someone has to disappear, he or she, or Mickey, or Alma, or all living creatures. But she finds him waiting for her at the restroom door.

"I'm sorry, Rissi, I've been acting like a love-struck teenage idiot," he says and wraps his arms around her. There are more people in the restaurant now, and she glances quickly at the faces, hoping she doesn't know anyone, and even more that they don't know her. Keeping her head down, she breaks away from his embrace and hurries outside to their table under the grape arbor. All the dishes have been removed and only her plate of roasted vegetables awaits her beside the bowl of cold yellow rice, but the taste of soap is in her mouth and she doesn't want to eat anything.

"I must be jealous," he says jokingly.

"You? I don't remember you being jealous."

"I don't remember you being a vegetarian, I mean married."

She smiles, how can she be angry at him? She'd rather not, now that she's the one making the choices. "That reminded me of the way I used to force my daughter to eat. It must have been awful for her, but I had to do it. I was afraid she'd die."

"Die?" he says in surprise. "You were really overreacting! Children don't die of hunger in situations like that."

"I made a terrible mistake. I thought I was saving her. She never asked to eat, was never hungry, and she didn't grow. I didn't know what to do."

"Maybe she just wanted to eat meat. If you'd fed her meat, she would have devoured it."

She shakes her head. "It's not funny, Eitan," she says, sounding like a schoolteacher again.

"Maybe, but it's not tragic either, assuming that nowadays you don't force her to eat anymore."

"Nowadays someone else is forcing her to do other things." Suddenly she feels an urgent need to share this with him. "I'm terribly worried about her, Eitan. I think she's in trouble."

Still slightly amused, he asks, "How old is she? It seems weird to me that you have children, I still haven't gotten used to it. Once, you didn't have children."

"Twenty-one," she says, just as his phone vibrates on the table.

"Sorry, it's the hospital." His tone changes, instantly growing more serious, as if this call is still about his sick mother. "So increase the dosage," he instructs, "I'll be there in a little while to see her." Is that why Alma's story doesn't bother him, because he's used to bad news, or is it because she isn't his daughter? "I have to go, Rissi. When will I see you again?"

"Tomorrow I'm busy until late."

"Day after tomorrow I have the kids."

She wants to shout, See me today, see me now, I'm not a teenager in love, I'm a mother whose daughter is in trouble, that's what I am.

But he has already stood up. "By the way, I'm going to a conference in Rome at the end of the month. Want to join me?"

"How can I join you?" she mutters.

"If you want it, it'll happen. We've suffered enough, haven't we? It's time to enjoy ourselves." He leans over and kisses her forehead, ruffling her hair slightly. "Sorry, Rissi, I warned you that today would be short, didn't I? I have to get back to the hospital."

"You didn't warn me, but that's okay," she says, and for the first time since meeting him again, she realizes how small a part he plays in her life. There will never be a total, absolute resolution. But that's all right, even if you stay here for another ten hours, you can't relieve the anxiety that's tormenting me now, and that's all right too, because you aren't supposed to, the mistake is in the expectation. Alone now, she sips the warm arak distractedly, and only when she has emptied the glass does she realize that she can't drive for a while, neither home nor to see her daughter. It isn't only because of the law, but also because she's dizzy and has a headache. She waves at Moussa and he hurries over.

"Is everything okay?" he asks. "Do you want some black coffee? Mint tea? Something sweet for dessert? That's how the doctor is, always disappearing in the middle of the meal," he tries to console her. He seems to be looking at her pityingly, and she wonders what else he knows that she doesn't. Does Eitan bring women here often?

But that isn't what's upsetting her now, and she points to the empty chair. "Please sit down for a minute," she says. "Do you have a daughter, Moussa?"

"Three daughters," he replies, "why do you ask?"

She finds herself continuing the conversation that has just been interrupted. "My daughter is twenty-one. I think she's in trouble. She's a waitress in a bar in Tel Aviv. She's distanced herself from us and from her friends, she looks different. I think her boss is controlling her. Maybe it's not really a cult in the accepted sense, but it's frightening."

As evening falls and lights come on in the village to the sound of birds shrieking for their chicks to return to their nests, she tells him everything she wanted to tell Eitan. He listens to her quietly and lights a cigarette, his pleasant young face focused on hers. "I'll make you some strong black coffee now," he finally says, "with a lot of sugar to give you strength. You should go to see what's happening with her, but not alone. You should go with her father."

"He won't want to come with me. I told you, I've been asking him for a few days, but he would rather ignore it."

Moussa says, "He'll go if you really want him to."

A petite waitress Alma's age comes over, and he orders a salad with a lot of lemon juice in it for her. "You have to build up your strength," he says, "to be strong when you get there." She eats obediently, surprised that the more she eats, the hungrier she is, she even wants to eat more of the yellow rice and roasted vegetables. His presence is soothing; finding it difficult to leave him, she asks for another cup of coffee. The darkness around her is now as thick and hot as the coffee he brews for her. People who live in the hills are unused to such nights of stifling heat, but the night they were told of her father's death was exactly like this one. She remembers being unable to fall asleep because it was so hot, and that's why she heard the knocking on the door and her mother's screams. She heard orphanhood bursting into the small apartment like a mob of rioters come to stage a pogrom.

Did she unwittingly bequeath that sense of orphanhood to her daughter? She looks westward, where the dying embers of light flicker on the plains behind the hills, where her Alma is. She must hurry before her light is extinguished as well. Just as she takes her phone out of her bag to call Mickey, he calls. "What's happening with you, are you still at work?"

Unwilling to lie on such a night, she says, "I was at a meeting outside the city. I have a headache. I can't drive home, and I don't want to drive home. I want us to go to Tel Aviv to see Alma. It's time, Mickey. Pick me up at the interchange." He doesn't answer right away, and she hears his heavy breathing. "Did you hear me?" she asks.

"I heard you, I'm thinking about it."

"There's nothing to think about, Mickey, I did the thinking for both of us."

"I don't like the way you take over everything."

"And I don't like the way you deny everything," she counters.

"Okay, I don't have the strength to argue with you. Give me half an hour." His voice is hostile and cold, he prefers being angry at her to worrying about his daughter. How stupid it is to expect that if one man disappoints you, the other will surprise you for the better. How stupid to expect anything at all.

FOURTEEN

Will that argument go on forever, or will it end sometime? It seems as if, until they take their last breath, parents will be arguing about who is to blame, who is the better parent, who is right and who is wrong. She has met so many couples like that over the years, only a few rise above it, and she and Mickey are apparently not one of them. He picks her up at the interchange in hostile silence. Is he angry about the drive itself, has the meeting place aroused his suspicion, or did he read the text in the morning and no longer suspects, but knows? She prefers to focus on their mission now and not think about it, to concentrate only on what they will say to their daughter, if she is there at all, or to the owner of the place if they meet him. Will they speak to him directly or simply try to feel him out? Or maybe at this point, would it be better not to say anything and give all their attention to what they see? If only she could speak to Mickey simply, the way she spoke to Moussa, ask his advice openly, plan their course of action together. Why is it so much easier to talk to a stranger, because clearly Orit, Moussa's wife, would be more comfortable consulting with Mickey than with her husband under certain circumstances. That is undoubtedly the most common and exasperating paradox of living together—moving closer in order to move away—so what's the point?

Closeness creates so much pain and sensitivity, wounds and scars, that every subject becomes too charged for a sensible conversation. But there is also no point in complaining to him now, she is clearly the last person who has a right to complain, considering her status as an unfaithful wife. Even if he doesn't know yet, she does, and her cell phone does, because it's ringing now. Pain is calling, and of course she doesn't answer, but even when she mutes the ring, the vibration incriminates her because she doesn't answer, because he doesn't stop, and sends a text that also vibrates in the closed car. His texts thrill her, but today he thrust a dead animal into her mouth and she is trembling.

"Are you cold? Should I turn down the air conditioner?" Mickey asks, and she says quickly, "Yes, a little." For some reason, he raises the volume of the music at the same time. "Dad's going back to his roots," Omer likes to tease him about his new devotion to Iraqi music, and she herself actually enjoys the new discs he has begun bringing home, though she never listens to them with much attention. Not too long ago he told her that he was sorry he changed his name from Moalem to the Hebrew name Eilam when they got married. She was quick to remind him that it wasn't her idea, even though she supported it, that for him, it was mainly a way to cut himself off from his father, adding that as far as she was concerned, he could change their name back to Moalem. He claimed that it was too late, and she felt once again that he was blaming her. Even now, he is trying to provoke her by playing the music of his ethnic forefathers, the music of the Jews of Babel, as he puts it. She, of course, won't ask him to lower the volume, even though she thinks the vocal cords of the woman singing in Arabic will break, because the singer refuses to calm down despite the violin's valiant effort to console her. She seems to be in terrible pain, at the summit of sorrow and lamentation, trying to draw them to her, to that place where eyes are open forever. We're there, we're already there, Iris wants to say to her, you're not alone, but the singer responds with a hoarse shout, you're not even halfway there, you have no idea what awaits you. Iris trembles again and turns to look through the window. The glittering towers of Tel Aviv are already beckoning them with their thousands of glowing eyes, extinguishing the stars in the sky with their light. How close Tel Aviv actually is, especially at night when the traffic thins.

Years back, they went there often, but ironically, since their daughter moved to Tel Aviv, the city seems to have moved farther away from theirs, just as their daughter has moved away from them. And now here they are, already navigating the busy, illuminated streets. So many beautiful girls are hurrying across the road in their light-colored mini-dresses, short shorts, and tank tops. The city looks open, vibrant, not the slightest bit worried. After all, it won't stop moving because of one young girl who came from another city and got herself in trouble, it has enough other girls to be happy about. Attractive young men fill the streets as well, so why did Alma chose a middle-aged man, the owner of a run-of-the-mill bar in the southern part of the city, instead of one of them? Why, in this place so full of life and freedom, did their daughter find slavery?

Or is it all only unfounded rumor, because now they are passing the place in their car. "You have reached your destination," the satnav announces, and it looks safe enough and well lit, with large windows facing the street, not trying to hide a thing. Mickey finds a spot with surprising ease in the adjoining parking lot, and only after turning off the music, the air conditioner, the lights, and the engine does he speak.

"So what exactly do you want to do, what's the plan?"

"There is no plan," she says. "We're out for a night of fun in Tel Aviv. We've suffered enough, it's time to enjoy ourselves, right?"

He laughs bitterly. "It really is time, but why in Alma's bar, of all places?"

She opens the car door. "Do me a favor, Mickey, put your lost honor aside for a minute and go along with me, okay? I hope I'm wrong and you're right, but we have to check it out."

"How exactly are you going to do that," he grumbles, "by going inside and asking her? Or him? Will you call them into the principal's office for questioning? Really Iris, I thought you were cleverer than that."

"For once, will you be with me and not against me? Stop competing with me? I have no answers for you, we'll just go in there and see what happens, okay?"

"Do I have a choice? I know you, you won't give up until you see that I'm right."

She takes his arm and slows them down on the sidewalk across the street from the place as they approach it, stepping carefully, as if they are in a minefield. Peering out at them from the adjacent display window is a naked doll, its plastic breasts protruding defiantly. A stray clothespin springs like a grasshopper around their legs, and she turns to look at an old woman hanging laundry through the window, bent over the lines. Now she's hanging an old flowered robe remarkably similar to the one Iris wore recently, and a streetlamp casts yellow light on the clothes swaying limply in the sea breeze as if drained of all their energy.

Most of the shutters they pass are closed, but coming from the shabby apartments above them is a jumble of human voices, both repellent and consoling, a quiet argument, moans of pleasure, a baby crying. There is some graffiti in Arabic along the length of the wall, and although she believes that language is a cultural bridge, she still hasn't had time to learn that one. Above it is an Israeli flag, somewhat tattered and torn, apparently left there since Independence Day more out of neglect than pride, faded by the summer sun. And here they are, in front of the window of the Sinai Bar, the mysterious arena of their daughter's life.

A woman of about sixty with dyed red hair is sitting next to the window, an open laptop on her table, two young couples behind her. From a distance, they can see several more figures leaning on the bar, and a waitress carrying a tray walking among the tables. But it isn't Alma, this one is blond and plump. Hasn't she started her shift yet? And where is the owner? They can see very little from outside, and perhaps it will be the same inside, but she pulls Mickey's arm and together they cross the street to the glass door that opens for them.

"The service here is not great," Mickey says when no one comes over to their table. "I'll phone Alma to come and take our order," he quips, and she says, "Very funny." She doesn't even notice that time has passed because she is carefully observing every single detail, forced to admit that she likes the place. It's homey and not too fancy, the music isn't too loud, the large blue couch in the corner even reminds her of their living room couch, and the waitress who finally comes over to them with menus is polite and pleasant.

"Would you like to hear about our specials?" she asks, and immediately recites the list in that familiar waitresslike manner. Should they ask her about Alma? Better to wait for the time being, introduce themselves only when they have no choice. She whispers to Mickey to be quiet, but he's busy with the menu anyway, unlike her, since she ate to her heart's content in a different restaurant not long before and isn't actually hungry.

"I heard that the lentils here are good," he says, and she's glad that he hasn't divulged his source.

"Everything here is good," the waitress says. Her teeth are slightly prominent when she smiles, and her hair, which from a distance looks pulled back, is actually as short as Alma's. She is wearing a black T-shirt and gray pants—is that the uniform in this place? Is it the cult uniform?

"Sorry I took so long to come over," she suddenly adds, even though they haven't complained. "We're short-handed tonight."

"Why, what happened?" Iris asks nervously.

"Just a few sick waitresses, but we'll manage." she says as she moves away.

"Let's cancel our order and drive over to Alma's apartment," Mickey says. "We won't find out anything here if she's sick. I'll call to see what's up with her."

But she stops him quickly. "Wait, don't call," she says, her voice so loud and grating that the people at the next table glance at her. Mickey, who also stares as if she has lost her mind, immediately makes a show of reading something on his phone and ignoring her completely.

More than twenty years, and she still hasn't solved the enigma of his face, she thinks, as she looks at him with displeasure. His face is crowded with large features that make for a very strong presence, large black eyes, a long nose, a wide mouth, but nonetheless he gives the impression of being gentle. She tries to focus on his face, to understand once and for all how that is possible, but the door opens right then and a man enters. No longer young, he is short, wearing white pants and a tight black T-shirt, and from the sudden tension, almost fear, she sees on their waitress's face, she knows immediately that he is the owner. He is followed into the restaurant by a noisy family that hides him from her sight, parents and two older children, a boy and a girl. They are a sort of reflection of her unrealized hopes, because the four of them are totally enjoying their outing together. They sit down at the table next to them, and she hears them laughing, teasing each other. The father pats the son's shoulder and the daughter and the mother chat and laugh together, and once again a sense of failure chokes her. Instead of chatting with her, her daughter is keeping frightening secrets. Instead of the four of them going out for a family dinner, they are spying on their daughter, at which they seem to be failing too, because she isn't here, there is no trace of her, and if she is sick, who is taking care of her? To all appearances, there is nothing worrying about the place except for her absence, so maybe it really is only a false rumor. As she looks around for the man in the white pants, he comes out of the kitchen, his face slightly red, his gray hair cut short, his eyes dark and intense. When the waitress walks past him, he grabs her by the arm and says something to her. From a distance it's hard to tell if the movement is violent, but when she comes to their table with their food, she is upset and her hands shake slightly as she places bowls of soup, an endive salad, and warm white bread on the table.

"Is everything all right?" she asks them the way waitresses do.

Iris replies with a question. "Is everything all right with you?" But she walks away and returns immediately with menus for the family at the next table, who apparently know the place and all its specials very well, because they order quickly.

She whispers to Mickey, "Did you see him? That's him! That's the Boaz she talks about."

But Mickey is engrossed in his pea soup. "You have to taste this," he says with pleasure, "you have never eaten soup like this. Now I understand why Alma barely eats at home." She looks at him hopelessly, but has to agree that at least as far as the meal is concerned, the chef on the other side of the closed door knows his stuff, she hasn't eaten such superb food in a long time. Should that make her feel better?

Now she sees the owner making his way to the neighboring table carrying a tray, helping the only waitress, who is collapsing under the burden, and he exchanges a few words and smiles with the diners. "You look fantastic, Boaz," the stocky man compliments him. "How do you manage to keep your figure? I wish I could." She doesn't hear Boaz's reply, he speaks in a quiet voice, slowly, but the fact that he is a person in the world, a person whom people know by name and speak to, calms her a bit. Now their main dish arrives, mung beans and polenta, which is absolutely delicious, and a risotto with asparagus that puts a broad smile on Mickey's face. He reads something on his cell phone as he eats, exactly as he does at home, and there is no doubt that this place has a homey atmosphere, she's ready to stretch out on the couch in the corner and take a short nap, but it's too soon to calm down, too soon to go, and apparently too late to expect Alma. They are left with no choice but to ask about her, otherwise they'll leave soon with full stomachs and no information at all, so when the waitress reappears to make sure that all is well and suggest desserts, she asks her, "Tell me, isn't Alma working this evening?"

Although she hasn't said she's Alma's mother, her question makes the waitress uneasy, who blurts out, "Alma? She's not here now."

"Obviously she's not here," Iris says with a smile, "but she still works here, right? When is her next shift?"

The waitress replies curtly, "I'm not authorized to give out information," and disappears without asking what they want for dessert. When Mickey finally looks up from his phone, she sees that, for the first time, he is worried too, and they anxiously watch the waitress walk away.

"She went to report to her boss that we asked about Alma," Iris whispers. She won't pass up an opportunity to be right, even though she would be so happy to be wrong, and very quickly indeed, two glasses of vodka arrive at their table.

"The drinks are on the house," the waitress says with a frozen smile and leaves. Iris looks around for the host and sees him sitting at the bar, a similar glass in his hand. He raises it to them with a smile and takes a sip, but she doesn't return the smile. She expected him to be hostile, but his amiability doesn't calm her, and neither does the fact that the waitress is openly avoiding them even though Iris is signaling her.

"What do you want from her?" Mickey asks, and she replies impatiently, her hand still waving in the air, "It's time for dessert, don't you want something sweet?

"Wait, don't drink," she warns him as he raises the glass to his lips, and he asks, "Why, is it poisoned?"

His question brings a wide grin to the face of the owner, who is approaching them with glass in hand, his black shirt clinging to his body, revealing a tensed, muscular back. Bending toward them, he asks, "How may I help you?"

His speech is slow, as is his glance, which is focused unwaveringly on their faces as if he has nothing to hide, while they do, spies who sneaked in pretending to be innocent diners. Without waiting for their reply, he pulls out a chair and sits down at the head of their table for two, equidistant from both of them.

"Where's Alma? Is she okay?" Iris asks quickly, not bothering to introduce herself.

He smiles serenely, exposing perfectly even white teeth. "Alma is fine, but I don't think you are. Why are you so stressed?" He emphasizes each syllable, his eyes fixed on her lips, waiting to hear what she has to say.

"Why am I stressed? Because I'm worried about my daughter!" she replies, already knowing that she will regret missing the opportunity to begin their conversation more pleasantly, regret that she attacked him right away without trying a friendlier approach first.

"To Alma," he says, raising his glass and drinking its contents in one swallow. "Drink up, it's great vodka." He smiles amiably at Mickey, who empties his glass. "It's very hard to live when you're worried all the time." He points to her full glass, "Look at how wound up you are," and turning to Mickey, "you probably agree with me." The beginning of an annoying smile appears on Mickey's face.

Looking at both of them angrily, she says, "I'm not worried all the time, I'm worried about my daughter now. She's changed since she started working here. I want to know what's happening to her, what kind of relationship you have with her, what working for you entails."

"It's not good to be so suspicious, it contracts the muscles of your soul," he says, again shifting the conversation to her, again fixing his eyes on her. His physical closeness oppresses her the way the closeness of an unpredictable animal would. "Look," he says, "you've come to a new place with your husband, you ate well, you had a drink, and you can't enjoy yourself! All that suspicion!" He clucks his tongue as if he is really and truly concerned about her welfare. "Look at how you respond to me the first time you meet me. Have I done anything to you?"

"The muscles of my soul are not the issue here," she says. "I asked you a simple question. What is happening to my daughter? Where is she now, for instance? We thought she worked evenings here, we came to see her."

He replies immediately, stressing every syllable as if she is deaf or dimwitted. "Alma is working now, but not here. She is doing very important work, spiritual work. You have nothing to worry about, I assure you. If she's changed, it's only for the better. Right now you still can't understand what this is about, you still don't have the tools, but she needs this, let her do it." He looks directly at each of them as if studying the impression his words are making, and then pulls a toothpick out of the holder on the corner of the table and begins to pick his beautiful teeth.

"Spiritual work?" she repeats in horror. "What does that mean? Where is she now? I want to know where my daughter is!"

Still picking his teeth, he smiles. "Tell me, Iris—your name is Iris, isn't it? Is the flower you're named after the child of the sun or of the seed that created it? Is Alma your child or a child of the cosmos? You raised her, educated her, worked for her, gave her everything you have, but now you don't have enough anymore, you don't have what she needs. Now it's time for you to release her, now it's time for her to work for herself."

"You can't tell us how to behave with our daughter," Mickey finally snaps out of his silence, his face heavy and gray, and he looks ill.

"Of course not," Boaz says quickly. "It's just a little advice, and it's not meant for you, but for your wife. You see your daughter, I know, and you're not alarmed by what you see, but your wife doesn't see. It's not easy to live with someone who doesn't see. By the way, where did you acquire your knowledge?"

"The Hebrew University," Mickey replies, confused.

But Boaz clarifies, "No, I mean where did you acquire your deeper knowledge?"

As Mickey wavers between rejecting the compliment and accepting it with open arms, she interjects, "Turning us against each other won't help you. What do you mean, spiritual work? What are you hiding?"

"I should ask you what you're hiding, Iris. But I don't really want to know. Look at you, you're practically collapsing.

Why don't you trust me?" He touches her arm with a gentle and surprisingly small hand. "Your daughter is training, she's doing very important work, she needs to rid herself of preconceptions, accumulations, attachments. Let her go, release her, she's not your property!"

His voice is firm and gentle, and he seems to believe totally in the truth of his words, neither avoiding nor denying, but proud of what he is doing. Should that worry her or reassure her? This is precisely how she tries to train her teachers to speak to their pupils, with gentle firmness. Would she have hired him? The fragrance of aftershave or men's perfume rises from his smooth cheeks and he runs his fingers through his hair in satisfaction. She hasn't met such a well-groomed man in a long time. Should that worry or reassure her?

"She's not your property either," she hisses, "and I'm not sure you remember that. I'm also not sure that everything that goes on here is legal. I'm about to call the police to check out this place."

He smiles as if he has heard a good joke. "You're calling the police because your daughter cut her hair? Because she doesn't come home every day? I can save you the call. That's the district commander and his wife at the next table, he eats here regularly. Do you want to talk to him? Please, go right over." He stands up nimbly and brushes an invisible crumb off his white pants. "I've had enough of this conversation." He looks darkly at them, as if accusing them of something serious. "You know what? Maybe you should talk to Noa. Come here for a minute, Noa'le," he signals the waitress. "Come over and explain to Alma's parents what we do here so they won't worry so much. I'm sorry to say that I couldn't do it, I give up."

With hands raised in surrender, he walks away from them and slaps the stout man on the back like an old friend. He seems to feel remarkably comfortable in his small kingdom, and she watches him in horror. She has never met such a person, and she feels as if his very existence in the world cancels out her own, challenges her world so much that she begins trembling uncontrollably. She puts her hand on Mickey's, who immediately responds by lacing his fingers through hers, and that is how the waitress finds them when she sits down in the seat he vacated. But unlike Boaz Gerber, who sat comfortably, his back pressed against the back of the chair, she perches uneasily on the edge of it, her eyes darting.

"It's awesome that you're holding hands!" she gushes. "I never saw my parents hold hands."

Finding it difficult to accept the compliment, Iris says, "It's rare with us too," dampening the girl's enthusiasm. "Explain to us what goes on here, what this 'spiritual work' is that you do."

"It's hard to explain to an outsider," she says with a quick, rabbity smile, the robotlike tone of her voice becoming almost excited. "I've been here for almost two years and I'm only just beginning to understand! Alma only came four months ago. You can't really learn something about one person's development by looking at someone else's. Noa is not Alma! Alma is doing her own thing! Why do you think that Noa is Alma?" she suddenly bleats.

"Of course you're not Alma," Iris says quickly. With Noa, she at least feels comfortable, trying to reassure her as she would a frightened pupil, while in the face of Boaz's smug confidence, she herself became a frightened, aggressive pupil. Was she too aggressive? Would the appearance of trust have made the conversation more productive? It's too late anyway, and she is in the midst of another conversation, no less important, so smiling warmly, she reassures Noa, "Naturally, everyone's development is different, but since you're an old-timer here, I'd love to hear about your experience, what you've been through since you came here."

"It's really hard to explain. At first, everything, like, falls apart?" she says, her lips moist, her slightly watery eyes moving between them. "You meet someone like him and you realize you've been living a lie? Not that you're, like, liars, you're her parents, but you don't know her, and she met someone here who could see everything that was holding her back and help her liberate herself from it. When I first came here and he told me all the things that were holding me back, I was in shock."

"What, for example?" Iris interrupts the confused, breathless monologue.

Noa answers quickly. "For example, I always knew I was a bad person!" she declares almost proudly. "I was born that way, it's not my fault, I was born a bad person who can't give. It gets in my way, not anyone else's! I can't love, can't empathize, I'm not a generous person, and no one would ever tell me that! They all stabbed me in the back. They said to me, you're good, you're fine. No one ever helped me. Until I met Boaz, no one dared to say to me, Noa, you're a bad person! You're a bad soul, you need to liberate yourself!"

"How did you liberate yourself?" Iris asks, stunned, trying to hide her horror, to conceal any criticism in her tone.

Noa sighs as if she hasn't been properly understood. "That's exactly what the spiritual work is!" she cries. "Boaz teaches us to set ourselves free, he teaches us everything he's learned in life. He makes us a gift of all the knowledge he's accumulated, bit by bit. I came looking for work and found a teacher, a real teacher, there's no other way to explain it!"

"I understand," Iris says softly. "I'm sure you're doing excellent work. But exactly what kind of work is Alma doing? Is she a bad person too?"

Noa shakes her head. "No, Alma's different! Alma's a delicate soul! But she's not open. She needs to open up! She's too restrained, she doesn't know how to free herself. Her ego is strong," she adds excitedly, her cheeks flushing, "she has to learn how to let it go, to, like, shed it? With the spiritual work she's doing, she's hewing her path herself! It's like being reborn!"

"Hewing?" Iris asks.

"Yes, hewing! Because she's turned into stone, just like me. Until I came here, I lived twenty-two years that turned me into stone. Now she has to hew away at the stone and turn it into something beautiful. It's hard, what she's going through, but it's the only way!" she adds passionately.

"What you're telling me is very interesting," Iris says, her tone contemplative. Then she adds casually, "Why are you short-handed this evening? Where is Alma now, is she sick?"

Noa shakes her head firmly. "She's not sick, she's fine, it doesn't matter where she is now, the important thing is that she's doing work, she's freeing herself from the preconceptions."

"What preconceptions?" Iris tries to wrap the question in a reassuring smile, but her lips seem to have ossified. She is apparently hewed out of stone too, and if only she hadn't asked, because Noa is already on her feet.

"I have to get back to the customers." She bows oddly in farewell. "All kinds of preconceptions, our lives are full of preconceptions, like the idea that we have to have possessions?

And attachments? Like we should be paid for working? Like we have to know someone before we sleep with him?"

She immediately returns to her professional, almost robotic voice as she turns her back to them and begins suggesting desserts to the family at the adjacent table. Mickey, who has been listening to the conversation with his head lowered, looks over at her slowly, and he seems shocked and upset. His eyes are red and the corners of his mouth turn downward as he says in a hoarse voice, "I want to get out of here."

"Me too," she whispers, almost laughing to learn how strong those preconceptions are, because it's a fact that of the entire flow of manipulative clichés, it is the last bit of information, served as dessert, that has defeated them. She wants to say, in a pathetic attempt at humor, that they apparently have much spiritual work to do, but the way he looks alarms her no less than the information they have just received.

He drops her hand, clutches his chest, and whispers, "I don't feel well. I have pressure in my chest."

"Oh Mickey," she says, frightened. "I'll call an ambulance."

But he refuses, "Don't get carried away, let's just go home." He takes some money out of his wallet, puts it on the table, and stands up heavily without waiting for the check, leaning on her as he walks. To their great relief, if it is at all possible to feel relief, they don't bump into the owner, who has apparently disappeared into the kitchen. Only Noa watches them in concern, but the sight of the money on the table satisfies her, and she waves goodbye as the door closes behind their defeated backs.

"Should we drive straight to the emergency room? What exactly are you feeling? Does your arm hurt too?" she asks as he holds on to a lamppost, panting.

"I have pressure in my chest, it's hard to breathe, I want to go home. Oh, Iris, I've never felt so humiliated in my life." With her arm around his waist, she leads him to the car, sits him down in the passenger seat, and tilts it back. When she sits down beside him, in the driver's seat, a hand knocks on the window, and she is so startled to see bills pressed against the glass that she opens the door instead of the window, revealing a pair of white pants glowing in the dark.

"You're my guests," Boaz says, "I don't take money from you," and he vanishes as the bills float onto her thighs.

FIFTEEN

Like a distorted mirror image of lovemaking, mourning shared
by a couple is not expressed in words, but only in moans and
sighs that rise from a tortured mind struggling against painful
knowledge. As they drive home, she realizes why this is so
much like the night she learned of her father's death. It is a
night of disasters, a night so cursed that, let not God inquire
after it from above, neither let the light shine upon it. Even
though their daughter has not died, she has been taken cap-
tive. How can they save her, and if she can be saved at all,
how damaged and battered will she be? Black winds envelop
the car as it ascends from the coastal plain to the hills, winds
of ignominy and ire, of disgrace and degradation. She can
barely see the road on that night of overwhelming grief. The
still-hidden moon makes a mockery of the meager illumina-
tion of the headlights and she drives with wide-open eyes, her
head almost touching the windshield.

Every now and then, the honking of a nearby car warns her that she is veering out of her lane, and she straightens the car in a panic. If only he could take over the driving, but he is in worse shape than she is; after all, she was ready for the news, while it hit him like a lightning bolt. He lies on his seat moaning, one hand on his chest, the other clutching the door handle.

"Iris, I have to throw up," he shouts suddenly. "Pull over to the side for a minute!" She groans. How will she get to the side of the road with all the traffic? Everyone seems to be fleeing Tel Aviv tonight, cars race forward on either side of them, and even if she does finally manage to pull over, the shoulder is so narrow it's dangerous. But why shouldn't a car hit them, she almost hopes for a moment, as she slows and turns to the side, exhausted. One blow will release them from this humiliating existence that has suddenly taken control of them, or perhaps it has always been there and only now do they see it.

Only now does she notice how close they are to the interchange where her car awaits her, where he picked her up a few hours earlier, when she still hoped that she was wrong, that she was exaggerating. It seemed as if years have passed since then, how old they have both become. She supports him as he gets out of the car and when he manages to stand on his own by holding on to a tree trunk, he asks her to move away from him. He hates to vomit, she knows, but his body firmly rejects all the food he had enjoyed so much. A sour smell rises from the bushes as he heaves, absorbed by the smells of the night, blending with the scent of fig trees, hay, exhaust spewing from the cars straining to ascend the hill, smoke drifting from a distant campfire. The stomach-churning fumes of roasted meat, burnt blood, rise in her throat. For a moment, she feels as if her tongue, moving in her mouth almost uncontrollably, is turning into the hairy tail of the animal she was forced to swallow. She drops to her knees, her head spinning, and lets the lump that has accumulated in her stomach fly out of her mouth. Now we too are divesting ourselves of preconceptions, we don't have to accumulate, we don't have to adhere to anything.

Like two pagans, they kneel on the main road under the black sky, offering up their vomit to the local gods, crying out for a miracle. He seems to be feeling a bit better, because he walks over to her with lighter steps. She hears them crushing dry branches on the rocky ground, but she can't lift her head, it's so heavy and painful. She too, it turns out, is made of stone, hewed out of rock, a rigid sculpture of a mother.

Shaking, she drops onto the ground beside her vomit as if it is all she possesses, seized by agonizing contractions from head to toe. It was on exactly such a night that Alma was conceived. She knew that for a fact because Mickey was on reserve duty and her longing to become pregnant was so intense that she was thrilled to discover that his only day off was the day she could conceive. She wasn't bothered by the memory of the night her father died, on the contrary, she actually hoped to erase that cursed memory by creating a tiny being just beginning to make its way in the world, to sweeten the world, at least their world. But now the taste of the world is horribly bitter in her mouth, as if she has been poisoned and is dying among the bushes.

"Let's go, Iris," he says, his voice muted and distant, seeming to rise from the bowels of the earth. "Come on, we can't stay here all night." She tries to take the hand he holds out to her as she sways on her knees. They both reek as if they are rotting bodies left on the road after a hit-and-run accident that hurled them out of sight. Almost twenty-two years ago, they lay naked on their bed in their first apartment. They hadn't seen each other for two weeks and the yearning they felt combined with her desire to conceive created the false impression of love. Showered and scented, lithe and lustful, they tried to fuse the gold of their love into a singular amalgam, and now they stumble to their car, heavy and rank, stiff and despairing. "I'll wash the car tomorrow," Mickey mumbles as he sits down at the wheel instead of her. All the way to the apartment, she turns those words over in her mind again and again, laughing wildly, "I'll wash the car tomorrow." There can be no better news than that, it seems to her, because there is no hope greater than that, there are no consoling words more profound than those.

She'll laugh even in her sleep, if she falls asleep at all. Alma's bed repels her as if it is infested with dangerous germs, plague, boils, the slaying of the firstborn. Her daughter is sick, and how will she be healed? Only that morning, she lay there on those sheets and said, "I found myself in Jerusalem." Who touched her on the way? Nausea rises in her throat again as she pictures the man in the white pants lying in this bed beside Noa and Alma, who lick his body from head to toe, purring like cats. She flees to the double bed, where Mickey, who has already come out of the shower, is lying with closed eyes. Tonight she prefers his snoring to the voices that rise from within her.

"What will you do tomorrow, Mooky?" she asks him.

"I'll wash the car."

She laughs hysterically, as she did in the shower, and now again in bed, wrapped in a towel because she doesn't have the strength to dry herself or put on a nightgown. He'll wash the car, he'll wash the car inside and out and everything will be fine. Maybe he'll use the hose to wash Alma inside and out as well, cleansing her the way the dead are cleansed before burial, and then he'll seal her orifices with wax. After all, she is in fact dead, it isn't a rebirth but a living death. Her laughter dies and she burrows under the damp sheets, her teeth chattering, cautiously approaching the heavy body beside her.

"There's a whale in bed!" the children used to scream happily, pretending to be frightened as they fled. But now the whale radiates pleasant heat and she presses up against him, sheltered in the shadow of his sleep. Where are you now, the little girl who ran away from the whale? What animal have you found in your bed tonight? From a distance, those Saturday mornings in winter return to her, the children jumping around their bed in their pajamas, the house heated, and the smell of vegetarian cholent wafting through the rooms. Usually it didn't end well, because Omer became too wild, but at first, you could still enjoy the warmth of their small bodies, the languidness of the morning when they didn't have to hurry off, the naturalness of the family. How had Eitan put it—"You built a home and a family." But she doesn't want to think about him now or read the texts he sent. She can't take comfort in him or yearn for him, can't see him and can't give him up, because of all the identities she has accumulated in her life, only one remains. She is Alma's mother, and that identity does not suit him, she felt that strongly when she tried to tell Eitan about her. Nor does it suit her to be Alma's mother at his side, but rather to be at the side of Alma's father, because on those Saturday mornings when Alma jumped happily around their bed, her cheeks red with excitement and her brown hair covering her face, Mickey was beside her. She tries to imagine pushing Alma's hair off her face, she wants to see her again, her glowing coal-black eyes, her pug nose and full lips, but when she is finally able to do so, she sees only an empty, featureless face and she cries out. She must have dropped off for a moment straight into a nightmare, and she flees to the living room, there's a whale in bed!

One by one, she takes dusty photo albums off the bookshelves above the couch—back then, they took the trouble to develop pictures and didn't bury them in the computer—and until dawn, she watches her daughter grow from the day of her birth to adolescence, searching for the seed of the calamity. There was always a secret in her face, and now, in retrospect, it seems fateful. But things need to be seen for what they are, stripped of the fiery clothes the future clads them in. With compassion and horror, she caresses the still forming face, covers it with kisses, don't worry, my sweet child, my poor little girl, you're not alone, I'll rescue you despite your protests. She feels as if she is working hand in hand with all the budding little girls in the pictures to triumph over the big girl who has grown from them.

But how will she rescue her? Will she imprison her in the house, or whisk her away to Paris or Berlin? How will she separate them? If Alma truly loves him, the way she loved Eitan in her youth, or more precisely, the way she loves him to this day, how will she separate them? What can she offer her daughter that will be as powerful as what she is experiencing with him, the total loss of body and soul in a union larger and deeper than they are? A biscuit cake? A heart-to-heart with Mom? Shopping at the mall? All those trivialities that made her so happy when she was a child no longer affect her, and even then, her happiness was fragile. She suddenly remembers her sixth birthday, the small surprise party they gave for her at home for only the immediate family, the grandmother and the still-single uncles. The living room was filled with balloons, a tempting pile of gifts lay on the couch, the cake was covered with decorations and candles, and even little Omer was calm. But when she came in—Mickey brought her from her ballet class straight to the surprise—and the light came on and everyone leaped toward her singing and shouting "Happy Birthday," she stood unsmiling at the entrance to the living room in her pink tutu and ballet shoes. It was clear that, although she wanted to, she was unable to be happy because she hadn't performed well in class and couldn't overcome her disappointment to make room for her birthday party. Iris clearly remembers the dawning, depressing awareness that her ability to make her daughter happy was already quite limited.

Until that moment, she had thought that if she agreed to buy her ice cream or gum, that if she took her to a movie or a playground, she'd be totally happy the way only small children can be. But it turned out that twenty balloons, five presents, a cake with candles, and a loving family could not erase her disappointment in herself. With tears in her eyes, she sat down on her special, decorated birthday chair, sorry as well about the disappointment she was causing all the guests. It was obvious that the gathering, which she absolutely did not want then, nearly doubled her sorrow, and Iris felt almost angry with her. We took so much trouble to do this for you and you don't even deign to smile. Now too, her anger flares up momentarily, after all we gave you, you're taken in by some sleek charlatan who spouts endless streams of nonsense the likes of which I have never heard before and you're ready to put your life in his hands. But her anger quickly turns into compassion and concern; after all, the fact that she has fallen so hard means that her distress is so deep. This is not the time for anger, but rather for action. She knows there are experts in the field, but she prefers to try by herself, to do everything to bring Alma close to her, to gain her trust, without judging or criticizing, and then to slowly spread doubt in her mind. It will take time and she may fail, but she will devote every minute, every fiber of her being, to the attempt. On the dawn of this new day, already blazing and blinding at its outset like a baby born an adult, she understands that her life has changed. Not only has her daughter lost her freedom, but she has lost hers as well, because her daughter has fallen ill with an acute disease, and until she is healed, she will be enslaved to her. But unlike parents enslaved to their sick children, taking them for treatments and seeing to their every need, she must do it with cunning, with deception, behind her daughter's back and against her will.

It is in the intense light flooding the living room that her eyes finally close, but the sound of a phone ringing insistently wakes her. Who is calling Mickey at five in the morning? Is there a glitch in the system again? With barely open eyes, she walks toward the sound. Where did he leave his cell phone and what secrets will she find in it? Only yesterday her truth was left bare at home, and this morning it's his. She manages to pull the phone from his pants, which are hanging on the bedroom door, at the precise moment it stops ringing, and the name on the screen both frightens and calms her.

"Mickey, Alma wants to talk to you," she says, shaking his shoulder.

He opens dull eyes and reaches out for the phone. "Hello," he mumbles sleepily.

"She hung up already, call her back."

He sits up heavily and leans against the wall. "I don't know what to say, you talk to her." His bitter breath wafts toward her.

"But she wants you, not me," she protests just as her phone rings on the living room table, and she hurries to answer it. "Alma?" she blurts breathlessly before checking the name, "Alma, is that you?"

In the silence, she hears a low male voice. "Rissi, I'm worried about you, you didn't get back to me. Are you okay?"

She hears Mickey approaching, ears perked to hear the conversation with their daughter. "Put it on speaker," he says, and she ends the call immediately. It never occurred to her that it would be Eitan, he never calls at this hour, and now she has no choice but to call Alma, to avoid arousing suspicion.

She is so relieved when her daughter answers that she says cheerfully, "Hi, Alma, we were cut off," as if they were in the middle of a cheery conversation.

"What are you talking about?" her daughter barks. "I called Dad, not you. What was that visit all about? What right do you have to follow me? Why didn't you tell me you were coming?"

Her voice is so frigid that Iris can barely find words. "We're not your enemies, Alma, we love you, we worry about you." But the words that only a few minutes ago were whispered in her ear cause her daughter to end the conversation she doesn't want, just as she herself did a moment ago, and she sinks onto the couch hopelessly. "You try," she says to Mickey as he sits down beside her, dropping his phone on the table, "you're the one she wanted to talk to."

"I don't know what to say to her," he repeats in frustration.

But she insists, "She'll do the talking, don't worry, the important thing is to maintain contact." He sighs, but in the end does what she wants.

"Hi sweetie," he says, "are you okay? ... What do you mean, ambush? We came to see you, we were sure you'd be there, and meanwhile we heard a little bit about the place, about the spiritual work you're doing. We were very impressed." His voice is convincing, and Iris listens in admiration, surprised he can pretend so well. She never actually saw him do it before. Does he also pretend this well with her? Does he know that she is keeping a secret from him, and is he keeping one from her? Heavy-handed, slightly clumsy Mickey, who speaks little, is breezing through a conversation that she, with all her educational experience, was unable to have. In the end, he even manages to persuade their daughter to come home in the next few days and tell them more about the important spiritual work she is doing.

"Hats off to you," she says, accompanying her words with the doff of an imaginary hat. "Well done, Mooky, I'm very impressed."

But he doesn't let the compliment turn his head. "She doesn't sound good, Iris, she's completely brainwashed." With a sigh, he stretches out on the large couch, crossing his arms on his chest. "I'm having a hard time breathing, I won't go to work today."

"Of course you won't. Let's go to the emergency room, we have to check this out."

"No, it'll be okay," he replies dismissively. "I'll go to the clinic later."

He lies silently on the couch in his underpants, a beached whale, breathing heavily, his skin smooth and tan, his thighs pressed together and his crossed ankles looking like a huge fin. His lids flutter over his closed eyes and he doesn't see Omer come out of his room with his usual morning sourness, his Mohawk jutting up from his head.

"What happened to Dad?" he asks angrily.

"We got home late last night and he's very tired," she says.

Omer eyes her suspiciously. "You look wiped out too. This family is falling apart, isn't it?" Without waiting for a reply, he adds, "Make me two sandwiches today, okay? And give me some money, I have a civics final after lunch."

"Oh, right, I completely forgot."

"You've been forgetting me a lot lately, Mom," he says, looking down at her.

When did he grow so much? She's losing him, the anxiety once again churning in her stomach, she's losing him and soon he'll be in the army. She picks up a sharp knife and cuts the still-frozen rolls in half. "Sorry, Omer, these things happen sometimes."

"It's okay Mom, I don't take it personally. Just tell me if you need help from me." He turns his beautiful back to her and goes to his room to get dressed, and she follows him with her gaze. When did he grow up so much, and not only physically, when did he turn into such an impressive young man?

She did it, she succeeded with him, and on this morning in particular, she realizes that she can feel pride, not only failure. She succeeded, and soon they will be forced to part, the army will take him. Is that why she devoted herself to him more than to Alma? Is that what this country does to mothers, raising their sons in the shadow of a sense that their time with them is limited? Or is it only her, whose father was taken from her by war? She beats the eggs furiously, what does one have to do with the other? He was just the kind of boy who required special efforts, it had nothing to do with the country or the army, she thinks, shaking her head again and again over the yellow liquid that is now solidifying and bubbling in the frying pan. She gave him more because he demanded more. Did he demand more because she allowed him to? Does the country demand more because its citizens allow it to? Good luck on your civics test, son, I passed my test with you beyond all expectations. She stuffs the hot omelet into the frozen rolls, wraps them quickly and puts them on the table. Her efforts bore fruit, and the Israeli Defense Forces, which devoured her father's scorched body, will devour that fruit hungrily as well. But why get ahead of herself, he hasn't even received his first induction order yet.

As she is dressing quickly, the smell of something burning spreads through the apartment. Smoke is rising from the frying pan. Omer reproaches her patronizingly, "Where's your head, Mom, you didn't turn off the gas!" He likes to see himself that way with her, strong and firm. She was omnipotent for too many years.

"What luck, Omer, you saved us," she says.

"I mainly saved Dad," he quips, "we're on our way out." They both look at Mickey lying on the couch immobile, only his eyelids still fluttering.

She goes over to him, puts her hand on his forehead, and says, "How do you feel, Mooky?"

"A little better," he mumbles, "but I won't be able to wash the car today, Iris, I'm really sorry to disappoint you."

She says softly, "I'll get over it, but only if you go to the clinic."

If it weren't the last day of the school year, she would have stayed with him, but she has so many things to do today, no matter how worried or tired she is. She calls every hour to make sure he's okay, and keeps asking her secretary for more cups of strong black coffee. She can't shake off the end-of-year sadness, the feeling that something has been lost prematurely, taken in the prime of its life. With bitterness in her heart, she listens to the teachers chatting cheerfully, looking forward to summer vacation, planning trips abroad with their families. She too has been offered a tempting trip, an invitation to join him at a conference in Rome, could anything in the world have made her happier? But there is no room for happiness in her life now, not that kind of happiness in any case. Don't rejoice at the passing of time, she wants to tell all the excited new graduates who come to say goodbye to her, and she looks fearfully at the children she has known since they were in the first grade. If only you could be frozen at the age you are now, your skin still smooth, before pimples and scraggly face hair, before the army. What does life have in store for you, my dear little girls, she thinks, hugging the twelve-year-olds about to set out on a new path, I wish you could remain little girls. Alma was once twelve years old and wore a school uniform, came home at lunchtime and told me how her day at school was, and even if she didn't tell me much, she didn't keep secrets from me.

When her office is empty for a moment, she closes the door and puts her head on her desk, trying to remember the summer Alma was their age and had completed the sixth grade, but nothing comes to mind. Apparently that entire year of Alma has been erased from her memory, and perhaps it never existed in it at all. She lost it because of her injury, because of the operations, the hospitalizations, the rehabilitation. Is that why she has lost her forever?

"Iris, someone wants you," Ofra says, opening the door gently.

"Tell them I'm busy," she replies angrily, but Ofra, who always looks after her zealously, says in a cryptic voice, "It sounds important."

"Everything sounds important," she grumbles, "but nothing really is." She lifts her head and sees him standing in the doorway of her office, embarrassed and unkempt, a thin, gray-haired man with a young man's eyes, wearing worn-out jeans and a faded T-shirt that looks left over from those youthful days. For a moment, she doesn't recognize him because he doesn't belong to this place or time, he doesn't belong to her, and the pain she's had all day becomes unbearably stronger. "Eitan, is that you?" she mumbles, "how did you find me?" She goes over to him, puts her arms around his neck, and rests her head on his shoulder in plain sight of her longtime secretary, who hurries out and closes the door behind her. Apparently her pride at being right about the importance of this meeting is greater than her curiosity about what it means.

"Eitan, my daughter's sick," she says, pressing up against him as if she is about to leave for a battle she will never return from, not to him.

He strokes her hair and whispers in her ear, "I was worried about you, I knew something happened. What's wrong with her? Can I help?"

"It's not her body, it's her mind. She's being controlled, I have to save her," she mumbles as his lips burn on her forehead, her hair, and her brain seems to be on fire. She has waited so long for him. Are they too late?

"My love," he whispers, "Rissi, don't give up on me."

She sighs, "Oh, Eitan, even if I wanted to, I couldn't." She loves him so much at this moment, the expression of sorrow and shock on his face as it was on the days he came to her from his mother's sickbed. As she looks at him, a flame of sorrow scorches her. She is so tired, it's the last day of the school year and she wants to sleep now, standing up, with her head on his shoulder and her hands on the back of his neck. How much she loved falling asleep in his arms, nothing separating them, breathing in the air that he breathed out. "We haven't slept together yet," she whispers, "I want to sleep beside you and never get up." She thinks of the frying pan she left on the fire that morning. We'll burn so intensely that we'll fuse together, no one will be able to tell that there were two of us. Day after day, night after night, we'll be together.

"Come to me tonight," he asks, "or tomorrow? It turns out the kids aren't coming."

"I wish I could, I have to help Alma, she lives in Tel Aviv." Even though she doesn't know how she will actually help her that night, or the next.

He sighs, "Okay, I understand, tell me if I can do anything." He kisses her forehead and lifts her head from his shoulder. "I have to get back to the clinic. Call me when you can."

She leans against her desk, swaying. Her office has never been so empty as when he leaves it, pale and sad, her old young man who was late in returning. She collapses onto the desk, yellow Post-its stick to her hair. I won't give up, Eitan, I just have to focus on Alma now—does he even know her name?—I'll help her and come back, wait for me. She wants to run after him, to promise him, persuade him, disappear inside him, but exhaustion and sorrow have turned her feet into stone. A moment later, Ofra opens the floodgates and the throng of pupils who have once again gathered at her door enters en masse. She stares at them in confusion, says goodbye, hugs them, wishes them good luck. She has hugged so many people that day, but her arms are still embracing his beloved back, for almost thirty years they have embraced.

"What was Dr. Rosen doing here? I hope he didn't come to enroll his son," the school guidance counselor says as she enters the finally empty office carrying a pile of files.

Iris asks in surprise, "You know him? How do you know him?"

"He treated my mother once," Daniella says, "and when he heard what I do, he told me a little bit about his son, who had just been expelled from school. Apparently seriously disturbed. I deliberately didn't recommend our school, I didn't like what he told me. Do me a favor, Iris, don't accept him, we have enough trouble without him."

"You have no idea how much," she says, but naturally, she has to know more. "What scared you so much?" The years have taught her to trust Daniella's perceptions.

"I had the impression that the child was lost," Daniella says, "and no one really cared. The mother was still trying to find herself. The father tried, but didn't know what being a father means. You know the type, terribly busy, feels guilty, buys presents instead of setting limits. Something there was not working."

"He told you a lot," Iris remarks, digesting the uncomplimentary information uneasily.

Daniella rolls her eyes and says, "That's my karma, people just look at me and spill all! I waited six months for an appointment with him. He seemed like God to me, and then it turned out that even God has problems."

"Did he help your mother?"

"By the time we saw him, there wasn't much to be done, but yes, he relieved her pain. He's a good doctor, and he's a good man, I think, just a bit lost, cut off. I remember him telling me terrible stories about his son with a kind of smile, as if he didn't understand what he was saying. There are gaps in him, he hasn't really grown up."

"Wow, you actually diagnosed him."

Daniella smiles. "Yes, he interested me. I saw him a lot during that period, mainly when my mother was hospitalized. He was very devoted to her, even came to her funeral."

"Really?" Iris says in surprise.

Daniella nods proudly. "I told you, he's a good person. In general, pain doctors are more humane."

But it wasn't his presence at the funeral that astonished Iris, rather the fact that she could actually have met him there, a year and a half ago, because she had been there too, crowded under an umbrella with some of the teachers, her boots sunk in mud. If only she had looked up, she would have seen him, and then perhaps they would have had more time together. A year and a half ago, she had more room for love in her life because Alma was okay then, a fine soldier on an intelligence corps base in the field, monitoring the border fence. Apart from the fact that Iris had to wash and iron her uniform every weekend, she took up a very small part of their lives. Had they ignored the warning signs? Their difficult child was usually Omer, and they took it for granted that she was a bit reserved, closed. Her love life was minimal: there was a huge Russian boy who came to see her occasionally until he disappeared, followed by another one, very much like him. Mickey gritted his teeth when they closed themselves in her room, but none of them lasted, none of them even stayed until morning. They thought she still wasn't mature enough, that she was a closed bud that had yet to blossom. It was unthinkable that it would be plucked before it opened—how had Noa put it, "Alma isn't open, Alma needs to open up." She shakes her head, how did it happen, how did it happen to us?

"What did you say?" Daniella asks as she arranges the files on the wall shelves, and Iris tries to pull herself together.

"Sorry," she says, "my head is somewhere else."

"That's for sure," Daniella says. "Where is it? When will you learn to ask for help? Aren't you tired of that rigid education of yours?"

"Definitely, but you really don't need my troubles, believe me."

Smiling, Daniella says, "What's wrong with other people's troubles? There's nothing like them to make you stronger. You're taking a vacation, I hope. Here or abroad?"

"Here, I want to stay with my daughter in Tel Aviv for a few days."

"That's great, I forgot that Alma's a Tel Avivian now!" Daniella cries a bit too enthusiastically. "How is the little princess? I haven't seen her in a long time."

Iris grimaces at the grating expression and says, "That's so unlike you, Daniella. When we start calling them princes and princesses, they're sure they deserve everything, and so are we."

"You're right, "but Alma was always so princessy, with her dark skin and long hair, like a little Queen of Sheba."

Iris blurts out, "She just cut off all her hair and dyed it black, and that's only the symptom."

Daniella picks up her bag angrily. "Damn, when they're little, we want them to grow up already, and when they grow up, we realize that it's much more difficult. Please call if you need help, okay? And don't accept Rosen's son, even if he promised you medical cannabis till the day you die. Bye for now."

She blows her a kiss, and after she leaves, Iris's small office is once again flooded with so many goodbyes, thank-yous and good-lucks that she forgets to call Mickey. When he calls her, she forgets that he isn't at work, and is surprised when he says, "You should come home, Iris, your daughter is here."

That "your daughter" means that their encounter isn't going well, because he tends to speak about Omer that way, she thinks on her way home after hurriedly finishing the last round of farewells. But she has no idea of how bad it actually is until the elevator doors open and the shouting blasts her ears. She sees Mickey lying on the couch, covered by a thin blanket, one hand clutching his chest and the other over his face. Her daughter, his daughter, is standing on the other side of the living room table screeching at him. She must have been doing it for a while because Iris has only just come in and hears her shouting the same thing over and over again, "You ruined everything! You ruined my life! How could you do it? Are you happy now that you ruined my life?"

She feels sorry for Mickey and wants to get between them, but she immediately changes her mind and walks over to her daughter. "Alma, I don't understand, explain to me how we ruined your life."

Alma replies hoarsely—how could such a small face contain so much hatred—"You! How can you even ask? You, with your nastiness and suspicion! How dare you come to a place that's mine and ask questions about me, insult the first person in my life who understands me, threaten to call the police on him? What were you thinking? Did you even think about me, or only about yourself, as usual?" Suddenly drained, she drops onto the small, flowered couch and says, "You ruined my life. With parents like you, it's better to be an orphan!"

What do you know about being an orphan, Iris wants to say, how dare you talk to us like that, but this isn't the time for predictable responses. She has to surprise her, not to spout the obvious. Alma's slender back bends and heaves, her face is buried in her hands—Iris has forgotten how tiny her daughter is, and for a moment is surprised at her smallness. She sits down on the couch beside her. She is still wearing the same dark clothes—how long has she been wearing them?—and she smells of sweat and cigarettes, and even slightly of urine.

"Alma'le," she says, putting a cautious hand on her back, "I'm so sorry if our visit caused harm. We were hoping to see you, to surprise you."

Her daughter straightens up, shakes her mother's hand off her back, and shouts, "Surprise? A surprise like that birthday party you gave me when I was six? You still don't know that I hate surprises?"

"I guess I don't," Iris mumbles, recoiling from the stench of Alma's breath. She was always so clean and well groomed, with her crop tops and short shorts, her barrettes and perfumes. "Tell me how it ruined your life," she asks, knowing she is provoking another attack.

Of course, her daughter shouts right back at her, "What is there to explain? You think Boaz needed that parents' meeting? That place is not a school! Now he's telling me, why should I have to deal with a little girl? Go back to your mommy and daddy, who know what's good for you, and you'll end up like them, it'll be great for you! He canceled all my shifts for a week!"

"I really don't understand his response," she says. "I mean, it's not your fault we came! Don't worry, we'll make up the difference in your salary."

But it's so difficult to say the right thing, it turns out, because her daughter jumps up again and looks at her, eyes flashing. "You think this is about money?" she says disdainfully, "You're even more materialistic than I thought!"

"You mean you don't work there? He doesn't pay you a salary?" she asks, clinging to the last vestige of outward appearances, to the calming certainties of the old world.

"You think he should pay me?" her daughter hisses. "I'm the one who should pay him for everything he's teaching me! I'm trying to repay him with work! But now that I don't have any shifts, I won't have any lessons either!"

"What lessons?" she asks, stunned.

Alma repeats her question, "What lessons? He teaches me! He's my teacher!"

"What does he teach you, Alma?"

Mickey interrupts in a broken voice, "So how do you pay your expenses, Alma?" She realizes that he is already expecting the worst.

But their daughter blurts out quickly, "I waitress some-where else in the morning, how much do I need anyway! All I need is to keep doing my spiritual work, and you ruined even that for me!"

"Please explain what that means exactly," she asks, trying to show real interest, without doubt or scorn.

Alma replies in a calmer voice, apparently caught be-tween the need to guard her privacy and the missionary desire of every true believer to spread the word of the new doctrine. "I'm learning new things about myself and the world! I'm learning to become free of my ego and reach the real me, to free myself from all the preconceptions! Don't think it's easy, it's like hewing stone!"

"Give me a concrete example, okay? I still don't really understand," Iris says, trying to hide the anxiety that the word "preconception" arouses in her.

Her daughter says, "For example, my laziness? You always accused me of being lazy, but now I know that it only looked like laziness, it was really ego! Understand? We talk openly about everything I feel is holding me back and I free myself of it! We break down the personality and rebuild it, but only with things we decide should be in it!"

"Wow, that's fantastic!" Iris says. "I didn't know that was even possible."

Alma continues eagerly, "Of course it's possible! For in-stance, I need to ask myself who the real Alma is because there are two people inside me, one good and one bad. Bad Alma is someone spoiled and too closed, who accumulates anger, who's used to receiving and not giving, who's locked up inside the experiences she knows. Her parents reinforced this bad Alma to bolster their own egos." She goes on talking about herself and about them in the third person, as if they weren't her audience. "Only now, thanks to Boaz, am I starting to know the good Alma, the real Alma!"

"Tell me about her," Iris asks unnecessarily, because her daughter continues speaking even without being asked.

"Good Alma is open, her instincts infinite! She has no limits! She can fall in love, try new things, she's free, she's curious. You always told me that I wasn't curious enough," she says, as if trying to placate her mother, and Iris listens to her tensely. How satanic and clever to make a person believe that one's weaknesses are one's true self. Nonetheless, she senses there is a glimmer of truth in all that nonsense because she has always wondered why her daughter is so closed, so passive, so restrained. What a strange life she has, Iris sometimes thought, not very different from the fish she raised in the aquarium. After school, she used to sit in front of the TV in the living room watching the series she liked, sometimes the same episode over and over again. She went out only with girlfriends on Friday nights, in the army as well. Even when she communed with the mirror, there was no satisfaction, only tension. "Look, my left eyebrow is shorter than the right one!" she once shouted when Iris came into her room with clean laundry and found her looking in the mirror, horrified. "And if it is, so what? No one's perfect," she replied, and naturally, Alma stopped sharing her minor distresses with her. But now she is definitely sharing.

Listening to her words, spoken in a more moderate, almost didactic tone now, Iris thinks the scene might give the appearance of normalcy—parents listening to their mature daughter telling them about her life and her studies—especially if you focus on the tone and don't dwell on the content. When she calms down a bit, she begins to feel hungry and tired, all the ordinary feelings that fade in times of danger, and she says, "Want to come into the kitchen and cook something with me, Alma? By the way, the food in your place is fantastic! We haven't had such a good meal in a long time." She tries to speak lightly, leaving out, of course, the information about their bitter vomiting on the road.

Alma, now stretched out on the couch, also seems ready to calm down, to abandon herself to the comfort of appearances. "I'll just rest for a minute," she says.

Iris gives Mickey an encouraging look—see, she's staying, she's less hostile. When they are willing to listen, she is willing to speak, and maybe, for the moment, that's more important than what she is actually saying. But he gives her a dark look in return, which she has to ignore, and she makes herself ask in a cheerful voice, "Want a salad? Maybe we'll fry some halloumi cheese?" Although they are lying motionless on parallel couches and don't answer her, she goes into the kitchen feeling a sense of relief.

Alma is here now, with them, and even if she came intending to admonish them, she is upset and asking for their help. If they are clever enough, they can get closer to her. They must not utter a single word of criticism, they have to show total acceptance, even in their body language. Iris leisurely sets the table for four. Omer will be home soon and they'll sit at the table the way they used to, passing the salad bowl, the cheese, the olives, the eggs, the bread. Tomorrow is the first day of summer vacation, not hers, of course, but still, she can allow herself more flexible working hours, a few days off here and there. If she focuses only on her daughter and doesn't think, even for a moment, of the opportunity she has been given to love once again, she may manage to feel a comforting sense, if not of happiness, then of satisfaction, the satisfaction of having avoided disaster.

Perhaps she'll lock her in the house and not let her out? She once saw a movie like that about the mother of a soldier, and took comfort in the fact that Omer was still a little boy. But Omer is no longer a little boy, and her anxiety about his impending induction into the army is growing more acute. And now it seems that even young female citizens need to be locked away occasionally in order to protect them from enemies, even unarmed, internal ones.

"Alma, Mickey, come to the table," she calls calmly, and to her joy, Alma jumps up from the couch immediately and sits down in her usual place. Does her improved mood have anything to do with the texts she has been receiving with such loud frequency, or is it because she feels that her mother is really trying to understand what she's going through? Mickey stumbles in after her, heavy and slow, wearing khaki pants and a gray undershirt that shows his huge, sagging chest. Even though Omer is late, she doesn't wait for him—for so many years, Alma was deprived because of his demands and now it's time for some affirmative action. When their plates are full, she says, "Tell me more, Alma, exactly how do you practice freeing yourself of your ego? Maybe it'll help me too."

"You bet it'll help you!" her daughter cries enthusiastically. "Everyone needs help freeing themselves of their egos.

"So how do you practice it?" Iris asks.

"There are lots of ways, everyone chooses the right one for them. I think it works best with sex."

"Sex?" Mickey chokes.

Alma explains with strange indifference as she eats, "Of course, sex is a tool and you have to practice using it just like you practice using any tool, with no connection to love or physical need. For instance, last week, my exercise was to sleep with a different man every night in order to reach the real me."

Iris puts a trembling hand on Mickey's knee and gives it a cautionary pinch—don't say anything, control yourself. Luckily for her, he is too stunned to speak, his mouth opens and he makes aimless chewing movements.

"Do you know those men, Alma?" she asks in a defeated voice.

"It doesn't matter, some yes, some no, like it doesn't matter who I serve food to in the restaurant. I'm learning to be generous with the most intimate things." She speaks with satisfaction, as if she isn't aware of how aberrant her words are. "I always felt that something inside me was holding me back. Boaz helped me to understand that the roots of my inhibition lie in sex, and I have to practice it in order to open up."

"You practice with him too?" she dares to ask.

"Of course not!" Alma says in horror. "He's not like that, he's my teacher! I can see that you don't understand what a teacher is!"

Iris continues nodding, as if a spring is attached to her neck, but it's impossible to feel relief, because sleeping with Boaz from morning till night would be much less appalling than sleeping with seven strangers in one week. That at least would be human, while what she is telling them now is monstrous. Still nodding, she admits in a faint voice, "I guess I don't understand, so explain to me what a teacher is for you."

"What's not clear?" Alma says impatiently. "We all need a teacher. School doesn't give us anything, Madam Principal. Don't take this personally, but we go out into life without understanding how the world works, how our minds work. School doesn't teach us how to live full lives, how to become part of the cosmos. We have to learn that by ourselves and we don't have the tools. At the age of twenty, we're already set in our ways. I was lucky enough to find my teacher and he gives me tools, he teaches me everything from the beginning, as if I was reborn in his hands. He's not an ordinary person, Boaz, he has abilities that we don't have." As she speaks, she keeps refilling her plate and her mouth—Iris has never seen her eat with such appetite, speak for so long. The tension between the innocent tone of her voice and the substance of what she is saying is staggering, as if entirely new norms have taken root in her. How did it happen so quickly? Will she ever be able to return to herself?

Iris's hands shake as she tries to move her glass of water to her lips, and the walls of the apartment seem to be shaking along with her. For a moment, she hopes it's the sign of an approaching disaster, an earthquake that will destroy the building and bury them under the ruins. But she'll settle for the direct hit of a missile launched from a hostile country, because no other solution presents itself to her. As she tries to decide what will be better for Omer, to be killed with them or to survive and be without a family, he bursts into the apartment, shouting happily, "I aced the civics exam, it was really easy." Only then does he see Alma. "Hi, Sis, what's up?" He ruffles her hair, but that isn't enough for her, and she stands up and hugs him.

"Mom, tell her to take a shower after we eat," he says with a laugh, reverting back to the snitch of a younger brother he used to be. "Thanks loads for waiting for me. Is there anything left to eat?"

In the commotion he creates around him, she takes her first glance at Mickey, and he looks devastated, his face gray, his cheeks sagging, his eyes downcast. "Maybe you should go to sleep, Mooky," she says gently. "You look really sick." He stands up in heavy silence, his eyes damp, and goes like a sleepwalker to the bedroom.

"Good night, Daddy," his beloved daughter calls after him in a voice that remains childish and innocent.

He stops for a moment, turns his moist eyes to her with such a sad and painful look that he seems about to burst into tears or begin wailing. "Good night, Alma," he says as if coerced, and continues on his way.

"What's wrong with Dad? Doesn't he feel well?" Alma asks, showing such extreme unawareness that Iris hopes it's pretense, a grotesque experiment being performed on human beings, perhaps another one of her guru's exercises. You insist that you're learning how the world works, she wants to hurl the words at her, but in reality, you've totally lost your ability to see what's happening around you! Do you think your father is supposed to feel good about what you just told us?

But she restrains herself, she has no choice. The aggressive comment might drive Alma away for a long time, so she replies, "Dad hasn't been feeling well for a few days now. He must have caught a virus. How about some ice cream, kids?"

Is there even any point to this deception? They aren't children anymore and she is no longer the benevolent mother making them happy with a huge surprise, ice cream, although both of them are amused, take on their roles and begin to bicker about their favorite flavors. "Next time, buy only Belgian Chocolate, who needs all that sorbet," Omer complains. "See, Alma took all the chocolate for herself."

She returns to her role as the impartial mother worrying about everyone's needs, saying with a smile, "You're not the only ones here, Omer, your father and I prefer sorbet. Alma, share the chocolate with your brother." But when Alma's phone rings, she suddenly abandons her bowl of ice cream, hurries off in alarm to her room, and closes the door. A moment later, they hear a heartbreaking cry, a wail of supplication.

"What's going on, Mom?" he asks, suddenly serious, and it's hard to believe that he was once a child.

"What you see, Omy."

"I don't like what I see. Your daughter's lost it. I don't know what she's taking, but it doesn't look good. Don't pretend you didn't notice."

"Of course I noticed," she sighs. "I don't know if it's drugs, but something is clearly wrong with her."

He asks, "What are we going to do?" surprising her once again with his mature approach, his involvement. But she mustn't become dependent on it, she mustn't turn him into a partner.

"Trust us, honey," she says, "we'll find a solution."

"I'm sure Dad is already working on something," he sneers. Is there a note of satisfaction at his father's disappointment in his voice now, after all the years Mickey was so strict with him and so gentle with his sister?

"What do you want from him? He doesn't feel well, he needs to sleep."

"He's not sleeping, Mom," Omer smirks, "he's playing chess. I see that this family fails the reality test big time."

Straining her ears, she hears the familiar tapping of the keyboard from the hallway, which is immediately drowned out by the loud voice coming from Alma's room. She hurries to her door and tries to overhear. "But I explained it to you, you canceled my shifts so I went to my parents' place." She hears her daughter pleading for her life. "How can I get there in fifteen minutes? It'll take me at least an hour!... Of course I want to come!... Yes, I'm leaving now... Okay, I didn't know." And she bursts out of her room, almost bumping into her mother, who is retreating quickly toward the kitchen.

"Mom, I have to go back," she says in a shrill voice, her cheeks wet with tears. "Please drive me to the bus station, I can't be late! Oh, it's eight already, what am I going to do?"

Iris puts on her sandals quickly and grabs her bag. "Keep an eye on Dad until I get back, okay, Omer?" Her son is busy with the ice cream left on the table. Then they are both in the elevator, in the car, and Alma, tense and frightened, doesn't take her eyes off her watch.

"You said he canceled your shifts," Iris says, her tone patient, "so why is he angry that you didn't go to work?"

"I probably didn't understand him right. I always have to be ready. I can't come home anymore because it's too far for him... Okay, let me out here."

"I'll let you out when we get there, I'm taking you to Tel Aviv." Though she really wants to take her as far away from there as she can, she finds herself driving obediently, as if she too has been caught in Boaz's trap and is now his collaborator.

This is how she used to drive her to pickup points all over the country when she was in the army, sometimes when it was still dark, always afraid she'd be late, always vaguely terrified of what would happen. They usually drove in silence, which she tried unsuccessfully to break, and here they are again, driving in the dark. She hasn't slept for hours, but she isn't tired, animal alertness has taken over, and she feels she is capable of anything now. For instance, she is capable of grabbing that man by his white pants and ripping him apart, running him over with her car, breaking his bones. She breathes heavily as she once again passes the place where she parked the day before. Is she doing the right thing? A short while ago, she wanted to lock her daughter in the apartment, and now she is driving her straight into the arms of danger.

Alma keeps looking at her watch as if she is trying to keep the hands from moving with her eyes, and she texts every once in a while, tapping the letters frantically. What can Iris tell her that won't sound like a criticism? "I'm sorry you're so upset," she finally says, "but you couldn't know he'd need you to work. He has no reason to be angry at you."

"Of course he has a reason," Alma defends him immediately, "it's all because of my ego! I was thinking about myself again and not about him. If I'd thought about him, I would've stayed close by in case he needed me."

"But he canceled your shifts!" she says, unable to hide her anger.

"He canceled because he's angry at me, but I should have known he wouldn't manage without me," Alma says proudly.

"He doesn't pay any of the waitresses?"

"How can he pay? He's up to his ears in debt, but he gives us a lot more than money. That's exactly how he teaches us to free ourselves from preconceptions!"

"Right," Iris mutters, and since her daughter is engrossed in texting, she doesn't try to keep the conversation going. She turns on the CD player, and Mickey's music trills in the car, lamenting a kingdom that no longer exists. The singer grows hoarser, her voice seems about to disappear. What does she see? What is she lamenting? Is it a young boy and girl that she sees, so alike that they could be brother and sister, sitting in the shade of a huge mulberry tree, dipping their feet in a spring? He went into the water and tried to persuade her to join him, but she was warming herself on the rock like a lizard. She might even have fallen asleep for a moment, and woke up when she felt his lips on her feet, licking her big toes. "Should we get married here?" he said suddenly, as if everything had already been decided and choosing the place was the only thing they still had to do. "I want my mother to make it to my wedding," he added, saying "my" wedding, not "our wedding," and that made sense to her as something between him and his mother, not between him and her. But when they went back to his house late that afternoon, surrounded by the honeyed air and tiny wildflowers, their pockets filled with leaves, they found his mother lying unconscious on the floor in a pool of vomit. They immediately called an ambulance that took her to the hospital, which she didn't leave until after her death. And so he broke his promise because the reason for it was gone, and the urgency along with it, even though for her, all of it still existed, and she even had two witnesses, the mulberry tree and the spring.

"What's this, are you going back to Dad's roots too?" her daughter asks sarcastically.

"Why not? It's wonderful music."

"A little weepy, no? Please drive faster. Why does the car smell of vomit?" She goes right back to her phone without waiting for an answer.

"We're almost there," Iris says, surprised that she remembers the way so well. Without missing even a single turn, she reaches the street, which looks darker tonight, almost deserted. But when she pulls up to the curb in front of the window of the bar, she suddenly feels as if she can't keep her eyes open for another minute. "Wait a second, Alma," she mumbles, "I can't drive back, I'm dead tired."

Her daughter looks impatiently at her. "So what do you want me to do?"

"Give me the key to your apartment, I'll sleep there and go home tomorrow."

"Oh Mom, really, my place is so crowded and dirty, it's not for you. Believe me, you won't be able to fall asleep there."

"I won't be able not to fall asleep," Iris insists. "Don't worry, I'm not going to conduct an inspection, I just need to sleep." She's glad to see that her daughter realizes that the argument will take up valuable time, and Alma takes her key, threaded on a black shoelace, out of her bag.

"Don't lose it," Alma says, as if she is the responsible adult. "I don't have another one, and don't lock the door so I can come in. Do you even remember where it is?"

Yes, she remembers the gray building even though she was there only once, when they came to take a look and approve the small apartment—two rooms, a hallway, and kitchenette—she wanted to share with a girl who'd already been living there for two years. Iris was thinking only about her daughter leaving home, she'd have her own place, and didn't pay much attention to the way the apartment looked.

In any case, she didn't have a good eye for real estate, but Mickey thought it was a bargain, and paid relatively easily. They agreed that in a few weeks, when she found a job, they'd split the rent until she started university, of course, and then they'd help more. It was a sort of incentive to encourage her to go to university. Now, as Iris looks for a parking spot on the adjacent streets, she thinks scornfully about the parents they were, at the calculations they made. How unimaginative we were, she thinks. People, it seems, are naturally unimaginative, it's a fact that disaster always surprised them. And not only disaster, their daughter surprised them for the better when she found work in the bar that very week, giving them the hope that during the year, she would be ready to apply to the university. But now she is showing them what work is and what an education is, giving new meaning to their bourgeois perceptions: work without pay, sitting at the feet of a mad charlatan who sends her on obscene missions. But there is no point in thinking about that now, she has to find a place to park and go to sleep. Or maybe first go to sleep and then find a place to park, that seems more realistic at the moment. Maybe she'll sleep in the car in one of the no-parking places and hope that the parking officer will take pity on her. But now she sees an empty spot in a crowded lot and leaves Mickey's car there. Her car is still on the highway, and tomorrow Mickey will have to pick it up after work so she won't be left without a car, because, she suddenly realizes, she will not be going home any time soon.

As she turns the key in the lock, she reads the names scribbled carelessly on the door, Noa Varshavsky, Alma Eilam, and the first one sparks a memory—Noa! The day after they signed the lease, Alma told them excitedly that her roommate had found her a job in the bar where she had been waitressing for two years and where she was really happy. They had been so proud of their daughter for finding an apartment and a job in a single week, and now she understands the trap. If Alma hadn't moved into this apartment, she wouldn't have fallen into the arms of that man, and they were here with her, looked in all the rooms, read the lease, wrote checks. If only they had ruled out this apartment, their life would be different now because this is where her roommate Noa, their waitress, ambushed her. She was apparently doing her assigned job of finding another victim, another girl who had turned into stone and now needed to hew the stone in order to find something beautiful in it.

"Isn't it a bit Spartan?" she remembers asking, but Mickey loved it. "She's my daughter, she'll make do with little," he said, sneaking in a dig at her, the way he usually did. "It reminds me of our first apartment." But she actually thought there was too much traffic outside, the apartment was too neglected and it was on the ground floor, an invitation to Peeping Toms and insects. Recalling their first apartment gave her no pleasure at all, but Alma and Mickey were so persuasive, and now, with a heavy heart, she walks into the place that proved to be a booby trap. She hasn't been here since then and it seems that the neglect has only spread and deepened, clothes tossed on the floor beside dust balls, dirty dishes on the bed, the sink filthy, and the toilet bowl even worse.

Tensely, she walks through the cursed apartment that ambushed a young girl only recently discharged from the army, who had just left home. But she has to admit that not every young girl recently discharged, who has only just left home, would fall into this trap. What is there about Alma that allowed her to fall—she'll think about that another day, the question now is how to save her, and even more urgent is the question of how she will fall asleep on that bed, in this room. Alma is right, this isn't for her. She collects the dishes and removes the stinking linens, looks in vain for others in the closet, and having no choice, she turns a relatively clean shirt into a pillowcase, a towel into a sheet, and does without a blanket on this stifling night. Tomorrow she'll buy her more linens, send these to be washed, buy detergents and towels, dishes and food. She'll scrub the toilet and the floor and make a nest for her daughter, even if it's a bit late for that. Before falling asleep in her clothes on the makeshift sheet, she sends a message to her secretary to cancel all her meetings for the next day and texts Mickey not to expect her tonight, hesitating near the letter P, yearning to write that she hasn't given up on him, that he should wait for her. The pain seems to spread from the letter to her fingers and she presses them tightly together. She mustn't write to him now, it might weaken her position with her daughter, she mustn't even think about him because it suddenly occurs to her at this moment of pain and dread that only if she herself relinquishes this man can she demand that her daughter relinquish hers.

SIXTEEN

What's the connection? She rebels when street noise intrudes into her sleep early in the morning, garbage trucks, buses, horns. She has become used to the quiet of the high floor they live on, and here she seems to be sleeping on a street bench. The sun is hot on her cheeks, passersby shout in her ears, their phones ringing constantly, motorcycles and cars exhale into her mouth, no wonder Alma has gone mad. But what's the connection, why does she have to give up the love of her life so that Alma can give up a psychopath who is abusing her? Nonetheless, when she reaches for the phone to see if he has texted, she once again feels the strange pain and she drops it, walks cautiously over to Noa's room, and peers inside. There they are, lying side by side on their stomachs on the low futon, still wearing their black uniforms, their hair cut short, exhausted soldiers in a small, insane army.

They must have only just returned, because the kettle is still hot. Maybe it was their voices that awakened her and not the street noises, but she doesn't want to wake up yet, she's on vacation in Tel Aviv. A few days off at my daughter's place, that's what she told her secretary, and she looks in vain for earplugs or at least cotton, and finally makes do with toilet paper that she rolls up and sticks into her ears to mute the noise. Slowly the sounds melt into a more bearable blend that enables her to drift into reverie, because she sees herself and Eitan walking behind his mother's coffin. An ominous, early summer sun beats down on their heads and she seems to hear a voice on a loudspeaker, surprised and almost annoyed, calling out, "A woman dies and the world turns upside down?" Then the funeral turns into Daniella's mother's funeral in the pouring rain. If only she had looked up she would have seen him, walking alone, a black umbrella over his head. How did she not see him? It wasn't a particularly large funeral.

If only she had seen him, she would have joined him under the black canopy of his umbrella and they would have left the cemetery together, just as they did almost thirty years ago, walking toward the parting that lay in wait for her exactly a week later, toward the worst summer of her life. Will he be at her side next summer? She yearns to call him now and tell him that they could have met again a year and a half ago, that they missed out on yet another year and a half. He needs to know that, he needs to mourn with her, because that might have been the right time. When she thinks of the last year and a half of her life, she has to admit that nothing happened in that time that justified losing the opportunity, nothing that gave it meaning. But what does one thing have to do with the other? How can she break the connection, separate Alma from Boaz and herself from Eitan, and not only from him, but from their history, because the young girl she once was demands that she right the ancient wrong, and the young girl who is her daughter demands that she release her from the trap. The two tasks seem contradictory, because in order to release Alma, she has to offer her stability, at least for the next few months. But it isn't about that, it won't be hard to create the impression of stability for her even in the present circumstances. No, it's about the magical, implausible connection that she can't break with her painful fingers.

When she wakes up again, the apartment is empty. They must have just left because the kettle is still hot again. Their voices awakened her once more after she fell asleep, and while her eyes were closed, the industrious little worker bees went out to do their additional jobs. When do they have time to focus on their spiritual work if they work for him without pay and also support him? How can they not see the shameful exploitation? She makes herself a cup of black coffee and gulps it down quickly, there is no time, the situation is intolerable and needs to be changed quickly. She has to buy bread, milk, fruit and vegetables, oil, rice, lentils, and pasta, because except for the coffee, there is nothing in the kitchen. She also has to buy pots and frying pans so she can cook for them, and detergents, of course, and sheets and towels. She has to buy a change of underpants for herself, a few simple summer dresses and flip-flops, she doesn't need to wear much in this heat, and she has to find a Laundromat, there isn't a single piece of clean clothing here. She puts all the clothes she finds on the floor into a quilt cover, adding Noa's clothes and sheets, as well as the towels from the bathroom, collecting all the filthy items rapidly, as if she is cleansing the apartment of all signs of idolatry. His pants are so clean and white, and they live in such squalor.

She goes out onto the sweaty, bustling Tel Aviv street, a heavy, filthy sack on her back. Why is the sack so heavy? Each separate article of clothing is light, but together, their weight is unbearable, and she wonders about the obvious, as if she has made a remarkable discovery in physics.

When she finally rids herself of the dirty laundry, it feels as if an unbearable burden has been lifted from her and she can now look at the colorful display windows, the street stalls that eventually turn into an outdoor market. She hasn't walked in the streets for a long time, usually shopping in an air-conditioned supermarket after she leaves the air-conditioned school, and here, the heat strikes a blow at her as does her life. How close the market is, summer fruit breathes on the stands alongside the hanging dresses that sway in the breeze coming off the sea. She can't keep wearing these clothes, the dirty blouse and the tailored black pants she wore to work yesterday stick to her skin, and she feels as if they are about to spontaneously combust. Without trying them on, she buys three tricot dresses, two short and one long, a package of underpants, a hairbrush and toothbrush, face cream, fruit and vegetables, groceries, detergents; and little by little a new burden accumulates, so she buys a red shopping cart and quickly puts everything in it. She feels strangely cheerful as the bags pile up, promising cleanliness, food, a home, simple, soothing chores like scrubbing sinks and toilets, washing floors, cooking, organizing cabinets. A few days off at my daughter's place. My vacation.

She never liked the vacations they organized for themselves every summer, mainly for the children—the recommended kind of family bonding—usually with Dafna, Gidi, and their children, and sometimes other families, in Israel and abroad, depending on their financial situation, Corfu, Ahziv, Eilat, Crete, Croatia, Lake Kinneret. She couldn't bring herself to admit that she missed work, that spending a prolonged period of time with people who weren't her family depressed her, and that sometimes spending a prolonged period of time with her family also depressed her. When the children were small, Mickey occasionally organized trips for just the two of them to the north or the south, for a night or two. She used to go along reluctantly, putting aside her reservations, although they usually enjoyed the rest and the relaxed conversations they could have when there were no children to interrupt them. Mickey was at his best on those trips, and she used to rediscover his sharp, dry humor, the pleasant quiet along with the surprising powers of observation. They made fun of the guesthouses they stayed in, which called themselves cabins even if they were made of concrete, with the clumsy jacuzzi placed like an altar in the middle of the room, with the embarrassing bathrooms that had almost no dividers. Once, they found peacock feathers and a rabbity fur tail in a closet, and Mickey placed it on his rear end and skipped around the room as she roared with laughter. But she could never erase her feeling that other couples, Eitan and his wife, for example, even though she knew nothing about them, enjoyed things together on a deeper level, because youthful memories of perfect love still glowed inside her, even though it never entered her mind that Eitan would ever return to her.

She acquiesced totally to the sentence imposed on her as confirmation that she was unworthy of him, as if his abandonment of her placed her in a lower caste, which of course reflected on her husband, who belonged to her caste, and also on their children. The submissiveness that dominated her after she recovered from her breakdown intensified, for some reason, during vacations, while at work, it disappeared completely, which is why she always secretly looked forward to getting back to her routine.

But now, pulling a full shopping cart along the streets of south Tel Aviv, far from her routine, she feels a pleasant vibrancy that is inappropriate to the troubling circumstances of her stay here. She relishes the freedom and the knowledge that no one knows her, whereas at school, she can't take a step without being stopped at least five times. Teachers, pupils, parents, they all require her attention, her answers, and that naturally reinforces her sense of worth. But now, for some reason, she doesn't need it, it's enough for her to be a woman pulling a shopping cart back from the market who sits down in a café and orders iced coffee and carrot juice, and actually, why not breakfast?

"Coming right up," the waiter says warmly. Everything in this part of the city is done with warmth. She has never been called such affectionate nicknames as she has in the last hour—dear, sweetie, baby, honey—and has never had so many people hoping so amiably that she has a good day, as if this is the last one of her life. Of course, it all appears completely staged, but at the same time, genuine, if not totally wholehearted. There is no doubt that a thin layer of warmth has been formed here, something she's not used to, and she enjoys wading around in it, like a toddler in a kiddy pool. And she enjoys eating the hot, fresh bread she slathers with spreads she doesn't recognize, but they are all absolutely delicious. She enjoys watching the passersby, most of them clearly foreign workers, and she is proud to have been the first principal in her city to enroll their children in her school.

When she finally sets out on her way again, she is surprised when someone suddenly stops her, even in this city. "Iris? Is that you?" And she looks up at a handsome young man with short blond hair and bristly cheeks. The eyes, green and slightly slanted, are familiar, but she can't remember from where until he helps her, saying with an amused grin, "I thought you'd never forget me! I was sent to you every day for punishment!"

"Sasha!" she laughs in relief. "You're all grown up! It's so good to see you! What's happening with you?" She calculates quickly. "You've already finished the army, right?"

"Yes, I'm on my discharge leave now. You won't believe it, but I was in a combat unit," he says with the pride of a rejected child who didn't fit into the system for many years.

"Good for you, of course I believe it. And what are you doing now?"

"I was accepted into the medical school in Tel Aviv, so now I'm looking for an apartment and a job."

She nods enthusiastically. "That's wonderful, Sasha, I'm so happy."

"To this day, my mom says that it's all thanks to you, Iris. Do you remember how you fought to keep me in school? They wanted to transfer me to a special education program! My mom told me that the parents threatened to take their kids out of school if you didn't get rid of me, but you didn't give up."

"That's right," she says, growing happier as the memory becomes clearer. "That was my first year as principal, and there really was enormous pressure. I remember that you were in my office constantly for almost the entire year. I'm so pleased, Sasha, this is such wonderful news. Your mother must be thrilled."

"Yes, Mom's on cloud nine. And what about you, Iris, how are things in school? And what are you doing in Tel Aviv?"

"I came to see my daughter—I mean to clean her house."

He blinks with interest, and says, to her surprise, "You mean Alma moved to Tel Aviv?"

"I didn't know you knew each other."

"I don't really know her, but I saw her a few times in the city."

"Here in Tel Aviv?" she asks fearfully, because who knows what he saw.

"No, in Jerusalem. I'd love to get in touch with her. What's her number?"

"Why don't you give me yours and I'll pass it on to her," Iris says quickly, afraid he might catch Alma at a bad time, in the middle of one of her insane missions. It's because he looks eager, because she might like him, that she has to wait for the right time. There aren't many opportunities in life, no one knows and understands that better than she does, and Alma has to get healthy before she is offered this one.

In the end, Alma will realize your dream, she thinks, mocking herself for the excitement she feels. Dreams are sometimes hereditary, like genetic diseases, this Sasha will be her Eitan and you'll relinquish yours. There appears to be a similarity, the light eyes, the thin face. She remembers how much she supported his mother, a new immigrant from Russia, and how they both fought for the boy, who was undoubtedly gifted but whose behavior was impossible. He was the most difficult pupil she had ever dealt with, the most violent and also the smartest and most consistently able to incite everyone around him. A day did not pass without complaints about him. He didn't let the teachers teach, constantly disrupted and provoked. She kept him close to her for days at a time because no one else could control him, and gave him various jobs to do, private lessons whenever she could, built a special class schedule for him, mainly sports and science. She tried to empower him, as they say, by providing more of the subjects that interested him and raising money for special courses and therapy, until he gradually settled down. She hadn't heard from him since he went on to middle school, and even thought they might have left the city.

She didn't have much time to find out because many like him came to the school, not exactly like him, but each a challenge, because the rumor that she performed miracles led endless numbers of parents with such children to her door. She had forgotten most of them, but she remembered Sasha very well, the way you remember your first, the way she remembered Eitan. Now that rejected child, the son of a poor, hardworking new immigrant, has been accepted to medical school, while Alma, the principal's daughter, hasn't even tried to get accepted anywhere because she would rather sleep with strangers and serve a psychopathic tyrant. The anger floods her again as she enters the apartment, changes clothes, pulls back her hair, and attacks the filth furiously.

Here and there, she sees a beautiful painted floor tile— strange how they are strewn haphazardly among the ordinary tiles. She wanders from room to room, beats the mattresses, sweeps, dusts to destroy any trace of the sick, moldy air, and scrubs the walls and windows with white sponges. She never cleaned her own apartment with such determination, attacking every corner, wiping away again and again all the dust that has collected. She finds only the most basic items in her daughter's room, as if she hasn't finished moving all of her possessions into it, but Noa's room is much more crowded, and she dusts the furniture, the carpet, the pillows, the CD player, and the books.

Obviously she has no right to touch her things, but it's too late, she can no longer stop. The entire apartment will be clean, no exceptions, and she'll clean Noa's room as if she were her mother. She thinks for a moment about that mother, who she is and what she knows about her daughter's life. Maybe she'll find some clue here that will enable her to contact the woman, to join forces with her against a common enemy. Probably all the information is on the computer on her desk, which she dares not turn on. So she glances at the few books, most of them children's books, for some reason—the Brothers Grimm fairy tales, *Winnie the Pooh*, *The Little Prince*, and beside them, *The Drama of the Gifted Child*, which she knows quite well, and resting, like cause and effect, on Osho's *In Search of the Miraculous*. Browsing through it, she is happy to find the name of its owner, Mira Varshavsky, which gives her a lead and a sense of a shared destiny. But she won't call her now, not until she has completely annihilated the filth and the stench, which return again and again, like drifting sand, not until the rag finally comes away unblackened and she wipes the floor with pleasure. The toilet bowl and the sinks are already shining, the new sheets have been put on the beds, the two large fans she bought are blowing through the apartment. Now it's time to cook a healthy meal for the hardworking girls. She fries onions on the old stove and adds cubes of tofu, cooks brown rice and steamed vegetables—they need vitamins, nutritional fiber—she'll make the salad when they sit down so it'll be fresh. She washes grapes and plums and puts them in a bowl on the small Formica table and imagines the girls sitting down and eating her food, happy she is there, chatting away comfortably about the day they've had.

That's exactly how it was with Alma and Shira, so many meals after they came home from the afternoon childcare center, or before ballet class, which became piano class, which became painting class. Dafna was always late, but that didn't bother her, on the contrary, Shira was so open and extroverted that Alma loosened up a bit when she was there, talked more about what troubled her and what made her happy.

You're such an idiot, she shakes off the memories now, what exactly do you think she'll tell you? Those aren't the stories I want to hear, but I'll hear it all anyway, just as long as they talk and take me into their world. She walked around the apartment again, smoothing a wrinkle on a sheet, hanging a towel, tasting the food, glancing at the clock. It will be night soon and they haven't returned, they must go from one job to another without coming home. She's waiting in vain, they'll come back near dawn, sleep until noon and go out to work again, they won't even have time to notice the nest she created for them. With a sigh, she lies down on Alma's bed, her back aching from the effort she isn't used to. She mustn't fall asleep and miss them again, just lie there with open eyes in front of the powerful fan.

Suddenly she feels as if the hair on her forehead is moving and she gets up to shift the direction of the breeze, but the strange movement continues as if her hair has taken on a life of its own. When she looks up and sees the long, thin legs appear from an eyebrow, exactly the same color as her hair, she jumps up in a panic, slapping wildly at her head to remove the frightening visitor, and there it is on the floor, a huge black spider walking with surprising, provocative slowness between her feet. Probably its life is as precious to it as hers is to her, but she steps on it with horror, and it withdraws into itself in acceptance, pulling in its legs, which walked along her scalp only a moment ago, and becomes an inanimate black ball. She stares at it in terror, she doesn't know very much about spiders, is it a black widow or a more innocent creature that just looks threatening?

No, nothing is innocent in this apartment, where the trap was laid for her daughter and which now mocks her efforts to turn it into a safe, pleasant place. What is the point in all that cleaning if when you're done, you find a giant spider on your head? That didn't happen on any of her school trips to the north and the south when she slept outdoors in a sleeping bag beside her pupils. But it happened now, in the gleaming apartment, in Alma's bed with its clean linens, and she flees the room, leaving behind the spider's corpse. There is no living room in the apartment, so she sits down, trembling, in the small kitchen, still slapping at her head to drive away any additional visitors. A burning sensation spreads over her scalp, and she calls Mickey, tells him every small detail of what happened, as if this were their biggest problem.

He listens to her with a patience that lacks all empathy. She always knew that in her guerrilla wars with the insect world, he would always stand with the insects, which he considers more helpless than she does. He always prefers to remove animals from the house gently instead of carrying out her death wishes for them. Now too, he interrupts her and asks, "How many legs did it have? It was probably a totally harmless furry spider. You didn't have to kill it, it's actually on your side. It eats cockroaches, which you hate."

"I don't know which I hate more, it was so disgusting, and it was after I'd cleaned for hours. I'm alone in the apartment with the spider's corpse. Alma hasn't come home, I don't know what to do here without her, and I don't know if I'll get to see her at all."

"So come home," he says joylessly, "if you don't feel there's any point in staying."

"I'm not sure yet. For the time being, I'll lie in wait for her."

"You see," he chuckles, "you're not very different from the spider you killed. It was lying in wait patiently for its prey. Just be careful that a giant foot doesn't crush you."

"Really, Mickey, that's a terrible comparison. I'm planning to devour Alma?"

"From her point of view, maybe."

She knows that now they are both remembering that night in the first apartment they rented together several weeks before they got married. It was a ground-floor apartment in a cheap neighborhood, bedroom, living room, and another locked room where the owners stored old possessions, and even though she tried to ignore its existence, it bothered her. One night, a tiny gray mouse scurried out of it just as they were about to turn off the light in the living room and go to sleep. She saw it first and ran screeching into the bedroom, closed the door behind her, and, terrified, barked orders to her future husband. "Kill it, Mickey, I won't come out if it's still here. I'm moving, I won't live with a mouse."

"Why should I kill it," he protests, "how should I kill it?"

But there was no pity in her heart, neither for the mouse nor for Mickey. "I don't care how," she roared, bloodthirsty, "just as long as it dies!" Unable to summon up the courage to oppose her, Mickey found himself undergoing the first test of his manhood she put him through, and because he gave up his principles for her, he was doomed to failure. He went after the mouse with the new purple broom they had bought a week earlier, when they moved in together. She sat on the bed, body contracted, eyes closed, and covered her ears to block out the whacks of the broom against the wall and the strangled squeals that might have been coming from the mouse or from Mickey, she couldn't tell. She wanted to be rid of them both, to escape through the window from the battle that seemed to go on for hours without a victor, because even when the wall grew silent and the front door opened and the cover of the garbage bin outside opened and closed, even when he came into the bedroom and said, "You can come out, the field is clear," his voice was weak and his expression bitter. And although she said, "Thank you, my hero, you saved me," they both knew it was a defeat. She tried to pull him to her, kissed his neck, his forehead, his lips, wanting to show him that, at least for her, he had passed the test and deserved a reward, but he pushed her away and moved to the far end of the bed. "Come to me, Mickey," she whispered in surprise, he had never refused her before. "Don't call me Mickey, call me Mickey Mouse," he said, lying immobile, breathing quietly, shaken to the depths of his being. They were so embarrassed by that battle that they never spoke of it again.

The next day, she sealed the door of the closed room with strong tape, as if hazardous chemicals might leak out of it, and when their lease was up, they left the apartment without the slightest regret. Ever since, she has made sure that they lived on a relatively high floor and tries not to ask for his help in her battles with the insect world. But if she does ask for it, she knows that he will pick up the bug gently and set it free through the window.

Now she calls him again and says, "Have you forgiven me, Mickey?"

"Not now," he says, "I'm in the middle." Then, exuberantly, "Yes!"

She laughs, "You won?"

"Yes, a great victory," he says, slightly abashed.

"Congratulations, you're such a little boy."

He surprises her by saying, "In response to your question, Iris, I've forgiven you, but not myself. That was the worst night of my life, my adult life, in any case."

But she has to contradict him. "Don't exaggerate, Mickey, it was worse at Alma's bar, and the day I was injured was worse, and so was the day your mother died." She continues to list their disasters, trying to absolve herself of the responsibility for the worst day of his life, but he won't surrender.

"There's no comparison, being angry at yourself is harder than being angry at fate."

"So who were you angry at when I was injured?" she asks, trying to trap him.

"Why do you always go back to that?"

"Because something from back then hasn't been resolved."

"You think everything else has been resolved?" he mocks. "You go back ten years as if what happened yesterday is resolved? I, for example, still haven't resolved the question of what you were doing at the interchange the night before last."

"So why don't you ask me?"

He answers quietly, as if talking to himself. "I don't believe in questions and answers anymore."

She has to stop there because if she has to choose either the closeness that has so suddenly and casually appeared between them or the safe distance that the lie creates, she still trusts the distance more, so she says, "I interviewed a teacher there who couldn't come to the city. She's on maternity leave with twins. You see, you're just not a dialogue person! If you just asked questions, you'd see that the answers are simple. She couldn't come so I went to her."

"Not now, I'm in the middle," he mutters, and she understands that he has started a new game instead of listening to her nonsense.

Her unnecessary lie chokes her and she sighs, "You're right, Mickey, there's no point in questions, and definitely not in answers. I just wanted to ask you to forgive me."

"Why are you talking about this now? I've already told you that I'm not angry at you. You are what you are, you couldn't have acted differently."

But she persists, "Not just about the mouse, Mooky." Is he engrossed in the game or in the things she doesn't dare say?

"You are who you are," he repeats finally.

The spider's corpse is still lying in wait for her in Alma's room, so she stretches out on Noa's bed after pounding it with a pillow to make sure it's insect-free, and then pounding the pillow itself. Evening is falling, but she doesn't turn on the lights. Does he know? Has he discovered the truth on her cell phone and is he waiting nobly for everything to end? Or were his words insignificant, because he listened to her with his usual distraction, absorbed in a game? For some reason, it makes no difference to her now, alone in the apartment with the spider's corpse, thinking sorrowfully about her father, because not only are dreams inherited, but also nightmares. While he was still alive and even after his death, her mother used to blame him for that. "Leave the child alone. Why are you infecting her with your fears?" she would admonish him when he took her in his arms to distance her from every insect, even if it was only a roach or a tiny spider. "Look at you, you're just like your father," she scolded her over the years, "what are you both so afraid of, two spoiled babies." But now, for some reason, she yearns to hear even those reproaches.

"Hello, Iris. You want talk to Mama? Mama in shower," Parshant tells her. "You want Mama call you after shower?"

And she replies, "Yes, please help her call," but as she waits, she thinks sorrowfully that she has been too late for a long time now, there is no longer any point in asking her mother questions about her childhood, about the very short time she had and meager memories she has of being a little girl with a father. For years she believed that there was no reason to hurry, there were always more important things to do, but in one elusive moment, it became impossible. Her mother is still with them in body, but not in mind.

Yes, she sighs, we will always be doomed to long for an earlier time, which did not have much to recommend it either. On her last several visits, she noticed, to her sorrow, an additional ebbing of her mother's mental faculties. She was immersed in a fantasy world, pointing to places in the room and describing sights and scenes she was imagining. The only witness to Iris's first years can no longer bear witness for her, and she must settle for her own early memories. Nevertheless, she still hopes she can get her to talk and extract some recollection from the muddle of words that comes out of her mouth.

"You won't believe it, Mother, I just had a huge spider on my head," she tells her, agitatedly. "Remember how afraid Daddy was of bugs?"

But her mother dismisses her words scornfully. "My father? He wasn't afraid of anything! After what he went through in the Holocaust, you think he'd be afraid of bugs?"

"I'm not talking about Grandpa Moshe," she says, slightly ashamed for some reason. "I mean my father."

"Your father? Who is your father? I don't think I knew him."

"You married him, Mother," she implores, "of course you knew him! Gabriel Segal, your husband."

Her mother repeats the name sourly, "Segal? It sounds familiar, but I really can't remember what all the neighbors were afraid of!" Iris can imagine the angry, childish expression on her face now. At first she sometimes suspected that her mother was pretending just to annoy her, and even now she is angry at her, as if she is deliberately refusing to give her what she wants. "What is so frightening about bugs?" she continues to jeer, "you step on them and that's that. Parshant and I aren't the least bit afraid."

Yes, her mother coped fearlessly with the terrifying creatures, ridiculing her squeamish panic, she couldn't abide squeamishness. Strange, for many years Iris attributed her masculinity to the fact that she was a widow, that she had to be both father and mother to her children, and only when she became an adult did she consider that it was her personality that had apparently determined her fate. She was direct and harsh, judgmental and opinionated, and she strongly condemned all shows of weakness in everyone, including her deceased husband.

As Iris grew older, her mother allowed herself to be more critical of her father, and her list of complaints grew longer over the years. "He never did anything with himself," she would say, as if after his death, she expected him to develop, to show initiative and resourcefulness. "He was a spoiled, lazy little prince, your father, and he had no ambition," she would occasionally say bitterly, convinced that with a bit of healthy resourcefulness, he would have been able to evade the artillery shell that hit his tank. It made no difference that dozens of other soldiers were also killed, including ones less spoiled than he. She found him guilty of his own death, and his mother even guiltier, for spoiling her only son rotten. "She never even let him make an omelet," she would sometimes tell her, "he didn't know how to change bedding and it took him two hours to put the duvet into the duvet cover. He was so used to having her do everything for him that he atrophied. She didn't prepare him for life. I'm sure that even when the tank started to burn, he sat there helplessly, waiting for his mother to come and rescue him. I have no idea how he survived the army at all. Someone must have always covered for him just because he had such a beautiful smile."

He really did have a gorgeous smile, astonishingly like Omer's. In most of the pictures they have of him, he is smiling, and only in the last one does he look serious, staring at the chessboard in concern, as if he knows he is going to lose very soon. She sensed that her mother enjoyed criticizing him because she was jealous of how much he loved their daughter from the day she was born. Sometimes she heard a hint of gloating in her voice when she told her how much he loved her, but their blissful years together were brief, cut off with a single blow, and life without him turned Iris into a hardworking, gloomy little girl who joylessly helped her mother raise two superfluous children. Every morning, her mother would get up early and go off to the clinic to "take blood," as she put it, leaving her to get her brothers ready for kindergarten and school alone while she sat in a chair and drew the blood of patients who waited in a long line, their arms extended to the needle and test tubes. The darkness was so deep and protracted that she remembered almost nothing of her childhood and teenage years, only the constant, dreary burden of existence. She learned how to make an omelet and put a quilt into its cover, how to diaper and clean, wash clothes and hang them up, do her homework with half-closed eyes. It wasn't until Eitan entered her life when she was sixteen and a half that it filled with light for a full year, until he too disappeared abruptly without giving her a chance to say goodbye. Lying in the silence in the strange bed, she wonders why she is suddenly thinking about all of that. She doesn't usually have time for memories, but now that she momentarily has nothing to do, that previous, fatherless existence has attacked her. She lay in the silence in her small bed just like this, taking her afternoon nap as her father threw on his uniform and went off to war. Of course he wanted to wake her with a hug and a kiss and words of love and farewell, but her mother wouldn't let him, better not to disrupt the routine, which was disrupted beyond recognition anyway.

What is the point of all this, she should focus on action, and she sits up and turns on the lights in the room. Should she try to talk to the other mother now, find out if she shares her trouble? How difficult it is to give someone such news, but perhaps she already knows, perhaps she knows even more than Iris and can help her with information, details, tactics. She obtains several phone numbers of women with the same name. "Hello, are you Noa's mother?" she asks in an authoritative voice, and when the answer is no, she apologizes quickly and ends the call.

But now a hoarse voice replies in a heavy French accent, "Yes, is everything okay with her?"

Iris reassures her, "Everything's fine, more or less. I'm Iris, the mother of her roommate, Alma. I'm in their apartment now." Then she explains unnecessarily, "I cleaned it and cooked for them. They work so hard."

"That's how it is when you insist on living in the middle of Tel Aviv," the mother says, her tone critical, a chilling echo of previous arguments, and Iris already understands that she won't be having the friendly conversation she hoped for between two mothers with a shared fate.

"Tell me, have you ever visited Noa at work? Did you meet the owner?"

She hears the woman's heavy tongue struggling to get out the words. "Yes, I was there once. I don't get down there very much, we live up in the Galilee." She sounds as if her mouth were full of nuts, leaving no room for syllables. "He seemed nice and the food was very good. What did we eat there?" she tries to remember. "Chicken and nuts, maybe. Samuel, what did we eat in Noa's restaurant?" she asks someone who is apparently sitting beside her, and Iris has to suppress a sudden fit of wild laughter. The thought of the nuts in her mouth turning into words seems hysterically funny to her and she chokes as she tries to replace the laughter with words.

"Hello, are you there? What did you say your name was?" the woman from the north asks.

Iris puts her hand over her mouth. What can she do to stifle the laughter? It seems as if only that spider's corpse can restore her ability to speak, so she goes into the other bedroom, and to her horror, the black ball is gone, as if the earth swallowed it up. Did it only pretend to be dead? "How can it be?" she asks in a smothered screech very much like the screech of the mouse that was crushed against the wall.

Noa's mother complains, "What are you talking about? I can hardly hear you, there's noise on the line."

Iris leaves the room, she has to get to the point, she'll think about the spider later. "Listen," she says, "I heard bad rumors about that bar. That Boaz they work for doesn't pay them and he's exploiting them in all kinds of ways. He's made himself a guru and is controlling their minds and their bodies."

Now it's Noa's mother's turn to screech. "How can that be?" Each in her turn is a mouse crushed against the wall.

"I'm really sorry to drop this on you," Iris adds sympathetically, "but I thought we could try to meet, figure out a way to get them out of there. I'm ready to drive up north to see you."

But to her disappointment, Noa's mother regains her composure quickly and rejects her firmly, as if Iris herself is the bad news.

"Listen," she says coldly, her accent already so heavy that every word seems to hurt her, "you people in this country get mixed up in everybody's business, but I come from a different culture where we don't stick our noses under the sheet. My daughter is already twenty-three years old, and if she's willing to work for nothing, that's her choice, and if she does all kinds of other stupid things, that's her responsibility, and I don't intend to get involved. I have my own life! You Israelis don't know how to let your children grow up," she preaches condescendingly. "You stay too close to them. Noa is a grown woman and so is your daughter. What they do is their business, and what we do is our business."

Completely stunned, Iris listens to her. "I'm so sorry I bothered you," she mumbles.

The woman kindly forgives her, not noticing the irony. Somewhere up north, she moves her heavy tongue, "No problem, we just have different mentalities. So good luck and goodbye."

Iris stares at the now-silent phone. She was wrong, those weren't nuts in her mouth, they were ice cubes. What a selfish woman, the way she rebuffed her, preferring to live her life with no unnecessary disturbances, to crush ice between her teeth and not worry about her daughter. Upset, Iris paces the apartment, bends to look under the bed, moves chairs. Where is the resurrected spider, is it still breathing in some corner of the apartment, lying in wait for her? She has to get out of here, she can't stay alone at night with the spider, dead or alive, and without showering, without changing clothes, she tears out of there, locks the door hastily, and hangs the key around her neck. The red tricot dress she bought in the market is sweaty and dusty and her scalp burns from the spider bite as she dashes out onto the sooty streets and is carried along in the stream of people without knowing where it's headed. This city has always been alien to her and now the sense of alienation intensifies with each moment, with each step.

She doesn't belong to the never-ending party on these streets, she wasn't invited to it and everyone seems to know, which is why they look at her, at her dirty dress, her bitter face. Is everyone really so happy, or are they just pretending? This is exactly how she felt when she recovered from her breakdown after Eitan and began walking in the streets again. This is exactly how she imagined seeing him everywhere, a new girl at his side who didn't remind him of that terrible year, of his mother's death.

Where will she go, where is she walking to so aimlessly? She thinks she's getting close to Alma's bar, and actually, why not? She'll burst into the place and start overturning tables and the plates of gourmet food will be hurled to the floor one after the other the way Alma's birthday cake was hurled to the floor. Then that Boaz will understand that the girl from Jerusalem is causing more damage than good and he'll throw her out of there. But how will Alma react, will she be able to endure it? For a moment, she sees her as her own young self, lying on her back, shrinking, being absorbed into the mattress, which was absorbed into the bed, which was absorbed into the floor, which was absorbed into the earth. She dare not force her to break off relations. She's her daughter, her flesh and blood, even if she always felt that they were so different. But perhaps they aren't really so different after all. For the first time, it occurs to her that she too has been enslaved all these years to a cruel tyrant, to her past, which has cast its long and bitter shadow over her life.

Her cheeks blaze from the heat, and her scalp itches as if the spider were still there. She scratches constantly, maybe it managed to lay eggs in her hair and dozens of small spiders have hatched from them. She remembers how she and Alma used to catch lice from each other because the lice they brought home from their respective schools created an endless closed circle, and they used to comb each other's hair with a fine-tooth comb, laughing with horror, giving the lice names. But even that ended after her injury, when she stopped teaching, when she cut her hair, when it turned out that she alone had been the source of the problem, because Alma didn't have lice from then on.

Horns honk only at her because she is the stranger here. How is she supposed to know how the traffic flows on this street, whether the danger comes from land or sea? The air is so damp and salty, perhaps she has already sunk into the sea and she needs to make swimming movements with her arms in order to save herself. But no one around her is swimming, and even so, they're not sinking. Is there a lifeguard on this street? She feels as if she's going mad, is this what the big city did to Alma?

Her feet hurt and she has to sit down, but the crowded cafés put her off. Everything that was pleasant during the day has become threatening at night, so she turns off the main street onto a side street and goes into a front yard in search of shelter. She doesn't belong here, she is filled with past sorrows and future anxieties, just like her city.

Exhausted, she sits down on the steps of the well-maintained building, and the black-and-white floor tiles, which resemble a chessboard, swim before her eyes. She needs help, she can't be alone tonight. Maybe Dafna is here today, she has already forgotten which days she goes to her Tel Aviv office. It seems as if weeks have passed since she said goodbye to her angrily at the end of their last meeting, pushing her away the way Noa's mother pushed her away today. No one thanks the bearer of bad news, but Dafna won't hold a grudge.

"Hi, Dafi," she says in a low voice, "do you happen to be in Tel Aviv?"

"I just drove onto the highway on the way home. Why? Where are you?"

"It feels like I'm in hell, or having an anxiety attack, and a giant spider bit me and Alma is sleeping with seven men in a single week and who knows what she's doing now."

"Oh, you poor thing," Dafna cries, "I'm on my way. Where are you?"

Iris walks out onto the street and gives her the address, then hurries back to the building, as if missiles are being fired at the city and she has to find shelter. She feels better now that she has some expectation again, the hope that their meeting brings, the knowledge that she will soon be picked up, that in Dafna's car she'll find the identity she lost here.

A short time later, Dafna picks her up wearing her Tel Aviv clothes, high heels, a pencil skirt, and silk blouse. "Are you cleaning houses to boost your income?" she says with a laugh. "Are the Board of Education salaries that low? No, don't hug me, you'll get my blouse dirty."

But Iris presses up against her, puts her head on her shoulder and her arms around her long, slightly wrinkled neck. "Thank you for coming," she says tearfully, "you saved me."

"Should I take you home?"

"No, my car is here, Mickey's actually."

"So Mickey will pick you up tomorrow somehow, you're in no condition to drive."

"No, he has to pick up my car at the interchange first."

"What interchange?"

"Forget it, it's too complicated, and it's not important. I have to stay, I still haven't finished here."

"It looks like this place finished you. Want to get something to eat?"

"Can we eat in the car?" She feels so protected in the clean, fresh-smelling car beside her beloved friend as she drives confidently through the streets, which suddenly look friendlier.

When Dafna parks, she hands Iris a lipstick and a bottle of perfume and says with a chuckle, "They won't let you in otherwise."

"It's okay, I have my own." But nonetheless she puts on Dafna's lipstick, which is darker than hers, and sprays herself with her strong perfume. "I'll turn into you," she says.

"No problem, as long as I don't have to be you."

Dafna has always been better groomed than she, knows how to hide her full body with flattering clothes. They used to laugh that their daughters were switched at birth because Alma was as fastidious as Dafna, Shira as negligent as Iris. Maybe we'll switch them back, she used to suggest sometimes, when Alma dragged her bored mother to buy her clothes or shoes, while Dafna forced Shira to try on clothes at the mall, even though she was totally indifferent about her appearance. Now, in her flip-flops, Iris follows her impressive friend to the impressive, beachside restaurant, her feet hurting, holding on to Dafna's arm, although she protests, "Don't overdo it, some of my clients are probably here and I'm taking a risk by even going in there with you."

"Order for me," Iris says when the smiling waiter comes over to their table. "As far as I'm concerned, you can chew for me too, I'm so exhausted." Then, as if talking in her sleep, she tells her everything, from the end to the beginning, because everything has always led there, to the beginning, to the guilt, to her.

"Drop the guilt," Dafna says, pouring water into a glass and handing it to her. "Feeling guilty is the most banal thing, it's ineffective, and not even true. You're a good mother to Alma, good enough, in any case. No one's perfect."

"That's what I used to tell Alma," Iris says, "that no one's perfect, but it apparently didn't help her."

Dafna persists, "You said what you thought, what's wrong with that? Today parents are afraid to be themselves, to say what they feel. You didn't like her obsession and you showed her that. What were you supposed to do, measure her eyebrows with a ruler? And even if you were young, even if you were busy and things were hard, that's normal, it's not a disaster. It doesn't explain what happened to her. There's also a lot of randomness in all this, so many different things are involved. She moved into that apartment, met that man, not everything's your fault, you can't control everything."

"So how can I get her out of it if I can't control anything?"

"First of all, eat, this salad is excellent. If it had shrimps in it, it would be even better. You have a lot of influence over Alma. If you keep at it, you'll succeed."

"Influence?" Iris chokes. "What are you talking about?"

"I see her differently, Iris, when she's at our place with Shira, she's different. She talks about you a lot, quotes you, she thinks very highly of you."

"Thinks highly of me? Maybe you're talking about when she was ten."

"Absolutely not, she was at our place not long ago and mentioned you. I don't remember the context, but it was lovely, even Gidi noticed it. It's nice to see you eating, by the way. You've suddenly turned anorexic on me."

"That's so surprising, what you said."

"Of course she's very attached to you, even if she doesn't show it. I remember now that after you were injured, I used to invite her to sleep over a lot and she always refused. She said she wanted to be at home to take care of you. It was heartbreaking."

"What am I supposed to do with all that now? It only makes me feel guiltier."

Dafna reproaches her, "Enough with the crime and punishment, I'm telling you this so you'll see that you have power over her, in the good sense, and that she loves you."

"Loves me?" Iris mutters, staring through the window at the darkening sea, an infinite, ominous well. "I never thought about that. It should be the most important thing, but it actually doesn't matter."

"Apropos of love, what about the love of your life?"

"Oh, it's complicated. You'll laugh at me, but all of a sudden, I'm afraid to get in touch with him because it might hurt Alma. I love him so much, but I feel that I shouldn't talk to him, even if it's not rational."

"Of course it isn't. What's the connection? You know I'm against breaking up the family, but anything that makes you feel better right now seems important. That's your cell phone ringing, isn't it?"

Iris takes it quickly out of her bag, it might be Alma, but it's him. "It's him," she whispers, "I shouldn't answer."

To her astonishment, Dafna takes her phone out of her hand and answers the call, smiling broadly. "Iris can't talk right now," she says warmly, "should I give her a message?...No problem, I'll tell her." She ends the call, her eyes flashing. "What a sense of timing that guy has," she chuckles, "how did he know when to call?"

Shaking her head, Iris says, "He already called twice today and I didn't answer. It would be irresponsible, Dafna, what if something happens to Alma now?"

"What is all this black magic, suddenly? It's not like you. Why make it harder for yourself? You're going through a complicated time, don't make it more painful for yourself, especially since he's going to be at a conference in Tel Aviv tomorrow."

"Eitan? At a conference in Tel Aviv?" she chokes. "How strange. Was that the message he gave you for me?"

Dafna chuckles, "I've seen stranger things in my life, there are no end of conferences in Tel Aviv."

"So what exactly did he say, that I should go to see him at the conference?"

"Something like that, that he'd be happy to see you, but only if you change your dress." Iris smiles at her, maybe she's right, maybe it's a sign that she should see him. The abstinence she has imposed on herself is unbearable, her suffering won't help Alma.

"What's with Shira, by the way?" she asks, more awake now. "How come we haven't heard from her for two hours already?"

"She has a date tonight with that guy. She listened to you and it actually worked. This is their second date."

"I'm so glad. Let's order dessert." But Iris feels an annoying twinge of jealousy. Shira has a date and Alma is sleeping with strangers, but she won't let that dull the sweetness of the fluffy cake. She'll see him tomorrow, she'll go to the conference. Her daughter loves her and she loves her daughter, but she loves him too, and maybe there is no momentous contradiction in that.

"Alma's building is fantastic, classic Bauhaus," Dafna says when she lets Iris off where she picked her up.

But Iris laughs, "That's not Alma's building. I didn't notice that you drove back here."

"So what were you doing here?" Dafna asks, but Iris finds it difficult to explain, to identify with the terrified woman who wandered the streets only a short time ago, and she directs her friend to the correct, ugly building. She suddenly feels slightly relieved, even the mystery of the spider and Alma's absence won't keep her from falling asleep. She'll see her in the morning, she has influence over her, she'll find the right words.

But how will those right words reach Alma if she doesn't come home? She wakes up every hour to an apartment whose tenants have gone, as if they have vacated it for her, and only when the sourish lemony light rises and the street traffic comes to life does she hear the door open. She listens tensely for their voices. Do they know she's listening and is that why they aren't speaking? Or are they too tired, because apart from the sound of flowing water and several quick whispers, she hears nothing. They don't eat the nutritious food or notice the shining floor, the polished counter, the bowl of fruit on the table. They are not in reality, they are above or below it. She lies on the bed silently, above the still-dying spider, and welcomes the new day, tense and excited. She'll see him again, she'll get up soon, shower and put on the short black tricot dress, she'll see him again in one of the seaside hotels.

She'll wait for him in the lobby, he'll come immediately and they'll go up to one of the rooms, where their souls will intermingle as they did in the beginning. Dafna was right, there is no reason to remove him from her life now, of all times. As she drinks her coffee, she sees Alma come out of Noa's room on her way to the small bathroom, wearing a black shirt, her skinny legs bare, and then she hears her brush her teeth.

"You're still here," Alma says uneasily as she pulls on her pants.

"You're going out already? Where to? You've hardly slept."

"To work, I have the morning shift," Alma replies coldly. "You always complained that I was lazy, now I'm working hard, and that's no good either?"

"Should I make you some coffee? A sandwich?" she offers.

"Coffee." Alma yawns widely, her eyes half closed, looking totally drained, so wrung out by the internal and external work she does that she accepts her mother's presence.

Iris hands her the cup and, like a devoted housekeeper, reports, "Today I'll bring your clothes from the Laundromat. Would you like to meet later? We'll buy you something pretty to wear?"

"I don't have time."

But to her surprise, Alma doesn't ask when she's leaving, when she'll return her key and vacate her Tel Aviv bed, which she has also taken over. Is it really out of tiredness that she doesn't protest, or deep down, does her mother's presence make her feel safe?

She goes out into the street again, the humidity striking her face like a used floor rag, exhaust fumes filling her throat, and walks to the parking lot, so excited about seeing him that the heat doesn't bother her. Nor does the ominous news broadcast waiting for her on the car radio or the high cost of the parking. The rendezvous awaiting her lifts her by the hair and raises her above reality. As she drives to the hotel where the conference on nerve pain is to be held that day, she suddenly realizes that this is exactly how her daughter must feel now, because that man, the owner of an inconsequential little bar in south Tel Aviv, rescued her from the boredom of her daily life and offered her change, an acrobatic leap over the reality of her life. No more TV sets, computer monitors, and radar screens, but roller-coaster days and nights, and that's why she's a prisoner, mesmerized by the terrible, exhilarating experience she is suddenly having, by the additional faces she never found in the mirror before. But she, her mother who brought her into the world, must teach her, just as she taught her to walk and talk and cross on the crosswalks, that we have to forge a peace treaty with reality as it is, with its heat and humidity, its dreariness and boredom, its high cost of parking and its news headlines—for only there are we free. She must teach her, even though she herself has only just learned that what appears to be life above reality is, in fact, enslavement.

The sea sparkles, winking at her with countless turquoise-white eyes, and she lingers in her car in the hotel parking lot. Hasn't she drummed it into the teachers and parents that only by setting a personal example can we truly effect change? If she does get out of the car and see him now, as she yearns to do, if she does take her life in that direction, she will have no right to expect her daughter to diverge from her path. It isn't black magic, it's education.

Is that his car moving toward her? If she sees him now, she won't be able to overcome her feelings—she is meant for him and he for her, the spring and the mulberry tree will testify to that. But a young woman gets out of the car and hurries inside to the conference, while she leaves behind the luxury hotel that overlooks the sea and drives with a heavy heart toward the ground-floor apartment that beckons to thieves, Peeping Toms, and insects, the apartment that suddenly became a booby trap. She drives slowly, as if in a funeral procession, despite the honking horns and passing cars signaling her, her heart as heavy as the price. She doesn't know how or even if she will justify it, because together and separately, she and Alma will have to learn about the beauty of reality as it is.

SEVENTEEN

Though they didn't eat a thing, she cooks again. Maybe she'll go out into the street with the full pots, distribute the food free to passersby, force them to eat the way she forced Alma, and while chopping onions, garlic, and eggplants, she tries to plan her next move. She has to get to Alma, but not she herself, she needs a messenger, so she browses through the contacts on her phone. She once had friends in Tel Aviv, but she hasn't kept in touch and feels uncomfortable calling suddenly, and mainly she doesn't want to have a meaningless conversation or share intimate information either. Her fingers are drawn to the newest number that joined her list of contacts yesterday, and before she can change her mind, he answers and she asks quickly, "Are you free tonight, Sasha?"

Surprised, he replies, "The truth is, yes, I am. Don't tell me that I'm going out on a date with the principal!"

"Not exactly a date, and not with the principal, just with a worried mother, okay? You must know all about that."

"Absolutely, my mom is always worried. Cool, so where should we meet?"

She tries unsuccessfully to remember the name of the café she saw next to Alma's bar. "I'll text you the address when I'm on the way, okay? How about seven o'clock?"

"Cool," he says again, still surprised. "A date with the principal, it's huge!"

She hangs up on his laughter and hurries into the shower, her body once again bitter and sweaty. Eitan is surely waiting for her, occasionally checking his phone. The conferees won't be looking out of the windows of their room on a high floor, from there everyone looks as tiny as grasshoppers, and so does their pain. No, she must immerse herself in the masses now like a foreign worker who has left behind everything she holds dear. Is there really no other way? Tonight, apparently, there isn't, and tonight is the night she needs help urgently, she can't wait anymore for the girls to come home at dawn. She dries herself quickly, combs her hair, puts on the long black dress, and leaves the apartment. In the muted twilight, she sees the desolation of the city, its heat undiminished by the evening, a sick, festering city that infects young girls with its disease. Night has not yet fallen to hide the dirt and congestion, the party has not yet begun. Again and again, she bumps into bike riders, baby-carriage pushers, and grocery-cart pullers, but now, for some reason, they seem as frightened as she. Does it have something to do with the news broadcast? She wants to talk to them, ask them to follow her in a long procession all the way to Alma's bar, where they will gather in front of the large window until Alma comes out of her own free will. Alma might actually be lonely, filled with anxiety the way Iris was yesterday, so she'll surround her with people.

Only it isn't to Alma's bar that she walks now, but to the one nearby that looks almost the same.

Do all these wretched places look alike? The waitress is skinny and appears stressed out. Does she also work for nothing, is she also battling her ego? Probably it's only because of the workload, it isn't easy to pay for an apartment in the middle of Tel Aviv. She listens distractedly to Sasha's plans for the future, he wants to be a psychiatrist, to treat children like him. She makes do with a frozen vodka, but orders the most expensive item on the menu and a huge beer for him, enjoys watching him as he eats and speaks, his sharp jaw moving rhythmically under his high cheekbones, his blue, slightly slanted eyes, his dark skin. He was such a breathtakingly beautiful child that people took pleasure in looking at him, but under the angelic mask was a devilish determination. "I'm sure you'll succeed, Sashinka," she says, "that's what your mother calls you, right? Even when you were eleven, you were the most determined person I'd ever met."

Chuckling, he says, "Determined to make everyone's life miserable."

"In the end, that seems to have been marginal. It's a fact that you managed to channel that determination in the right direction. At meetings, we always used to say that you'd be either the head of the Mafia or the prime minister."

"It turns out that's more or less the same thing. Hey, this is great beer, can you order me another glass?"

"Leave room for the rest," she says, "our night is just beginning." When he looks at her in embarrassment, she laughs, "Don't worry, Sashinka, I'm not into younger men. I need your help with Alma." As he eats, she explains what she needs him to do, simply sit in Alma's bar, text her about what's going on, and wait for the moment when he can be of use to her. "I want her to feel protected, to know there's someone else watching, that she doesn't have to face him alone. Do you understand?"

The longer he listens to her, the softer his expression becomes, and she sees in his face the sensitive, volatile child he once was, so hurt when he felt wronged. Now it seems as if the wrong has been done to Alma, and that, along with the wrong she is doing to herself, hurts him personally. "Thank you for your faith in me," he says with emotion, his eyes moist. "I'll do what you say, I'll sit there all night if you want me to. You know there's no one in the world I owe as much as I owe you. I only hope it helps."

"Thank you, sweetheart." Her third day in the city and she too is tossing about cheap terms of endearment. "It has to help. I don't have any other ideas at the moment." Then she gives him some money and says, "Order whatever you want, stay there as long as you can."

"Should I try to talk to her?"

"Maybe, if it isn't forced. I trust you, kid."

He stands up slowly, apparently finding it difficult to leave her. Then he bends down and pats her shoulder in an awkward gesture of encouragement. "It'll be okay," he says with a smile, but his eyes are moist. "I believe in miracles, and also in mothers. Just look at me."

Yes, she smiles as she watches him walk away in his striped shirt and cargo pants, his huge light-colored sneakers, you really are a miracle. Most of the staff were sure that in only a few years he would be in a center for juvenile delinquents. Teachers came to her in tears and parents called constantly, threatening to take their children out of the school if he wasn't expelled, as he had been from several other schools. Then there was his mother, who worked hard in a pharmaceutical factory, helpless and also frightened of him. How could Iris expel him and cause her to lose more days of work, how could she transfer him to a special education school when she sensed his rare mind, his extraordinary abilities under the hooligan's mask he showed the world. So she took him under her wing and patiently and firmly dismantled the wall of obstacles he had built. He occasionally disappointed her and she almost broke, but she couldn't give up on him. Even when he hurt one of the hamsters in the animal petting corner she had cultivated, she believed him when he said that he had just wanted to see its inner organs. "He'll be a surgeon one day," she promised his terrified mother, "don't worry, believe in him, in yourself and in us. We'll show him the path and he'll take it."

Now, with a heavy heart, she recalls that year. Even without him, her job would have been almost impossible, what with the supervisor who was just waiting for her to fail, the staff of burnt-out teachers, and the difficult pupils, but she didn't give up. Of course, her Alma paid the price, because when she came home exhausted, she didn't have any patience or interest left. Perhaps there was a rare cosmic justice in the fact that the boy who had drained her mother's patience was now mobilized to save the girl who had been neglected because of him, who had become a child of the cosmos.

And here comes his first report. "I'm sitting at the bar, Alma looks wiped out, the other waitress is more interested in me, the boss is wearing white clothes, sitting at the bar next to me, can I punch him in the face?"

She reads and rereads the words until another text appears: "Rissi, the conference is over now. Can you meet me?

319

Let me help you." All those letters spin around her, asking for her attention, and her fingers hesitate above the keyboard. "My love," she types, again feeling that if she sends the text, Alma is lost, and if she doesn't send it, Alma will be saved— or perhaps she's wrong?

Perhaps she should learn from Noa's mother. "I have my own life," she had proclaimed, "what we do is our own business." Alma will gain nothing from her loss, but nonetheless, she erases the words, then immediately retypes and sends them, her heart pounding. But she is answered immediately with a question mark and a smiley, realizing that she has mistakenly texted Sasha instead of Eitan. This, she is convinced, is incontrovertible proof that she must put her own wants aside until she saves Alma, even if this act is so much more formidable as compared to her small mistake. She puts her phone in her bag to avoid being tempted and orders another frozen vodka. Then she immediately takes it out again because, after all, she's waiting for reports, and the knowledge that Eitan is waiting for her reply lies heavily on her. Is she taking revenge on him for having left her?

Instead of answering him, she texts Alma: "Hi sweetie, you must be tired. When will you get home? I'm waiting for you." Then she updates Sasha, "I texted Alma," and Sasha replies, "She has no time for texts, she's running back and forth, the place is mobbed." To her surprise, she receives a quick, curt reply, "Don't wait for me, go back to your house," and when she reports to Sasha, he sends her a blurry picture. But she recognizes Alma's cell phone with its red cover lying on the counter next to a white sleeve, and she understands that it wasn't Alma who replied, but Boaz. Her anger mounts when she realizes that her text led Boaz to interrogate Alma aggressively, and she is being raked over the coals that very moment. She can barely keep herself from jumping up and running over there—it's so close—to drag Alma out of that place. No one can stop Sasha, who will be happy to display the power of his fists by landing a few punches on the owner's face.

Forget everything I once preached to you against violence and finish off that man, she'll whisper to him, but she has to wait, the time isn't ripe yet. She calls Mickey to let him know what's happening, and she is startled to hear how alert and calm he sounds. He's helping Omer study for his civics final, he tells her, knowing it will make her happy. "He has a good head," he says, almost surprised, and she decides not to disrupt their pleasant time together with bad news from Tel Aviv.

"Lovely," she says, "so we'll talk later."

Once again she reads the text, "Don't wait for me, go back to your house," scrolling back over the few texts they have exchanged. How many of them were actually written by him? "I'm busy, sorry," "I'm at work," "I have a really crazy day, I'm doing a double shift and have to close up too," "Can't make it Friday," "Can't make it Saturday," "Can't make it Sunday." Why did she agree to give him free access to her cell phone? Is he also sending texts in her name to the men she sleeps with at his behest? She shakes with rage, how did this happen to Alma, how is this still happening to young girls, young women, in the twenty-first century, after all the revolutions? Her grandmother was married off against her will to a man who turned out to be violent, she was prevented from getting an education, kept from achieving independence. But Alma, whose parents are so anxious for her to enroll in university, who sees a model of equality at home—how can she be so willing to give up her freedom?

"Are you cold? Should I lower the air-conditioning?" the waitress asks.

She mumbles, "It doesn't matter, I'm cold on the inside."

But the waitress won't stop: "Do you want a cup of tea? Maybe soup? We have great celery soup."

Iris orders both tea and soup even though she wants to get out of there, even though she doesn't know where she will go. There is no place where she can escape the unbearable feeling, because for some reason, Boaz's control over her daughter's phone horrifies her even more than his control over her mind. Her throat contracts and she breathes heavily, as if she has been exposed to hazardous materials and is beginning to die an agonizing death. Once again she reaches for her phone, maybe she'll call Eitan anyway, maybe he's still in the city. What's the point of a personal example that no one knows about, that saddens her so much, that tortures her, because she is meant for him and he is meant for her. The spring and the mulberry tree will testify.

Maybe she'll ask the solicitous waitress to tie her to the chair so she can't call, the way Odysseus commanded his sailors to lash him to the mast. Who knows how she'll respond; after all, even in this city, which has seen everything, this will undoubtedly be an unusual request. But she is in an unusual situation and she is the mother of a daughter who is in an unusual situation, and isn't that, in fact, what her daughter has chosen, to shackle herself completely?

This place is almost empty for a reason, the soup is bland and the tea tepid. But that's fine with her, no commotion around her and no one to look at her apart from the waitress, who comes over to her again now and asks mechanically, "Is everything okay?"

Iris nods resentfully. People have stopped listening to what they say, have stopped looking around and exercising good judgment. "Does it look to you like everything is okay?" she rebukes her, then apologizes, "I'm sorry, it's nothing personal, it's just that those questions are so unnecessary."

"Sorry if I bothered you," the waitress says, swinging her long, chestnut hair as she walks away. Alma's hair used to be exactly like that, almost to her waist. The day before she went into the army, she cut it for the first time, not really short, but it was still not an easy parting, the first in a series of partings that continued into the next morning when, tired and tense, they took her to the induction center. She burst into tears, and when Iris hugged her, she was surprised at how fragile her body was, and even more, at the way she clung to them, unable to say goodbye. When her name was called and she stepped onto the bus, her shoulders shook under her shortened hair, and they stood there and waved at the bus as it moved into the distance, then walked silently back to their car feeling a vague sense of disaster.

"Calm down," they told her in the teachers' room, "what can happen to a girl? Wait until you send a boy into the army, that's the real hell." But she didn't calm down, she waited anxiously all day for the phone call that didn't come till evening, when Alma sobbed loudly, "Mom, get me out of this place, I can't stay here another minute." They both tried to persuade her, "All beginnings are hard, you'll adjust, don't worry, you can always leave." She did adjust in the end, but they were surprised at how difficult it was for her, apparently an indication of a weakness they had not been aware of.

Several months after that morning, when she was driving her to the central bus station, she suddenly said, "You know, a day doesn't pass when I don't think about that bus ride the day I was drafted. It was so awful, I don't understand how I stayed there, how I didn't get off in the middle of the road. It was the worst day of my life." She always said the most important things at the most inopportune moments, which seemed to minimize their importance and allowed no time to delve deeper into them.

Did they dismiss her difficulties too easily? Because the moment she seemed to be adjusting, they also adjusted to her absence, to her empty room, her empty bed, which became a convenient refuge, and even before she adjusted, they had occasionally rebuked her for her inordinate complaining. "You can't believe how terrible it is here, it's like the Warsaw ghetto!" she cried one evening, calling from boot camp, and Iris, unable to hold back, reproached her, "You should be ashamed of yourself for comparing the two! I won't listen to that kind of talk. You're either ignorant or spoiled or both!" Then Mickey added gently, in his didactic tone, "You're only in the army to keep the Warsaw ghetto from ever happening again," and Alma laughed bitterly, "You really shouldn't count on me, I can barely hold my rifle. It's bigger than I am."

"Everyone contributes to the best of their ability," Mickey said. "Stick with it, Alma, don't give up on yourself." She didn't give up on herself, but in some elusive way, they gave up on her. Since she seemingly overcame her difficulties, they didn't ask themselves why it was so hard for her, not the physical conditions but leaving home and childhood, which was more painful for her than for her friends. It apparently still is because it's a fact that she needs a jailer to tie her hands and feet to keep her from going back home, to separate her from her parents and forbid her from seeing them or even replying to their texts.

Now she recalls an evening when that difficulty was as distinct and palpable as Alma herself. It confused and worried her, but a few days later, she let it go because you can't worry all the time, you always deal with the most urgent and present concerns. You walk through the world with a giant spider on your head unaware that it's there.

They visited her one weekend, and since the base was far away, they rented a room for the night in the family lodgings at her recommendation. She greeted them with her usual fragile happiness, which faded quickly, and although she had asked them to come, they already felt, even before dinner, how much they oppressed her. Iris tried, as she always did, to lighten the family mood, and with forced cheerfulness took out of the cooler the food she had worked hard to prepare at night after an exhausting day at work, hawking her wares as if she expected cheers. "Corn quiche, pasta salad, spinach pastries, lentil salad, halva cake. Who's hungry?" she asked like a kindergarten teacher, setting the card table in the yard with plates, glasses, silverware, and napkins, proud of herself for not having forgotten anything. But perhaps she had forgotten the most important thing?

They seemed like a nomadic family that evening, carrying their food, eating habits, and neuroses with them from place to place, the outer trappings of a family, mother and father, son and daughter, sitting around the table as if they were home. But they weren't home, they were on an army base where their daughter belonged, while they were transient guests, merely visitors, and so there was a painful division between her and them even as they sat together and ate, even when they spoke, and mainly when they wanted to go to sleep. She was tired after her night of cooking, and Mickey was tired after long hours of driving, so they moved in and out, preparing themselves and the room for sleep. Alma, however, stayed in the yard, even though she had to return to the soldiers' quarters.

"Want to sleep with us?" Iris asked when she saw how difficult it was for her to leave, and Alma said, "I don't know, is there room for me?" Iris pulled out a folding bed for her from under her bed—Omer was already sound asleep on the one that had been under Mickey's—and Alma stood there hesitantly until she said, "Never mind, I'll go back to barracks." But she didn't, she remained standing in the doorway instead, watching Iris as she undressed and put on her nightgown. Then she said again, "So I'll go back to my room," but she went back outside and sat down on the grass next to the card table like a faithful watchdog, and Iris, who couldn't close the door while she was still there, went outside in her thin nightgown. "Is something bothering you?" she asked, "do you want to talk to me about something?"

"We can talk if you feel like it," Alma said, and Iris asked her a few questions, which she answered briefly, about the training course, her girlfriends, the job she would have. When she realized that her daughter didn't feel like talking, she said with an apologetic smile, "I'm very tired, I cooked half the night," and Alma replied quickly, "So go to sleep Mom."

"But what about you, aren't you tired?" Iris asked, and Alma said, "Yes, I'm tired," but once again her words did not lead to action. "So good night, sweetie," Iris said as she stood up, "we'll talk some more tomorrow."

"Good night, Mom," Alma said, and remained seated, watching her mother leave with a mysterious air of expectation. But it wasn't a particularly good night because she couldn't fall asleep. She tossed and turned with worry, unable to understand what Alma had actually wanted, afraid to go and see if she was still there, beside the card table, her profile sharp and sad, a little girl in uniform.

Now she is ready to believe that if she had stayed with her all night and hadn't given in to her tiredness, she might have prevented her from falling into the trap that will demand concessions of her much more painful than one sleepless night.

That's how it is, she sighs loudly, we'll always miss the previous stage in the obstacle course of our lives. But she won't think about that now, maybe it's only a temporary concession, only a postponement. After all, she waited decades for Eitan to come back to her, and a few more months won't matter, he'll wait for her just as she waited for him. But apparently even thinking about him put Alma at risk, because now, to her horror, Sasha texts, "It doesn't look good," and she replies quickly, "What's happening?"

"She changed into a short dress, put on a lot of makeup, is leaving the restaurant now," he texts. "Follow her!" she writes, but he is more levelheaded than she, "Not a good idea, it'll make her and the people here suspicious. I have to stay."

She admits that he's right, but she herself has no problem arousing suspicion, they already think she's weird, at best, so she stands up quickly and announces, "I have to run, how much do I owe?" The waitress walks over to the cash register with annoying slowness and she tries to hurry her along.

"Please, I'm in a big rush, my daughter is in the emergency room," she hears herself say, and immediately pulls out a large bill and doesn't wait for change. Mickey would go crazy at the waste of money, he would completely lose it if he were with her now, he would run down the street screaming, just as she is now, "Alma, where are you? Alma, wait for me!" She hasn't dared to run since the injury, but now she wobbles on her platinum pelvis, feeling the fractured bones that the best surgeons had labored long hours to repair coming apart again. "Alma, come back, Come home!"

Of course, she has no idea whether the street she is running on will bring her closer to or farther away from her daughter, or whether her shouts can be heard over the noise of the cars, conversations, and music in the open cafés. Nonetheless, she keeps shouting and ignores the looks she's getting, keeps shouting as if she were alone in the streets, her eyes darting around in search of a skinny girl in a short dress, a needle in a haystack. Until her feet, surprised by the running, collide with a bump in the street that suddenly becomes the sidewalk and she falls flat out, as unyielding as a tree trunk, her hands flailing in helpless shock. In a flash of understanding and acceptance, a few seconds before her body meets the sidewalk, she realizes that the crash is inevitable.

Those were precisely the seconds she didn't have that morning, the seconds when the understanding and the injury are joined. No bird sang, no bull roared, no hawk soared, only she soared over the roof of her smashed car, observing the inhuman scene of human pain from a bird's-eye view. She remembers that she silently parted from her mother and Mickey and thought about her father, who would reach out from the sky and gather her to him, because they were the same age then. But she utterly and surprisingly forgot to bid farewell to her children, forgot that she even had children, while now, she can think only of Alma. Where have you gone, what are you doing, when will you come back?

"Alma," she groans, lying immobile on the sidewalk, on her stomach, her hands at her sides as if she has lain down to sleep, and the passersby who hurry toward her from every direction ask, "Are you okay?" How strange everyone in this city is, they see a person who is totally not okay and ask her over and over again if she's okay!

"Can you get up?" they ask. "Did you hit your head? Do you want us to call an ambulance?" She hears a mixture of voices and questions that she doesn't understand, that she understands but can't answer, can answer but doesn't want to. She is too tired and it's time to go to sleep, she had too much to drink and she needs to sleep, it doesn't matter where. She's safer here on the sidewalk than in Alma's bed, and she turns onto her back with an effort, runs her tongue around the inside of her mouth to check that her teeth are intact. Her body is strewn with pain the way the sky is strewn with stars, and she sees them for a moment when she blinks. It's strange that the stars are so clear in the middle of the city, but they won't keep her from falling asleep, nothing will keep her from falling asleep now, not even the talking going on above her head as if she were a baby or a frail old woman.

"She was just in our place! Her daughter's in the emergency room!" she hears someone shout, and is momentarily alarmed, Alma's in the emergency room! That's why she was running after her in the streets, to save her from disaster, Alma's in the emergency room! Then she remembers the waitress, who has apparently just finished her shift. "What hospital is your daughter in?" she asks as she bends over her, the ends of her long chestnut hair brushing against Iris's cheeks. She always taught her pupils that our lies come back to haunt us, and that's what's happening to her now. Sometimes lies turn into a truth that works against us, she used to say, exaggerating to make the warning stronger, and now that exaggeration is shaking her to her core. Whom did Alma go to meet, where did he send her so heavily made up? This city is full of drunks and junkies, she has to rescue her, she can't sleep here. She'll ignore the stars of pain and continue searching for her, if she scours street after street, she will undoubtedly find her one day. She tries to lean on her left hand, which hurts less, among all the pairs of legs that have gathered around her. At least ten people circle her, as if they are about to begin prayer.

If only she can spring up and float above the streets. When they look down at her, they'll find that she's gone, that she left nothing behind, and they'll have to go back to minding their own business instead of hers. Perhaps Noa's mother is right, people here are busybodies. Now another pair of legs joins the crowd, particularly large feet in light-colored sneakers, another busybody leaning over her. But how does he know her name?

"Iris! What happened? Did you fall? I've been looking for you."

She groans, "Sasha, I lost her, I couldn't find her."

"She'll come back," he says. "Let me take you home." The disappointed crowd disperses instantly, the passersby have gathered in vain, have given their time in vain, and now the event is over before they can enjoy it to the fullest. "That man is dangerous," Sasha says, sitting down on the sidewalk beside her and lighting a cigarette. "I would have crushed him with my hands, then I would have stepped on him, kicked him, and thrown him in the garbage."

She laughs despite the pain and says, "You're back to your old self. That's exactly how you spoke when you were a boy."

He gives her an embarrassed smile, apologetic and proud at the same time of the child he once was, and justifiably so. He was brave and tenacious, believed that he was surrounded by enemies and refused to surrender, and now his presence beside her imbues her with a remarkable sense of power. How did he suddenly appear in her life like a walking miracle, how did she even think of fighting this battle without him?

"So how are you feeling?" he asks, studying her carefully as he crushes a cigarette butt with his gigantic foot. "How bad is the pain, where do you hurt? I took a medic course in the army."

"My right hand, my right knee, my ribs."

He checks her hand and asks, "Can you move your fingers?"

"Yes, but barely."

"Your hand is really swollen. We'll call an ambulance to take you to the emergency room."

"Absolutely not, let's wait till morning. Please, Sasha," she implores as if she were a little girl and he her father.

He probes her hand and says, "Okay, we can go to the clinic tomorrow. It depends on how much it hurts you."

"I'd rather wait," she says gratefully. "Help me up?"

Slowly and carefully, he picks her up from the sidewalk and stands her on her feet. A taxi has already parked next to them, and he helps her lie down on the back seat for the short ride; in a few minutes they reach the gray building. He pays the driver, bends over her, and in an instant she is in his arms like a bride being carried by her groom into their new home on their wedding night. Her head rests on the striped shirt that covers his broad chest, his skin is smooth, his heart strong. Oh Eitan, she sighs, we thought that we were godlike, that we could return to the past and correct all our mistakes.

At the building entrance, he freezes in place and she feels his muscles tense. She shifts her gaze and sees her daughter sitting on the steps, wearing a very short yellow dress, her made-up eyes wide with shock at what she sees. She jumps up and runs toward them. "I told you I didn't have a key!" She blurts out the complaint that has apparently been waiting on the tip of her tongue, but immediately gets a grip on herself and asks, "What happened? Who's that? What's going on here?"

"You'll find the key in her bag, Alma," Sasha says. "Your mother fell. She went out to look for you and she fell."

Alma obeys angrily, foraging around in her bag. "To look for me?" she barks as she turns the key in the lock. "Why was she looking for me?" Only when the door opens and the light comes on does she look at him and point an accusing finger. "It's you! You were at the bar just now! What's going on here?"

"Where's your bed, Alma?" he asks impatiently, as if he is the responsible adult and she an annoying child. "Your mother needs to lie down first and get treatment before she can answer your questions." She obeys him again and points to her bedroom door. As Iris listens to them, she realizes that they are talking over her head, like the people on the street, but this time she likes it, she likes it so much that she is ready to sink into sleep and let Sasha explain everything however he wants to. Alma has seen them now, and he won't be able to sit there pretending to be a customer anyway, so her long-term plan has just been ruined, leaving only the present, this night, when her entire body has been battered. Did she ever have anything but the present? she wonders, but she has refused to submit to it, tried to control it with all her newsletters, with all the plans she made, and now it says to her: I am not an echo of past memories, I am not a bridge to future plans, I am all you have, the essence of your existence. Trust me, because you have no choice.

But how can she trust it? The pain and anger are growing stronger every minute. It has all been for nothing because after she cleaned, cooked, shopped, and organized with a sense of joyous omnipotence, after she decided to appoint herself her daughter's housekeeper in the hope that it would help her get used to her presence, she has all at once become useless, ineffective, and inefficient, an unnecessary burden.

Why did she have to look for her, instead of waiting here to welcome her when she came back, to feed her and put her to bed, and do so with patient consistency, day after day. I'm here for you no matter where you've been and what you've done, the important thing is that your mom is waiting for you in a clean home with a nutritious meal. Only now, after crashing onto the sidewalk, has it become clear to her that she planned to do exactly that, and she realizes sadly that she will have to return home very soon and stay there as long as she needs help, because even if she has no broken bones, her movement will be limited. Obviously she can't clean or cook or take care of anyone, which makes her presence in this apartment in this city pointless, and she shakes her head with growing anger just as Sasha comes over with a small bowl and some cotton. "We have to clean your wounds," he says, bending over her bare knee and gently swabbing it with cotton soaked in soapy water. Then he moves on to her fingertips, where the cuts and scrapes also turn out to be superficial, and he once again checks the movement of her fingers. "Maybe you just came down hard but didn't break anything," he says. "I'll bandage you for the time being, it'll help with the pain tonight, and tomorrow we'll go check it out. Do you have any bandages here?" he asks Alma.

Alma shakes her head, an expression of horror on her beautiful, made-up face as she looks at the wounds. "Never mind," he says, "in the army we managed without bandages. Do you have a shirt you don't need?" She looks in the closet and reluctantly hands him a black tricot shirt, her slave uniform, and Iris is mesmerized by his movements as he tears it into strips with his huge hands. Isn't this the same as the ritual of tearing the clothes at a funeral, a symbol of the family's pain and sorrow? She pictures Eitan's torn shirt, the tear so long that his chest was exposed when he knelt down at the pile of earth and cried out, Come back to me.

But now, in her living present, this tear might signify hope, not mourning, and she finds herself mumbling a prayer, "May you be torn away from him, may you be torn away from him in the same way, amen."

This is how I dreamed of binding you to me so it would hurt less, she wants to tell Alma, as he winds the black strip around her hand, pressing her fingers together and lessening her pain. After he ties several strips tightly together and hangs it around her neck as a sling for her hand, Alma smiles, "It's so funny that everything's black! She looks like a dominatrix—all she needs is a whip!"

Sasha, studying Iris with satisfaction, also laughs. "Yes, it's kinky." Iris likes the way he keeps a certain distance from her daughter. The moment they seem to be getting closer, he says quickly, "Okay, I'm gone, call me in the morning, Iris." He leaves without even glancing at Alma. He is so huge that his absence makes the room seem larger.

"Who's that? Where'd you find him?" Alma asks, unable to control her curiosity.

"He was my pupil once, I bumped into him by accident on the street." Iris hopes that her vagueness will allow some flexibility about the sequence of events, making it appear that she met him after she fell, but her daughter insists on knowing exact details.

"So you sent him to the bar?" Alma leans on the doorframe, her tight dress exposing her back, and looks at her with suspicion in her eyes, which emphasizes their intense blackness.

In an effort to change the subject, Iris asks, "Do you happen to have any painkillers?"

"No, I don't have painkillers," she replies hostilely, her voice growing louder. "Why should I have painkillers? Did I know you'd come here? Did I know you'd fall? Why can't you be careful?"

Iris absorbs the hurtful words and says quietly, "Why are you attacking me like this?"

"I'm attacking you? You're attacking me! Did anyone ask you to move in here all of a sudden? Why don't you take care of yourself? I can't stand to see you like this, with all those bandages!"

"I completely understand you," Iris says, trying to hide the sorrow, the humiliation. "You don't have to see me, I'll ask Dad to come tomorrow and take me home."

To her surprise, her daughter stamps her foot and bursts into tears, sits down on the edge of the bed and covers her face with her hands, her bare back shaking. "Sure, this gives you an excuse to run away! Is that why you keep hurting yourself, so you can run away from us?"

Iris listens in shock, it has been years since she saw her cry this way, like a baby having a tantrum. "Alma, what do you want? Help me to help you!"

"I don't need your help," her daughter sobs, "I have other people who help me, I have a teacher who teaches me how to live! You were right, I wasted my life in front of the TV, you're always right, but you have nothing to offer me and he does!"

"Calm down, Alma," she says, desperately seeking the right words. "You barely slept at night, come on, eat something and go to sleep. We'll talk some more tomorrow, okay?"

But her daughter leaps up and screams, "I won't be here tomorrow!" The makeup running from her eyes in crooked black streams makes her face look cracked. "I'm leaving, I can't bear to see you lying in bed like that again! Why don't you watch where you're going? I'm going back to work, my shift isn't over."

Iris tries to sit up, to take her hand. "You're not going!" she says in her most authoritative voice, but her daughter jerks her hand away. How can she reach the door before her and block it with her body if she can't even stand on her feet and feels crushed under the weight of the pain? With tears welling up, she pleads, "Alma, don't go, I need you here now, I can't stay alone."

"What do you need?" She turns around and walks back suspiciously, eyes averted, both of them breathing heavily.

"Maybe I have some painkillers left in my bag," Iris says. "Can you please look?"

Alma shoves things around in the bag, hands her a few stray pills she finds on the bottom. As a child, she loved searching through her mother's bag for surprises, gum, candy, a new lipstick. She and Omer used to squabble about who would do the foraging, and then left it sticky and messy. Now, however, she drops it in the middle of the room because her phone begins ringing in her own bag and she goes into Noa's room and closes the door, but Iris can hear her voice, trembling and agitated.

Is he demanding that she come back? What will she do? She has no more ammunition against him now, if Alma decides to go, she can't do a thing. She tries helplessly to eavesdrop, how can she leave her here until morning? She hears the door open and her daughter come out, upset, though she still doesn't look as if she's planning to leave. "Alma, bring me a glass of water," she asks. And if you're hungry, there's lots of food." It seems that only now does her daughter notice the changes in the small apartment, still undecided about how to react. Will she rebuke her for violating her privacy, or will she enjoy the change, because after all, she always loved cleanliness and order, soft sheets and fragrant towels.

"It doesn't suit you to be earth mother," Alma says wryly, but comes from the kitchen with a glass of water for her and a full plate for herself, and sits down beside her on the edge of the bed. "I didn't have time to eat today," she says as she chews hungrily.

Iris asks cautiously, "You girls don't eat at work?"

"Usually yes," Alma replies with her mouth full. "But I left early today, because I saw your message, you wrote that you were waiting for me." Iris is surprised by the simple words, which belong to a totally different reality. What's happened to us, my sweet little girl, if the most normal words sound so incongruous, but she doesn't dare say anything. She was barely able to keep her from leaving the house and she's afraid of another flare-up, so she just looks at her daughter quietly. She seems to be pleased with the way the apartment looks, but chooses to hide her satisfaction, and Iris hides her own satisfaction at the fact that she's here, beside her, chewing and swallowing.

"Is he angry at you for leaving early?" she asks, cautiously choosing her words, and Alma gives her a quick glance as if trying to understand whether it's a simple question or a jibe.

"Of course he's angry," she replies candidly, "he said that I've given in to my ego again, but it felt right to come home. I didn't give in to my ego, I just didn't want you to wait for me, I know you hate to go to sleep late."

Iris listens to her, her lips trembling with emotion, but she won't tell her that the behavior she is working so hard to justify is taken for granted in the other reality that isn't theirs. "I'm glad you came back," she says, "you must be tired. I'm sorry I took your bed, but there's room here for both of us."

"Don't be silly, I'll sleep in Noa's bed."

But Iris coaxes her, "Why? You should sleep here so you won't wake up when she comes," and she shifts her aching body toward the wall. To her happiness, her daughter is too tired to argue, and she turns off the light and lies down beside her without changing clothes, without washing her face or brushing her teeth. How quickly she has adopted the lifestyle of a survivor, but Iris doesn't say anything. She makes herself small and tries not to move, a fly on the wall of her life tonight, a mother on the wall, and from there she listens to

Alma's rapid breathing, to the sound of her own phone ringing. Despite the pain in her wrist, fingers, and knee, she feels the beginnings of such intense satisfaction that she doesn't know which is stronger, the pain or her satisfaction at Alma's choice that night, which might signify the beginning of recovery. That would turn this pain almost into joy, a miraculous gift that we must suffer to attain. What other gifts come with both pain and joy apart from giving birth to a child—even when you're screaming in agony, you don't forget for a moment that you are giving life.

Sometimes once is not enough, sometimes we have to give our children their lives over and over again, to keep the fire of life burning within them, help them over and over again to choose life, the gift we gave them, though they never asked for it. That is what she is trying to do now, that is why she is in so much pain, just as she was during her daughter's birth that cold night when her young body split open in torment to part from the creature that was living peacefully inside her. Even though they were reunited, that parting was so difficult, as are all the predetermined partings imposed by nature, which dictates the duration of pregnancy and child rearing, of life itself, sometimes even of love. Yes, the pain of being ripped apart from each other was stronger than the joy of their reunion that night. Her torn, emptied body mourned the primal connection it had lost and the baby cried constantly, mourning in Mickey's arms as he rocked her gently and sang her the melancholy childhood songs his mother had sung to him in Arabic.

That was, of course, the first of many partings and reunions life placed in their paths, and for them, the sorrow of the parting has always been greater than the joy of the reunion, which was usually elusive and tentative. But now, as they lie in the same bed for the first time in many years, she feels the full power of this reunion, even though her daughter is sleeping and she herself is drifting off.

Waves of pain encircle them, drawing the map of their lives that overlaps only partially where her pain cast its shadow over Alma's life and Alma's pain cast a shadow over hers. So many partings still await them. Oh, Eitan, she sighs, how terrible the absence of choice was when you doomed me to a whole life without you, and how difficult the choice is now, when there is no longer a whole life left, there will never be a whole life anymore, not even with you. She tries to pull herself together, in dreadful situations, one must not think that far ahead, at the most she'll think about tomorrow morning. She'll need an x-ray, which may lead to a cast, or even worse, surgery. She'll have to tell Mickey to come and pick her up, Alma's away all day and she'll need help. But even that future is too far away for her, only the present moment exists, this moment when she closes her eyes and falls asleep despite the pain. She isn't even sure she has really fallen asleep when the front door squeaks open and intense yellow light floods the room, accompanied by a shriek.

"Alma, get up fast, you're really in trouble, honey! Call Boaz, he is so pissed off at you." She opens her eyes and sees Noa standing in the doorway, also wearing a short dress and heavily made-up. Although she sees Iris, Noa persists, now in a lower voice, "I have to wake up Alma. believe me it's for her own good."

"Over my dead body," Iris says firmly. "Tell Boaz that I wouldn't let you wake her up."

But Noa pleads, "Alma will be angry at you when she finds out, she's not allowed to sleep when he needs her, it's for her own good!"

"You should go to sleep too, Noa'le," Iris says.

Noa steps back hesitantly, "I don't know," she mumbles.

Iris cuts her short. "But I do know, everything is fine. Turn off the light and go to sleep. By the way, I spoke to your mother earlier and she said she really misses you. She'd be happy if you came home soon."

Noa freezes in the doorway and says dubiously, "She said that? That's not her style."

"You'd be surprised, people change. Especially mothers."

EIGHTEEN

Has the big bad wolf taken advantage of the time she slept to steal her little lamb, her beloved, lost little lamb, who lay close to her all night, quiet and warm? If there was any progress, no sign of it remains, because now the bed is empty, the apartment is empty. How quickly she has grown accustomed to the noise of the bustling street. It's almost noon when she gets out of bed, walking heavily, holding on to the furniture and walls. The short distance to the kettle, the toilet, her bag, her phone, her medication is so long and agonizing. Every movement drills into her bones and she already longs to return to the bed, but there is no relief when she lies down again. Her fingers are swollen and black-and-blue under the black bandage, her knee is throbbing, and her ribs shudder at every breath.

Anxiously, she checks her messages, but there is nothing from Alma. Did she erase whatever they achieved as she slept? For one happy moment, she thought she had managed to get him out of Alma's way, to bring her closer to her, but that was only an illusion. She went back there, went back to her evil ways and left her here, betrayed, with her unnecessary pain. She has never felt so powerless, not even after the injury, because then, her primary mission in life was to recover, while now, it is to save Alma, and she can't do that while lying uselessly in her bed. Dejected, she checks her other messages: Mickey, her secretary, Sasha, and one of her teachers, nothing from Pain. Has he given up on her? Will she try to reach him now that she has failed anyway, will she let him bandage her wounds? I only understand incurable diseases, he said, and they both laughed like children. Is Alma incurable?

A strong sense of foreboding paralyzes her once again, her fingers were injured for a reason, and she calls Mickey instead. His voice is warm and devoted, as it usually is when they aren't under the same roof. "I've been worried about you, Irissi, Alma told me you fell." And she is momentarily surprised that he even knows Alma, so alone did she feel at night, as if she were a single parent.

"When did you talk to her?" she asks. "How did she sound?"

"About an hour ago. She sounded fine. A little confused, but less hostile. How are you?"

"Not great. You should come this evening to take me home, okay? I can't be here alone, I'm almost completely bed-ridden again. Mickey, this must be my karma."

After a brief hesitation, he says, "I actually think you should stay there. I had the impression that she's happy to take care of you. Let her take care of you, why not?"

"But she's always at work, or whatever you call it. You don't want me at home?"

"At work? She told me she would stay home to take care of you. I thought that was a really positive development."

"So what if she said it? Lying also seems to be part of her spiritual work," Iris grumbled miserably. "She didn't stay here, but if it's hard for you to come, I'll take a taxi, and if you don't want me at home, I'll find a hotel."

"What am I going to do with you, Iris? Isn't it about time to let go of your fear of being abandoned?"

"What are you talking about?"

"You know very well what I'm talking about. I have no problem driving there tonight. I just thought it would be good for her to take care of you, good for both of you."

"So what if you thought that?" she grumbles.

Just as she is searching for a way to redeem the conversation, the door opens and her daughter comes in, her hands full, wearing the same dress but no makeup. "I brought you painkillers," she announces.

"Thank you," Iris says, her voice melting with gratitude. "You didn't go to work?"

"No, you said you couldn't stay here alone."

"Sorry, Mickey, you're right," Iris whispers into the phone, but he has already hung up, and he is right about that as well.

Alma really does seem happy to take care of her, even if she makes an effort to hide it, but Iris is still worried about her. Her voice is strident, her gestures exaggerated, and she bought grapes even though the small apartment is full of grapes. She asks her mother over and over again if she wants coffee but forgets to bring the glass of water she asks for. She wanders around the apartment aimlessly, and when her phone rings, she goes into Noa's room and closes the door, avoiding Iris's eyes when she comes out.

"Alma, come and sit here for a minute," she finally calls out to her.

"In a minute, I'm making us breakfast." She hears her frantically opening and closing the fridge, cutting vegetables. She was never enthusiastic about cooking, but she has accumulated experience as a waitress, and now she appears in the doorway with an enticing tray of sliced bread, cheese, vegetables, grapes of course, and coffee. Iris praises her as if she has performed a miracle, and makes room on the bed for her and the tray.

"You know what I just remembered?" Alma says, seated beside her, leaning against the wall and filling her mouth with grapes.

Iris looks expectantly at her rapidly moving jaws. "What did you remember?"

"Never mind," Alma says dismissively, "maybe it never even happened. I just remembered the first morning you came home from the hospital. I got up really early to make you breakfast and arranged everything nicely on a tray for you, but you didn't want it, or maybe it just seemed that way to me."

"Oh Alma, I'm so sorry, I don't remember anything like that, but I was so groggy from the morphine. Why didn't I want it?"

"You were nauseous, you didn't want us to come into your room at all. I was so anxious for you to come home, but even when you did, we hardly saw you. Come on, don't cry. Now I'm sorry I told you."

"I'm not crying," Iris mumbles, "I never cry," and then she bursts out laughing at the contradiction between her words and her actions. "Forgive me, Almush, that was a terrible time. I didn't want you to see me suffering. When you were with me, I tried to show you that I was fine, and that was so exhausting. It's hard to be a mother who isn't functioning, it goes against the essence of motherhood. And it was even harder to be a mother who needs to be taken care of."

"But I wanted to take care of you, I wanted to give you a nice surprise after disappointing you, to show you that I know how to take care of you."

"Disappointing me? Of course not! Why did you think I was disappointed in you?"

"I don't know," Alma says, "for not being the best student? For not sticking with any of my afternoon courses? For watching too much TV? I wanted you to see that I was good at taking care of you. I bought a cookbook and learned how to make a few things for you, but you didn't want them."

"Oh Alma, I had no idea. I remember that at first, I really preferred to be alone, but when I started to feel a bit better and tried to join the family again, I found you pretty indifferent."

"I give up quickly, you know. I don't stick with things. By the way, who's Eitan?"

Iris, suddenly unable to breathe, mumbles, "Eitan? Why do you ask?"

"You must have been dreaming about him. When I woke up I heard you mumbling something, like you were calling him?"

"Really?" Iris dissembles. "He's someone I loved thirty years ago when I was even younger than you. It's strange that I suddenly dreamed about him."

"My dreams go backward too. This last year, I dreamed a lot about the attack, that you were, like, injured and I was trying to save you and was injured myself."

Shaking her head, Iris says, "Why didn't you tell me, how come we never talked about this?"

"It was hard for me to talk. I was too closed. Boaz helps me open up. Thanks to him, I can say a lot more today."

Trying to hide her disappointment at the enemy's reappearance, Iris forces herself to ask softly, "How exactly does he help you?"

"It's part of the spiritual work, changing things about myself that bother me. I felt that my life couldn't go on the way it was, that here I had a chance for real change."

Iris says gently, "I understand," even though she mostly wants to scream: but why this particular change? How can you not see how twisted it is? But it's better not to utter a single word of doubt right now, this isn't the time for preaching, only for quiet, steady giving. She will take care of her daughter and her daughter will take care of her, and perhaps that way, they can slowly defuse the bomb that has been laid at their doorstep.

"I'm glad you're sharing this with me," she adds. Suddenly, she doesn't know what else to say, because on the one hand, her daughter is here, beside her, slowly growing closer to her, but on the other, someone else is pulling her strings, as if she were doomed to raise her along with a stranger, a dangerous one, as Sasha said.

Just as she thinks about him, Alma asks, "What about your pupil? When is he coming?" For the first time, it occurs to her that his presence might interest her, and perhaps, as she explained to parents many times, several elements are usually needed to achieve change when none of them can do it alone.

"Sasha? I really should get back to him. My phone is here on the bed, isn't it? Maybe under the tray?"

Alma finds it in the sheets and stares at the display. "Pain called," she says. "Who's Pain? Sorry I looked, it just caught my eye. Since when does Pain have a phone number?"

Iris sighs, she can easily improvise a lie, after all, she's been specializing in it recently, but her lies have come back to haunt her. "It has to do with what I told you before about my first boyfriend," she admits, "I met him by accident in the pain clinic a few weeks ago."

Alma listens with interest, then says, "You met him out of the blue after thirty years? So that's why you dreamed about him last night! It really does sound like a dream."

"You're right, it has nothing to do with reality." Iris chooses her words cautiously now that she has been found out. "It's kind of an escape from reality."

"What's wrong with escaping?"

Iris hesitates a bit before replying, "When you escape, you're not free."

"But what about love?" Alma persists for some reason. It's strange that she's so interested, strange that she doesn't identify with her father as usual.

"Love has many faces, sometimes it's cut off from life like a kite without a string. You know it's gliding in the sky, but you have to let it go because you don't want other things that are more important to you to fall."

"Oh, Mom, that's sad," Alma sighs.

"I've seen much sadder things in my life." Is this really how their love story will end, or are these words meant only for her daughter?

Now is not the time for decisions, it's the time to wrap her wounds with the bandages Sasha brings with him as he enters the apartment, and though it hurts to move her fingers, it is possible, so she refuses once again to be examined. "I'm sure I didn't break anything, I'm just banged up. I know because I have something to compare it to," she assures him, "let's wait another day." She is glad to see that, though he is watching Alma, he keeps his distance.

Her daughter, relaxed and charming, offers him the remains of their breakfast. "Even if you don't look like someone who would be satisfied with leftovers," she giggles.

Sasha takes a slice of bread and vegetables and smiles, "For starters, this is great." As he eats, he tells her about apartments he's seen recently, and she recommends one Web site or another. Actually, she tells him, a room in a friend's apartment is available, not far from here. As Iris watches them surreptitiously, she sees them glowing with the beginnings of life. Despite everything, they shine with the miraculous glow that might still heal the damage, or at least hide it. Their skin is so smooth, and under it, their bodies are young, their bones mend quickly, and despite everything, Alma is still naive, still believes in love. Iris doesn't listen to what they say, merely looks at the light reflecting off their skin, their bare arms, the sunbeams dancing on their foreheads, the golden radiance glowing above their heads like halos.

Would she return there if time flowed backward, as it does in dreams? Would she return to that day, the most wonderful day in her life, when it was neither too hot nor too cold? Their blossoming wadi has become a building project that houses hundreds of people, people who love and suffer, who are born and die. It is only in her memory that the wildflowers bloom once again, but if she was visited by such happiness once in her life, it might return one day, perhaps even today. She shakes her head, she has grown so used to reaching into that empty place that her fingers have been lost in the deep, hollow pocket of her life, and now, when she puts her hand in her other pocket, it is full to the brim. The sun dazzles her and she can't see anything. Even when she closes her eyes, the light penetrates her lids, a gold blanket spreads over her, a weave of gold threads absorbs her pain. She hears steps in the room, a faucet is turned on and off, dishes are washed, words are whispered, doors are opened and closed, car horns beep, voices rise in angry arguments, street noises blend with the noises in the apartment.

It's her cell phone ringing, or maybe on the other side of the window, on the sidewalk, another woman will answer for her? She reaches out from within the twilight of her sleep and gropes blindly for the smooth phone. Someone must have answered, because she hears the sound of crying. Is it her daughter? "Come back to me, come back to me," he pleads, and she shakes her head in puzzlement. What is he talking about? Who is he talking to? She died almost thirty years ago, right before your eyes, she died slowly, lingering so you could say goodbye. "Rissi, come back to me," he continues, and she opens her eyes to the last rays of the sun. "I know you never stopped loving me," he says, his voice somewhat steadier.

"I will never stop loving you," she hears herself whisper, but he doesn't hear her.

"You promised me you would come back," he persists, "that you would give us a second chance."

"Maybe there are no second chances, only a first chance for something else."

It's strange that he doesn't hear her, because she hears him so clearly when he says, "I have to hang up, I'm waiting for you."

She drops the phone and calls out in the suddenly darkening room, "Alma? Where's Alma?" Has the call she answered unthinkingly caused a disaster?

But there is Sasha standing in the doorway, saying, "Alma went to work."

"Oh no!" she screams. "Why did you let her go?"

"Her boss was here, didn't you hear the shouting?"

"No," she moans. "I didn't know what I was hearing, whether it was from here or from outside, I must have fallen asleep. What are we going to do, Sasha?"

"Believe in her, Iris, like you used to tell my mother, we'll show him the path and he'll take it."

But she protests, "This is nothing like that, you were still a child."

"She's still a child too. Go back to sleep, Iris, I'll stay here for the time being. She asked me to wait for her."

Everyone is waiting for everyone else, she thinks, and no one comes. Is this the chance we were given, the chance to part? Because the storeroom burned, there was nothing to hide the moon. She hears herself muttering all sorts of sayings. It feels as if Eitan is lying beside her and she is trying to tutor him for his exams. The past has passed, she says to him, everything has changed and nothing has been resolved. We think that cause precedes effect, but it is always the effect that leads to the cause. We were together day after day, night after night, and so I too was enslaved, controlled by a cruel, uncompromising tyrant. The past controlled me, and I have no idea why I am speaking in the past tense.

"Did you call me?" Sasha says, coming over to her, and when she shakes her head, he says, "I'll be right back. I'm going out for a minute to see an apartment not far from here."

"Just check to see that there are no mulberry trees and no springs there."

He chuckles, "What are you talking about?"

"I'll explain when you come back. It's an old story with one beginning and many endings."

To her surprise, he returns immediately. Is it because he wants to hear her story? His large body is on the threshold. "Irissi," he says, "you took a really bad fall."

She laughs, "Is that you, Mickey? I've been waiting for you! Don't worry, it could have been much worse."

"No doubt about it, we've already seen that."

"I'm sorry, Mickey, I didn't understand you properly before. You're right, it really is better to stay here for the time being."

"I'm not sure anymore. It looks worse than I thought. You have to get x-rayed."

"But it hurts less already, and the sun here is so pleasant, it'll heal me. And it isn't too hot or too cold here."

"The sun set a while ago," he says with a chuckle, and his broad face seems to split into two, a sort of miraculous masculine birth.

Then a young voice says, "Hey Mom, what's all this weird talk?" For some reason, she is extremely excited to see him, as if they haven't seen each other in years, and she reaches out toward him.

"Omy! I'm so glad you came, how was your civics exam?"

"Awesome," he says. "Dad nailed it. The questions on the exam were exactly the same ones we worked on together."

"That's wonderful!" she says. "Aren't you the lucky one!"

"Not really, look at the letter I got today." He hands her a folded page with a depressing logo embossed on it, a thin olive leaf coiled around a wide sword, imprisoned inside a star, so familiar to her from childhood, because that symbol decorated most of the letters that reached their home. Concealed beneath it were sorrow and loss in the form of invitations to camps and special fun days for the children of fallen soldiers, meetings of widows and bereaved parents.

But still, she doesn't understand, and asks, "What's this?"

"Don't you see? My first draft notice!"

"Draft notice? Already? But you were just born!"

With her swollen, throbbing fingers, she unfolds the form and reads an invitation, or more accurately, an order, for Omer Eilam to appear at the Jerusalem recruitment office in accordance with the national service law on such and such a date, which will arrive only too soon. They even provided him with a travel pass and a new acronym, NMSR—New Military Service Recruit.

Omer Eilam, the letters crowd together for her on the memorial plaque, bending their heads in suppressed pain, and she shakes her head. How do they even know he was born? After all, it was a strictly private matter, only she and Mickey and the midwife were there, and not a single representative of the army or the state, so what do they want from him now? And how do they know exactly where he lives? They even know the postal code, which she always forgets.

"Now that he finally learned civics, he stops being a civilian," Mickey jokes.

But she crushes the flickering letters into a small paper ball and says, "I won't allow it, Mickey, enough, I've given enough! I gave my father, I gave my body, I won't give my son. We'll hide out here, at Alma's place."

Mickey looks at her, surprised. "It's not like you to talk like that, Iris, you with all your educational messages! And why do you even think this is about you?"

"So who is it about, the country?" she says.

"First of all, it's about him," pointing at Omer, who sits down on the edge of the bed, rubbing his shaved temples.

"I'm not even me anymore," Omer mutters. "I'm just an NMSR. What the hell is an NMSR anyway?"

Mickey says, "I've already explained it to you twice, New Military Service Recruit."

"New Military Service Slave is more like it."

Mickey sits down beside him and puts his hand on his shoulder. "Calm down, it's only your first draft notice. You still have time to get used to the idea, right Rissi?"

"What did you call me?" she asks. She never let him call her that, but now, for some reason, it doesn't bother her. The past has opened, she suddenly feels. Is this the chance she has been given? The chance to open the sweet, suffocating, cursed cavern of the past and let its contents blend with the sun, the wind, and the voices of the present?

"What's this, family day?" she suddenly hears Alma's voice. How did she not see her enter in her yellow dress like a sunbeam?

She calls to her apprehensively, afraid that their presence might cause her to run back to where she just came from. "Alma, you're here? When did you come in?"

"I just came for a minute to make you dinner," her daughter says, walking over to her.

Iris says, "Look," handing her the crumpled paper ball as if asking for mercy.

"What's that?" Alma asks suspiciously, then recognizes it. "What an honor, your first draft notice! I'm so glad that's all behind me! Don't worry. Believe me, if I survived, you will too."

She tosses him the threatening paper ball, and Omer grumbles, "How can you even compare the two," as he catches it and tosses it back.

"It'll make you less spoiled," she teases him as the ball rolls under the bed next to the spider's corpse. "And it's about time."

"I'm spoiled? Look who's talking! You're the one who's spoiled! 'Mom, make me a half-ponytail, I won't go out of the house without a half-ponytail!'"

"Don't remind me of that!" Alma warns him, her face darkening. "For years I thought that Mom was hurt because I wanted a half-ponytail!"

Omer says, "You're kidding! I was sure it was because I was hiding in the bathroom! How long has it been Mom, ten years?"

"Ten years and seven weeks," Iris says, looking at them in surprise. The caverns of the past have opened for them as well, its stories blending with other events, woven into the large fabric of their lives. How can it be that they never talked about it, she thinks, what have we actually been doing until now?

"It has absolutely nothing to do with either of you," Mickey sighs. "It's all my fault because I left early."

"So honestly, why did you leave early?" Alma asks.

He looks into her deep black eyes and says, "It's an old story—"

Iris interrupts him. "Mostly, it doesn't matter anymore. I recovered, can't you see that I recovered?"

"You're not very convincing with all those bandages," Omer says.

Alma sits down on the bed beside them and says quietly, "This time it really is my fault."

"It's not your fault," Iris says, "it's thanks to you." Is this the chance she has been given? Not the chance to love him again, but to love her life for what it is, not to long for what it isn't.

"Where did I put that?" Mickey suddenly asks himself, rummaging through in his pockets. "You got a letter today too, Iris, I completely forgot." He pulls out a thick, wrinkled piece of paper. "I found it on the windshield of your car when I picked it up at the interchange." He hands it to her, his expression inscrutable, and she pales at the sight of the clear letters, blue on white, "Come back to me."

"Come back to me? Now that's really something," Omer says with a chuckle, looking at her suspiciously and then at his father.

To her surprise, Alma comes over to her, takes the paper from her hand, and without looking at it, crumples it into an ever-smaller ball. "It must be a mistake," she says.

Iris looks at them, her gaze moving from one to the other. They are here now, they are present. "It's not a mistake," she says, "it's an old story."

Zeruya Shalev was born at Kibbutz Kinneret. She is the author of four previous novels, *The Remains of Love*, *Love Life*, *Husband and Wife*, and *Thera*, and a book of poetry and two children's books. Her work has been translated into twenty-five languages and won multiple awards including the Corine International Book Prize, the Welt Literature Award, and the Prix Femina étranger.

Sondra Silverston is a native New Yorker who has been living in Israel since 1970. Among her published translations are Amos Oz's *Between Friends*, which won the 2013 National Jewish Book Award for fiction, Eshkol Nevo's *Homesick*, which was long-listed for the Independent Translation prize, and works by Etgar Keret, Ayelet Gundar-Goshen, Alona Frankel, and Savyon Liebrecht.